VICTIM

VICTIM

ROBERT WANGARD

AMP&RSAND, INC.

Chicago • New Orleans

ISBN 978-0-9985222-1-0

Design
David Robson, Robson Design

Published by
AMPERSAND, INC.
515 Madison Street
New Orleans, Louisiana 70116

719 Clinton Place
River Forest, Illinois 60305

www.ampersandworks.com

———

www.rwangard.com

Printed in U.S.A.

In memory of Captain and Max,
both kind and gentle souls
who loved the lake

ONE

The man with the ponytail and star-spangled do-rag nestled in the brush along the lake and kept the crosshairs of his scope trained on the jet skier's torso as he zigzagged across the flat water toward him. Each time the jet skier turned, he sent sheets of water spraying skyward and momentarily disappeared from view. When he reemerged, the crosshairs found his torso again. The man's forefinger twitched as he watched the jet skier come closer.

Fifty yards from shore, the jet skier throttled back and the angry whine of his machine softened as he coasted to a stop. The man watching him fought to control his emotions and wiped his eyes to clear his vision. He sighted through his scope again and adjusted the controls to sharpen the focus, centering the crosshairs on the jet skier's torso and holding steady. Then he raised the crosshairs to the man's head for a few moments before dropping them back to his torso. His forefinger began to tighten, slowly, slowly, slowly. Finally, he dropped his head and squeezed his eyes closed.

When he heard the jet ski rev up, the man raised his head and followed the rider with his eyes as he headed south. He brought his scope up again, this time centering the crosshairs on the skier's back. He kept them there as the skier weaved back and forth across the water until he became a speck in the distance.

The man lowered the scope and breathed deeply several times to relieve the tension that gripped his body. Then he slipped the scope into its padded sheath and put on a pair of wraparound sunglasses and rose to his feet. He glanced around as he walked to his pickup where he stowed the scope in a canvas duffel bag and stuffed the bag under a tarp that hung partially across his tailgate, concealing his license plate. He'd inflated his orange kayak before he left home, and now he pulled it from his pickup's box and carried it to the water.

He took twice as much time as he needed to screw the two sections of his paddle together. When he was finished, he walked down the narrow sand beach and tried to appear preoccupied with other things. He knew someone might see him and would assume he was looking for unusual stones. Being seen wasn't a problem, though. In fact, it was good. That's what he wanted, to be seen.

After a while, he returned to his kayak and launched it and began to paddle. He forced himself to concentrate on his surroundings as he moved noiselessly through the water. On shore, he heard a brace of crows squawking from a dead tree, and just ahead of him he saw a heron flying low over the lake. The peacefulness calmed him and he began to think through his plan again.

An hour later, the man returned to his launch point and glided onto the beach. He fussed with his equipment for a couple of minutes and then carried his kayak to his pickup and hoisted it into the back. He made sure the end of the tarp continued to hang down over his license plate and started out the single-track dirt road to the highway. Apparently hearing his truck, the woman with the straw hat and blue shirt and brightly-decorated gloves who always seemed to be working in her flower garden looked up. He stared straight ahead and gave no sign that

2

he'd noticed her. He glanced to his right, but didn't see the other woman. The one who never seemed to be outside, but he suspected observed everything in the area. The invisible woman.

A half-mile north on M-22, he turned left onto a seldom-travelled road that branched off the highway, away from the lake. When he was comfortable he'd gone far enough, he stopped and went to the rear of his pickup where he removed his do-rag and ponytail wig. He stuffed them in the duffel with his scope and put on a worn baseball cap. Then he deflated the kayak, folded it, and stored it under the tarp. He pulled the end of the tarp back so that his license plate showed again. When he was finished, he turned around and got back on M-22.

Pete Thorsen sat on his screened porch with a collection of Chuck Berry's greatest hits playing softly on his Bose music system, his laptop open on a table next to him, and a yellow legal pad resting on one knee. He stared absently at the lake as he thought about the best way to begin his article about Viking longbows for *The Fjord Times*. For inspiration, he'd positioned his replica longbow across the arms of a wicker chair in front of him.

He couldn't help but smile when he thought about the bow's history. Some years earlier, he'd taken a trip to Norway with Harry McTigue, his long-time newspaperman friend. After visiting a museum filled with historical artifacts from the Viking Age, he'd become enamored with the longbows from that period, and the museum's curator introduced him to an elderly craftsman named Ulf who carved bows that meticulously resembled those used by the storied warriors. When he was finally able to persuade Ulf to make a bow for him, he quickly learned that it wasn't as simple as grabbing a piece of yew wood and beginning to carve. First, Ulf emphasized, they had to decide on an appropriate draw weight. Pete knew nothing about draw weights, so Ulf sized up his six-two, two-hundred-five-pound frame and proposed one that Pete later discovered might have been appropriate for a Viking warrior his size, but was a tad optimistic given his twenty years behind a desk as a lawyer.

It wasn't the bow's draw weight that tickled Harry, though, it was the special fixtures at the ends. Ulf had never been out of Norway, but he was an aficionado of black and white American movies, notably gangster films. Al Capone, in particular, fascinated him, and when he found out that Pete and Harry were from Chicago, he took it upon himself to come up with something Pete could use in close combat in the urban jungle if the need should ever arise. His innovation was the sharpened steel fittings at the ends of the bow, steel being Ulf's sole concession to modernity. Harry never tired of ribbing Pete about strolling through Chicago's streets in a pinstripe suit with the menacing Viking bow slung over his shoulder.

Pete jotted down several possible openings for his article and was finally getting into it when he heard the whine of high-powered engines on the lake. He looked up, and far out on the water, spotted two motor boats running side-by-side, heading east. The smaller one was pulling ahead in what obviously was a race. Pete wondered if his friend, Bud Stephanopoulis, was at the helm of the lead boat. He was meeting Bud later that afternoon for one of their periodic one-on-one basketball games, and was sure he'd hear all about it if it were. If there was one thing Bud liked more than basketball, it was his latest water toy.

He jotted down a fourth possible opening, and then began work on an outline for the entire article. The Chuck Berry CD had run its course and he didn't insert a new one in the player. It was quiet on the lake, too, and his thoughts were flowing better than they had earlier. After an hour, though, his enthusiasm for writing began to wane. He checked the time and saw he still had over an hour to kill before meeting Bud.

Pete got up and stretched and picked up his longbow. He pulled the bowstring back a couple of times, then got his arrows and went out to the small range he'd set up in the wooded area behind his lake house. He'd strategically positioned three army surplus silhouette targets among the trees and bushes at various distances. After repositioning one that had blown over in the wind, he stepped back and eyed the targets.

He pulled the bowstring back a few more times to regain the feel. Finally, he nocked an arrow, and after running through in his mind the basics of form, drew the bowstring back to his right jaw and let the arrow fly. It grazed a young sapling, altering its course and causing it to completely miss the intermediate-range target. *Rust*, he thought. He nocked another arrow and tried again. This time he barely caught the shoulder of the target. Not good, but better than his first attempt. He pulled the bowstring back a couple of times without an arrow, then nocked a third one and let it fly. It grazed a bush and again missed the target. *You stink*, he muttered.

As Pete stared at the targets, a motivational gimmick he used to employ came back to him. His Chicago law firm was going through an internal power struggle at the time, and as the firm's managing partner, he was the primary target of insurgents led by a mid-thirties-something partner named Marty Kral. When he was at the lake in those days and wanted to let off steam, he began to visualize Kral's sneering face on the targets. Visualizing again, he drew the bowstring back and let an arrow go. *Thunk!* Not dead center, but safely within the target. He nocked another arrow and let it fly. *Thunk!* Center ring this time.

Pete was enjoying himself now. He was in the zone and pounded one arrow after another into the targets as he relived his battles from the old days.

TWO

Pete kept his eyes riveted on the drawstring of Bud's shorts. He was in the classic athletic stance with knees flexed and feet comfortably apart, on the balls of his feet and ready to move in either direction. Bud faked with the ball, then faked again. Pete held his position and didn't go for the fakes. *Stay down*, he reminded himself, *stay down*. Bud did a quarter pivot and began dribbling. Pete slid his feet to stay between Bud and the basket. Suddenly Bud rose to execute a jump hook. Pete came out of his defensive stance and jumped straight up in an effort to block the shot, but the ball sailed over his outstretched hands. He spun around to face the basket, arms outstretched again to block Bud's path. The ball rattled around the rim and spun out. Pete felt Bud's weight on his back as he grabbed the ball.

"Foul," Pete called as he dribbled away, looking over his shoulder at Bud.

"Bull," Bud said in a snarly tone, "that wasn't a foul! I barely touched you!"

"You were all over my back, for crissakes."

Bud waved a hand and scowled as Pete dribbled into the backcourt. In his college days, Bud Stephanopoulis had been an All-American basketball player at the University of Minnesota and was drafted by the Boston Celtics in the first round. He tore up his knee in his rookie season, and after two operations and over a year rehabbing, he was cut by the Celtics and gave up his dream of a professional basketball career and went into investment banking. Pete, who'd barely made his high school basketball team and gave away five inches to Bud, reveled in the rare moments when he bested him on the court.

Pete dribbled toward the basket. Bud blocked his progress at the free throw circle and swiped at the ball a couple of times with a big hand. Pete made the mistake of picking up his dribble and pivoted away from Bud to retain possession of the ball. Bud didn't move so Pete pivoted back to face the basket again and jab-stepped with his left foot. Bud didn't go for the fake. Pete jab-stepped again, then stepped back and let his jumper go. Bud timed it perfectly and swatted the ball back at him. Pete ducked as the ball whizzed past his head.

Pete turned and saw the ball lying on the grass, off the court. He looked at Bud and said, "Jesus, you mad or something?"

"You called that crappy foul on me that wasn't a real foul."

Pete just stared at him. That was typical Bud. Nothing he ever did on the basketball court was a foul, but on the other hand, if his opponent got within two feet of him, it was a flagrant. Pete shot him a look and went to retrieve the basketball. He brought it back and handed it to Bud with both hands. "I don't want you to call a foul on me," he said sarcastically. Bud smirked.

A half-hour later, Bud had won the game twenty-one points to eight. "It's been fun," Pete said. "Thanks for suggesting it." Inside, he was still irritated by Bud's self-serving notion of what was or wasn't a foul.

"How about a game of H-O-R-S-E before we hang it up," Bud suggested. "I'll even let you go first."

Pete was dragging and mopped his brow with a sleeve and considered it for a second. H-O-R-S-E neutralized Bud's height advantage which gave him a big edge in one-on-one games. He said, "You're on."

Pete took the ball out to what would be three-point range in the professional game. He dribbled a couple of times, then jumped and let the ball fly. Swish, nothing but nylon. He retrieved the ball and took it back to where he'd shot from. "Right here," he said, pointing to the spot. "A jump shot."

Bud took the ball, spun it around in his hands a couple of times, and let it fly. The ball clanged off the rim.

"That's 'H' for me," Pete said smugly. He went to three-point range again on the other side of the court and stood with his back to the basket. After dribbling a couple of times, he turned and released the ball. Another clean swish. When the ball went through the net, Pete did his best Michael Jordan impersonation, shrugging and shaking his head, implying that he just couldn't miss.

Bud's turn-around jumper caught the rim and spun out again. "I think that's 'H-O' if my spelling is right," Pete said.

Bud's lips tightened as they always did when he was irritated. "Okay, hotshot, let's see how you do closer in."

"I've got one more shot from outside. Straight in," Pete said. Bud shot him a disgusted look.

Pete jab-stepped to his left, then jab-stepped to his right, and finally let the ball go. This time it rattled around the rim, but caught enough iron to go through the hoop. Pete held both hands waist high with forefingers extended, like he was firing a pair of six-guns, and backed up cockily.

Bud missed his shot from the same place. "H-O-R," Pete said.

They traded shots for the next twenty minutes until the score was finally Pete "H-O-R-S-E" to Bud's "H-O."

"You going to throw the ball at my head again just for old time's sake?" Pete asked tauntingly.

"Screw you."

Pete smiled at him. They walked toward their cars in silence.

"You want to stop at my place for a drink?" Bud asked in a more civil tone.

Pete glanced at his watch. "You promise you won't throw something at me?"

Bud grinned at him. "Now that I think of it, I do have a new set of knives."

Pete followed Bud to his house on Shorewood Drive. It was an imposing structure constructed in a peeled-log style with a three-car garage and a stone patio with a splendid view of the lake. Steps — ninety-two of them according to Bud — led down the bluff to where he kept his impressive array of watercraft. From above, it looked like a private marina. Bud spent a few minutes showing Pete around even though he'd been to the house several times before.

"Sorry, I don't have any of that Thor's Hammer stuff you always drink. Gray Goose okay?"

"Gray Goose is fine. But light on the Goose and heavy on the tonic."

Pete enjoyed the view while Bud mixed the drinks. He returned with Pete's vodka and tonic and a martini with a bunch of olives for himself. He took a sip and popped a few mixed nuts in his mouth and crunched on them.

Pete said, "I always forget how nice this place is. How long have you had it?"

"Since shortly after I started coming here. I was still with Harrison Stryker LLP at the time."

"Is your house in Panama built in the log cabin motif, too?"

Bud chuckled. "No, it's classic Caribbean all the way. White stucco walls, tile roof. You ever been to Panama?"

Pete shook his head. "Never."

"You should come down sometime. I'm usually there from October until the following May. I don't know how the hell you stand the winters up here."

"You forget, I was born in the wilds of northern Wisconsin. The weather here is child's play compared to what it is up there."

"That's right, I forgot. You're one of those wild-eyed Scandinavians who thrives on the frozen tundra. I'm from Greece where the weather and everything else is more civilized."

Pete let the barb go and said, "How did you wind up in Panama? Why not the Bahamas or someplace like that?"

"A senior director at Harrison Stryker had a place down there. He was kind of a mentor to me. He had me down a few times and I got to like it. When the place I now own came on the market, I snapped it up. There's a nice mix of people in the area—Americans, Panamanians, some Mexicans, quite a few Europeans. All with money."

"Is your director friend in the same area?"

"Used to be. He died five years ago. When he was alive, we had a Panama office that he ran for ten years before his death."

Pete took another sip of his vodka and tonic and gazed out at the lake. It was nearing the longest day of the year, and with Crystal Lake being at the western edge of the eastern time zone, the sun was still well above the bluffs that surrounded the water. He said, "I remember you were just on the cusp of fifty when you hung it up. I still don't know why you left so young."

Stephanopoulis shrugged. "Investment banking is a young man's game. Or these days, I guess I need to say 'person's game.' I started with a small firm, then moved to Harrison Stryker where I spent most of my career. I know it's hard to believe, but I was a young buck once. Bankers make a lot of money, but you pay a price for it. Sixteen hour days aren't unusual. You're in your prime in your thirties and forties. When the Big 5-0 starts staring you in the face, the powers start to nudge you so they can elevate the younger blood. How about you? You're not much younger than I am, and you're not practicing law anymore."

Pete shrugged. "I wanted to do something else with my life."

"Gosh, what an enlightening answer."

Pete laughed.

Bud continued to look at him, obviously waiting for more.

Pete felt uncomfortable talking about personal stuff—the sudden death of his wife, his mentor who went off the deep end one night and shot a younger partner, then had a heart attack and died in jail before he could stand trial—so he shared only part of the story. "When I joined our firm, the legal profession was still seniority oriented. That system had its flaws, but then things changed with a vengeance and all of the firms found themselves with a cadre of younger guys whose only goal in life was to make money. In my case, I'd worked my way up to managing partner of our firm when all of this started happening and I found that trying to maintain a balance was a losing proposition. After while, it gets old."

Bud nodded. "Jesus, before I retired, I remember sitting around in a conference room talking about this deal or that deal. Most of the other people in the room looked like they were still in high school, cracking their gum and checking their Blackberrys every fourteen seconds."

Pete said, "So the pre-pubs got together one day and threw you out, then flipped a coin to determine which of them would get your office."

"They didn't *throw* me out. I'd made enough money that I could afford to give them the middle finger salute and walk out and not look back."

They sat quietly for a couple of minutes. The sun was finally sinking below the bluffs on the west end of the lake and the water's surface took on a silver sheen.

"Do you miss it?" Pete finally asked. "Or do you have what we in the legal business call an 'of counsel' relationship that lets you ease out of things gradually?"

"Oh, I had the usual three-year transition agreement that called for me to be available to help the firm with deals and all of that. I'd go to the office and sit in on some meeting or other. Maybe a merger we were advising on or something I knew more about than all of the pre-pubs, as you call them, combined. They'd just give me vacuous stares whenever I made a suggestion and go on with their conversation. After a while, I got to be happy to just draw my check at the end of each quarter and not let it bother me."

Pete swirled the ice cubes around in his glass and looked out at the lake again.

"You ready for another?" Bud asked.

"Thanks, but two's my limit. Too many empty calories."

"Calories? Shit, with that thimbleful of vodka you like in your drinks, there can't be more than ten calories in one of them."

"Ten calories of vodka and a hundred plus calories of tonic."

Bud looked at him and shook his head and went inside to mix another martini. The conversation about the past had put Pete in a pensive mood, as had thoughts about what was in store for the following day.

Bud came out the sliding glass door balancing his fresh drink and a tray with pretzels and nuts and several ground sirloin patties. He said, "I don't know about you, but I'm hungry enough to eat a rhino. If you don't want a burger because you're worried about what it will do to your delicate little body, I'll eat for both of us."

Pete smiled and watched Bud fire up the grill and scrub the grate with a wire brush. Then he said, "Picking up on our conversation, to be honest, I sometimes wish I'd stayed with the firm a little longer."

Bud glanced over his shoulder as he placed the patties on the grill. "You wouldn't have been happy from everything you tell me, with the younger crowd gnawing at your heels all the time."

"You forget, unlike some nameless weak-kneed Greeks, I was capable of kicking butt if I had to."

"Hah! You must have been tougher then than you are on the basketball court now."

"Umm, how do you spell H-O-R-S-E? H-O . . . H-O . . . What's the rest?"

Bud chuckled. "You were just lucky you managed to find the hoop with those three-pointers. You know that old saying, even a blind hog finds an acorn now and then."

"Sure, sure," Pete said, smirking.

Bud flipped the burgers over and said, "Seriously, do you really miss your old law firm?"

"Once in a while. I put a lot of time and effort into getting to where I was. I wasn't like you, with a rich old man who coddled you from birth."

"Rich? You call owning a crummy Greek restaurant rich?"

"Yeah, but there's the restaurant's income and then there's that other income from the skim. Everybody knows how you Greeks operate."

Bud grinned. "Shoot, without the skim, the seven kids in our family would have had to emigrate to one of the Scandinavian countries and live off the welfare state. Except it's too friggin' cold up there."

They ate their burgers and talked some more and Bud had two more drinks. Eventually, Pete pried himself loose and drove home. Darkness had set in and the sky was alive with stars and a half-moon was rising over the lake. Pete felt morose in spite of the splendor. He wasn't looking forward to the trip to Bloomfield Hills.

THREE

When the man who planned to kill the jet skier got home, he carried the duffel bag and the deflated kayak to the storage shed where he unlocked the padlock and went in and closed the door behind him. It was dark inside, but the small windows on each side of the building let in enough light for him to see even with the flimsy curtains covering them. He moved the rack with the Sunfish sailboat away from the workbench, then pulled the workbench back from its place along the wall and removed the large piece of pegboard. Finally, he detached the hunk of insulation that was directly behind where the workbench had been to expose the compartment and stared at the rifle for a long time.

He'd driven all the way to Tennessee to attend a gun show in a tiny burg fifty miles outside Nashville to buy it. There were closer gun shows, but he'd learned from Internet sources that the Tennessee show was one of the more lax ones with little in the way of background checks or record-keeping procedures. In fact, he hadn't actually *attended* the show; he'd bought the rifle from a bearded backwoodsman in the parking lot outside the small convention center. It had been a cash transaction with no identification requested and none volunteered. He suspected that the man who'd sold him the rifle had purchased it the same way.

The man pulled on a pair of latex gloves and took the rifle from the compartment, hefting it and running his hand over its stock, testing the sound suppressor he'd purchased separately to be sure it was securely attached. The seller had described it as a Remington 700 XCR Compact Tactical Rifle chambered for .223 caliber ammunition, and had thrown a box of ammunition into the bargain. It might not have the same firepower as some of the AR weapons on the market, he said, but it was more accurate. He'd already taken the rifle deep into the woods several times to practice and satisfy himself that it was as accurate as the man had said.

He returned the rifle to the compartment and put the duffel bag and inflatable kayak in. Then he reattached the insulation, rehung the pegboard, and pushed the workbench against the wall. Finally, he moved the rack with the Sunfish back into position. He eased the shed door open a crack and scanned the area. Seeing no one, he stepped out and snapped the padlock back in place.

The man felt drained as he walked toward his front door. Inside, he stripped off his khaki T-shirt and baggy camo cargo shorts, feeling relieved to get out of them. He didn't like the clothes, but they were part of his plan. Once more, and if all went well, they'd be disposed of like everything else. He took the T-shirt and shorts to his washing machine, dropped in a packet of detergent, set the load to light, and pushed the start button.

The hot water felt good as he let it cascade over his shoulders for ten minutes. He changed into his regular clothes and went to his kitchen where he got a frozen dinner from his refrigerator. He waited for the microwave to heat it up, and then took his food to the living room couch and clicked on the evening news. It was a presidential election year and the presumptive nominee of one of the parties was being interviewed by a reporter. He changed channels in the middle of the interview, and found one where a local anchor was just getting into a story about a robbery at a community bank in a nearby town. He clicked the off-button on the remote, and after he finished eating, he took the plastic tray to the kitchen and dumped it in the garbage.

He slumped on the couch in front of the television, but didn't turn it on again. He leaned back, stretching, and tried to think. A while later, he went to the closet and got the cardboard box and carried it back to the couch. For the next hour, he sorted through the contents and alternately felt exhilaration and anger. Then he leaned back and closed his eyes and dozed off. He felt disoriented when he woke up again, and after collecting himself, he took the box back to the closet and went outside.

Darkness had come, and overhead, the night sky blazed. He got in his pickup and drove, thinking about whether he'd overlooked anything. From what he'd read, if he ever came under suspicion, the authorities almost certainly would seize his laptop computer and scour it for evidence that could be used against him. He'd used the laptop to research gun shows and weapons and telescopic scopes and sound suppressors that could be attached to a rifle barrel. That's why after he'd returned from Tennessee, he'd meticulously wiped his laptop clean of fingerprints before smashing it to bits with a sledge hammer. To provide an additional layer of protection, he'd divided the scrap into two piles and buried the material in the woods a mile apart. No one was likely to be out there before hunting season, but he raked dead leaves over the excavated areas to camouflage his digging.

When he got to the lake, he followed the road until he reached the west end. He was tempted to go in the access road, but he knew that wouldn't be wise. Going kayaking during daylight hours was one thing; to be seen skulking around at midnight was another. He continued on and drove along the south shore of the lake until he had to pick up the highway to Beulah and Benzonia.

He stopped at the new public access spot, which was deserted except for a pickup and SUV, both with boat trailers attached. Probably fishermen out for some night fishing. He sat with his driver's-side window down for a long time, gazing at the shimmering light on the lake and listening to the sounds of the night.

FOUR

Pete navigated local highways and wound through small towns until he reached the Interstate that would take him south to Bloomfield Hills near Detroit where Julie's private boarding school was located. It was a familiar route and one he'd driven many times over the past four years, most recently a week ago when he'd gone down to attend Julie's graduation festivities.

Memories washed over him as he motored south. His stepdaughter had reached the end of another chapter in her life. And in his. In the fall, she would be off to Cornell University which was much farther from home than the boarding school she'd been attending. She was also eighteen now, which changed a lot of things.

As he turned into the school's campus, he was again struck by how much it looked like a prestigious small college — stately brick and stone buildings that exuded a feeling of permanency, a clock tower that soared over the other buildings, a stream that meandered through the grounds complete with two rustic wooden bridges, grassy lawns everywhere, athletic fields and courts tucked unobtrusively into the landscape. On the way to Julie's dorm, he passed the campus police station. Seeing it brought back unpleasant memories that colored the mostly good times.

The restrictions on non-permit parking had been relaxed for the week to make it easier for parents to move their sons and daughters out of their dorms. He rounded the corner of a building and bedlam greeted him. The lot he usually parked in was a tangle of SUVs and sedans with a handful of pickups thrown in. Parents seemed to be everywhere, carrying boxes and suitcases and sound equipment of various kinds to their double-parked vehicles. Students hugged each other and tearfully promised to keep in touch. Pete kept an eye open for a parking spot as he cruised slowly through the area and called Julie on his cell phone to let her know he'd arrived and would be up as soon as he found a parking place.

On this third trip around, a SUV with a pole lamp extending out its rear window backed out of its parking space, and Pete moved aggressively to claim the spot, ignoring the hostile glares of other parents who'd been eyeing it as well. Pete walked up the stairs to the second floor of the dorm where Julie's room was located. Her door was open and he saw an impressive collection of suitcases, boxes and other items like her golf clubs in the center of the room. Julie was sitting on a chair with her knees tucked up and her folded arms resting on them, gazing out the window.

He knocked and walked in. She looked his way and said without smiling, "Hi, Dad."

"Something wrong?"

"No, I'm just feeling down. Leaving and everything."

"Hey, look," he said, trying to cheer her up, "this is the end of one chapter before you go on to the next. It's an exciting time." He hoped his voice sounded buoyant because his mood was as much in the dumps as she seemed to be.

"That's easy for you to say. You don't have to worry about whether you'll like your new roommate or whether Cornell will turn out to be the right place for you or whether you'll have enough money to come home for Christmas." She paused before continuing. "I can just see it now. I'll be sitting alone in my room eating Cheetos or something because airline tickets at that time of the year are so expensive."

"Come on, young lady. You're going to love Cornell. And do you really think I'd leave you alone to eat Cheetos at Christmas? What happened to that independent-minded, spirited young woman I know and love?"

"Oh, I know it's stupid. Come on, Dad, let's get this stuff loaded up before some parent firebombs your car to get your parking spot."

Each of them grabbed a load of the stuff littering her floor and carried it out to Pete's Range Rover. Julie ran her hand over the dark blue finish and looked at Pete and said, "You know, if you hadn't been with me, I would have walked all over the parking lot looking for your old green thing."

"The green Range Rover is history, Sweetie. Blue's the new family color."

"If you'd bought a new car instead of one that's three years old, you could have stuck with green."

"When you buy a new vehicle, you don't know what you're getting. This vehicle was owned for three years by a fastidious gentleman who really took care of it. He took the buyer's risk out of it for me. Plus, he gave me a good price and knew I'd continue to care for it. It was win-win on both sides."

"That's it, isn't it? You got a good deal."

"Hey, we can either stand here debating my economic habits or we can get the rest of your stuff and get out of here before someone does more than firebomb my new Range Rover. If I have to replace this one, I might wind up with canary-yellow the next time."

"Eeek! Canary-yellow?"

Pete gave her a sly grin and headed for the back door of her dorm. An hour later, they finally had all of Julie's possessions loaded in the Range Rover. Julie made a final sweep through her room to make sure she hadn't missed anything, said tearful goodbyes to a couple of friends she bumped into in the hall, and they were off.

As Pete backed out of the parking slot, another father with determination plastered on his face like a Halloween mask was already wedging his way in. Pete was thankful to escape the bedlam, but just before they exited the campus, Julie said, "I know you probably want to get on the road back to the lake, but do you suppose we could take a half-hour and walk around the campus for the last time?"

Pete looked at her quizzically.

"This might be the last time I'm here. I'd just kind of like to, you know, say goodbye and everything."

"Sure," Pete said, knowing that the school would be all over her as soon as she graduated from college, trying to get her and other alumni back on campus to restoke school spirit and pry financial contributions from them.

Julie suggested a place to park, and they set out on their walking tour of campus. Julie kept up nonstop chatter as they strolled through the grounds, recounting this experience and that one. When they came to the soccer field, Julie relived a match against a neighboring school, traditionally a soccer powerhouse, when she'd scored all three of her team's goals as they shut out their rival. Pete remembered that game as well because it was on parents' weekend. He'd rarely felt prouder of his daughter.

As they walked past the library, Julie grabbed his arm and said, "Remember when those two goons followed my girlfriend and me and we had to run to get away?" She giggled. "I never did find my cell phone."

"I do remember. I believe the police ultimately decided it was probably just a couple of seedy looking guys passing through." He'd never told her about the heart-to-heart conversation he'd had with Vinnie Zahn about the incident and the armistice he'd brokered to avoid a recurrence.

"It was scary, but nothing like the time someone stuck a knife in my door during the middle of the night. That *really* freaked me out."

"That was different. I think I told you the knife incident was the handiwork of the wacky sister of a former client of mine who's in prison for sabotaging her ex-boyfriend's hang glider wing and causing serious injuries to him. The sisters were estranged, and the wacky one thought she could patch things up by going on a vendetta against me. Now she's in prison, too."

"Dad, since you moved up to the lake, it's been one thing after another. You really need to assess what you're doing and see how you can avoid these problems."

Pete touched his daughter on the shoulder and said, "Now hold on, young lady. I was representing the woman who was the root of the trouble *pro bono*. I'd known her for years and liked her and we had a good relationship. Then she turned crazy and blamed me for her problems. When you're a lawyer, you get involved with a lot of people. Ninety-nine percent of them are upstanding citizens and good people, but once in a while one will turn out to be a wacko. Believe me, if I'd known Robyn was in the latter category, I'd have cut ties with her long before the problem ever came up."

"I'm not *blaming* you, Dad. I'm just saying that you seem to get involved in a lot of these situations."

Pete was about to say something, but Julie remembered some other more pleasant memory and began to relive it. A half-hour later, after more memories and a few tears, they were finally in Pete's Range Rover again winding their way through town to the Interstate.

Julie was quiet, like she was exhausted from her journey down memory lane, until she asked, "What was the name of that woman you hired to watch my dorm after the knife incident?"

Pete thought for a minute, then said, "Rae Acton, I think."

"That's right, Rae." She was quiet again for a while, then asked, "Could we stop and say goodbye to her? And thank her for everything she did for us?"

Pete tried to avoid rolling his eyes, thinking that payment of her fee was all the thanks Acton expected. He tried to keep the irritation out of his voice and said, "I don't think we can just drop in on her unannounced."

"I wasn't thinking about dropping in *unannounced*. You keep driving and I'll call her. Then she'll know we're coming."

Pete held his tongue, and out of the corner of his eye, he saw that she was searching her cell phone's directory. "Here it is," she said, her voice brimming with excitement. She held the phone up to her ear. She said to Pete, "Her office isn't far from here, right?"

"Right," he responded, hoping Acton was out of the office.

"Rae?" Julie said. "This is Julie Sable, Pete Thorsen's daughter. My Dad is with me and we're in the car headed home because I just graduated from school. We'd like to stop and say goodbye and thank you for everything you did for us."

Julie listened for a few moments, then said, "Wonderful! We'll be right over." She listened some more, then added, "No, no, my Dad knows where you are. We'll see you in a few minutes."

Julie ended the call and said to Pete, "She's in her office and sounded as excited to see us as we are to see her. This will really be a nice send-off."

Pete had already resigned himself to another side-trip and changed course to head for Acton's office. It was in the town of Clawson, over a pizza joint. They arrived ten minutes later and Julie bounded up the stairs to Acton's office. Pete followed at a slower pace, and when he got to the second floor and walked in, Julie and Rae were embracing like it was a reunion of two close friends who hadn't seen each other in twenty years.

When they disengaged, Acton said, "Hello Pete. Good to see you again."

Acton looked the same as the last time he'd seen her. Five-five, stocky, dirty blonde hair that looked like she cut it herself, a black turtle neck over dumpy black pants, very little makeup.

"Nice to see you, too, Rae."

"Your daughter has grown into quite a young lady since the last time I saw her."

"And turned eighteen to boot. She makes all of her own decisions now."

"Not *all* of the decisions," Julie said, blushing a little. She said to Acton, "Do you have any new cases going?"

"I always have new cases going, honey. I have to pay the rent on these pricey digs." A sly grin crept over her face and she waved a hand expansively.

"I know my Dad will think I'm asking too many personal questions," she said shyly, "but do any of the cases involve, you know, using your piece?"

Pete remembered the first and only time Julie had met Acton. She seemed mesmerized by the fact Acton carried a handgun. Acton played along and told stories that Pete suspected were at least partially fiction, but sounded exciting. Julie hung on her every word.

"Honey, since you've graduated now, do you have plans for college?"

"I'm starting Cornell University in the fall," Julie said with a combination of pride and a touch of trepidation.

"And you're going to study what? To become a lawyer like your Daddy?"

Julie, suddenly pensive, said, "I haven't decided yet. I plan to take general courses my freshman year. After that, I'll map out a direction."

Pete kept quiet.

They chatted for fifteen minutes more, with Pete surreptitiously checking his watch, and then said their goodbyes. Julie was quiet until they were on the Interstate, then said earnestly, "I think I might add private investigator to my list of possible career options after college."

Pete glanced her way to see if she was kidding. "I thought you were thinking of becoming a neurosurgeon. Or a journalist. Or Heaven forbid, even a lawyer."

"Those are on my list, too. I'm just trying not to limit myself."

FIVE

It was after five o'clock when Pete pulled into his driveway. Julie jumped out of the car and ran down to the beach, kicked off one of her flip-flops, and tested the water temperature with her toes. She came back and announced she was going for a swim. Pete diplomatically suggested that she might want to help him unload the car first. After needling him about how overly disciplined he was, Julie pitched in and helped carry her possessions into the house and store them in a spare bedroom. Then she changed into her swimsuit and grabbed a beach towel.

"Are you coming with me?" she asked.

"The water's still too cold for me."

"Pansy," she said, elbowing him playfully in the ribs.

Pete watched as she exuberantly ran down to the water, and without hesitation, plunged in. She surfaced and screamed as she jumped up and down, "It's cold! It's cold!"

He smiled.

She plunged in again and swam with a strong overhand stroke. She tread water for a while and called to him, "It's not bad once you get used to it!" Then she began to swim again. Fifteen minutes later, she waded out of the water and grabbed her towel and wrapped it around her. She walked toward the cottage, shivering, and said, "That was nice."

"If it was so nice, why are you shivering?"

She came back at him and said, "Hey, it's only mid-June." She looked thoughtful for a moment, then added, "This isn't a personal best, though. I think my record was before Memorial Day one year. I'm going to get a lot of swimming in this summer before I leave for college. That and roadwork. I have to get in shape for soccer."

"Harry called while you were swimming. He wants to treat you to a welcome home dinner. Why don't you get dressed and dry your hair? I told him we'd be at the restaurant by seven."

When they walked into Rona's Bay Grille, Harry McTigue was already sitting at his usual window table. He saw them and hoisted his egg-shaped body from his chair and started across the room toward them with a duck-like gait. He engulfed Julie in a bear hug, then stepped back, beaming, and admired her.

Pete smiled as he watched them. Besides being his closest friend, Harry owned and published the town's weekly newspaper, *The Northern Sentinel*. He had no children of his own, and doted on Julie.

"Look at you," Harry gushed. "All grown up. You'll be the prettiest managing editor in the country." He let his smirk show as he glanced at Pete and added, "Or the most beautiful neurosurgeon."

Pete didn't take the bait and let it pass.

"Your father tells me you've decided on Cornell University."

"Yes. I'm *so* excited." Then her glow faded a bit. "And a little nervous as well."

"Why nervous?" Harry asked. "You've been a star at everything you've done so far. I'd be shocked if that didn't continue." He put his hand over hers and his round face showed boundless pride, as if he were in Julie's bloodline and responsible for many of her achievements in life to date.

Julie said, "It's so nice of you to say that, Uncle Harry. But I was looking at the profiles of incoming students at Cornell. They *all* look like they're stars."

Harry scoffed. "I've seen enough of you in recent years to know you'll shine with the best of them."

Julie's face brightened. "Are you still going to be my tutor if I take some creative writing or J-school courses?"

Harry, who'd been filling that role for the last two years of Julie's high school career and reveled in it, said, "You've gotten to be so skillful with the English language that you probably don't need help from a broken-down newspaperman anymore. But if you think I can help . . ." He looked like a puppy waiting for her to toss him a stick.

Rona Martin, Harry's long-time lady friend and the restaurant's owner, came over to join them. She was a tall woman with a thick mane of sun-streaked hair and warm eyes. Her waist might have filled in a bit over the years, but she still turned a lot of heads. Julie adored her as much as she did Harry.

Their conversation meandered through a host of topics, including the presumptive nominees of the two major political parties for president in the November elections. Harry, who tried to be meticulously even-handed in his coverage of politics, solemnly told of how he'd received letters and emails from people both on the left side of the political spectrum and those on the right, each taking him to task for favoring the other side.

"You must be striking a perfect balance, then," Julie said.

Harry, without appearing to beat his chest too obviously, pushed his half-glasses up on his nose and smoothed the fringe of gray hair that ringed his head and solemnly declared that the importance of even-handed treatment of candidates for public office was something he'd learned in his first year of journalism school. In fact, he said, he kept a quote from his former professor on his desk to remind himself of that journalistic obligation.

They got their dinner orders in and moved on to other topics. As Harry pushed his empty plate away, he looked at Julie and said sagely, "You know, an important benefit of college—apart from getting a first-rate education, of course—is that it fosters the breaking away process."

Pete had been content to let the others carry the conversation, but when he heard Harry's comment, it struck a nerve and he frowned. He'd been down in the dumps for a couple of weeks, brooding over what was ahead. It was one thing to have a son or daughter go off to college if you had five children. It was something else if you had just one.

"I remember how it was with me," Harry continued. "My dad was a prominent journalism professor—he was still teaching at Northwestern at the time—and he liked to give me advice about what courses to take and how I shouldn't join a fraternity and blah, blah, blah. Between you and me, I let everything go in one ear and out the other. It was *my* life and I wanted to make my *own* decisions. Even if I agreed with what he was saying, I still wanted to do it *my* way."

Pete sat stone-faced and listened as Harry packaged and repackaged his advice that Julie should use her college years to become her own person as well as to get a solid education. Pete chafed and waited impatiently for him to wrap it up and move on to something else. He saw Bud Stephanopoulis walk in and seized the opportunity to change the subject. "There's Bud," he said.

Harry stopped talking and looked across the room to where the lanky ex-basketball player was about to slide onto one of the bar stools. He called, "Hey, Bud!"

Bud saw them and came over. He smiled when he saw Julie and said, "Well, look who's here."

Julie had known Bud for years and was particularly captivated by his fleet of watercraft. She jumped up from her chair to give him a hug.

Bud grinned fondly. "A new high school graduate, I understand."

"Why don't you grab one of those chairs over there," Harry said, pointing to the nearby table, "and join us. We were just giving Julie our perspectives on college life, breaking away from family and becoming your own person, that kind of stuff. The things we all learned the hard way. Maybe you've got some wisdom you'd like to add."

Oh God, Pete thought, *can't you talk about something else?*

Bud dragged a chair over and sat next to Julie and signaled to the bartender, Frankie, to bring him a drink. He looked at Julie again and said, "My only advice is to have fun. Don't be a slave to your work regime and sacrifice the college experience. And—red letters here—don't think you're going to get a fat professional sports contract and you'll be on easy street the rest of your life. It can all vanish in a nanosecond." He was obviously referring to his own experience.

"I don't think I'm good enough to be a professional athlete," Julie said, with a hint of blush lighting up her cheeks.

"That's not what your father tells me. He says you're a lights-out soccer player who's capable of leading the country to the World Cup title, plus you're a good enough golfer to go on the LPGA Tour right now."

"Did you say those things, Dad?"

Pete rubbed his chin and looked at Bud. "If you say I said those things, I don't want to call you a liar. But tell me, had I been drinking?"

"Thanks a lot, Dad!"

"Just kidding."

"What's your handicap these days?" Bud asked.

"Seven. I was down to four, but I've slipped."

"I bet with some work and a good instructor, you can reach red numbers. You've got a beautiful golf swing."

"Thanks!" She looked at Pete. "Did you hear that? Maybe I should try out for the golf team at Cornell, too."

Pete shrugged uncomfortably. "Why not?" he said.

They switched to other subjects and Bud had a second drink. When the waiter brought his roast beef sandwich to go, he stood to leave and said to Julie, "I just got a new WaveRunner. One of the really high-performance models. Want to go out tomorrow? Say three o'clock or so?"

"Dad, are we doing anything tomorrow?"

Pete shook his head. "Nothing planned."

"That would be wonderful," she said to Bud. "I can ride my bike to your house to get some exercise."

Pete was tired from the day so they wrapped up dinner with Harry and Rona a half-hour later. On their way home, Pete said, "Just a suggestion, but you might want to keep Bud under control tomorrow. Jet skis can be dangerous."

"Oh, Dad. I've been out with him a dozen times and everything was just fine. You worry too much."

"Part of my job description."

SIX

The man who planned to kill the jet skier knelt in the brush along the shore and placed his burlap-wrapped rifle on the ground beside him. He put the two sections of his kayak paddle on top of the rifle to camouflage it in case someone should come up behind him unexpectedly. His orange kayak was inflated and leaning against his pickup like it usually was when he was about to go on the lake.

After glancing over his shoulder to make sure no one was close by, he raised the binoculars dangling from a strap around his neck and scanned the lake. Then he searched the trees around him. His feigned bird watching was a subterfuge, like the kayak. He listened intently for sounds of an engine on the lake as he continued to gaze around. Through the trees, he saw the woman in the straw hat working in her garden again. He looked at the closest cottage on the other side of the access road, where the invisible woman lived, and wondered if she were watching.

Ten minutes passed, then twenty, then a half-hour. *What if he didn't come today?* The palms of his hands felt moist and he wiped them on his camo shorts. When it got to be an hour, anxiety began to set in. *Maybe he should abort and try again another day.* He scanned the area with his binoculars again. Still no one in sight except the gardener. And in her cottage, the invisible woman ...

The man tried to take his mind off the time by watching birds. A cardinal perched on the branch of a nearby tree, its scarlet plumage gleaming in the sunshine. He trained his binoculars on the bird, studying it as it looked around with herky-jerky movements. The cardinal flew off and he switched his attention to a couple of other birds. He didn't know what they were, but he pretended to study them.

He checked his watch again; he'd been there for an hour and a half. *How much longer could he wait?* Sooner or later someone would come along, maybe with a folding chair to sit on the narrow beach and read. That would be a disaster. Even if scumbag showed up, he wouldn't dare unwrap his rifle because he might be seen. If he did manage to get the rifle into position, he still wouldn't dare fire with someone sitting fifty feet away. The woman digging in her garden, or the invisible woman spying on everyone from an upstairs window, that was one thing. But someone sitting almost right in front of him? He knew the rifle emitted some sound even with the suppressor.

As he forced himself to wait, his hands began to tremble and he gripped one with the other to make them stop. He glanced around to make sure no one was coming in on the access road and scanned the lake yet again. Still no sign of scumbag's jet ski. Then he thought he heard something in the distance and his pulse beat faster and he eagerly swept the lake with his binoculars. Seeing nothing, he concluded that his mind was either playing games with him or the sound he thought he heard came from the highway.

Then he heard it again, a droning sound. He raised his binoculars and studied the horizon. Far to the east, maybe two miles away, he saw twin dots on the water coming toward him in looping patterns. Slowly they morphed into a pair of jet skis. He saw that the one in the lead was black. *That has to be him!* As they came closer, he saw that the figure on the black jet ski was a tall man. *It's scumbag!*

He was confused, though. The times he'd observed scumbag before, he was always alone. He trained his binoculars on the figure on the second jet ski, the red one. It looked like a woman, and his mind raced, trying to get his arms around what was going on. *Would both of them stop where scumbag usually stopped?* And if they did stop, would it be too far out for him to get a shot? When he practiced, he'd always fired at targets from fifty to a hundred yards away. What if they stopped two hundred yards out? Or what if they didn't stop at all? He wasn't confident he could hit a moving target.

As he agonized over the possibilities, a small sailboat came into view on his right. It was on a northbound course and was right in the area where scumbag usually stopped. The day was essentially windless and the sailboat seemed to barely move. Further out, the jet skis continued to swoop and turn, heading directly toward where he was lying in the brush. He studied the figure at the helm of the sailboat. It looked like a young boy, maybe a teenager, with shaggy hair and a skinny frame. He seemed oblivious to everything around him.

The angry whine of the jet skis' engines filled the air and the man watching clamped his hands over his ears to shut out the noise. Closer in, the small boat was directly in front of him now and its sail intermittently blocked his view of the jet skis as they came closer. *Jesus Christ, kid, move!*

While he watched, paralyzed with indecision, the sailboat slowly moved north so the man had an unobstructed view of the jet skiers again. They slowed as they approached the shore and the din of their engines subsided. Then they stopped and the riders appeared to be talking to each other. To his left, the sailboat slowly moved out of his field of vision. He glanced over his shoulder to confirm that he was still alone. *Would he ever get a better chance?*

He let the binoculars hang from their strap again and his mind felt disengaged from his body as he unwrapped his rifle with the telescopic sight and the sound suppressor. His hands trembled as he propped the rifle on the stump in front of him and sighted through the scope and adjusted it to sharpen the focus. After first centering the crosshairs on scumbag's torso, he moved them up to his head. *No, no, take the big target!* He moved the crosshairs down again. His vision blurred and he lowered the rifle and wiped his eyes with the sleeve of his T-shirt. *Do it for crissakes!*

He took several deep breaths to steady himself and focused on his target's torso again, aiming for the mass of his body. His hands continued to tremble, but the tree stump steadied his rifle. His finger tightened on the trigger. *Squeeze,* he reminded himself, *don't jerk.*

Pffft! He closed his eyes when he heard the muffled sound.

Again, he told himself. *Shoot again!*

He opened his eyes and worked the rifle's bolt action and sighted through the scope. *Pffft!* He saw the man slump to one side. He worked the bolt again and squeezed the trigger a third time. *Pffft!* Again. *Pffft!* The man slid toward the water. *Pffft!* He heard his fifth shot ricochet off metal. He fired again.

The scope's crosshairs moved to the woman and centered on her face. *Who was she?* He watched her stare at her companion as he sank into the water. His vision blurred again and his heart pounded wildly. He took his finger off the trigger and looked around. Still no one except the gardener.

He had to get out of there! He rose to his knees and wrapped his rifle in the burlap and searched the ground frantically for the brass shell casings. He found three of them and crammed them into one of his pockets. *How many shots had he fired?* He continued to search around the stump, but didn't find any additional casings. *I can't spend any more time looking!*

He grabbed the burlap-wrapped rifle and the kayak paddle and headed toward his pickup. Out on the water, he heard the woman's sobbing shrieks over the soft purring of the jet skis as he placed the items in the pickup's box and covered them with one end of the tarp. He turned to look at the woman again; her eyes were still focused on the water beside her companion's jet ski. He hoisted the kayak into the pickup and forced himself to walk casually to the driver's-side door and climb in.

His hands trembled and he fumbled around until he finally got his key in the ignition switch and the engine sprang to life.

Pete watched through his telescope as the lead jet ski carved graceful turns in the water and the one trailing fifty yards behind followed in his wake. He saw pink on the second jet skier, the color of Julie's bathing suit, and immediately became irritated. When Bud took Julie jet skiing, she always rode on the seat behind him, but he was certain that was her riding alone this time. *What's she doing?*

Bud slowed to a stop when he got close to the western shore of the lake and waited for Julie to pull up alongside him. Pete watched as they sat side-by-side, apparently talking, and was about to leave his telescope when he saw Bud tilt sideways on his seat, like he was reaching for something. He waited for him to sit up again, but he didn't. Instead, he slid off the jet ski into the water. Pete could see Julie staring at him and his first thought was that Bud had suffered a heart attack.

Then he saw Julie power up her jet ski and head south toward him, staying near the western edge of the lake. For someone not experienced with jet skis, it looked like she was coming at a reckless speed. Suddenly she veered to one side, like she was trying to avoid something, and her jet ski kicked up a spray of water. He saw her either thrown off the machine or jump as it lurched sharply to the left.

Oh Christ! Pete bounded down his front steps and ran to the beach. Without a power boat, he thought his best option was to run down to where Julie was rather than waste time trying to find help. He kicked off his shoes and started through the shallow water, skirting the piers that jutted out every now and then. He slipped on a rock and sprawled head-first into the water, then righted himself and resumed running. His heart pounded and his thighs ached.

He was a hundred yards away from Julie now, and he could see her bobbing in the water, buoyed by her life jacket. He continued to run even though his legs felt leaden and his chest felt like it was going to explode. He circled another pier and found himself in chest-deep water and began to swim with a furious overhand stroke. When he reached Julie, she was crying and he grabbed her.

"What happened?"

She grabbed him and held on and said between sobs, "Bud's hurt."

SEVEN

"**D**id he have a heart attack?"

"He's hurt!"

"I understand that, but do you know what happened?"

"I don't *know* what happened! He just fell off his jet ski and didn't say anything when I asked him what was wrong."

Pete got Julie to shore and spotted two beach towels drying on a nearby pier. He grabbed one and wrapped it around her and held her until she was shaking less. He looked at the jet ski she'd been on. It appeared to be still running.

"Will you be okay for a few minutes while I go down and check on Bud?"

She nodded and pulled the towel tighter around her.

He saw a folding beach chair leaning against a nearby tree and brought it over for her to sit in. Then he borrowed the other beach towel and wrapped it around her legs.

"Stay here," he said. "I'll be right back."

She nodded again.

Pete waded into the water, and when it became too deep, he swam the rest of the way to the jet ski. After a couple of tries, he managed to hoist himself onto the seat without tipping the machine over. The handlebars resembled those of an exercise machine he worked out on at the health club. He studied the controls and managed to get the jet ski moving forward.

He steered away from the shore and looped around to head north, then accelerated. The engine whined as he skimmed over the water at a speed that was faster than he was comfortable with. He throttled back and steered more toward deep water in case there were hazards he couldn't see. When he got close to Bud's jet ski, he throttled back even more and looked at Bud as he circled around him. His head was tilted back and to one side, but his face was out of the water because of his life jacket. He wasn't moving. Worse, there seemed to be blood in the water. Blood wasn't something he associated with a heart attack.

Pete pointed the jet ski toward shore and gave it some throttle again. As he got close, it occurred to him that jet skis likely were driven by propellers like ordinary power boats and could get messed up if they chopped into sand and rocks. He decided not to worry about it and didn't throttle back until he was ten feet from the beach. The jet ski glided up on the sand and came to a lurching stop. He shut down the engine.

He didn't have his cell phone with him, so he knew he had to find a telephone to call the sheriff's office for help. He squinted through the foliage in both directions, searching for the nearest cottage, looking for someone who was outside. He spotted a woman working in her flower garden, and trotted that way through the bramble and trees.

"Ma'am, excuse me. There's been an accident involving a couple of jet skiers and I need to call the sheriff's office right away. Can I use your telephone?"

The woman looked up with a start and seemed alarmed to see a man in water-soaked clothes and disheveled hair standing right behind her. Instinctively, she raised her garden tool in defense. Pete noticed and said,

"I'm Pete Thorsen. I have a cottage just down the shore. Sorry for my appearance, but I had to jump in the lake to rescue my daughter."

The woman continued to size him up. "You said some jet skiers had an accident?"

"Yes."

"Those things are dangerous, you know."

"I know. I need to call for help."

"Oh, my," the woman said, like his words had finally sunk in. "This sounds like an emergency." She walked to the door of her cottage, opened it and pointed to the telephone on the counter. "I'll wait out here," she said as she stepped to the side to let him pass. "Don't forget to dial one and the area code first," she added.

Pete rushed in and grabbed the telephone and dialed the sheriff's office number. He knew it by heart after having called many times over the years. When a deputy answered, he identified himself and told him what had happened. "You better get someone down here as fast as possible," he said.

That led to the usual barrage of questions that always seemed to come when a citizen called to report something. What happened? Were there witnesses to the incident? Was it an accident or was something else involved? Pete finally convinced the man to send an ambulance and worry about the details later. He told him where Bud was located.

The woman was waiting by the door, and when he came out, she said, "I overheard your conversation. It sounds awful. They should pass a law making those jet skis illegal."

Pete only half-heard the woman's words because he was thinking about Julie and he wanted to get back to her. He saw an older model sedan standing in the woman's driveway. "Could you do me another favor after the ambulance gets here?" he asked. "My daughter witnessed the accident and she's very upset. She's about a half-mile away. Could you give me a ride?"

Her suspicious look returned. "Your daughter? You're not making sense, young man. How could she see the accident if she's a half-mile away?"

"She was with the man who was injured when the accident happened."

"I don't understand."

Pete was just about to tell the woman to forget it when he heard a siren. A minute later, an ambulance with its lights flashing bumped in the rough access road. He hurried over and explained to the EMTs what had happened. Satisfied that he'd done what he could, Pete decided to jog back to Julie rather than field twenty more questions from the woman in the straw hat. He started toward M-22 at a trot.

"Sir!" the woman called. "I guess I could put off my gardening and take you to your daughter if you want."

Pete looked back at her. "That's nice of you. Can we go right now? I'm worried about her."

He stood by the woman's car and fidgeted as the woman went into her cottage to get her keys. On her way out, she locked up like she was leaving for a month-long vacation in Europe. He glanced at his watch impatiently. Finally, they piled into her sedan and she started out her driveway. He cringed when she almost hit a tree navigating the narrow driveway.

"What did you say your name was?" the woman asked.

"Pete Thorsen."

"And you say you have a cottage on Crystal Lake?"

"Yes. About a quarter-mile beyond where my daughter is."

As she drove down the highway at a speed suitable for a funeral procession, Pete learned that his chauffeur's name was Lydia Vreeland and that her family had been coming to the lake since early in the twentieth century. He half listened to her stories about the old days and how much everything had changed. He tried to gauge approximately where Julie was, and when he thought they were there, he asked Lydia to turn in a driveway marked by multiple names on a wooden sign. Pete thanked her and got out and walked to where he could see the lakefront in both directions. He spotted Julie sitting in the beach chair wrapped in the borrowed towels about fifty yards up the beach and headed toward her.

"Did you find out what happened to Bud?" Julie asked.

"There's an ambulance there now with two EMTs and they were checking him out when I left." He didn't say anything about the blood because he didn't want to spook her.

"You don't know if he's dead?"

"I couldn't tell. I know he didn't drown because his life jacket was holding his head out of the water. Let's wait to see what the EMTs and the sheriff's people have to say."

Her look suggested that she thought he hadn't done everything he could to help Bud. "Why didn't you at least pull him out of the water?"

Choosing his words carefully, he said, "The worst thing you can do with an injured person is to move him if you don't know what you're doing. As I said, I checked to make sure his face was out of the water and then called the sheriff's office. Let's see what they say."

Julie still didn't look satisfied.

"Let's get home and find some dry clothes," Pete said. He started to walk and Julie shuffled along behind, still wrapped in the borrowed towels and staring down at the sand. Pete waited for her to catch up.

"When there's an accident, don't the police usually want to talk to people who witnessed it?" she asked.

"Usually. When I called the sheriff's office, I told the deputy on duty to ask Detective Tessler to stop at our house and we'd tell him what we know."

They started to walk again. Julie was quiet for most of the way, but then said, "Why did you ask the deputy to have Detective Tessler come to see us if Bud had a heart attack? I thought detectives were only involved if there was a crime."

"Julie, look, I know you're upset. I'm upset, too. I don't know whether Tessler will stop by or not. I just gave the deputy the message in case he *does* come out. I suspect someone will come, though. We're the only witnesses to what happened."

"You aren't a witness. You weren't there."

"I was watching the two of you through my telescope."

She looked surprised and stared at him for a few moments. "You were watching us?"

"I was sitting on the porch working on my article. I heard the jet skis and I looked through my telescope. That's how I knew you were in trouble."

She studied him some more and shook her head. "You don't trust me, do you? What are you going to do when I go off to college? Lurk around campus with your telescope and watch me as I walk between buildings to my classes?"

"Julie . . ."

"Now I know what Uncle Harry was saying last night about breaking away. You talk to him all the time. Maybe he can explain a few things to you. Young people don't like to feel like they live in a police state and are being spied on all the time."

Pete clenched his teeth, but didn't say anything. He heard a power boat out on the lake and turned to look. The boat seemed to be headed toward where Bud's jet ski was and he assumed it belonged to the sheriff's department. He quickened his pace to catch up with Julie.

When they got to their cottage, Julie said, "I'm going to lie down. Let me know if your detective friend just *happens* to show up and wants to interrogate me. I'm sure you'll want to witness *that*, too." She disappeared inside.

Pete shook his head, but didn't say anything again and a few minutes later followed her. He went to the porch and watched through his telescope for ten minutes, but couldn't tell what was going on down the shore. Then he went upstairs to get cleaned up and change clothes. On his way downstairs, he saw that Julie's bedroom door was still closed. He went out to his porch and peered through his telescope again. The sheriff's department boat was anchored out in the water, but Bud's jet ski had been moved to the beach.

He logged off his computer and stuck his paper materials back in the file folder. Then he sat in his favorite chair and wondered some more about the blood he'd seen in the water.

EIGHT

An hour later, Joe Tessler's unmarked Acura sedan pulled into Pete's driveway and parked behind his Range Rover. The detective got out and glanced up at the screened porch.

"Come on up," Pete called.

While a trim man, Tessler walked on his heels so it sounded like a person twice his weight was clomping up the steps. He let the screen door slam behind him and came to the porch where Pete was sitting and dropped into a chair. He brushed his wing of dark hair away from his forehead and said, "Your buddy Stephanopoulis is dead."

Pete grimaced. "I was afraid of that. A heart attack?"

Tessler shook his head. "He was shot. At least four times from what we can tell."

"Shot," Pete repeated, stunned.

"Judging from the brass one of our guys found on shore, he was killed with a high-powered hunting rifle. A .223 it looks like."

Pete digested that and said as much to himself as to Tessler, "That explains the blood."

"What's your point?"

"When I went down there, I saw blood in the water. I assumed Bud had hit his head on the jet ski when he fell off and it was coming from a cut."

Tessler shook his head again. "Gunshot wounds. Your daughter was on the other jet ski, right?"

"Yes. They'd rendezvoused and were talking when it happened."

"Did she hear shots? Or see anyone?"

"If she did, she didn't tell me. She's upstairs. You might want to talk to her yourself. She's pretty shaken up by what happened."

"Our deputy told me you witnessed the incident, too."

"Only from long distance." He told Tessler about watching Bud and Julie with his telescope and seeing Bud fall off into the water.

Tessler scribbled in his spiral pocket notebook. "Do you think I should talk to your daughter now? Or should I come back?"

"It's up to you."

"We'll need to talk to her at some point. As far as we know, she's the only one who witnessed the whole thing up close."

Pete went to get Julie, and when he returned, said, "She'll be here in a minute."

It wasn't a minute, but Julie eventually walked out on the porch dressed in a loose-fitting T-shirt and denim shorts. Her still-damp hair was pulled back in a ponytail. She'd met Tessler before, but Pete introduced him again.

Tessler started off with some soothing words, and after brushing his forelock back from his face again, he said, "I understand you were on a separate jet ski following Mr. Stephanopoulis."

"What happened to him?" she asked, ignoring Tessler's routine statement that he obviously just wanted her to confirm.

Tessler glanced at Pete, then said, "Someone shot him."

Julie looked at him for a few moments like she didn't really believe him, then clamped her hands over her face and said, "Oh my God!" Tears began to run down her face.

Tessler waited for her to get a grip on herself. Finally he said, "I know it's hard, but I need to ask you some questions. You're the only eyewitness we have."

She wiped her eyes and kept shaking her head.

It was an awkward moment and Pete wanted to go over and comfort her, but given the way she'd lashed out at him earlier, he knew that probably would be a mistake. Better to let Tessler handle it.

Tessler said in a gentle voice, "If you'd prefer, I can come back later."

She took her hands away from her face and looked at him and said, "He's dead, isn't he?"

Tessler nodded.

"No!" she said and her hands returned to her face.

Tessler looked at Pete, obviously seeking guidance. Finally, he said in a low voice, "I'll come back later, Julie."

She continued to sit with head bowed and her hands covering her face, shaking her head.

Pete knew he had to say something. "I agree that later might be best, Joe."

Julie lifted her head and looked at her father and said in a snappish voice, "Why don't *you* tell him what happened. I'm sure you know everything. You admitted you were spying on us."

"Sweetie, I wasn't *spying* on you."

"Stop calling me Sweetie! I'm eighteen, not eight. I'm not a child anymore."

"Sorry."

"You want to control everything I do," she continued, looking defiant.

Pete knew better than to argue with her when she was in this frame of mind and just kept quiet.

Julie got up and grabbed a wad of tissues from a box on a nearby table and sat down again. She wiped her eyes and said to Tessler, "Okay, what do you want to know that my father the spy hasn't already told you?"

Pete knew he had to get out of there before he said something he would regret. He got up and said, "Do you want something to drink, Joe?"

"Water, thanks."

"Julie?"

She just glared at him.

Pete went to the kitchen and took his time before he returned to the porch with three bottles of water. Tessler was in the middle of taking Julie through the chronology of what had happened that afternoon. Pete placed two bottles of water on the table between them.

"So you rode your bike down to Bud's place. What time was that?"

"About 3:30 p.m."

"Did you go out on the jet skis right away?"

She sniffled. "Do you mean both jet skis?"

Tessler looked puzzled. "Yes, the ones the two of you were on when Bud was shot."

"No. Bud had just gotten a new racing-model jet ski. A WaveRunner like his other jet skis, except it's a lot more powerful. He took me for a ride on it."

Tessler waited for her to continue.

She sniffled again. "When we got back, I asked him if we could switch positions so I could take the controls. He wouldn't let me, but after we talked about it for a few minutes, he agreed to let me follow him on one of his less powerful jet skis. I'd operated that one a couple of times before."

"Okay, then you both were on jet skis headed west, right?"

"Yes, Bud had a route he liked to follow. When we got to the western end of the lake, we were sitting on our jet skis, talking. I was glad to rest because I was nervous and stressed out after holding the handles of my jet ski."

"That's when Bud was shot, when you were sitting on your jet skis talking?"

Tears started to stream from Julie's eyes again. She dabbed at them with a tissue and said, "Except I didn't *know* he'd been shot. He just slumped in his seat and finally fell off into the water."

"Did you hear shots?"

She dabbed at her eyes again and shook her head. "I didn't hear anything. Except our jet ski engines. They were idling as we talked."

"Did you see anyone on shore?"

She shook her head again. "I didn't really look, though. I was concerned about Bud and kept looking at him."

"What did you do after he fell into the water?"

"I don't remember exactly. I was so confused. All I thought about was getting back so I could tell Dad and get some help for Bud."

Pete listened to her account and was relieved that she was referring to him as "Dad" again and not as "the spy."

Tessler turned to Pete and said, "And after you got Julie to shore, that's when you said you went down to see what was wrong with Bud, right?"

"Right. Like I told you, I saw what appeared to be blood in the water."

Julie's eyes widened and she said in an accusing voice, "You didn't tell me about seeing blood."

"You're right, I didn't," Pete said. "I told Joe that I thought Bud might have hit his head and cut it when he fell off the jet ski. I had no idea he'd been shot."

"You still could have told me," Julie said, not letting it go.

"Maybe I should have, but I didn't want to make it sound worse than it was until we knew all of the facts."

"Treating me like an eight-year-old again," she said disgustedly.

Pete chafed at her continued sniping, but didn't say anything.

"Anything else?" Tessler asked.

"I used a telephone in a nearby cottage to call your office," Pete said. "You know the rest."

"Well, I'm going back to the scene," Tessler said. "I'll let you know what else we find out."

When Tessler was gone, Pete said to Julie, "What would you like for dinner?"

"I'm not hungry." She got up and walked through the living room to the stairs leading to the second floor. Seconds later, he heard her bedroom door slam.

NINE

When the man who'd shot Bud Stephanopoulis got back to his house, his heart was still thumping, but his anxiety level was down and he was able to think more clearly. *He'd finally done it,* he kept reminding himself. He checked to be sure no one was around, then unlocked the padlock that secured the shed door and went inside and began moving things around to get at the hidden compartment.

He went outside again and tried to look casual as he walked to his pickup, like he was about to move gardening supplies from his truck to the shed. He carried the inflatable kayak inside and stuffed it in the compartment, and went back for the burlap-wrapped rifle, the paddle, and the duffel bag. He exhaled deeply after he'd closed the shed door behind him, relieved to be out of sight again.

He began to store the items in the compartment, but after thinking about it, rearranged everything and put the rifle in first. He was about to put the duffel bag in when he remembered the brass shell casings and fished them out of his pocket and put them in a Zip-Lock bag and added the bag to the items already in the duffel. Then he placed the duffel on the compartment's floor and leaned the paddle sections against the wall. Finally he stuffed the deflated kayak in and flattened it with his foot. He stared at the stuffed compartment. It was only temporary, and he knew the reordering would do him no good if he came under suspicion and the compartment was discovered before he'd disposed of the items. However, not having the rifle visible immediately somehow made him feel better.

The same worries he'd had when he searched the ground for shell casings returned. *How many shots had he fired?* He removed everything from the compartment and unwrapped the rifle and extracted its ammunition clip. Then he worked the rifle's bolt action and a shell casing flew out. He scrambled around until he found it under the workbench.

He was breathing hard when he rose to his feet again and his chest felt tight. He stood in the dim light and tried to focus his mind. He was certain he'd filled the magazine with five rounds of ammunition and inserted another round in the chamber so he wouldn't have to work the rifle's bolt action for his first shot. He checked the Zip-Lock bag in the duffel and confirmed that there were three shell casings in it. With the one in his hand, that made four rounds. Two casings were unaccounted for and must still be at the scene.

His hands began to twitch again. What if the authorities found the other two casings? As a precaution, he'd wiped each round of ammunition with a cloth, but what if he'd missed something and they found a fingerprint? He tried to remember whether he'd ever been fingerprinted but couldn't think of an occasion. He'd been ticketed for speeding on the Interstate a few years earlier, but they didn't fingerprint you for that kind of offense, did they? What if the authorities began to suspect him for some reason? If he were arrested, they'd certainly fingerprint him and might be able to identify him as the shooter that way.

As he stood in the semi-darkness, he wondered if he should go back and try to find the other two casings. No, that would be too risky. Someone might see him. Even if he wore his disguise, the risk was too great. He'd just have to take a chance that the casings weren't traceable to him.

He consoled himself with the fact that scumbag was dead. At least he thought he was.

He put everything back in the compartment and restored the insulation and rehung the pegboard and shoved the workbench and the sailboat back into their usual positions. Then he stepped back and surveyed everything. It looked like the typical cluttered shed, which was what he wanted. For his own safety, though, he had to get rid of things just as he'd planned. The question was how. He'd thought of burying the rifle and other items in his garden where fresh earth wouldn't look suspicious. That would be convenient, but he thought about a story he'd read where the accused person had buried the murder weapon in his garden. That turned out to be one of the first places the authorities looked. He had to come up with something better.

He locked up and walked to his house, feeling a mix of emotions. Relief that it was over and terror at the consequences of what he'd done. The scumbag deserved it, though. As a matter of fact, his death came too quickly. It should have been slower, more agonizing. But he'd done it the sure way, the certain way, if not the most satisfying.

Inside, he stripped off his T-shirt and camo shorts and threw them into the washing machine and started the cycle. Disposal of the clothes was one thing he did have a specific plan for. Two black plastic bags stuffed with other clothes he wanted to get rid of rested in the corner. He planned to add the T-shirt to one bag and the camo shorts to another and take them to the Goodwill drop-off in Traverse City in separate donations. As the washing machine ground away, he wondered if he should wait on the clothes until he was sure scumbag was dead.

Out of habit more than hunger, the man looked through his refrigerator for something to eat. He settled for a bottle of Zero Water and drank it while he turned on the television just in time to catch the "Breaking News" segment reporting that a man had died while jet skiing on Crystal Lake. The cause of his death was unknown, the anchor said, saying his body had been taken to the morgue for an autopsy. Then the anchor turned to a different story.

The man clicked off the television and leaned back with his eyes closed, breathing in and out deeply, trying to relax. He opened his eyes again and stared at the ceiling and wondered when the investigation would begin. And how aggressive that idiot sheriff would be. He felt the need to move around, to be active.

He went outside and stared at his shed for a long time and wondered if he should begin disposing of things that night, when it got dark. He hated this time of the year when it stayed light so long. He preferred night, when the stars were visible and everything was quiet and peaceful. He walked around the shed, observing, thinking. When he got to the front again, he yanked the padlock to make sure it was securely locked.

After eating some leftover chicken, Pete moved to his porch with a glass of wine and put a Sam Cooke CD on his Bose system. He kept the sound turned down so he wouldn't disturb Julie in case she was trying to sleep. He was worried about her. She hadn't been out of her bedroom since Joe Tessler left.

He sipped his wine and tried to make sense of Bud's shooting. He could be prickly at times, and on occasion even something of a jerk, but as far as Pete knew, he was reasonably well liked around town. He drew a complete blank when he tried to come up with the names of people who might want to kill him.

After filling his wine glass again, he dialed Joe Tessler's cell phone number. He wondered if the sheriff's office team had found anything when they scoured the area where they thought the shots had come from. Tessler didn't answer and Pete didn't leave a message. Joe would see from Caller ID that he'd called, and if he were inclined to talk, he'd call back.

Darkness was setting in, and Pete debated whether he should check on Julie. After putting it off a couple of times, he climbed the stairs and rapped on her door.

"Julie? Can I bring you something?"

Hearing no response, he knocked again. "Julie?"

Pete was about to open her door and see if she was sleeping, when she said, "I don't want anything. I'm trying to sleep."

"Okay, let me know if you change your mind."

He returned to the porch and changed the music on his player to one of his all-time favorites, the late Johnny Cash. He turned the volume up slightly and sat down again and poured another glass of wine and listened as Johnny worked his way through "I Walk the Line" and "Folsom Prison Blues" and "Jackson." He hummed along with the lyrics.

The music made him think of his old army buddy, Jimmy Ray Evans, the person responsible for turning him on to oldies. The previous year, Jimmy Ray, at the time a disc jockey in a small southeastern city, had shown up at his lake house unannounced, ostensibly to get away from the music scene for a while, but as Pete later discovered, really to escape a North Carolina sheriff who was after him for personal reasons. Pete managed to get Jimmy Ray out of that scrape, and the last he saw of him was when he was headed for Mobile, Alabama to take a job at a radio station owned by a woman he was bedding.

If someone had shot Jimmy Ray, with his weakness for booze and penchant for getting involved with the ladies, he almost could understand it. But he'd never seen those traits in Bud Stephanopoulis, except maybe the liquor part. He wondered what he'd be able to get out of Tessler when he called back. He thought some more about people who might have had it in for Bud.

He looked at his watch again and saw that it was after 10:00 p.m. It was getting close to his bedtime, and he was torn between letting Julie sleep off her grief or knocking on her door again. He decided to take another stab at father-daughter communication.

He rapped on her door and called, "Julie?"

No answer.

"Julie? I'm going to bed soon. Can I get you something? Or we can talk about this afternoon if you want to."

When he heard no response, he eased her door open a crack. The room was dark, but with the light from the hall, he could see her lying on her bed curled into the fetal position.

"Are you okay?" he asked.

"I told you I'm fine and that I don't want anything! Now leave me alone, please!"

"I'm not going to leave you alone as long as you keep acting this way. You need to eat something and get ready for bed. You'll feel better in the morning."

No response.

"Julie?"

"I told you, I'm not hungry and I don't want to talk."

"If you don't want to talk, fine, but you should eat."

Silence.

"You keep reminding me that you're eighteen. You need to start acting like it."

More silence.

"I'm not leaving until we talk," Pete said.

Suddenly she sat up in bed and looked at him. "If we talk, you won't like what I have to say. Now please, leave my room!"

"You're acting childish, Julie."

"Oh, am I? You know what, Dad? *You're* the reason Bud is dead."

Pete stared at her in the semi-darkness and was speechless for a few moments. Finally he said, "That's ridiculous."

"Is it? Do you remember those things we talked about when we took that farewell tour of my school yesterday? How some goons chased me because of something you got mixed up in? How someone stuck a knife in my door because of something else you were involved in?"

"Julie, I explained both of those incidents."

"Oh, sure, you gave me your convenient explanation, but you know what, I don't believe you anymore. Wayne," she said, referring to her biological father, "told me that you've been involved in one thing after another like this. He's right!"

Pete had been locked in an ongoing battle with Wayne Sable for years, and after the knife incident, he'd taken Pete to court in an effort to deny him all contact with Julie, citing Pete's allegedly reckless lifestyle that endangered Julie's well-being. The judge denied Sable's motions, in part due to his own wanton ways, but obviously Sable hadn't let the matter drop and had been working on Julie. Pete knew, though, that this was the wrong time to get into a discussion of Sable's attempts to influence her for his own selfish interests.

"Be logical, Julie. How could I be responsible for Bud's death?" Pete asked. "I was a mile away when he was shot. I don't even own a firearm."

"You and Bud must have been involved in something. That's probably why someone killed him."

"You know that's not true."

"Well, you wanted to talk, *Dad*. Now we've talked and you know what I'm thinking."

Her comments hurt. He said quietly, "Goodnight, Julie. I'll see you in the morning."

He went back to the porch and sat down again and stared at the lights around the lake for a long time. Then he went to his wine rack and got a fresh bottle of Pinot Grigio. He opened it and settled back in his chair and resumed staring at the lake while Johnny Cash sang about the "Ring of Fire" in his gravelly voice.

TEN

ete woke the next morning with a flannel mouth and a drummer beating a staccato rhythm in his head. One glance in the bathroom mirror confirmed that he looked as bad as he felt. He wanted to retreat to a dark corner and sulk, but knew from experience that a morning run would be a better tonic.

He brushed his teeth and changed into running clothes. On his way downstairs, he saw that Julie's bedroom door was still closed. He left a note saying he'd gone for a run and would be back in an hour. He clamped his favorite "Save the Boat" cap low over his eyes and headed out.

Each time his foot landed, it seemed to reenergize the drummer at work in his head. He did his best to ignore the throbbing and concentrate on the splendor around him. When he came to South Shore, he veered left and followed the road that hugged the south side of the lake. The sun was still low in the sky and cast a sparkling sheen on the water as he loped east. Dog walkers were out in force, and occasionally he'd meet a group of ladies who were power walking and chatting animatedly. He looked straight ahead and didn't do anything to invite conversation.

He passed the public beach and thought about Bud Stephanopoulis's place which was a few miles ahead just off Shorewood Drive. He wondered if the sheriff's department's forensic people had searched the house yet. Or if they intended to search it. He was tempted to stretch out his normal routine and run past the house to see if there was any crime scene tape indicating that they'd been there, but decided against it. Even on a good day, that would be a little much.

Pete continued on for a while, then turned around and headed back. He was dragging when he got to his driveway and walked the rest of the way to his house. He smelled bacon frying as he climbed the steps. That was a good sign because it meant Julie was up. He walked in and saw her in the kitchen with a white apron protecting her shorts and T-shirt and said, "Good morning."

Julie looked up and repeated a bit sheepishly, "Good morning."

"That smells good. Are you cooking for two?"

"Uh huh. Scrambled eggs and bagels and fruit. And a few strips of bacon. I thought you'd be hungry after your run."

"Wow, aren't you sweet."

She looked at his sweat-soaked T-shirt and wrinkled her nose. "Gads, did you jump in the lake or something?"

He grinned and said nothing about last night's wine working its way out of his body. "Are you saying you won't have breakfast with me unless I clean myself up?"

She resumed cracking eggs into a bowl. "If you can be in and out of the shower in fifteen minutes, your timing will be perfect. More than that and everything will be cold and you'll have to eat by yourself."

"I'll be back down in fourteen minutes, max."

He took a quick shower, brushed his damp hair, slipped on a pair of clean jeans and a polo shirt and went downstairs again.

Julie looked at him and checked the kitchen clock. "Not bad for an old man. You look a lot better, too. I like that facial stubble. It gives you a 'with it' look."

Pete flashed his grin again. "I'll tell you, daughter, all along my route this morning I had to dodge lovelies who were trying to strike up a conversation."

Julie looked at him and came over and engulfed him in her arms and buried her face against his chest. "I'm sorry about last night," she said. "I was just so freaked out by what happened."

Pete put his arms around her, too, and fought to control his emotions. "Hey, no apologies necessary. It was a bad day." He kissed the top of her head.

She pushed back gently. "We could stand here all gooey, or we could eat this delicious breakfast I spent hours slaving in a hot kitchen to prepare."

"I opt for breakfast."

"You made the right choice, Buster."

Julie dished up two plates and carried them to the porch where she'd set a small table for two. Then she tore into her breakfast like she hadn't eaten in a day, which she hadn't. Pete wolfed his down as well. He was feeling better after his run, but mostly because his relationship with his daughter seemed to be back on track.

She took a bite of her bagel and looked out at the lake while she chewed and then looked back at him. "So what's your plan? Are you going to help Sheriff Richter and his people investigate Bud's murder?"

He hadn't expected such a direct question, and he frowned. After a few moments, he said, "I don't think they need my help. Or want it for that matter."

"This is the kind of situation where you get involved, isn't it? Where a friend is in some kind of trouble? Or in this case, where he's been murdered."

"Let's see how it plays out," Pete said, uneasy about being put on the spot.

"I think you should try to help if you can. Bud was your friend. And kind of my friend, too. But if you *do* get involved, you have to promise me you'll be careful. I think that's the reason I lashed out at you last night. If I lost you, I don't know what I'd do."

Pete got a lump in his throat. That's when Joe Tessler called.

"Pete, I was scrolling through my missed calls and saw your name."

"Just checking in to see if there was anything new on the Bud Stephanopoulis shooting."

"Thanks for getting right to the point rather than beating around the bush like you usually do. Trying to pretend that you called to ask about my love life or something."

"How *is* your love life, Detective?"

Tessler laughed. "Glad you asked. It's picking up after last night. When we have more time, I'll tell you about this gal from Manistee I've been seeing. I took her to the Little River Casino last night. You ever been there?"

"Once," Pete said, thinking about an old love, Lynn Hawke.

"We'll have to compare notes sometime. But before we get sidetracked with romantic stuff, Frank asked if you'd be willing to come to our office and give us some background on Stephanopoulis. Plus, of course, share any observations you might have on the shooting."

Pete didn't say anything for a moment, then, "Every time I talk to your boss, he seems to horse me around. This isn't going to be one of those times, is it?"

"I'm sure it's not. We're just trying to piece together a picture of the vic and see if anything jumps out that might kick-start our investigation."

"Okay."

"So you'll come? Frank and I are both in the office now."

Pete thought about his schedule for that morning, which like most mornings since he moved north, was conspicuously free of obligations. "Will an hour from now work?"

"Perfect."

"Do you want Julie, too?"

"Not right now. She was pretty clear about what happened when I talked to her yesterday. How is she by the way?"

"Fine," Pete said, not wanting to get into a prolonged discussion of the subject with his daughter sitting across the table from him.

When he ended the call, Julie said, "So, do they want to talk to me again?"

"Not right now. They might want to later, though."

Julie had seemed almost back to normal, but now she looked at him with an annoyed expression again. "Is this a case of them thinking that a teenager isn't able to contribute anything?"

"I don't think that's it. You were very thorough when you talked to Tessler yesterday. What they're looking for today is some background on Bud. Joe probably didn't see any need for you sit through that."

"Okaaay. If they think of anything a vacuous teenager might know, please tell them they know where to find me." She got up from the table, dumped her dishes in the sink with a clatter, and went up the stairs to her bedroom.

Pete shook his head. He did a quick clean-up of the kitchen, and went upstairs himself to put on a better shirt. On his way out, he rapped on Julie's closed door and said, "I should be back in a couple of hours."

The County Government Center was in Beulah, at the east end of the lake. Pete parked and went to the sheriff's office and asked for Joe Tessler. Tessler came out a couple of minutes later and led him down the hall to one of the interview rooms. It wasn't the same room he'd been in during his past visits, but looked like a clone. Windowless, a laminated table that was too large for the room, plastic chairs, scuff marks on the walls from chairs being pushed back and rubbing against them, no artwork.

Tessler motioned for Pete to take one of the chairs across the table and sat down close to the door. Sheriff Franklin Richter came in a few minutes later and took a seat one chair away from Tessler. Richter was a workout freak and his body showed it. He wasn't particularly tall, maybe five-ten or five-eleven, but had a massive torso that seemed disproportionate to the rest of his body and the fabric of his uniform shirt strained under his muscles. His cherubic face gave him the appearance of being ten years younger than he actually was. As always, his brush-cut hair was moussed and perfectly styled.

Pete had a history with the sheriff that went back a half-dozen years, and they weren't exactly fond of each other. Richter looked at Pete and smirked. "Right smack in the middle of it again, huh Thorsen?"

Pete rolled his eyes and looked at Tessler.

Tessler, who often tried to act as peacemaker between the two, seemed to read his thoughts and quickly jumped in. "Frank, as we discussed, Mr. Thorsen knew the vic for quite a few years. To get the ball rolling, I suggest we have him start with when he first met him and take us through yesterday. Then he can share his thoughts about who might have had a motive to murder him."

Richter's expression suggested that he'd prefer to have a little more fun at Pete's expense, but he waved his hand for him to proceed. Pete repackaged what he'd told Tessler the previous afternoon, adding more detail. Then he summarized what Julie had said about the incident and his own observations.

"So to put a finer point on it," Richter said, "Stephanopoulis and your daughter were on their jet skis at the western end of the lake. They'd stopped fifty or seventy-five yards from shore and were talking to each other. Stephanopoulis was shot while they were talking. No one heard shots or saw anyone fire them. Does that accurately sum it up?"

"Pretty much."

Richter looked at Tessler and said, "We're going to want to talk to his daughter to see if she has a different perspective."

"I already talked to her once. What she said is spot-on with Mr. Thorsen's version. I decided not to bring her in today because she's really upset from the experience. We can always talk to her again in the future if we see a need."

That seemed to satisfy Richter. He looked at Pete again and asked, "How long did you say you knew Stephanopoulis?"

"Ten or twelve years. I first met him when my wife and I starting coming to the lake."

"How would you characterize your relationship? Were you close friends?"

Pete considered that. "We were friends, but not what I'd call close friends."

"Which means?"

"We played basketball quite a lot when we were both up here. Had dinner and drinks once in a while. Sometimes I'd see him around town and we'd talk. That sort of thing. But we weren't close in the way that best friends are close"

"You must have been pretty close if he took your daughter jet skiing."

"I don't see your point. A lot of people around here take other people's kids tubing or water skiing or whatever. That doesn't necessarily mean they're good friends."

Tessler jumped in and said, "Lucky Julie wasn't riding behind the vic yesterday."

Pete had thought of the same thing.

"I understand that Stephanopoulis was quite a basketball player."

"He was. All-American at the University of Minnesota. Drafted in the first round by the Boston Celtics."

"Then he went into investing banking, right?"

"Yes. He was with a small firm for a while, then that firm merged with Harrison Stryker LLP in Philadelphia. He made a bundle of money and retired young."

"Did you ever do legal work for Harrison Stryker? Or for Stephanopoulis personally?"

"No to both questions. I didn't really know Bud when he was at Harrison Stryker or I might have tried to get some of their business."

"You didn't do any estate planning for him?" Richter persisted. "I'm told that rich guys need a ton of that kind of work, although I wouldn't know about that myself." Richter shot a look at his detective who he obviously viewed as a kindred soul financially.

"I'm not an estate planning lawyer. I could probably do a simple will and not much more. Bud was a smart guy. I'm sure he needed something a lot more sophisticated than what I could offer. He probably used a specialist at one of the big firms in Chicago or Detroit or somewhere."

Richter stared at his notes, then looked up and said, "Stephanopoulis had a place in Panama, right?"

"That's what he told me."

"Were you ever down there?"

"Never."

"Did he ever have any of his Panamanian friends up here?"

"Possible, I don't know. If he did, I never met them."

Richter looked at his notes again. After a few moments he said to Tessler, "Detective Tessler, do you have any other questions for Mr. Thorsen?"

"Just one. Since we talked yesterday, has anyone come to mind who might have a motive to kill the vic? Someone with a serious grudge against him, for example? A family member maybe?"

Pete shook his head. "I've thought about that, but I've come up blank."

"If you do think of someone, you'll let us know, right?"

Pete nodded.

"Alright," Richter said, "I guess this wraps it up for now. Thanks for coming in." He got up and left the room.

Tessler expelled air from his lungs, as if he were relieved. He looked at Pete. "I thought the two of you got along pretty well today."

"Are you suggesting that this might be the dawn of a new chapter in sheriff's department-citizen relations?"

"You never know." Then Tessler added, "Do you want to see Sheree's photograph? She's the woman I told you about when we talked on the phone." He was already reaching for his wallet.

"Sure."

He plucked a photograph from the wallet and handed it across the table. It showed Tessler posing with his arm around the waist of a brassy-looking woman in a top that few people would describe as modest.

Pete nodded approvingly, and asked, "What's her full name?"

"Sheree Starr." Tessler spelled Sheree and emphasized that Starr had a double 'r,' like the old Green Bay Packers quarterback. "Kind of unique," he said. "I like the way the name rolls off the tongue. Sheree Starr."

"Sounds kind of like . . . an entertainer," Pete said, choosing his words carefully.

Tessler furled his brows for a few moments, then said, "Yeah, maybe. I could see her name on a theater marquee somewhere. I don't think she's ever been in show business, though."

"Umm."

"We had this shot taken at the casino last night. She has a copy and I have one."

"Have you known her long?"

"Last night was our third date. You never know about these things, but I have a feeling there might be a spark there."

"Is she aware of your complications down in Chicago?"

Tessler frowned. "You mean with Taty?"

Pete nodded. As far as he knew, Tessler was still married to Taty, which is what he called his estranged wife.

"I haven't told Sheree about my status yet. I was thinking, you know, that if we develop a relationship, it might stimulate some action on my part."

"So you've about gotten Taty out of your system."

"I really don't know if I'm there yet, but I'm working on it. Tell you what, when we both have the lunch hour free, let's get some sandwiches and go to our favorite thinking spot and talk about it."

When Pete got back to his lake house, he found a note from Julie saying that she'd gone to a friend's house and would be back that evening. He was glad that she'd gotten out. He was concerned about her sinking back into a dark mood after their last conversation that morning.

Pete grabbed something to eat and settled down on his porch with his laptop and the file folder that contained his raw material for the article he was writing for *The Fjord Times*. As he tapped the keyboard, something caught his eye down the lakeshore. He went to his telescope and scanned the area and saw three people walking around near where Bud Stephanopoulis was shot. The sheriff's department crime scene team, he assumed. He was tempted to go down and "inadvertently" run into them, but quickly put the thought out of his mind. With his luck, Sheriff Richter would be there and he didn't need the hassle.

He went back to working on his article, but periodically returned to his telescope to check on what was happening along the lakeshore. When he reached the point where his heart was no longer in his work, he grilled a burger and sat on the porch and ate it and thought some more about Bud's murder.

ELEVEN

Pete glanced at Julie who was slumped against the passenger-side door, dozing, as he drove north toward Sleeping Bear Dunes National Lakeshore. She'd gotten home late the previous night after spending much of the day with her friend from school, Sarah Kettering, whose family had a second home on the north side of the lake. He'd stayed up until she got home. She'd been friendly enough, although hardly effusive. To keep her mind off the shooting incident, he'd talked her into an outing at Sleeping Bear and then lunch in Traverse City.

Julie stirred as he navigated the winding road in the national park and parked in the small lot close to the overlook that featured a magnificent view of the sand dune and the nearby lake. They walked across the short bridge to the observation deck and she leaned on the rail and gazed out. After a few moments, she said, "I remember the first time you and Mom took me here. I think I was three or four."

"Do you remember how old you were when you first climbed the dune?"

"Seven. You guys climbed to the top with me the first time. I wanted to go again, but you were both tired out so you sat on a bench and watched me go by myself. Do you remember that?"

"I do. You waved to us from the top."

Julie gazed out some more and was quiet. "I still miss Mom," she finally said.

Pete put his arm around her and gave her a squeeze. "I miss her, too."

After admiring the scenery a while longer, they left and followed the winding road again out of the park. When they passed the base of the imposing sand dune, Pete asked Julie whether she wanted to climb it, but she begged off, saying she had the entire summer for that kind of thing.

They continued on to Traverse City, following the West Bay into town. Julie was dozing again and Pete tapped her shoulder and said, "Hungry?"

Julie blinked and seemed disoriented. "What time is it?"

"Noon."

She shook off her drowsiness and said, "Could we go someplace where we can sit outside?"

Pete thought for a moment. "How about the West End Tavern? It's right ahead. They have an outdoor patio."

"Fine."

Pete circled through the parking lot twice before he found an open spot. They managed to get a patio table looking out at the marina, and both of them ordered iced tea with lemon.

Julie sipped her tea and gazed at the jumble of watercraft. She looked at Pete and smiled. "Who needs the Riviera when we have this? Have you ever been to the Riviera, Dad?"

"Once, when I was in the army in Germany."

"Was it something like this?"

Pete thought about it. "Sort of. Maybe a touch swankier."

"You mean fancier?"

"Yeah, maybe that's a better word. A lot of the rich and famous go there."

Julie eyed him. "You weren't rich and famous in those days. At least according to what you told me."

"I'm still not, but the army owned a couple of hotels that they made available to GIs at *very* cheap rates. I went there with two of my buddies for a long weekend."

"Did you see any rich and famous people while you were there?"

"To three poor soldiers, everyone on the Riviera seemed rich and famous. We just didn't know who they were."

"That sounds exciting. Maybe you should have stayed in the army. You could have been a general by now."

"I don't think there's a path for a spec four to be promoted to general."

"What's a spec four?"

"It's short for specialist fourth class. The E-4 pay grade. It's like a corporal."

"Umm."

"Besides, if I'd stayed in the army, I wouldn't have been able to afford you."

After they ordered their lunches, Julie looked at Pete with an impish smile and said, "I'm not *that* expensive, am I?"

Pete put his hand on hers and said, "If you are, Sweetie, you're worth every cent."

He saw a woman in a navy suit with tortoise-shell glasses holding her dark hair back walking toward the door that connected the patio and the inside of the restaurant. He called to her. "Susan!"

She saw him and came over to their table. "Pete, I haven't seen you in ages."

"Susan, this is my daughter, Julie."

Susan Ettleman shook Julie's hand and said, "Hello, Julie. I've heard all about you."

Julie flashed a slightly embarrassed smile and said, "Only the good parts I hope."

"Off the charts."

"Could you join us for a few minutes?" Pete asked Ettleman.

She looked at her watch and said, "If you'll let me visit the ladies' room first."

While they were waiting for her to come back, Julie asked, "Is Susan another of your girlfriends?"

Pete laughed. "No, she's a woman I used to help me on a legal matter a few years ago. I've only seen her a couple of times since then." He didn't want to tell her that he'd also gone to Ettleman on a professional basis when he was having problems adjusting after seeing a man known as the Colonel blown away in his own house with a shotgun.

"What does she do? She doesn't look like a clerk at K-Mart."

"She's a psychiatrist."

"A shrink."

"In layman's terminology."

Ettleman came back and sat down. She looked at Julie and said, "You're in college now, right?"

"Starting in the fall."

"Where are you going?"

"Cornell."

"You're kidding. I did my undergrad work there."

Julie's eyes came alive. "Did you like it?"

"Loved it. Have you been on the campus yet?"

"Once. When Dad and I took my college tour."

Ettleman smiled and looked at Pete and said, "You couldn't talk her into going to the University of Wisconsin-Madison, huh?"

Pete smiled. "That was one of the schools on her secondary list. In case she didn't get into one of her first choices."

Julie acted like she hadn't heard his zinger, and began bombarding Ettleman with questions about Cornell. Pete left to use the men's room, and when he came back, they were still talking about college life in general and Cornell in particular.

"Dad," Julie said, "Susan told me about all of the weight she put on in her freshman year because she didn't eat right. She said that happens to a lot of freshman girls. That's scary."

"That shouldn't be a problem for you, though," Ettleman interjected. "You've been in boarding school so cafeteria food won't be a new experience. Besides, colleges have gotten savvier and most of them now offer salad bars and healthier eating options. That wasn't the case when I was in college."

Ettleman and Julie talked about college life some more, and then she looked at her watch again and said, "I'm sorry, I have to go." She looked at Julie and said, "Let's have lunch before you leave for Cornell. We can talk about college from the female perspective without prying male ears listening in." She rapped Pete playfully in the shoulder with the back of her hand and smiled at him and got up.

"By the way," she said, "I see your little lake community has made the news again. A man was shot while he was jet skiing or something?"

Pete's eyes flicked toward Julie and he chose his words carefully. "That's right. The sheriff's department is investigating. I haven't heard whether they have any suspects yet."

He was aware of Julie's eyes on him. "I don't know why you're being so coy, Dad," she said. She looked at Ettleman and said bluntly, "The person who was shot and killed was a man named Bud Stephanopoulis. He was a friend of Dad's, and I was jet skiing with him at the time he was shot."

Ettleman's expression showed her compassion and she said softly, "Ooooh, I'm so sorry."

Pete kept quiet.

Ettleman asked Pete, "Do you still have the same sheriff in your county? The tall guy who looked like he should have been in one of the old Marlboro television commercials?"

"Bill Haskins? No, his former first deputy, Frank Richter, took over when Haskins decided to run for, I believe, the state senate. Then Richter got reelected for another term."

Ettleman looked pensive. "I liked Haskins. I consulted on a case of his way back when."

"Maybe you can consult on this case, too," Julie said. "I'm sure Dad will be all over it even though he pretends that he knows almost nothing about it right now."

Pete held his tongue again.

Ettleman looked from Julie to Pete and back to Julie. She dug around in her purse and found a business card and handed it to Julie.

"Let's have that lunch before you leave for college," she said. She squeezed Pete's hand and left to join her companions who were waiting by the door looking very impatient.

The waiter came by and asked them if they wanted dessert and they both passed. Pete paid the bill and they walked to the Range Rover without saying anything. On their way out of Traverse City, Julie continued to look straight ahead. When Pete turned to go west, she said, "That was kind of sneaky, Dad. I really don't need a psychiatrist, you know."

Pete glanced her way and said, "I don't recall saying that you did."

"Then why did you oh so casually just arrange for us to bump into your friend, Susan Ettleman?"

"I didn't arrange anything. Susan happened to be having lunch at the West End Tavern at the same time we were. It's a popular place."

"Right."

"Look at it this way. You wouldn't have all of those insights into Cornell if you hadn't met her."

TWELVE

Joe Tessler must have been eager to talk about his latest love, because when Pete called the next morning and proposed lunch, he not only accepted without hesitation, but even suggested they go on the early side so they'd have plenty of time to talk. Pete picked up the sandwiches at Ebba's Bakery, and when he managed to escape the clutches of Ebba Holm who'd been pumping him for information about the investigation into Bud Stephanopoulis's shooting, Tessler was already waiting for him at the curb with his Acura's motor idling.

They circled around Betsie Bay and headed for the scenic overlook outside the small town of Elberta. The high season for tourists hadn't arrived yet, so the overlook was free of vehicles except for a panel truck with the area cable television logo and a Harley Davidson motorcycle. Pete glanced Tessler's way because he knew from experience that Joe viewed the overlook as his personal domain for important lunch conversations and got more than a little hostile if he found intruders there. The cable guy parked at the far end eating his lunch wasn't likely to be a problem, but the Harley couple . . .

Tessler unwrapped his sandwich and took a bite, eyeing Mr. Harley and his tattoo-blanketed flabby arms and scruffy beard with a snarly expression as the biker moved along the cable in front of them that separated the parking area from the steep drop off. He was snapping photographs of his black-clad companion with his iPhone as she struck various poses. Unlike her man, who looked like he inhaled two boxes of doughnuts for breakfast every morning, she seemed to rely too much on Camels and Diet Cokes and not enough on food.

Pete suppressed an urge to chuckle as he ate his lunch and watched Tessler out of the corner of his eye. One of these days, the detective was going to jump out of his car, stick his shield under some trespasser's nose, and give him a choice between moving on or spending the night in the county jail. The Harley couple finally wrapped up their photo shoot, and Tessler flashed a middle-finger salute at them as they roared off.

His expression took on a more civilized tone again as he gazed at the scene below him. The wind had picked up from the day before, and kite surfers skimmed over the waves inside the breakwater. Their orange and yellow and pink kites billowed in the air, and waves pounded against the breakwater and sent sheets of water spraying skyward. A large alabaster lighthouse anchored the outer end of the breakwater and lorded over its domain. Not far away, its younger candy-cane-striped brother stood ready to carry out its orders.

"Jesus, this is something, huh?" Tessler said as he stuffed the last of his sandwich into his mouth. "This would be a great place to take Sheree someday. Maybe have a little picnic lunch or something. Some wine and cheese, maybe some fried chicken."

"She'd probably like that."

Tessler crumpled his sandwich wrapper and spent an inordinate amount of time wiping his hands with the only napkin he had left. He balled it up and scrubbed his fingers again and eyed the extra napkin on Pete's lap. "You going to use that?" he asked.

Pete handed the napkin to him.

Tessler continued his scrubbing routine with the fresh napkin, and when he was satisfied that his hands were grease-free, he said, "Do you want to see Sheree's picture again? I didn't give you a chance to really study it in our office."

Pete nodded and reached for the photograph. Tessler pulled it back, apparently concerned about Pete's greasy hands.

"Why don't I hold it," he said, extending his arm again so the photograph was in front of Pete. "Let me know if you want it closer."

Pete studied the photograph again, trying to be polite. When he thought he'd admired it long enough, he said, "Very nice. I can see why you might want to put Taty behind you."

"You never met Taty, did you?"

"Not in person, but I feel I know her because I drove past her apartment enough times."

Tessler scowled. "One time you said you drove past, but later you admitted you hadn't."

"I explained that. I wanted people to think I was in Chicago and not in Wilson, North Carolina."

"You could have confided in me and I wouldn't have told anyone. I thought we were friends."

"Listen, I didn't want to put you in an awkward position, okay?"

"I still wish you'd handled it differently," Tessler groused.

Pete was itching to get to the investigation of Bud's shooting, but didn't want to seem too eager to change the subject. He said, "So, where are you going to take Sheree on your next date?"

Tessler's face turned thoughtful. "I've been trying to think of something. I want it to be special, you know?"

"I have an idea. Why don't the two of you take a day off and go to Sleeping Bear. You don't have to climb the dune if you don't want to. There are lots of places you can get great views of the lake and the surrounding area without doing that. Maybe take a bunch of photographs including some selfies of the two of you so you'll have more than one photo of her. Then you could pass through Traverse City on your way home and have lunch or dinner, depending on what time it is. Maybe try a place called the West End Tavern. It's right on the water overlooking a marina. It's as close to the Riviera as you're going to get in this part of the country." He was pleased with the way he'd worked Julie's observations into the recommendation.

Tessler looked thoughtful for a while. Then, "If I had a regular job, that would be a great idea. But with Frank on my tail every day, if I told him I wanted to take a day off, or even a half-day for crissakes, he'd have my final paycheck cut and I'd be history in five minutes."

Pete clucked in sympathy. Sensing an opening, he said, "The Stephanopoulis shooting is keeping you occupied, huh?"

"Only about a hundred and ten percent of my time. The other forty percent I spend on my other cases. You know that night me and Sheree went to the casino? We had to go at ten o'clock at night. I didn't get home until almost three the next morning. Didn't even have a chance to, you know, fool around or anything. Needed to get a couple hours of sleep before I had to be back at it, you know?"

After agreeing about the injustice of it all, Pete pushed some more. "Any developments in the case?"

Tessler looked Pete's way and shook his head several times. "I can't talk about that, Pete. Frank issued strict orders that no one in the department can say anything about the case except him."

"A complete lock-down, huh?"

"You remember that old television program where they had the cone of silence? That's a sieve compared to the gag order Frank has on."

Pete nodded. "Well, I know from my CID days that an investigation sometimes *has* to be conducted in secret. By the way, my daughter knows we're having lunch today. She said to ask you whether you want to talk to her again."

Tessler looked thoughtful. "Maybe. I'm trying to get my arms around possible motives for the shooting."

Pete sensed another opening and said, "When I was picking up the sandwiches, Ebba Holm told me there's a rumor circulating that the shooting might have been a random act and not a premeditated murder."

Tessler's head jerked toward him and he asked, "Where did she hear that?"

"It wasn't clear. She claims she heard it from a couple of people. She didn't mention any names."

Tessler continued to look interested. "Did she say anything else?"

"Not that I remember. The random act theory is what sticks in my mind. You know how Ebba is, she talks your leg off. I was just trying to get out of there so I wouldn't keep you waiting."

Tessler's face turned dark and brooding. "The rumor is that your pal, Harry McTigue, is coming out with a big story about the case in his next issue. He doesn't know crap about what's going on, but we heard that he's planning to write something about the shooting maybe being a random act, too. Do you know anything about that?"

"I'm a contributing editor of *The Northern Sentinel.* If I start blabbing around what Harry might be planning to write and the Traverse City paper or some other daily picks it up and breaks the story first, I've lost a friend. Remember, his paper is a weekly and he has to keep news under wraps until his next issue comes out so he isn't scooped."

Tessler scowled. "You think I'm going to scoop him? I'm law enforcement, for crissakes."

"I know, but he's touchy."

"This isn't something he should play around with. A story about the shooting being a random act could spook people and get them to thinking that maybe the lake isn't a safe place anymore. They'll start thinking there's some loon out there picking off people just to get his jollies. People will stop letting their kids go to the beach, they'll stop boating and fishing, they'll be afraid to jog or walk their dogs. The economy in this area depends heavily on tourists and people who are seasonal residents. They start staying away and we've got big problems."

"I agree that it wouldn't be good. But . . ."

"Are you willing to try to get Harry to deep-six the story? Or at least tone it down? You might be the best one to talk to him because the two of you are friends. If me or Frank try, he'll accuse us of trying to manipulate the press."

Pete thought about it for a few moments. "If I were to say something, I couldn't mislead him."

"Will you at least try?"

"Let me see if I can find some way to get the point across without deceiving him."

"Thanks, you'll be doing the community a favor." He looked at his dash clock and said, "I got to get back."

On their way back to Frankfort, Pete asked, "If I do something for you, are you willing to do something for me and tell me what's happening in your investigation? I feel I have an interest in it because Bud was my friend."

Tessler shook his head a couple of times. "Like I told you on the bluff, I can't talk about the investigation."

"Let me understand this. You want my help to keep a story you're worried about out of the paper, but you won't tell me what's going on with the investigation. Do I have it right?"

"It's not my call. Frank is afraid of people starting to talk before we're ready to move. I can't argue with his thinking."

"Joe, let me ask you a question. When have you ever told me something in confidence and later found that I'd told someone else?"

Tessler swiped some specks of dust off his dashboard. "I can't think of anything at the moment, but—"

"But crap. You can't think of anything because it's never happened. And here's another question for you. There've been only a handful of serious crimes in this area in recent years. How many have I had a role in helping you solve?"

Tessler glared at him. "You shouldn't have played a role in solving *any* of them because you don't carry a shield. Even though you act like you do sometimes."

Pete stared back at him for a few moments, irritated at the comment. They were almost at his office.

Tessler stopped at the curb and said, "You mad at me?"

"Why would I be mad?"

Tessler shot a look his way. "I didn't mean to sound ungrateful or anything. You've given us a lot of help on some of our cases even if Frank won't admit it."

Pete didn't say anything.

"Just so we understand each other, though," Tessler continued, "I've bailed your butt out of trouble a few times, too. You realize that, don't you? That kind of evens things out, doesn't it?"

Pete knew he'd overreacted and said, "I do realize that. I'm grateful, too, and didn't mean to imply otherwise."

"We make a damn good team. I just wish our department had enough in its budget to hire you as a part-time detective so there'd be two of us working these cases."

"Can you imagine Frank's reaction if you suggested something like that?"

Tessler didn't say anything, but shook his head disgustedly.

Pete started to get out of the car, but Tessler said, "If you've got a few minutes more, I'll tell you where we're at with the Stephanopoulis case."

Pete tried not to appear surprised.

"The only conditions are that you don't breathe a word to anyone else. And that you'll see what you can do with Harry. Deal?"

"Like I said, I'll try, but I can't make promises. Harry can be prickly when he senses somebody is trying to influence him. He views it as impugning his journalist integrity."

"I know, I know. I know the old coot myself, remember? But you'll try, right?"

"I'll try."

Tessler brushed more specks of dust off his dash. "We're looking at a suspect named Gaz Ramczyk. Do you know him?"

"Gaz?"

"It's some kind of nickname."

Pete thought for a few moments, then shook his head. "I don't think so."

"He's a former army guy who pulled several tours of duty in Afghanistan and, maybe time in Iraq, too. He came back here a couple of years ago and now rents a place out on River Road. Most of the time he's unemployed and hangs around the Union Street bars in Traverse City a lot."

"Did he know Stephanopoulis?"

"We aren't sure, but we don't think so. We do know that he has, or at least claims to have, that stress disorder thing. He—"

"Post-Traumatic Stress Disorder?"

"Yeah, that's it, PTSD. The condition that fools around with your mind. There've been a lot of cases around the country where people came back from the war zone with that condition and committed violent acts. Ramczyk has been drawing disability payments from the government, and people tell us he's off the rails, mentally. That's what got us thinking about the random act theory. Maybe Gaz was hanging around the lake, looking for a target because of his mental condition. He could have shot any one of a number of people. Motorboaters, sailors, people tubing or waterskiing. Maybe even someone at the beach who was just wading out in the water. Stephanopoulis might have just been in the wrong place at the wrong time."

"Interesting."

"We also interviewed some people who live in the area where Stephanopoulis was shot. They told us that a man fitting Ramczyk's description hung around there a lot. I guess he likes to kayak and launches by the end of the access road. On the day Stephanopoulis was shot, they saw him there with his orange kayak. We put this together with the PTSD thing."

"Have you talked to Ramczyk?"

"Wait, there's more. Frank has lived in this area his entire life. He remembers Ramczyk from his high school days. He says the guy was a delinquent back then and is worse since he got out of the army."

"Umm."

"Getting back to your question, we want to search his place before we question him so he doesn't get rid of evidence. We just got the warrant."

Pete nodded. "Any other suspects?"

Tessler's cell phone burred. He talked for a few moments, then ended the call and said, "I have to get back. But talk to Harry and see what you can do to, you know, shape the story he's planning. And again, don't mention a word about the other stuff."

THIRTEEN

After taking care of a few things at his office, Pete walked down the street to *The Northern Sentinel*'s offices. Harry was huddled with a slender man who had closely cropped brownish hair that was thinning on top and dark-rimmed glasses that gave him a studious appearance. He looked like he was approaching middle age.

Harry looked up when he walked in. "Pete, let me introduce you to another one of the *Sentinel*'s contributing editors, Jeffrey Talbot. He's a teacher at our high school and writes the poetry column we started running a few months ago."

"Nice to meet you, Jeff," Pete said, extending his hand. Talbot shook hands, but his expression looked pained.

"He prefers Jeffrey," Harry hastily said. "Jeffrey, Pete writes feature stories for us now and then on local history subjects. The old logging days and stuff like that." Harry got an impish grin on his face and added, "Once in a while he tries to sneak other things past me, like fiction pieces claiming that the Vikings had an influence on this area even though everybody knows those people never got past Vinland."

Talbot's eyes widened a bit. "The Vikings here in Michigan? That's fascinating. How did you get into that?"

"I'm Norwegian on both sides of my family. I'm getting back to my roots in my senior years."

"You're Norwegian on one side and only part Norwegian on the other," Harry corrected him. "You told me your mother had some Swede in her."

Talbot seemed more interested in storylines than bloodline purity. "The Vikings had a big influence on my ancestral home. That's England as you might guess from my name. Did you ever read *The Sagas of the Icelanders?*"

"Parts. In translation."

"You really should read them in their entirety. They're fascinating. I always tell my students they should set aside time to read the great works. That's what I do with the Lake Poets. Every time I read a poem by Wordsworth or one of the others, I discover something new. It's exhilarating."

Pete nodded his agreement.

Harry and Jeffrey Talbot finished their meeting and Talbot left after telling Pete a second time to be sure to get a copy of *The Sagas of the Icelanders* and read it all the way through. When he was gone, Pete asked, "What kind of feedback are you getting on the poetry column?"

"Better than I expected, to be honest. A large segment of our readership consists of seasonal residents who have places on the lake. Many have one, two, even three college degrees. They're hungry for content that goes beyond fires or village politics or the annual crowning of the Coho Queen."

"So you're going to continue it?"

"For the time being at least. Talbot can drive me crazy at times, though. He keeps pushing me to expand the column to a full page. I'm concerned that might be too much and I've dug in my heels."

"Umm. How about the Stephanopoulis shooting? What are you planning for the next issue?"

Harry's eyes lit up. "That's front-page material everyone's interested in. I did a draft of a follow-on story, but I think it comes off as flat with nothing really new. Except for maybe the murder weapon. I'm afraid readers will skim the first couple of paragraphs and then go on to something else because they don't see anything they don't already know."

"The murder weapon was .223 caliber hunting rifle, right?"

"I guess that's what they've concluded. From what I understand, one or more of the bullets didn't pass all the way through Bud's body and the medical examiner found it. Or them."

"They also found some of the brass by a tree stump. There's not much question it was a .223."

Harry made a note of that and said, "Whenever I ask people at the sheriff's office, they give me the standard line about the investigation just getting underway."

Pete's laugh had a sarcastic tone. "That doesn't sound like Richter, does it? Usually he's giving press conferences and throwing out the names of suspects before the body is even cold."

"Not this time. Even Cap isn't talking. Not on the record, not off the record and without attribution." Harry looked at him and added, "You're pretty tight with Joe Tessler. Has he said anything?"

"Nothing you don't already know," he lied.

Harry looked at the legal pad on his desk and made some doodles on it and drummed his pen for a while. He looked up at Pete and said, "You know what's buzzing around in my noggin? That Sheriff Richter and his people might know something they don't want to get out."

"Like what?"

"When I talked to Cap, he was closed-mouth like I said, but he let something slip. You know how the guy is, always taking potshots at Sheriff Richter behind his back. He's never gotten over the fact that Richter was appointed acting sheriff when Bill Haskins resigned. He thinks he's the one who should have been appointed because he was senior to Richter in the department. Anyway, during our conversation, he said something that made me think. I don't remember exactly how he put it, but it led me to believe that the department might be looking at someone who might have shot Bud without having a specific motive."

"Interesting. Have you tried to confirm that with Richter?"

"Are you kidding? Sheriff Richter would can Cap on the spot because he'd assume the information came from him."

Pete thought about it. "That's a pretty flimsy thing to base a story on if you not only can't name your source, but you're also not even sure what Cap was saying."

"Do you know Cody Baker, the guy who owns Cody's Fin & Fur? He's second only to Ebba Holm when it comes to keeping a finger on the pulse of the community. He stopped in yesterday and told me there's a rumor circulating that a maniac might be out there using people for target practice. He claims people are getting spooked. This is the off-season for hunting, but he says he's never been busier. According to him, people are coming in, buying guns of all types, stocking up on ammunition."

"I barely know Cody, but you seem to be telling me he said basically the same thing that Cap implied."

Harry nodded.

"Didn't you just say, though, that Cody's a gossip?"

"There's no question he's a gossip, but he also has his ear to the ground."

"That still doesn't seem like much to base a story on."

"That's two sources," Harry said defensively.

"Hardly sources. You're not even sure what one of them said, and you admit that the other is a gossip."

"People buying guns and ammunition isn't gossip."

"What happened to Harry McTigue the journalist who just reports the facts? If you get into the speculation business, you're going beyond the facts, aren't you? As editor of the *Sentinel,* you're responsible for the content. You're not some blogger who's trying to stir up his base by serving them red meat."

Harry glared at him. "It's so nice to have someone who has no training or experience in journalism preach to me. I've only been in the business for thirty years."

"I didn't mean to preach to you. I was just trying to point out the pitfalls of going with a story that isn't based on facts you've actually confirmed."

Harry stared at the top of his desk and drummed his pen some more. "The madman theory bothers me," he said.

As their conversation droned on, Pete felt conflicted about deceiving his friend on the one hand, and on the other, not fueling rumors that could be damaging to the community, particularly since it sounded like news about Gaz Ramczyk would soon get out. Choosing his words carefully, Pete said, "How about this for an approach? You can base the bulk of your story on the facts as you know them. When you think about it, you actually know quite a lot. You know where Tessler and his people believe the shots were fired from. You can run down and take a couple of pictures to accompany the story. I'd prefer that you not involve Julie more than necessary, but maybe you could get a quote from her about what happened. Then you could finish with a paragraph or two saying that the motive for the shooting is unclear and include some carefully crafted words about the random shooting possibility without actually calling it that. A wordsmith like you should be able to put the right spin on it."

Pete could tell from the look on his face that he liked the idea. "You know, Thorsen, I knew there was a reason I hang around with you."

"If something happens in the case before you go to print," Pete continued, "you can modify the story to include the latest developments."

"And I wouldn't have to even identify Julie by name. I could just say something like, 'An area woman who was jet skiing with Stephanopoulis . . .' Something like that."

"I think you're on the right track."

When Pete got home, he sat on his porch and looked down the lakeshore toward where Bud's shooting had occurred. Somewhere along the lake, children shrieked as they played. Images of Julie and Bud talking while their jet skis idled side-by-side flashed through his mind again, and he shuddered. If the shooting had been random, why had the killer chosen Bud and not someone else?

Pete shook off his dark thoughts and wondered about Lydia Vreeland, the woman who'd let him use her telephone that day and then given him a ride back to where Julie was. Tessler hadn't said who he'd talked to in the course of his investigation, but his guess was that Lydia probably was one of them. He felt the need to do something, and went outside and jumped on his bicycle.

He pedaled north on M-22 until he came to the access road just past Lydia's driveway, then bumped along the path through tall grass and brush until he came to the lake. He leaned his bike against a tree and walked to the beach and looked around. He didn't see crime scene tape cordoning off any part of the area and wondered what that meant. He spent ten minutes poking around, and after satisfying himself that he wasn't likely to discover something the forensics team had overlooked, he glanced toward Lydia's cottage, but didn't see her outside. Her car was parked in the driveway, though, which indicated she was likely at home. He went over and knocked on her door. Hearing no answer, he knocked again and called, "Mrs. Vreeland?"

A few moments later, he heard footsteps and a sleepy-eyed Lydia Vreeland came to the door. She blinked a couple of times and stared at him through the screen. "Can I help you?" she asked.

"It's Pete Thorsen, Mrs. Vreeland. You let me use your telephone that day the jet skier was shot and then gave me a ride, remember?"

She blinked some more.

"The day of the shooting?"

Suddenly a look of recognition came over her face and she said, "Yes, of course, you're my neighbor."

He didn't want to get into a debate with her about whether people who lived more than a mile apart qualified as neighbors so he just said, "Right."

"How is that daughter of yours? I remember you were worried about her."

"She's fine," he said. "Do you have a few minutes to talk to me?"

"Of course. Come in and we can sit on the porch. I made iced tea earlier. I'll get two glasses for us."

While Lydia was in the kitchen, Pete stood at the screen and looked out. Even with all of the trees surrounding her cottage, Lydia still had a decent view of the lake and the end of access road.

"Nice view," he said when she came back with their iced tea.

"Thank you. This cottage was built in 1927, you know. Of course, it's been updated since then." She squinted in the direction of the lake and added, "I should have someone come and thin some of the trees, though, so I can see the water better." She babbled on about her mother and grandmother and great-grandmother having all been gardeners and horticulturists, emphasizing how much they loved flowers and trees. She pointed to various trees and then told him which ancestor had planted which one.

Pete listened patiently and waited for an opening to raise what he was really interested in. When he found one, he asked, "That day the jet skier was shot, did you see anyone in the area who looked suspicious? You were gardening as I recall."

"That's the same question the police asked me."

"What did you tell them?"

"It's real woodsy around here, as you can see. The only people I saw that day were people who live around here. I see them all the time."

"No one who looked suspicious, huh?"

Lydia shook her head about seven times. "No one who looked suspicious," she repeated.

"How about gunshots? The jet skier was shot several times. If the shooter fired from this area, someone should have heard shots."

Lydia went into her head-shaking routine again. "I didn't hear any gunshots, either."

Pete considered what she'd just told him and asked, "Since you've lived here for a long time, I assume you know the neighbors. That cottage in the woods north of here, on the other side of the access road, do you know those people?"

Lydia wrinkled her nose. "That's Harriet Marlowe."

"Why the disgusted look?"

Lydia went into her head-shaking routine and her voice became low, like she was about to divulge a secret she didn't want anyone to overhear. "Harriet's a busybody and a terrible gossip. I've known her for fifty years. Not a good person. Not good at all."

"I think I'll walk over and talk to her."

Lydia looked at him like he was deranged. "Why?"

"I'm trying to piece together what happened the day of the shooting. Because of my daughter."

"You'll be wasting your time. Harriet will just make up some story to make herself seem important. You can't believe a word that woman says."

"I'll keep that in mind." He got up to leave.

"I suppose I could walk over there with you and introduce you two," Lydia said, getting out of her chair and following him.

"You don't have to do that. I can introduce myself."

Lydia suddenly looked geared for battle. "I'm going with you so that woman doesn't try to pull something," she said sternly. "I told you, you can't trust her."

Pete avoided rolling his eyes and acquiesced, fearing he was stepping into the middle of a long-standing feud. On their way through the trees to the Marlowe cottage, Lydia kept up a running monologue about "that woman." Her voice became more hushed as they got closer.

When they got to Harriet's door, Lydia did everything but nudge him aside to establish that she was the one in charge. She pounded on the door with her walking stick and called in a loud voice, "Harriet, open up, I have a gentleman here who needs to talk to you." When Harriet didn't respond in ten seconds, Lydia pounded again, more vigorously this time. "Harriet?"

Finally the door opened and a dour lady in ill-fitting brown slacks and a rumpled blouse with some kind of pattern opened the door and stared at Lydia. Lydia stared back. "Did you hear what I said?" she asked. "This man needs to talk to you about the jet ski shooting."

Harriet eyed Pete for a while and said, "You don't look like a deputy."

"I'm not, Mrs. Marlowe. I'm —"

"He's a lawyer, Harriet," Lydia said, finishing his sentence for him. "His daughter was almost killed when the jet skier was shot. He's doing what any responsible father would do. He's helping the police investigate the case."

Harriet tried to brush Lydia aside and said, "Is the man able to speak for himself?"

"Ladies," Pete said as the two women stared daggers at each other. "Mrs. Marlowe, if you have a few minutes, I'd like to ask you a couple of questions about the day of the shooting."

"I already told the police everything I know."

"And what would *that* be?" Lydia asked, her voice dripping with disdain.

Harriet put her hands on her hips and said, "They asked me if I saw any suspicious-looking people around that day and I told them who I saw, that's what." She shot Lydia a smug look.

"Who did you see?" Pete asked.

"I saw the man with the kayak. The one with a ponytail like some men have these days and one of those funny things on his head. Like a little flag."

Lydia waved a hand to show her dismissal of Harriet's observation and said, "I saw that man, too. He's not a suspicious looking person. He comes to the lake all the time. This is where he puts his kayak in the water."

"Oh, he's not suspicious? Then why was he hiding in the brush by the water? And why did he leave right after that man fell off his jet ski? And why, Mrs. Smarty-Pants, didn't he ever put his kayak in the water? The police certainly thought *that* was suspicious when I told them about it."

Lydia was obviously on her heels after hearing Harriet's revelations. Finally she said, "I could have told them about *that* man, too."

Pete interjected and said, "What kind of vehicle was the man driving? He obviously couldn't carry a kayak on a bicycle."

"A truck, he was driving a blue truck. The kind with one of those boxes behind where the driver sits. He carries his kayak in that box."

Lydia acted like Harriet wasn't even there and said to Pete, "She doesn't know what she's talking about. The man with the ponytail drives a *black* pickup. Or maybe very dark gray. Definitely not blue." She gave Harriet a look that indicated she thought she'd regained the upper hand in their war of words.

"What time of the day did all of this happen?"

"It was the late afternoon. I know because that's when I water my flowers. I was watering and just happened to notice everything I just told you."

"She wasn't watering her flowers," Lydia said to Pete, the disdain dripping from her words. "She was peeking out her window, spying on her neighbors like she always does."

"Lydia, you —"

Pete cut her off. "Anything else, Harriet? Did you notice the license plate on the truck or anything?"

"I didn't see the license plate because it was covered with a piece of cloth that was hanging out of that box in back. I'm certain it was a Michigan license plate, though."

Lydia rolled her eyes. Again, she talked to Pete as though Harriet weren't there. "How could she know it was a Michigan license plate if she couldn't even *see* the plate? It could have been a Wisconsin license plate or an Indiana license plate or an Ohio license plate."

"How about gunshots," Pete asked, trying to control the conversation. "Did you hear any?"

Harriet looked out at the lake and her eyes gleamed conspiratorially. "I thought I might have heard something."

"What?" Lydia demanded. "Either you heard gunshots or you didn't hear gunshots. I live right over there and *I* didn't hear any gunshots and I've got better hearing than you do."

"I didn't say for sure that I heard gunshots. I just said I *might* have heard some."

Pete eventually managed to separate the two combatants, and with Lydia as his guide, he talked to a couple of other people in the area, but none of them had seen anyone suspicious that day or heard gunshots. Pedaling back to his cottage, he thought about the man with the ponytail that both Lydia and Harriet said they'd seen. He wondered if telling Harry about him would breach his confidentiality promise to Tessler.

FOURTEEN

Pete was in his office the next morning trying to make progress on his article and waiting for Joe Tessler to return his call when his outer door opened and three people walked in. His eyes immediately fixed on the sullen-faced younger man with the ponytail and patriotic do-rag who trailed behind the other two. His clothes looked like they'd been slept in.

The woman in the lead, an older lady in a plain dress adorned with small flowers and bobbed gray hair held in place by bobby pins, knocked on his inner doorjamb and said, "Mr. Thorsen, we're sorry to interrupt, but we have something important we'd like to talk to you about. If you have some time."

She stood in front of his desk with a hopeful look on her lined face. The wiry man at her side, her husband he assumed, looked uncomfortable being there, and had the earmarks of a working man—large gnarled hands, a blue chambray shirt hanging loosely over his K-Mart work pants, a grimy cap with a John Deere logo.

Pete knew why they were there. And also what his answer was going to be. Deciding he should be polite, however, he cleared off the client chairs he'd been using as auxiliary filing space and asked them to sit down and offered coffee or water. Then he settled in behind his desk again and steepled his hands and braced himself for what he knew was coming.

The woman scooted her chair closer and looked at him with earnest red-rimmed eyes and said, "I guess we should introduce ourselves. I'm Ruth Ramczyk and this is my husband, Jacob." She pointed to the man with the ponytail and said, "This is our son, Alfred. Everyone calls him Gaz. That's a nickname he got in high school on account of his football coach always saying he was faster than a gazelle." Gaz, who'd pushed his chair back to separate himself from the rest of the group, continued to count the floorboards and didn't say anything.

"I've never talked to a lawyer before so I really don't know how to start," the woman said.

"Just tell me in your own words what the problem is," Pete said in as soothing a tone as he could muster.

Ruth glanced at her husband, then said, "Have you heard about the man driving the jet ski who was shot?"

Pete nodded to show he had.

Ruth choked the words out and tears began to trickle down her cheeks. "The police think Gaz might have had something to do with that."

Neither her husband nor Gaz said anything. Jacob just continued to fidget with his hands and Gaz stared at the floor.

Pete played dumb and asked Gaz, "Did they accuse you of the shooting? Or did they just question you? Ask where you were at the time, that sort of thing."

Gaz didn't say anything, but after wiping away her tears, his mother said, "They say they have eyewitnesses who saw Gaz at the place by the lake where the shots came from. They say he knows guns, too, because he was in the army for six years."

Pete thought he knew who the eyewitnesses were and said, "Did they—the so-called eyewitnesses, I mean—say they actually *saw* Gaz shoot the jet skier?"

"They said the eyewitnesses didn't have to see actual shooting." She pulled a piece of paper from her purse and put on a pair of reading glasses and read from her notes. "They said a circumstantial case is all that's necessary and that they have a good case against Gaz. The important thing, they said, is that eyewitnesses placed him at the scene at the time of the shooting. They knew Gaz was getting disability benefits, too, and said he shouldn't be getting those payments and that they'd use that against him along with the other things. They said if Gaz would confess to the shooting, they might be able to persuade the judge to go easy on him."

"Where were you at the time Bud Stephanopoulis was shot, Gaz?"

Gaz just continued to look down and didn't say anything.

"Do you know where he was, Mrs. Ramczyk?"

Ruth Ramczyk looked embarrassed. After a few moments, she said to her husband, "Maybe you should tell Mr. Thorsen, Jacob."

"He said he was with a whore."

Pete saw Ruth Ramczyk wince at the words even though he suspected she knew what her husband was going to say.

"Where?" Pete asked.

"Traverse City," Jacob mumbled.

"What's the woman's name?"

"He says he don't know her name."

Pete knew he should move on because Mrs. Ramczyk seemed to be getting more and more upset and she was dabbing at her eyes with a tissue again. Tessler had mentioned a search warrant, and Pete asked, "Does Gaz live with you?"

"He has his own place," Mrs. Ramczyk said.

"Have they searched it yet?"

She sniffled and said, "That's what they did this morning. It wasn't even light out. They came in and took a bunch of his guns and some other stuff. They did say they'd give us a receipt for everything they took."

"Were you there during the search?" Pete asked Gaz.

Gaz didn't say anything so his mother answered for him. "He was sleeping when the sheriff's people came. They put handcuffs on him while they were doing the search. They wouldn't let him take his medicine or anything."

Pete's desk phone rang. Pete saw that it was Tessler returning his call and let it go to voicemail.

"That's okay, you can answer your telephone," Mrs. Ramczyk said politely. "We can wait."

"Thanks, I'll return the call later. Obviously, they didn't arrest Gaz because he's here."

"They told him they were going to evaluate all of the evidence they have, but that it didn't look good for him. They warned him not to try to leave the county. They said if he did, he'd be running away to avoid prosecution and that would be added to the other charges."

As Pete listened to Mrs. Ramczyk, he thought about the most diplomatic way to tell them he couldn't represent Gaz. As she perched on the edge of her chair and looked at him anxiously, he said, "I'm sorry, Mrs. Ramczyk, I'm not a criminal lawyer. I won't be able to represent your son."

"Your sign outside says that you're a lawyer."

"But I'm not a *criminal* lawyer. I do corporate work, helping companies with their problems and transactions. I don't even do much of that these days. If the sheriff's office regards your son as a suspect in the Stephanopoulis shooting, he needs a specialist who knows the ins and outs of criminal law and procedure. I'm afraid I'm not that man."

Mrs. Ramczyk persisted. "People we talked to told us you've helped other people in the community who were in trouble."

"I have gotten involved in a couple of cases, Mrs. Ramczyk, but even then, the person accused of the crime usually hired a lawyer who does criminal work full-time to represent him in court. Again, I'm just not qualified to do that kind of work."

She slumped in her chair, clearly dejected. Her husband continued to fidget and didn't say anything. An awkward silence hung in the air.

Pete finally raised something he hadn't intended to raise. "There's another problem in this case, too. I was a friend of the man who was shot. Because of that, I don't believe I could aggressively represent Gaz even if I *were* qualified."

Suddenly Gaz leaped to his feet and picked up the chair he'd been sitting in and threw it toward Pete. The chair struck the desk and wood splintered, sending his mother's coffee mug flying and coffee sloshing over papers. Gaz grabbed the damaged chair and swung it again, smashing it on the desktop. Pete turned away just in time as a leg broke off and grazed the side of his head.

"Let's get out of here!" Gaz screamed at his parents. "I'm tired of listening to this piece of crap! I don't need a friggin' lawyer!"

Ruth Ramczyk appeared immobilized by her son's violent outburst. Jacob was on his feet, trying to restrain Gaz. Gaz shook him off and continued to scream at Pete. "Friggin' shyster!"

Jacob Ramczyk tried to push his son toward the outer door leading to the street and finally succeeded.

Pete's cheek was numb from being struck with the chair leg, and he touched it with a finger. He saw blood and wiped his cheek with a tissue.

Ruth Ramczyk continued to look bewildered and finally murmured in a voice so quiet he barely heard it, "Sorry." Tears gushed from her eyes again.

"He needs help," Pete said, recalling his conversation with Tessler about PTSD. "Otherwise, he's going to hurt someone." He deliberately avoided any reference to Bud Stephanopoulis.

"Will your face be okay?"

He dabbed at his cheek again. "It's fine. Did you hear what I said about Gaz?"

"He didn't take his meds this morning because of the search. Usually he doesn't do things like this. He's just kind of disinterested and everything."

"Has he had professional help? A psychiatrist or someone who deals with these kinds of problems?"

"He went to a government person when he first got out of the army. He doesn't go anymore, though."

"You need to get him to start going again, Mrs. Ramczyk."

"I keep saying things to him, but it doesn't help. Jacob doesn't support me. He thinks a man should be able to deal with these things himself."

"From what little I know about PTSD, I don't think that's realistic."

Mrs. Ramczyk shook her head and sat there with a confused expression on her face. Finally she said, "I don't know what to do. I thought maybe you could help him, but now I don't know." She sat with her head down for a while, then looked at him and said, "Do you think Gaz shot that man?"

"I have no way of knowing. I always thought that people suffering from PTSD were most at risk of hurting themselves, but I just don't know. He needs professional help, that much is clear. And he needs a criminal lawyer. Even if the sheriff's people didn't arrest him this morning, he's got problems and he needs someone who can protect his rights. Also, you should tell him that if the sheriff or his detective or someone else comes to see him again, he shouldn't say anything without a lawyer present."

"Could you talk to the sheriff and tell him that?"

Pete shook his head and said, "I'm not representing him, so it wouldn't do any good. Just pass on what I said. And get him a criminal lawyer." He grabbed a piece of paper that wasn't soaked with coffee and wrote the names and telephone numbers of a criminal lawyer he knew in Traverse City as well as of his friend, Ira Manning, in Chicago. As an afterthought, he added the name of the area's public defender and her contact information.

Mrs. Ramczyk looked at the names, then folded the paper carefully and put it in her purse. She got up and said, "I guess I should go so you can get help for your face. The hospital in town does a good job with those things. Jacob and I will pay the cost if you'll let me know how much it is."

"I'll probably just put some antiseptic on it."

"You sound just like the men in my family. None of them like to go to the doctor for anything, either."

FIFTEEN

After Mrs. Ramczyk left, Pete went into his bathroom and examined his face in the mirror. Blood had continued to trickle from the wound, and he had a long dark streak down his cheek. He wet the end of a towel and cleaned the blood off and examined the wound again. The cut was an inch long, and judging from the surrounding redness, he was going to have a nasty bruise.

Pete considered just putting a Band-Aid on the cut, but then thought he might have wood slivers in his cheek and drove to the local hospital to have it attended to professionally. The nurse grilled him about what had happened and continued to look skeptical when he stuck to his story about tripping over some files on his office floor and hitting his face against a chair when he fell. The size of the bandage the nurse originally applied made him look like he'd just lost an encounter with an irascible grizzly, and he talked her into replacing it with something smaller.

He checked his voicemail when he got back to his office. He'd returned Tessler's call before he left for the hospital, but didn't have any messages from him. He walked down the street to *The Northern Sentinel* and caught Harry sitting at his desk with his feet propped up and a pensive look on his face.

Harry saw the bandage and frowned and said, "Another bar fight?" By another, he was obviously referring to the time the previous year when Pete had caught a punch in the side of his head when he was trying to break up a fight that erupted when his friend, Jimmy Ray Evans, made moves on another man's lady friend at a local bar.

"Not exactly," Pete said. "Have you had lunch yet? I can tell you about it over some food."

Harry scowled. "I've been sitting here listening to my stomach growl. Rona has been on my case about losing a few pounds. She's given her chef orders to only make me an alfalfa and clover salad if I come to the restaurant for lunch." He grimaced and his expression turned dark. "I can't stand that California crap."

"I won't tell her if you join me for a roast beef on rye from across the street. Or if you prefer, you can skip lunch and watch me eat."

Harry's eyes grew fiery. "If you eat, Mr. Viking, I eat. But I have to be back in an hour. I have a ton of work to do on the paper."

They got sandwiches from Ebba's Bakery and found a bench near the marina. Harry was inhaling his sandwich before they sat down. He mumbled through a mouthful of sandwich and potato chips, "You going to tell me about your face?"

Pete recounted the visit he'd had from the Ramczyk family that morning and how Gaz, who hadn't uttered a word, suddenly erupted and threw a chair at him.

Harry's eyes grew large and he brushed his napkin back and forth across his mouth a few times. "Did he apologize for losing his temper?"

"I don't think apologizing is something that occurred to him. My impression was that he had other things he wanted to do to me."

"As a legal matter, can you press charges for assault against a guy who's your client?"

"He's not my client. I told the Ramczyks I wasn't a criminal lawyer and couldn't take his case."

"That's rich," Harry said after he'd swallowed. "Not being a criminal lawyer hasn't stopped you all of those other times."

"Name one case where I've represented someone accused of a crime?"

Harry scoffed and said, "I could probably name a few if you'll give me a minute, but one for sure is that Billy Bob guy you represented last year."

"His name is Jimmy Ray. And even with him, the only reason I told the sheriff I was his lawyer was so I could get in to see him at the jail and hear his side of the story. If the case proceeded, I was going to bring in Ira Manning to represent him."

"Okay," Harry said, not sounding convinced.

"There's another factor here, too. Bud Stephanopoulis was a friend of mine. Like I told the Ramczyks, there's no way I could represent a man accused of murdering him."

"You're always giving me that pap about how everyone, no matter how vile his actions might be, deserves a primo defense. Have you changed your tune?"

"No, I haven't changed my tune. Everyone *does* deserve a good defense. That's our system. I just don't have to be the one who provides it."

Harry finished off his sandwich. "Getting off the philosophical stuff, do you think Ramczyk killed Bud?" he asked

"I have no idea." Pete told him about his conversations with Lydia Vreeland and Harriet Marlowe the previous day. "Their descriptions of the man they saw at the lake the day of the shooting fit Gaz like a glove. They saw him in the area before, too."

Harry eyed Pete's half-full bag of potato chips, but refrained from helping himself to some. "Do Sheriff Richter and Joe Tessler know all of this?" he asked.

"Almost certainly. Someone from the sheriff's department interviewed the women before I spoke to them. Plus, they searched Ramczyk's house this morning."

"In other words, Gaz is a suspect."

"Clearly." Pete didn't mention anything about what Tessler had originally told him about Ramczyk.

Harry's eyes began to gleam like he was onto a major news scoop. "Jesus, I've got to rewrite my story to include all of this. This changes everything."

"When does your next issue come out?"

"Two days."

"Okay."

Harry peered at him suspiciously. "The Great Censor isn't going to tell me I can't report any of this, is he?"

"Not as long as you don't report or cite me as your source. I don't want Joe Tessler to think I breached anything he told me in confidence."

Harry eyed him some more. "Did Joe tell you they were looking at Gaz Ramczyk as a possible suspect?"

"Not directly."

"What's that supposed to mean?"

"Just what I said."

Harry studied him some more. "You knew they were focusing on Gaz, didn't you?"

Pete just looked at him.

"Why won't you admit it?"

"What difference does it make? News of the search is going to be all over town by the end of the day, if it isn't already. Like I said, just leave me out of any story you write. Oh, and I think you'd be doing the community a disservice if you write something that suggests Ramczyk may be a lunatic who likes to pick off innocent jet skiers. Or sailors or children on the beach or whatever."

"Are you going to give me another lecture about responsible journalism?"

"No, I'm just making a point."

"Do you know something else you're not telling me?"

"Completely off the record and not for use in your story with or without attribution?"

"Just tell me for crissakes. We're friends, okay."

"I'm serious, Harry. I'm going to tell you something, but it would be irresponsible to spread it around."

"Okay, okay, I agree. Now what's the big secret?"

"The word is that Gaz has PTSD."

"The disorder some returning veterans have?"

Pete nodded. "Sheriff Richter doesn't believe it, though. He thinks Gaz has always been a bad apple and is faking it."

Harry seemed to chew on that for a while. "So, if Gaz shot Stephanopoulis, he *could* have been committing a random act of violence."

"Possible, we don't really know at this stage. I do know that if you speculate about this, you'd being doing a disservice to Gaz as well as to the community."

"Who told you about the PTSD thing?"

"Tessler. And Gaz's mother when the Ramczyk family came to see me this morning. She justified his eruption in my office by the fact they'd him cuffed when they searched his place and he couldn't take his meds."

"Do you think it's true? That he has PTSD?"

"After what I saw in my office, I'd have to say there's a damn good chance. There definitely seems to be something wrong with him."

"So he *could* have just randomly shot someone and the person who got in the way was Bud Stephanopoulis."

"Harry . . ."

Pete was sitting on his porch looking out at the lake when Tessler called back. "You're a hard guy to get ahold of," he said.

"I could say the same about you. Anything happening on the case?"

Tessler didn't answer for a few moments, then, "A few things. Are you in the middle of anything? Frank would like you to come in again so we can get more background on Stephanopoulis."

"I told him everything I know when I was in before."

"Maybe, but he'd like to hash things over again."

"Is there something I should know, Joe?"

"You know Frank, he likes to play detective in these things. He's trying to figure out a motive for the shooting."

"You mean beyond his notion that Ramczyk is a maniac who goes around shooting people?"

"The random shooting theory is just one of the possibilities we're looking at. We're looking at everything. That should make you happy. You're always criticizing us for jumping to conclusions too soon."

Pete let the barb pass and asked, "What did you find when you searched Ramczyk's place this morning?"

Silence, then, "News of the search is out already?"

"Probably. A couple of hours ago, Gaz's family tried to hire me to represent him. Things like that get around pretty fast in a small community."

More silence. "You aren't going to tell me you agreed, are you?"

"I told them I wasn't a criminal lawyer and begged off."

"That's refreshing. Your stock with Frank is going to go up a couple of notches. He always complains about you sticking your nose where it doesn't belong. I think that's why you and him have problems."

Pete didn't say anything.

"Why did they come to you?" Tessler persisted. "Why not some other lawyer?"

"There's only one other lawyer in town, remember? Maybe Mrs. Ramczyk knows what he's like."

"Oh yeah."

"Anyway," Pete said, "Bud Stephanopoulis was a friend and I'm not interested in representing a man who's accused of murdering him. My daughter was also caught up in this thing, as you know. You saw the way she reacted when she heard Bud had been shot. She'd go berserk if she found out I was involved in the case on the side of someone who's accused of being the shooter."

"I'm glad to see you're being smart for a change."

"Getting back to my question, did you find anything when you searched Gaz's place?"

"The usual stuff. A bunch of guns, that sort of thing. We're in the process of analyzing everything."

"Any .223 caliber rifles?"

"We're still analyzing things."

"Stock response, right?"

"Call it what you want. We're just trying to be professional."

"Is that why you didn't arrest Gaz? You've got suspicions, but your search didn't turn up any hard evidence?"

"C'mon, Pete, enough with the interrogation. Are you willing to come in or not?"

"What time?"

SIXTEEN

When Pete walked into the sheriff's office an hour later, he gave his name to the deputy behind the desk, and a few minutes later, Tessler came out to get him. He stared at the bandage on the side of Joe's face and frowned. "You didn't tell me you'd been beaten up. Did Mrs. Ramczyk hit you?"

Pete laughed. "No, but her son did."

Tessler's eyebrows raised. "He was there too?"

"All three of the Ramczyks were there. Gaz and his parents. At one point in our conversation, Gaz got upset and threw a chair at me."

"Jesus, that sounds like assault."

"Maybe."

"Maybe, crap. That's slam dunk an assault. You going to file a complaint against him?"

"I don't know yet."

"What do you mean, you don't know? With the other stuff we've got on him, adding assault charges might help break him down."

"I didn't know that the law was supposed to break a man down. I thought you were supposed to search for the truth and then give the perp, as you like you say, his day in court."

"Get off your white horse, Pete."

Just then Sheriff Richter came down the hall looking even more agitated than usual. "What the hell are you guys doing standing around in the hall talking? I've been waiting for you in the interview room."

Before Pete or Tessler could say anything, Richter saw the bandage on the side of Pete's face and his scowl turned to a smirk. "Nick yourself shaving this morning counselor?"

Tessler put a hand on Pete's arm before he could reply and said to Richter, "Let's go down to the room and I'll explain there."

When they were settled in, Tessler briefed the sheriff in on what happened when the Ramczyks visited Pete that morning. After he finished, Richter said, "I'm glad you're finally wising up and not agreeing to represent every piece of scum who shows up on your doorstep. There may be hope for you yet."

"That's the nicest thing you ever said to me, Sheriff."

"When we finish, you need to fill out a complaint form against Ramczyk for assaulting you. We can't have thugs like that walking into a citizen's office and throwing chairs at him."

"Like I told Detective Tessler, I don't know if I want to press charges."

"Why not? The maniac could have really hurt you."

"He's suffering from PTSD from what I understand. That might explain his actions."

Richter scoffed when he heard that. "PTSD, my rear end. I remember this guy from when he was in high school. He was a delinquent then, and he's worse now because he's been in the military and has been schooled in the use of violence. He's just using the PTSD thing as a smoke screen."

"Medical professionals disagree. They've even prescribed meds to help Gaz control the symptoms of his disorder."

"That's a bunch of bull."

"I thought you were a law enforcement officer, not a psychiatrist."

"I don't have to be a psychiatrist to know a homicidal nut when I see one. Assault is small potatoes compared to the other thing we're going to get him for, but it's still a serious offense. It also shows his violent tendencies."

Pete stared at him. "If you had a good case against him for the murder, you would have arrested him by now."

"Am I hearing this right? You're the one who's always ragging on us about being too quick to bring charges. We take our time, and now you criticize us for that, too."

Tessler, apparently seeing the conflict between the two escalating, tried to tamp things down and said, "Frank, Mr. Thorsen told me he has another appointment and I promised our session wouldn't take more than an hour. He's been here fifteen minutes already. Maybe we should get to the questions you have about Stephanopoulis."

Pete and Richter continued to glare at each other until the sheriff finally looked down at his note pad and proceeded to take Pete through a series of questions that were basically a rehash of those he'd asked the first time. Finally he broke new ground. "Do you know a man named Tomas Esteban? He goes by Tom I understand."

Pete thought for a few moments, then said, "No, I don't believe so."

"That's interesting," Richter said, drumming his pen on the table. "Esteban was a good friend of Stephanopoulis's and Stephanopoulis was a close friend of yours, but you're saying you don't know Esteban?"

Pete shook his head. "Maybe it's someone he knew from Panama. Bud had a house down there if you'll recall."

"Esteban *is* from Panama. He's also has a home on the eastern end of Crystal Lake."

Pete shrugged and said, "Sorry, don't know him."

Richter drummed his pen on the table again. "Interesting," he repeated. "Our investigation has disclosed that Stephanopoulis and Mr. Esteban had a legal disagreement over investments of some kind. You're a lawyer and were a friend of Stephanopoulis's, but you're saying he never asked you for legal advice concerning that disagreement?"

"We talked about this the first time I was in. I never did *any* legal work for Mr. Stephanopoulis."

"Okay," Richter said with a look that telegraphed he didn't believe him. "Next question. Do you know a woman named Kelene Brill?"

Pete scowled. "Sheriff, what's going on here? Are you going to sit there with the telephone book and spit out the names of people and ask me if I know them?"

"My question was whether you know Kelene Brill. Yes or no."

"No."

"Okay." Richter made a show of looking over his notes for a while.

Pete, continuing to wonder what was going on, asked, "Would you mind telling me who Kelene Brill is?"

"She's a woman Mr. Stephanopoulis knew."

"Oh, that's very helpful," Pete said sarcastically. "Is she from around here?"

"Yes."

When Richter didn't say anything more right away, Pete asked, "What you're telling me is that you've got suspects in this case besides Gaz Ramczyk."

"Let's just say that we have other persons of interest. Do you know what that means?"

"Yes, I know what a person of interest is. Let me ask you this, why are you being such a hard-guy with Ramczyk if you're looking at other people?"

Richter stared at Pete for a long time. "A man was shot in cold blood in broad daylight while jet skiing on the lake. People in the community are beginning to worry that there may be some fruitcake out there who's picking off people just for the fun of it. We know the way we're leaning, but we're also trying to determine whether something else might have been going on."

"And you're—"

Richter cut him off. "That's all I'm going to say."

Richter looked at his notes again and pulled out several sheets of paper he had tucked in his legal pad. He looked at Pete again and said, "Once again, do you stand by your statements that you've never represented Bud Stephanopoulis?"

Pete rolled his eyes. "For the last time, yes, I stand by my statements, okay?"

Richter slid the papers across the table to him and asked, "Then how do you explain this?"

Pete scanned the document. It was a three-page letter on his professional letterhead that was addressed to some outfit named Aegean Capital Partners LLC. He flipped to the last page and saw his signature. Philippe Stephanopoulis was shown as one of the persons copied on the letter.

SEVENTEEN

Pete studied the letter. He knew Philippe was Bud's formal first name, but he'd never heard of Aegean Capital Partners LLC, nor of the securities offering referred to in the opinion letter.

"I never wrote this," Pete said.

"Is that your letterhead?"

"Yes."

"Is that your signature on page three of the letter?"

Pete studied the last page again. "It must be a forgery. I had nothing to do with this."

Richter smirked. "Remember that letter you wrote to our governor last year when you were trying to stop us from extraditing that fugitive friend of yours back to North Carolina? I kept a copy of that letter in our case file. I dug it out last night and compared your signature on that letter to the signature on the one you're holding. I'm not a handwriting expert, but the signatures sure look identical to me."

"I told you, I never wrote this opinion letter and never signed it. And to repeat, I've never done legal work for Bud Stephanopoulis or for any business entity with which he was associated, including Aegean Capital Partners LLC. I never heard of the securities transaction referred to in this letter, either."

"Why am I not shocked to hear you say that?"

Joe Tessler was staring at the tabletop, seemingly embarrassed as the give and take between Pete and the sheriff continued.

"Can I keep this?" Pete finally asked, holding the letter up.

Richter shrugged. "Feel free. I have copies."

"This interview is over," Pete said, "and I'm leaving. But let me ask you something. Am I one of your persons of interest, too?"

"Not for the shooting. We know you didn't do that. But we think you might have been mixed up with Stephanopoulis in some way that went beyond casual friendship. Those two people I mentioned—Tomas Esteban and Kelene Brill—they've both made demands on the late Mr. Stephanopoulis for fraud and other claims relating to the securities referred to in this letter. I suspect other complainants will crawl out of the woodwork, too. We're trying to figure out what role you played in all of this."

"I can clear that up for you. I didn't play *any* role."

Richter shrugged again. "All I know is what I see, and I see a letter on your letterhead that was signed by you and it relates to an investment product some people think is fraudulent."

Pete glared at Richter for a long time, then said, "I came here in good faith to answer your questions about Bud Stephanopoulis and wind up being grilled about people I've never heard of and then accused of securities fraud. Even for you, this sets a new standard for flailing around."

Richter's eyes narrowed and his face grew red. "To set the record straight, counselor, we're not flailing around. We're investigating whether a homicide committed in our county was a random act of violence by a nutcase, which it may turn out to be, or an act motivated by financial fraud that was perpetrated by the vic. Financial fraud in which you might have participated. I'd say that's pretty damn sound law enforcement work."

Pete got up and walked out.

Pete was still seething when he got home. Julie was sitting on the porch sipping a Diet Coke and listening to one of his oldies CDs. "This is pretty good even if the music is a century old," she said when he walked in.

He forced himself to be civil and said, "Correction, young lady, maybe a half-century old. At most. Did you have a good time at Sarah's?"

"Wonderful. We finally had a chance to talk. At school, we were always so busy with classwork and sports and everything that we never seemed to have time to just talk about things. It was great to catch up."

"Mmm."

"You know, in two short months, I head east and she heads for UCLA. We'll be thousands of miles apart and have new friends and everything. We both want to be sure we keep our friendship going."

"Why did she decide to go to UCLA?"

"They have a great film program there. She wants to get into the business."

"Mmm," he murmured again.

He went to the kitchen to get a bottle of water and returned to the porch and sat down in a chair and gazed out at the lake. Julie frowned, like she'd just noticed his bandage for the first time. "What happened to your face?"

He decided not to say anything about the Ramczyk's visit, so he told her the same story he'd given the nurse at the hospital.

"Is that why you don't seem to be your usual self, because your head hurts?"

He fished the legal opinion Richter had hit him with out of his portfolio and handed it to her.

She skimmed it and looked up at him. "What's this?"

"That company, Aegean Capital Partners LLC? It apparently was owned by Bud, or at least he was associated with it. I never heard of it before, and I had nothing to do with the legal opinion."

"Okay, but I still don't understand."

"From what I gather, Bud was peddling some form of investment products on the side. He must have gotten ahold of copies of my letterhead and ran off copies of the legal opinion on it and forged my signature."

"That's awful. Why would he do that?"

"As part of the documentation for the securities he was selling, obviously. Either he was trying to save money on legal fees, or he knew no lawyer would give an opinion on the securities so he dummied one up and forged my signature."

"I thought Bud was retired."

"So did I. But it looks like he might not have been. Not completely, at least."

"Who gave you this letter?"

"I just had another meeting with Sheriff Richter and Joe Tessler at the sheriff's office. I was expecting to talk about Bud some more, but Richter hit me with the letter and implied that I was involved with Bud in his fraudulent investment activities."

Julie shook her head several times. "Did the sheriff say anything else about the case?"

"As usual, he was lurching all over the place. One minute his prime suspect is a veteran named Gaz Ramczyk, who's supposedly suffering from PTSD, and the next minute it's some investor who lost money in one of Bud's deals."

Julie looked at him wide-eyed for a few moments. "Do they have any suspects?"

"Ramczyk, obviously. They searched his place, but haven't arrested him yet. I don't know if they have any others although Richter threw out a couple of names when I was down there."

She looked at him some more, then said, "You know what Dad, I think you could use some help trying to figure out what's going on. I have the summer free . . ."

Pete forced a grin and said, "And you're looking to build your resume in case your career choice is private investigator, right?"

"Be serious, Dad. Bud was my friend, too. But the point I'm making is that two heads are better than one when it comes to figuring things out."

"Well, that's certainly true."

"For scheduling purposes, I should warn you that I'm not going to be available for the next three days. Sarah and I are going camping on Beaver Island for two days," referring to a nearby island in Lake Michigan. "Then when I get back, I'm having lunch with Susan Ettleman so we can talk some more about Cornell."

"Busy, busy."

"After that, I'm free. Mostly at least."

"I'll keep that in mind."

Julie's face grew somber. "I've been thinking about that day on the jet skis again. Sarah said I was screaming in my sleep. You know, I could have been shot that day instead of Bud. That totally freaks me out."

Pete went over to her chair and put his arm around her shoulder and gave her a squeeze. "It's just a hunch, but I have a feeling that whoever shot Bud was after him for a reason. Just about the entire sheriff's office is working on the case. I'll bet they arrest someone soon."

Joe Tessler called while Julie was taking a nap and Pete was sitting on the porch brooding about his latest confrontation with Frank Richter. "Pete, I want to apologize for this afternoon. I was in a real bind and—"

"Cut the crap, Joe. You work for the guy. That's just the way it is."

"I know you're upset. I thought Frank was going to ease into the letter, not drop it on you like a ton of cow doo-doo."

"So you admit you knew about the letter."

"Well, yeah, I knew about it, but Frank threatened me if I said anything to you in advance. He knows we talk about things once in a while and gets pissed about it. I—"

"Anything else you want to tell me?" His voice was cold and had an edge to it.

"No, just to apologize for—"

"I'll talk to you later, Joe."

After Pete hung up, he sat on his porch and brooded some more. *What had Bud been up to? And how had he gotten copies of his professional letterhead?* He tried to recall the times Bud had been in his office. He also wondered about the signature. If it had been forged, it was a damned good job because it certainly looked like his.

Pete left a note for Julie and got on his bike and headed for Shorewood Drive. The sun was just settling below the bluffs and a silvery sheen covered the water. He soaked up the beauty and thought about the telephone conversation he'd just had with Joe Tessler. It wasn't Joe's fault that he had a jerk like Richter for a boss, and he felt bad about the way he'd jumped on him.

He came to the end of the road along the lake and veered right and then left again to get onto Shorewood. He felt the strain in his thighs as he pedaled up-grade until he came to Bud's driveway. He straddled his bicycle and trained his binoculars on the house and wasn't surprised to see police tape strung across the front door. If Richter had the opinion letter, he'd assumed that his people had been in Bud's house, scouring it for anything that might be relevant to their investigation. The lights framing the front door were on, but the inside was dark.

He'd been in the house several times and knew there was a side door that opened into a mudroom. There was also a sliding glass door that led to the patio. He couldn't see if there was police tape across those doors, but assumed there might be. He knew the house had a security alarm system, too. He wasn't concerned about that, though. One night after dinner in town with Bud, he'd gone back to his house for a nightcap and had watched him disarm the system using a key panel inside the side door. He remembered Bud laughing about how he could never remember security codes or computer passwords, and so he'd programmed his system using a number he wouldn't forget—the year he'd been drafted by the Boston Celtics.

As Pete studied the house, he wondered if the forensics team had taken all of Bud's documents with them when they'd searched it.

EIGHTEEN

After helping Julie assemble her camping gear for the trip to Beaver Island, Pete dropped her off at Sarah's house before stopping at *The Northern Sentinel* to see what Harry knew about Tomas Esteban and Kelene Brill. Talbot was with him again.

"Jeffrey and I are going over ideas for his column in the next issue of the *Sentinel*," Harry said. "We'll be another fifteen minutes or so. You can join us if you like."

"Thanks, I think I'll catch up on the latest news until you're free." He picked up a copy of that morning's *Sentinel*. Front and center was a story about the Bud Stephanopoulis murder under Harry's byline. It chronicled how the shooting occurred, stated that the weapon used was a .223 rifle, and summarized what was known about the investigation to date. The story included several quotes from Sheriff Richter, including that his people had identified a local man as suspect and had searched his home and confiscated several weapons. The story didn't mention Gaz Ramczyk by name. It also didn't speculate that the shooting might have been a random act of violence rather than a premeditated murder.

Harry apparently had taken his sermon to heart. There was nothing in the story about Bud's financial activities or the claims against him for the obvious reason that Harry didn't know about them.

Pete alternated between thinking some more about his session with Frank Richter and Joe Tessler the day before and half-listening to the conversation between Harry and Jeffrey Talbot. Talbot was taking another run at trying to persuade Harry to expand his poetry column, and Harry was resisting while trying to remain patient and polite.

Finally, they wrapped up their meeting, and on his way out, Talbot said to Pete, "Have you thought any more about *The Sagas of Icelanders*? That's a bit outside my scholarly area, but I'd be happy to collaborate with you if you have an idea for a piece. Maybe if we combine forces, we can persuade Harry to further upgrade his fine newspaper." He looked Harry's way and winked.

Pete nodded. "Let's think about it."

When he was gone, Harry said, "Jesus, could you imagine having him as one of your high school teachers? He'd probably make you carry a copy of the complete works of the Lake Poets back and forth to school."

Pete smiled. "You heard him. His mission is to help you upgrade your fine newspaper."

Harry rolled his eyes. "He's smart as hell, though."

"On other matters, I thought your story about the shooting struck just the right tone."

Harry's face brightened. "You think so?" he asked.

"I do. And I think you made the right call by not speculating about the shooting possibly being a random act of violence."

"When I wrote the story, I kept thinking that it seemed incomplete. But you didn't get that impression, huh?"

Pete shook his head. "I thought it was a solid piece of reporting."

"Umm."

"I have a question for you. Do you know a Tomas Esteban or a Kelene Brill? Esteban goes by Tom."

Harry's eyebrows knit together. "I know who Tom Esteban *is*. I can't say I really *know* him. Kelene Brill, I've never heard of. Why do you ask?"

"Our friend Bud Stephanopoulis apparently was leading a double life. He told you, me, and everyone else he was retired, always implying he had more money than he knew what to do with. But I just found out he was promoting financial products of some kind right under our noses, and the two people I just mentioned are some of his investors. According to Richter, both are claiming investment fraud. I also gather that his people are looking into whether a disgruntled investor might have been the shooter."

Harry's attention was obviously focused now. "Unbelievable."

Pete nodded. "And, I know for a fact that my friend Bud was dummying up legal opinions on my letterhead, with my signature, and distributing them to investors as part of the package. Richter gave me a copy of one of the letters."

Harry just shook his head. "What kind of investment products was he selling?"

"I don't really know. All I know is that some investors, at least, are claiming they're fraudulent."

"Do you think they were like what that guy Bernie Madoff was selling?"

"Could be, I don't know."

"How did Sheriff Richter happen to give you the opinion letter? Is he accusing you of something?"

"Not the murder, obviously. But he told me flat out that he wonders if I was involved in Bud's fraudulent investment activities."

"He won't take your word that you had nothing to do with the opinion letters, huh?"

Pete's expression turned incredulous. "Are you kidding? He sat there with that 'gotcha' look of his when he handed me a copy of the opinion with what looks like my signature."

"Financial crimes—fraud and the like—are federal or state offenses, not local, right?"

"Yes, but how long do you think it will take him to call in the federal or state people if he thinks he's got me?"

Harry's lips tightened. "I know you don't want to hear this, but I've been telling you for years that you ought to patch up relations with the sheriff. I—"

"Cut the sermon, Harry. He's a jerk and both of us know it. I just don't let him push me around like a lot of people do."

Harry didn't say anything.

"Getting back to Tomas Esteban, what do you know about him?" Pete asked.

Harry's eyes widened all of a sudden and he said, "Don't look now, Pete, but I think that's Gaz Ramczyk staring at us through the window."

Pete kept looking straight ahead, like he was still carrying on a conversation with Harry, but shifted his eyes to the left and caught a glimpse of the man looking in. No question it was Ramczyk.

"Keep talking like you don't know he's there," Harry said.

In a couple of minutes, Ramczyk disappeared.

"Jesus," Harry said, "that was spooky. People look in the window all the time, but when you know the person is suspected of shooting somebody and he looks in at you . . . That's scary as hell."

"I didn't want to turn my head so I didn't get a good look at him. What was he doing, just looking in?"

"Standing there, staring at us. Maybe I ought to start keeping my blinds down. I'm going to have nightmares over this one."

"Has he ever done that before?"

"Not that I've noticed. Sometimes people I know will knock on the window and wave and move on. This guy just stood there and stared. It gave me the willies knowing who he is and that there might be something wrong with him."

"Maybe I'm the one he was staring at."

"Yeah, maybe, but now he knows that we're friends . . ."

"Keep an eye out. If you see him again, let's figure out what to do."

Harry shuddered. "Esteban. He's a seasonal resident who lives in a condominium complex on the east end of the lake. I remember him, because a couple of years ago, he and some of the other condo owners filed a lawsuit against the developer. I don't remember exactly what they were claiming, but Esteban was the spokesman for the group and I interviewed him over the phone a couple of times and wrote some stories about the dispute. I'm pretty sure I never met him in person. I remember that on the telephone, he spoke so quietly I could barely hear him. He had this funny voice. Not timid, really, but kind of thin. Like you shouldn't mess with him, you know what I mean?"

"Do you have his address?"

After punching a few keys on his keyboard, Harry gave him Esteban's address and telephone number.

"But you said you don't know Kelene Brill."

Harry was tapping away at his keyboard and said, "Just a minute, I knew there was something else about Esteban. Besides the condo dispute, he was accused of killing somebody's dog a while back. Apparently, the guy likes to roam around at night and one morning, a guy found his dog with its neck broken. The dog owner was convinced that Esteban did it and filed a complaint. I don't know what happened. The complaint never went anywhere."

"Umm."

"Kelene Brill I've never heard of, like I said." Harry pulled a copy of the local telephone directory from his desk drawer and scrolled through the names. "She's listed," he said. He gave Pete her information.

"Are there other people who invested in these phony deals of Bud's?" Harry asked.

"I assume so, but I don't have any information about them."

Harry studied him. "I have a feeling that Pete Thorsen the Great Censor is about to turn into Pete Thorsen the Great Sherlock again."

Pete frowned.

Harry grinned like he knew he was onto something. "This is the hook you've been looking for to get into the case, right?"

"I haven't been looking to get into the case."

Harry continued to grin and said, "Okay, if you won't admit to the hook, how do you plan to go about clearing your name?"

"I don't know."

"Are you going to do some poking around, as you like to say?"

"I told you, I don't know."

NINETEEN

He did know, though. He puttered around his office for the rest of the day and then went home and made dinner. After tidying up the kitchen, he found a pair of black jeans and a black T-shirt and tossed them on his bed. Then he located the collapsible black nylon bag he sometimes used when he had to carry documents that wouldn't fit in his briefcase, and broke open the packaging of his new mini-flashlight that had a variety of features permitting him to change the focus and luminosity. He inserted batteries and tested the flashlight.

The last item he needed was the gift from Adam Rose, his private investigator friend. He shoved the clothes on the closet hang bar to one side and dropped to his knees and reached in and slid a panel on the wall to the left and took out the small black case. He unzipped it and looked at the thin implements and identified those he thought he'd need. Then he rearranged the implements in the slip pockets so he wouldn't have to search for the right ones while he was on site. He rezipped the case and added it to the pile on the bed.

He sat on the porch, and even though the light was beginning to fade, he didn't turn on a lamp. He was on edge and kept checking the time even though it was darkness and not the hour that would dictate when he'd leave. He'd been through this a couple of times before and remembered the tension he always felt while he waited. That feeling was back. He put a Chet Atkins CD on his Bose music system and listened as the master caressed the guitar strings, trying to relax.

When it was finally dark enough, he changed into the black clothes and grabbed the rest of his equipment. He stopped in the kitchen for a pair of latex gloves, and on the way out, took his navy windbreaker and a dark cap. He got his bicycle out of the garage and organized everything and headed out, trying not to second guess what he was about to do. The other times, he'd always had someone with him who knew the ropes. This time he was alone. He kept rehearsing in his mind what he would do when he got to Bud's house, but his thoughts always drifted back to the consequences if he were caught.

The lights around the lake winked at him as he rode along South Shore. Traffic was light, and when a pickup or SUV did come along, it hugged the other side of the road in a display of courtesy. He encountered no joggers or dog walkers. He came to the place where the road veered away from the lake and zigzagged onto Shorewood. Sweat beaded on his forehead as he pedaled up the hillier terrain.

When he came to Bud's driveway, he untied the bundle behind his seat and hid his bicycle in the bushes on the opposite side of the road. He started downgrade toward the house, his eyes taking in everything, watching for humans or dogs that might be outside. Periodically, he took deep breaths to calm his nerves. The front door lights were still on, but otherwise nothing. When he got closer, he saw there wasn't any yellow tape across the mudroom door like there was in front. Only one of the neighboring houses had lights on.

He quickened his stride as he passed through the dimly-illuminated area at the front of the house. Everything was still clear when he reached the mudroom door. He pulled on the latex gloves and unzipped his tool case and looked around again and listened for sounds. He didn't hear any and switched on his flashlight, holding it in his teeth to free up his hands. Then he began to work with his implements. The five minutes it took him to manipulate the lock's tumblers seemed like an hour. When he heard the final click, he brushed the sweat from his brow with a sleeve and turned the knob. The door opened noiselessly and he stepped inside and closed it behind him.

He ran his hand along the wall, searching for the control panel, knowing he had just seconds to disarm the system if it were active. His pulse beat faster as he turned on his flashlight again. He saw the panel and quickly stepped over and punched in Bud's security code, then stood back and listened. There were no sounds of any kind. His pulse raced again as he tried to remember whether Bud's system used a silent alarm.

He'd given himself fifteen minutes inside the house to do what he needed to do, and he knew he couldn't squander the time by standing there agonizing over the alarm. He adjusted his flashlight to broaden the beam and made his way towards Bud's study. The door was open and he stepped in and looked around, being careful to keep his flashlight aimed at the floor to minimize the chance that someone outside would notice light filtering through the blinds. He tightened the cords as a precaution and stepped over to the bank of file cabinets along the wall and opened the top drawer and scanned the labels on the file jackets. They contained materials relating to the house and to Bud's fleet of personal watercraft.

The second drawer looked like it had what he was interested in—documents relating to the various investment offerings of Aegean Capital Partners LLC. He carried the file jacket for the most recent deal to Bud's desk and began to look through it. He found copies of the offering memorandum, a list of the investors, and various related documents.

As he pored over the documents to get an idea of what was involved, a dog broke into a frenzy right outside the house. Startled, Pete clicked off his flashlight and sat motionless in Bud's desk chair. The dog continued to bark and howl and snarl, like it had cornered an animal of some sort right outside the walls. From the way the sound rose and fell, the dog was racing back and forth outside the house. He wondered if his flashlight beam had been visible from outside and attracted someone's attention.

Pete continued to remain motionless in the dark room and tried to decide what to do. He didn't have many options. With the dog just outside, he knew he was effectively trapped. The clock in his head ticked away, eating at his allotted time, as he continued to listen. Then a light flashed against the window. Pete slid behind the desk, hoping it had nothing to do with his presence in the house. He heard the muffled voice of a man commanding the dog to be quiet. When he didn't hear anything else for a few minutes, he clicked on his flashlight and checked the time. He'd already been in the house fifteen minutes.

He waited a few minutes more, then resumed looking through the folder, knowing he had to pick up the pace. The sub-file labeled "Legal Opinion" was empty, probably because Sheriff Richter had taken the contents. He carried the file jacket back to the cabinet and took a different one relating to another deal. It did contain the legal opinion. There were multiple copies, all on his letterhead and all with his signature. He took a couple of copies of the opinion plus samples of each of the other significant documents, including the offering memorandum and a list of the investors. He crammed the documents into his nylon carry bag.

The bottom file drawer contained documents relating to Bud's legal affairs. As Pete hastily sorted through the file jackets, he noticed that one sub-file contained documents involving claims by investors. He knew he didn't have time to review the documents individually, so he took a handful and added them to those already in his bag. Then he came to several file jackets labeled "Harrison Stryker LLC." As best he could tell, they all related to Bud's departure from the investment banking firm.

He glanced at his watch again; he'd been in the house for a half-hour, double his allotted time. He took a handful of the Harrison Stryker documents and added them to his carry bag. Then he put everything back in the file cabinet and looked around to make sure there weren't any signs that someone had been in the house and rifled through the files. He retraced his path to the mudroom and reactivated the security system. When he opened the door a crack and looked out, the dog didn't break into a frenzy again and everything looked clear. He locked the door from the inside, slipped out and pulled it closed behind him. He hurried up the driveway to where his bicycle was hidden, resisting the impulse to run.

He coasted down the hill, and when he was on South Shore again, he pulled over and leaned his bicycle against a tree. Then he took a roll of reflective tape from his pocket and peeled off his windbreaker and put strips of tape across the front and back. He got on his bicycle again, and as he pedaled along, the anvil pressing on his chest began to feel lighter.

Pete spread the documents on his kitchen table and began to study them. He couldn't tell exactly what had happened when Bud left Harrison Stryker LLC, but it seemed clear that his departure from the investment banking firm had been less than amicable. Harrison Striker apparently had been sued in one or more class action lawsuits brought by investors in connection with investment products sponsored or underwritten by the firm. The firm settled the lawsuits, but because it had insufficient capital to cover the amount of the settlement, it looked to individual partners, of which Bud was one, to make up the difference. Bud had resisted contributing, raising all sorts of arguments, including that he wasn't a partner in the firm at the time the class actions were filed and that he had no voice in the decision to settle. Eventually, however, Bud was forced to contribute $7.8 million.

Not long after, it looked like Bud began to promote investment deals on his own. The legal opinion on the first one for which he had documents had been given by a Detroit law firm. For subsequent deals, Bud used the bogus legal opinions on Pete's letterhead. Pete compared those opinions with the one given by the Detroit firm. The language was identical.

All of the investment products had been structured to be exempt from the registration requirements of the federal and state securities laws. He scanned the investors list for one deal. Tomas Esteban and Kelene Brill were both on the list, as were investors from Panama, Detroit and Grand Rapids. Tucked among the documents were emails or letters from Esteban and Brill demanding their money back. One letter from Brill made reference to parts of Bud's anatomy, suggesting there might have been more than an investment relationship between them.

Pete wondered how carefully Richter and his people had examined the documents. He knew that things that jumped out at him as a lawyer wouldn't necessarily be evident to someone without legal training. He also knew from experience that the eyes of laypersons often glazed over when faced with lengthy legal documents composed in arcane language.

Even without a complete set of documents, the ones he had supported his conclusion that Bud *had* been leading a double life. His motivation seemed to be financial. The capital call on Harrison Stryker partners obviously had put a major dent in Bud's wealth. He couldn't tell for sure from the documents he had, but he suspected that the investment products Bud had been peddling in recent years were similar to those that had gotten Harrison Stryker in trouble.

Besides Tomas Esteban and Kelene Brill, he wondered how many other disgruntled investors were out there. He also wondered whether Sheriff Richter might be on the right track for once.

TWENTY

The man who'd killed Bud Stephanopoulis paced around his living room with the television remote in his hand and the sound turned down, waiting for the ten o'clock news to come on. For days, he'd been tuning into the morning news and then the early evening news and finally the late news, each time hoping to catch something about the sheriff's office's investigation into scumbag's shooting. Occasionally there'd be a brief update that said essentially what had been reported previously, followed by the usual statement about the investigation being ongoing.

He stopped pacing when the late news anchor appeared on the screen and turned up the sound to hear his words. The lead story involved the continuing efforts of a real estate developer to get the necessary approvals to construct a building complex on Front Street in Traverse City that would be several stories higher than the surrounding structures. The anchor droned on about the opposition to the project and a reporter interviewed two lawyers who gave their opinions on the finer points of the applicable zoning law. The man grew increasingly impatient as the story segment switched to a collection of local citizens, some of whom maintained that the project would change the unique character of Traverse City and others who argued that the opponents were merely trying to prevent progress and lamented the tax revenue the city would lose if the project were killed.

Finally the anchor moved on to another story and then another. When he called on other reporters for the weather and sports, the man knew the program was nearing its end. He slumped in a chair as the anchor went into his sign-off story about a man who'd broken into the local animal shelter and made off with nine dogs.

Nothing about the Stephanopoulis case. *What was going on?* The man knew that eyewitnesses had told the sheriff's people they'd seen someone who matched the thug's description in the vicinity of where the shots had come from. He also knew they'd searched his house and questioned him. Everyone in the community knew the guy's history as a bad actor, too. He didn't understand what was taking them so long.

The man thought about the rifle and other items hidden in his shed. Every day, he'd come up with a new plan for disposing of them, but they were still there because after thinking about it some more, he saw some deficiencies. Everything had been going so smoothly, too, and now it had ground to a halt. He needed to get rid of the stuff before that worthless sheriff knocked on *his* door and started asking *him* questions.

He turned off the television, took his car keys, and went outside, hoping a drive would help clear his mind. He got into his Toyota SUV and started the engine. The vehicle still felt strange to him. He'd sold his pickup, which he'd just gotten used to, at CarMax in Grand Rapids for cash, taking less than he thought it was worth. Then he'd used the cash to buy the Toyota he'd seen parked in a front yard with a "For Sale" sign on it. He thought his plan was foolproof, but now he began to worry that maybe the pickup could be traced back to him.

As he drove aimlessly along back roads, he realized he needed to get a grip on himself. He thought about Gaz Ramczyk some more and tried to think of whether there was anything else he could do. He knew where the thug lived and decided to drive past his house, hoping some ideas would come to him. He changed directions, and a half-hour later, he came to Ramczyk's driveway. The moon provided enough light for him to see, and as he peered in, he didn't see any vehicles parked by the house. He proceeded on, and a quarter mile up the road, he made a U-turn and drove past again to confirm that he hadn't missed something.

On his way to Ramczyk's place, he remembered passing an abandoned farm on the opposite side of the road, and when he came to it, he turned in and parked behind an old machine shed. He walked back to Ramczyk's property and stood in the neglected cherry orchard and studied his house some more. Then he edged closer and stopped and looked around again. *The thug must be out, whoring around somewhere.* When the man cleared the orchard and was passing the house, he saw white shapes just ahead of him. The shapes turned out to be white crosses arranged in neat rows, each at the head of a rectangular mound of dirt. Like a series of burial mounds.

He tested the mound closest to him with the toe of his boot. The soil was soft, like it had been newly formed. He stepped forward and read the inscription on the nearest cross: "Cpl. Rafael Ramirez," and below the name, "Died in Afghanistan, January 14, 2014 in the Service of his Country." The rest of the crosses had other names and similar inscriptions. He stared at the memorial a while. Then he backed out, using one foot to scrape dirt across his footprints.

TWENTY-ONE

After Pete got back from a run along the lake, he toasted a bagel, and while he ate it, he called Julie. When she answered, he said, "Good morning. Are you having a good time?"

"Beaver Island is wonderful, Dad. Did you know that a king once lived here?"

"I did. A self-proclaimed king as I remember." He was referring to James Strang whose "reign" occurred in the nineteenth century when he headed a religious colony on the island.

"He was shot. That's regicide, you know. I learned that in school."

Julie babbled on about the things she and Sarah had done on the island and their plans for that day until they had to catch the ferry back to the mainland. By the time he was off the telephone, he felt as though he'd sat through a travel monologue narrated by a representative of the local Chamber of Commerce.

Pete looked at the stack of documents he'd pilfered from Bud's house on the table next to him, and smiled when he thought about Harry's comment that he was using the bogus legal opinions as a hook to get into the murder case. If Harry knew what he'd done, he'd preach to him for an hour about how reckless he was and then gloat for a year about how he knew exactly what he was doing. The fact was, though, Pete did have an increasing feeling that Bud's murder was somehow connected to his financial shenanigans, and that unraveling one would probably also shed light on the other.

He knew he couldn't get so caught up trying to unravel the puzzle of Bud's murder that he took his eye off the ball. Knowing Richter, it wouldn't surprise him if the he contacted the Securities & Exchange Commission or the state securities authorities to try to implicate him in Bud's fraudulent schemes if he sensed an opening. Beyond that, there was the risk of civil lawsuits by disgruntled investors as well and he had to protect himself. If it turned out that also helped solve the murder case, well, that was a bonus. He dialed Angie DeMarco's direct number at his former Chicago law firm.

"Pete," Angie said when she answered, "you're calling to tell me you're in town and want to have dinner with me at Gibsons, right?"

Pete chuckled. "I'd love to have dinner with you, but it'll have to wait because I'm not in Chicago. I called to ask for a favor."

A pause, then, "Favors don't come free you know."

Angie DeMarco had been one of his closest allies when he was at Sears & Whitney and she'd succeeded him as managing partner. They stayed in touch after he moved north and both of them enjoyed the banter and innuendoes whenever they talked. He always suspected that Angie, who was in an unhappy marriage, had something in mind other than just banter.

"I'm aware of that," Pete said, "and the payment is dinner the next time I'm in Chicago. With one of those giant gooey deserts Gibsons serves tossed in."

"I'm going to hold you to that. Okay, what's this favor you want? I have to be in court in forty-five minutes."

Pete told her about Bud's murder and how it had come to light that he'd been using legal opinions dummied up on Pete's letterhead as part of his scam investment solicitations.

"If we were on Skype right now, you'd see that I'm sitting here shaking my head. People always call Chicago the murder capital of the world these days, but on a *per capita* basis, I think your little burg is besting us. Every time I talk to you, someone else has been bumped off up there."

Pete chuckled again. "I think that's overstating it. But here's what I need. A handwriting expert to examine the legal opinions and provide evidence I can use that they weren't signed by me."

"Do you have an original copy of one of the opinions?"

"No, but I have a pretty good copy."

"Send it. I'll have a guy I know look at it. I can't make any promises, though. Without an original . . ."

When Pete was off the phone with Angie, he sorted through the documents he'd taken from Bud's house and selected the clearest copy of the bogus legal opinion. He put it in an oversized envelope so he wouldn't have to fold it. Then he changed clothes and gathered up some things and headed for town and the FedEx drop. And after that, he was going to visit two of Bud's unhappy investors.

Pete pulled into the condominium complex where Tomas Esteban lived and located his unit at the far end and parked. It looked twice as large as most of the others, like two units had been consolidated into one. It also had a shed. The door was open and he heard scuffling inside. He called, "Mr. Esteban?"

Eventually a medium-height man with a deep tan wearing a faded pink polo shirt and Bermuda shorts with some kind of reptile-skin belt emerged from the shed. He seemed surprised to see Pete standing twenty feet away, like he hadn't heard his voice.

"Mr. Esteban?"

The man's eyes flicked towards Pete's vehicle and back to him. "Do I know you?" he asked in that strange thin voice Harry had described.

"We've never met. My name is Pete Thorsen."

Esteban peered at him some more and tugged at his shirt collar. "Are you with the sheriff's office?"

"I'm not. I know you talked to the sheriff's people about Bud Stephanopoulis. I also know that you had a financial relationship with Mr. Stephanopoulis and a disagreement with him over some investments. That's what I'd like to talk to you about."

Esteban's eyes darted around and he seemed to be gathering his thoughts. "I'm not going to talk to a stranger about my personal affairs," he finally said. He not only had a thin voice, but he appeared jumpy.

"Look, Mr. Esteban, we've both been taken advantage of by Bud Stephanopoulis. I think it would be in your interest to talk to me."

"Who said he took advantage of me?"

"I know he did."

Esteban put on a pair of reflective sunglasses that had been hanging by a bow tucked into the neck of his polo shirt. "Please leave," he said. "I have things to do."

"I only need ten minutes of your time."

Esteban turned around and slipped the padlock's hook through the hasp on the shed door, clicked it, and gave the padlock a yank to make sure it was secure. He started to walk toward the front door of his condo unit.

"You know Stephanopoulis is dead, right?"

Esteban opened his door, stepped inside, and closed the door behind him.

Pete thought about leaving, but then reconsidered and decided to take another run at him. He walked to the door and knocked and said, "Mr. Esteban, I'm not leaving until we talk, so you might as well open the door."

He heard no answer, so after a couple of minutes, he knocked again and called, "I'm still here, Mr. Esteban. We should talk."

No answer again. Just as he was about to knock a third time, a golf cart pulled into Esteban's driveway and the man driving called,

"Mister, this is private property. You've been asked to leave. Please do it now."

The driver got out of the cart, causing it to rock because of his weight, and walked toward him. He was a hulk of a man who looked like an out-of-shape professional wrestler. Pete didn't move.

"Did you hear me?" the Hulk asked.

"Do you live here?"

"Yes, smart guy, I live here. I'm also the condominium manager. Mr. Esteban called and said you were harassing him and refused to leave. You need to leave right now or I'm going to call the sheriff and press charges."

"I have to talk to Mr. Esteban about a business matter."

The Hulk stepped closer to him. "What's it going to be, leave or a date with the sheriff?"

Pete knew that pressing matters wouldn't do any good so he said, "Okay, I'll leave, but I suggest you ask Mr. Esteban to call me." He handed the Hulk one of his business cards. "And for what it's worth, I happen to know the sheriff personally. I also know that his people have already talked to Mr. Esteban once. I think I'll tell them they should talk to him again."

"I don't know what you're talking about."

"I suspect Mr. Esteban knows. It's more serious than killing somebody's dog."

Hulk stood with a puzzled expression on his face as Pete slipped past him and walked to his car and got in and drove off. He smiled and had to remember to thank Harry for the information about the dog. Either the Hulk didn't know about the incident, or he wondered how the hell Pete knew.

TWENTY-TWO

Pete thought some more about Esteban as he drove towards Kelene Brill's house, and wondered what Tessler's take on him was. Maybe he'd call Joe after he finished with Brill. He owed him an apology for the way he'd acted the last time they talked anyway. That might be a good excuse.

Brill lived in a ranch house with gray siding and a lawn that was in need of mowing. It had an attached garage at one end, and like so many of the houses in the area, a storage shed toward the rear. Pete parked and went up the walk and knocked. The inner door was open and the smell of cigarette smoke seeped through the screen.

A woman he assumed was Kelene Brill appeared in the doorway. She didn't open the screen door, but seemed to be sizing him up. Finally she said, "You don't look like the UPS man."

He smiled. "No brown, right?"

"And cuter, too. Do you want to introduce yourself?"

"I'm Pete Thorsen, Ms. Brill. I'd like to talk to you about Bud Stepha-nopoulis if you have a few minutes." Even through the screen, he could see her expression harden when she heard the name.

"What about?" she asked in a tone that suddenly was churlish.

"I understand you were one of the investors in financial products pro-moted by Mr. Stephanopoulis's company, Aegean Capital Partners LLC. I—"

"Did you bring my check?" she asked.

"No, but—"

"That's all I'm interested in. I want my money back. With interest, obviously."

"I'll explain what you have to do to get it back if we can talk for a few minutes."

She continued to stare at him through the screen. "Who did you say you were?" she asked.

"Pete Thorsen," he repeated. "I'm a lawyer here in town."

"Are you that slimeball's lawyer?"

"If by slimeball you mean Bud Stephanopoulis, no, I'm not his law-yer, but I knew him fairly well."

Kelene Brill's scowl grew more pronounced. She said, "Get me my money back. Then maybe we can talk."

"Mr. Stephanopoulis's estate is going to have to be probated. From what little I know about the situation, you and the other investors very well might have claims against the estate." Pete wasn't a probate lawyer, but he knew the basics. What he didn't know was whether there would be any assets in Bud's estate to satisfy claims. At least after those claims with priority were satisfied.

"I don't want to go through all of that. All I want is my money back. He took advantage of me."

"It's not that simple, Ms. Brill. Since Mr. Stephanopoulis is dead, everything *has* to go through the probate court."

"My girlfriend knows about these things. She said she read in the *National Enquirer* that when Bernie Madoff went to jail, people got their money back."

Pete sighed. It seemed that Harry wasn't the only one to invoke Madoff's name, but as far as citing the *National Enquirer* as the authority . . . "Okay," he said, "I wish you luck. I'll cross your name off the list of people who are interested in joining my group. Thanks for your time." He turned away and started back to his car.

Kelene Brill called after him, "If I file a claim, when will I get my money?"

Pete stopped and looked back at her. "It's not up to me. But I do know that if your case isn't effectively presented to the probate judge, you have a zero chance of recovering anything."

She hesitated for a moment, then said, "How much will you charge me?"

He went through the pretense of thinking about her question. "I haven't decided yet. If you and the other investors don't recover anything, I won't charge anything. If you do recover, I'll probably ask people in the group to reimburse my expenses. It would all be agreed in advance."

"Why wouldn't you charge a fee?" she asked suspiciously.

"Bud Stephanopoulis was a friend of mine. If he did something wrong and it looks like people like you have valid claims against him, I might try to do the right thing and help them recover some of their money without charging for my services."

"Aren't you noble." Her words dripped with sarcasm.

Pete shrugged. "Call me if you want to talk. I'm in the telephone book." He started toward his car again. He was thinking that his bluff hadn't worked when he heard her call to him a second time.

"I guess I could talk to you for a while. If it doesn't take too long. I have a date."

Pete retraced his steps and she let him in. Without the screen blurring her image, he saw that Kelene Brill was a middle-aged woman with some mileage on her. Her blonde hair had seen too many strip jobs, and her skin showed the years in spite of her makeup. Her perfectly oval eyes looked like they'd had work done on them, though. The way her body was packed into her tight black pants and blood-red blouse with the top two buttons undone suggested that she probably was telling him the truth about the date.

When he was inside, she looked him over more closely and asked, "What happened to your face?"

Pete was getting tired of the question, but gave her the same explanation he'd given the nurse at the hospital and Julie.

She moved closer and touched the bandage lightly with one finger. "She didn't do a very good job. Do you want me to replace it?"

"No, but thanks for the offer."

"Are you sure?" She touched the bandage again.

"Yes, it's fine."

"I'm not a registered nurse, but I've had a lot of experience taking care of people. It wouldn't be any trouble."

"That's very kind of you, but I have to change it in the morning after I shower. I think I'll leave it until then."

"How about a drink then?"

It was only four o'clock in the afternoon and a little early for alcohol as far as he was concerned so he said, "Just water, please."

She looked disappointed at being turned down for the second time in less than a minute and headed for the kitchen. He heard ice cubes drop into glasses and liquid pouring over the ice and a knife slicing into something on a cutting board. While he was waiting for her to come back, he glanced around her living room and noticed a handsome wooden plaque on the end table by the couch opposite him. He moved closer and saw that the plaque's brass inset said, "Honors Graduate in Self-Defense Skills." It had been awarded by some outfit named "The Up North Self-Defense Institute." He was looking at the plaque when Kelene Brill came back.

"I just got that," she said, her pride showing. "Are you impressed?"

"Very. What did the program cover?"

She nodded. "Everything. It's a program for women. Shooting guns, the martial arts, other things."

Pete's antennae began to rattle. "Did the Institute supply weapons for the shooting part? Or did you use your own?"

Kelene handed him the water and sat down and plucked a cigarette from a silver case and held it in the air between long fingers with perfectly manicured red nails. She lit it and took a long pull. "I don't have a firearm yet," she said as she blew a stream of smoke into the air. "I'm going to get something, though." She took another drag on the cigarette.

Pete pursed his lips and nodded.

"Women have to be able to protect themselves these days, you know," she continued. "The world is full of rapists and murderers and thieves."

"Have you had any problems?"

She took another long pull on her cigarette and squinted as she blew more smoke into the air. "There's this guy I used to date. I think he's stalking me."

"If he came around and you thought he was threatening you, could you shoot him?"

Kelene took a sip of her drink with a lemon-peel slice curled over the edge of the glass and gazed across the room. "Sure. When a man breaks into your house, it means he's trying to hurt you. You have to hurt him first. That's what they taught us at the Institute, 'Hurt, don't get hurt.'"

"Okay," Pete said, "enough of that. How did you meet Bud Stephanopoulis?"

She gave a little grunt and looked away and took another draw on her cigarette. "Ah, back to the slimeball."

Pete didn't say anything.

She blew more smoke over her shoulder. Pete hated cigarettes, but tried to keep his feelings under control. He knew he couldn't very well tell Kelene Brill she couldn't smoke in her own house, especially when he was trying to pry information out of her.

"We used to see each other once in a while." Another drag on the cigarette and more smoke.

"I see," he said, happy that Brill was acknowledging something he'd already gathered from the documents. "By seeing each other, I assume you mean you were dating."

"Yes. Did you know slimeball very well?"

"I thought I did."

"He'd say or do anything to get a woman into bed. Talk about your future together, things like that."

"Umm."

"He used that log mansion of his as a tool. He'd tell you about how he was going to remodel the place to create this humongous master bedroom with double baths that would be bigger than most people's houses. All a bunch of bull." Her eyes flicked around the room.

"How did you happen to invest in the Aegean Capital Partners deal?"

"We were . . . together . . . one night. You know, talking and stuff. He said he was putting together this investment pool for selected friends of his. High net worth individuals he called them. According to him, the pool would provide a guaranteed annual return of ten percent with an upside—his words—of up to twenty-two percent. That was *annually*, understand. I had some money from the settlement with my third husband that was, like, earning *nothing* at the bank. I asked him if I could invest in the pool. He pretended to resist for a while, then gave in and said he'd take my money because we were so close. All a bunch of bull. Bull!"

"How long ago was that?"

She thought for a few moments. "Two years. About."

"Did you get your ten percent annually?"

She threw her head back and blew another stream of smoke into the air and laughed a sarcastic laugh. "For the first three months, I got the equivalent of *fourteen* percent. I was so happy I bought slimeball a ring. A nice big man ring with a polished Petoskey stone. A wonderful ring."

When she didn't continue, he said, "And then?"

"Then the return dropped to eight percent and slimeball with my ring on his finger told me I'd get makeup payments as soon as his company's cash flow improved. It never seemed to improve, and pretty soon I started to get four percent. Finally, I asked for my investment back, but he pointed to some language in the investment agreement I'd signed. It said I couldn't withdraw my investment for the first five years. He said it wouldn't be fair to the other investors to make an exception for me."

"Did you continue to date him?"

"Well, sure, there aren't many men with money in this part of the country. How could I *not* keep dating him?"

"When you first invested, did you ever go to meetings with other investors?"

Kelene plucked a fresh cigarette from her case and lit it. "A couple of them. Or maybe it was three. He called them launch parties. You know, just before we put our money in. The first one was really nice. A huge smoked salmon on a silver tray with lemon and a lot of little crackers and tiny forks. Lots of other stuff, too. Pheasant slimeball claimed, but I think it was really chicken."

"Was a man named Tomas Esteban at any of the launch parties?"

She took a deep draw on her new cigarette and seemed to think for a few moments. Then she said, "The Mexican?"

"I don't think he's Mexican. I believe he's from Panama."

"Whatever. He looks like a Mexican."

"I don't think his nationality is important. What I'm getting at is, I gather he knew Bud fairly well. Was that your impression?"

Kelene shrugged. "I thought he was a weirdo. That funny voice and everything. I checked him out. There's a story about him and some dog, too. Who'd do that to a dog?"

Pete nodded.

"Now Esteban hates slimeball's guts just like everyone else and wants his money back, too. I think he invested a lot more than I did."

"How much?"

"How would I know?"

"But your sense is that he was a big investor, right?"

She looked at him as she took another draw on his cigarette. "What does this have to do with me getting my money back? You're beginning to sound like that policeman who was here, pumping me for information. He kept asking if I knew someone who might have wanted to kill slimeball. Asking a lot of questions about the Mexican and everything."

"I'm interested in that, too. If the probate judge knows that one of the investors killed Stephanopoulis, he's not going to be inclined to award him a refund of his investment. I don't want to include someone in my group of claimants if there's a chance he's the killer. I'm concerned he might taint the group."

"How would I know if that weirdo is a killer?" she said, shaking her head. "He could be. He looks the type. He killed that dog, didn't he? I just know *I* didn't kill slimeball. I might have cut his woo-woo off, though, if I had the chance."

Pete suppressed a smile and didn't say anything.

She continued, "If you were a friend of slimeball's like you say you were, you must know that he couldn't keep his zipper up if he saw a bunch of heifers in the pasture, must less when he was around women." After another draw on her cigarette, she added, "Disgusting."

Pete got up from the couch and said, "Thanks for your time, Ms. Brill. I'll let you know if I'm going to do anything with the investor group."

She snuffed her cigarette and rose to her feet as well. "You don't have to be so formal. Everyone calls me Kelene. You should, too. Now that we've gotten to know each other."

"Fine, and you can call me Pete."

"Pete and Kelene. That has a nice ring to it."

Pete sensed that Kelene was looking to expand her social horizons and started for the door.

"Do you have any favorite restaurants around here?"

Pete thought for a few moments. "There are a lot of places in Traverse City. If you don't want to go that far, Rona's in town is very good. Then there's The Manitou on M-22, which is one of my favorite places."

Kelene looked wistful. "I've heard of those places. My date wants to go to a place called The Big Apple. Have you heard of it?"

"I have. It's more of a hamburger place."

Kelene scowled. "That's what I thought."

"If you want to go somewhere a little more upscale, go to The Glenwood. It's south of The Big Apple a few miles."

Kelene's face brightened. "Slimeball took me there once. I really liked it."

"Suggest that as an alternative then."

The scowl settled back on Kelene's face. "I think he's trying to get by on the cheap. I should start calling him El Cheapo."

"Tell him it's a special occasion. You're dressed like you're going to a tony place."

The brightness returned. "You know, I've gone out with Steve nine times now, and he's never said anything that nice to me. He just wants to have a quick hamburger and come back here and . . . you know."

"Work on him. This might be the night."

She rolled her eyes. "Right. He says he's saving his money to buy a business."

"What kind of business?"

"Plumbing. He wants to buy out this old man he works for."

"Being an entrepreneur isn't all bad."

She wrinkled her nose. "Going from a two-man plumbing business to a one-man plumbing business is *bad*."

"Maybe the business will grow. There's a lot of demand for good plumbers."

She acted like she hadn't heard his last comment and said, "I know I shouldn't ask this since we just met, but are you one of those high net worth individuals that slimeball used to talk about?"

"Hardly."

"Then why aren't you going to charge our investment group a fee for your services?"

Pete felt himself getting sucked back into a subject he thought he'd finessed and said, "Like I said, I'm just trying to do the right thing and help people if I can. If I decide to represent them."

"I have a good feeling about you, Pete. Just so you know, Steve and I don't have an understanding or anything. I'm free to date other men."

TWENTY-THREE

Pete was still smiling to himself when he parked in front of *The Northern Sentinel*'s offices. Kelene Brill was a real piece of work. Still, he was glad he'd gone to see her. Their conversation had confirmed some things he thought he knew, but wasn't sure about. And he'd learned some other things.

Harry started yapping at him as soon as he walked in the door. "Where have you been? I've been trying to reach you all day. Didn't you get my messages?"

"I got them. That's why I'm here."

Harry's eyes narrowed as he stared at him. "You've been fishing, haven't you?"

Pete laughed and said, "No, I haven't been fishing. I had to see some people and I've been tied up most of the day. Anything happening?"

"Anything happening? Jesus, you must be the only one in the friggin' county who hasn't heard. This morning, the sheriff and just about his whole department descended on Gaz Ramczyk's place for another search. They found what they think is the rifle used to kill Bud. I guess

Gaz has some kind of memorial in his backyard and he'd buried the rifle under one of the fake graves."

Before Pete could say anything, Harry rattled on.

"And who should drive in while the sheriff's people were digging around in the memorial? Gaz himself. He went nuts when he saw what they were doing. He grabbed a shovel from one of the deputies and started swinging and screaming at everyone like a madman. He hurt two of the deputies before the others got him pinned to the ground and put cuffs on him."

"Where's Gaz now?"

"They're holding him in the county jail on a bunch of charges, including assaulting the officers with a deadly weapon."

"You said that two deputies were hurt. Do you know how bad?"

"Bad enough that they had to take them to the hospital. I was just there covering the story, but I couldn't get in to see them. A nurse told me that one deputy has a six-inch gash on the side of his head that required a gazillion stitches and the medical people think he might have a serious concussion. I guess the other one's banged up, too, but not as bad."

When Pete didn't say anything right away, Harry asked, "So what do you think?"

"Have they filed murder charges against Gaz?"

"I don't know, I was hoping you'd heard. I called Cap as soon as I heard the news, but he wouldn't talk. I guess Sheriff Richter still has got the gag order on. I pieced together what I know by talking to the EMTs and a nurse at the hospital."

Pete nodded.

"No observations? This is big news."

Pete shrugged. "Sorry."

Harry studied him. "I'm not trying to pry or anything, but what were you were doing when I couldn't get ahold of you?"

"I told you, I was talking to some people."

"People who you believe might know something about this case?"

"Maybe. I went to see Tomas Esteban and Kelene Brill."

Harry rolled his eyes. "I suspected it was something like that. Not that it makes any difference now, but what did they say?"

"A lot of people hated Bud. Esteban and Brill are two of them. I suspect there are more."

"Money, right?"

Pete nodded.

"Was I right when I speculated the other day that Bud might have been peddling Ponzi schemes like Bernie Madoff?"

"You were spot on from what the Brill woman told me. Esteban wouldn't talk to me."

"Why not?"

"You'll have to ask him. He's strange, just like you said. I hung around for a while, making a pest of myself. I thought he might eventually relent and talk to me. He didn't. He called the condo association manager on me."

"You're kidding."

"Nope. A blubbery guy in a golf cart showed up while I was camped on Esteban's doorstep. He threatened to call Sheriff Richter if I didn't leave."

Harry chewed on that for a few moments, then a grin creased his face. "Jesus, wouldn't it have been something if the sheriff had come and arrested you? I would have had to go down to the jail and bail you out."

"You would have come, right?"

Harry grinned again, then his expression turned sober. "This whole thing strikes me as bizarre," he said. "Bud was retired and everybody knows he was rich as sin. Why would he get involved in Ponzi schemes?"

"Everybody *thought* he was rich as sin. Maybe he wasn't. Or maybe he was rich, but he wanted more. There are a lot of stories about people like that." Pete wasn't about to divulge how he knew that Bud was in a financial bind, even to Harry.

Harry got a faraway look in his eyes. "He always struck me as a good upstanding citizen. Generous when it came to good causes in this region and everything."

"Good upstanding citizens don't go around dummying up legal opinions on his friend's professional letterhead and then using the bogus opinions to help solicit investors in scam investments."

"Maybe there's some explanation."

"Do you think I should ask him?" Pete said caustically.

Harry shot him a look. "We don't know for sure that what Bud was selling was Ponzi schemes. We're just speculating. A lot of legitimate investments go south for any one of a number of reasons."

Pete shook his head. "Trust me, they were Ponzi schemes."

Harry looked thoughtful for a few moments before he said, "Now that Sheriff Richter appears to have the killer locked up in his jail, do you intend to keep poking around as you like to say?"

Pete shrugged. "I still need to clear my name."

Harry rolled his eyes.

"Do you think I have a choice?"

"Yeah, you do. We both know that what you've been doing has as much to do with Bud's murder as it does with clearing your name. Now that Bud is dead, the unhappy investors might just file claims with the probate court and take their chances there. If they don't recover all of their investments, they might chalk it up to experience."

"Or they might take a shot at me."

Harry rolled his eyes again. "I think this is another case of you not being willing to accept the facts even when they're staring you in the face. You're a smart guy. You must know that Sheriff Richter isn't *always* wrong. It looks to me like he has a pretty strong case against Gaz based on what happened this morning."

"You might be right."

Pete left his Range Rover where it was parked and walked up the street to his office. He checked his telephone messages. One was from someone named Lila McKenzie who identified herself as a lawyer from Detroit and said she'd call back. The name didn't ring a bell with him.

The other messages were all solicitations of one kind or another and he deleted them.

He dialed Joe Tessler's cell phone number and waited. A few moments later, Tessler answered. "You're calling to apologize, right?"

"I am. I acted like a jerk. It's not your fault. You're in a tough position."

"Apology accepted. It's nice to know you weren't calling to pump me about what happened at Gaz Ramczyk's place today."

"You can tell me about that, too."

"I'm in my car. Let me pull over," Tessler said. Moments later, he said, "So what have you heard?"

"Just that you guys were playing Gestapo this morning and desecrated a man's personal memorial and he got irritated."

"You're always so charitable the way you put things."

"Sorry, just trying to keep the conversation light. Can you give me the details?"

"How much do you know? I don't want to duplicate things."

"I got the basics from Harry. A bunch of the department's deputies and you, I assume, went out to Ramczyk's place and searched the memorial he'd created behind his house. Gaz came home while your people were excavating. He went wild and hit a couple of the deputies with a shovel and put at least one of them in the hospital. He's now in your jail on assault charges. I'm not sure whether it was before or after Gaz exploded, but at some point, your team found a rifle buried in one of the mock gravesites that you believe might be the weapon used to kill Bud. That's the crux of it."

"The gag order is still on, so anything I tell you has to be kept strictly between us, okay?"

"We already have an understanding, remember?"

"What you said is basically true. One of the deputies Ramczyk hit has a big gash running from his temple down along his cheek where the shovel hit him. Blood was everywhere. He likely has a concussion, too, based on what I hear. They're keeping him in the hospital overnight for observation. The other deputy is banged up, too, but not as bad."

"Did it happen as I described?"

"For the most part. Ramczyk drove in while we were digging in the memorial. He came over and seemed calm at first. Then he erupted and all hell broke loose. He grabbed a shovel from one of the deputies and started swinging. We were lucky we had seven people there and were able to get him under control before he killed someone."

"Then you found the rifle. Have you established that it's the one used to kill Bud Stephanopoulis?"

"They're running tests now. But it's a .223 caliber, which is the same as the murder weapon. If there's a match on ballistics, Mr. Ramczyk is in big trouble."

"Are his fingerprints on the rifle?"

"They're testing for that, too. My gut tells me they will be."

Pete thought about it for a while, then asked, "You searched Ramczyk's place a few days ago. Why didn't you search the memorial then?"

"I guess you haven't seen it. It looks like a miniature Arlington National Cemetery. Rows of white crosses with names on them, a little white fence around the site, flowers on each of the fake graves. It seemed like hallowed ground and we didn't think we should go digging around in it."

"What changed your mind?"

Tessler hesitated, like he was searching for the right words. "This is one of the things we don't think is public yet. We got a tip from a citizen saying he saw Ramczyk digging in his memorial late at night right after Stephanopoulis was shot. He thought he should tell us."

"Who called? A neighbor?"

After more hesitation, Tessler said, "I can't give you his name. It was an anonymous call."

"Anonymous. Can't you trace those things and find out who the caller was?"

"We've been trying, but nothing yet."

"Doesn't this strike you as a little strange?"

"What's strange about it? Police get anonymous tips all the time. That's how we get a lot of our information. Someone who calls anonymously usually has information about the crime, but doesn't want to be involved for one reason or another. That's perfectly understandable."

"It's understandable if the tipster lives in a gang-infested area and is afraid of retribution. I don't think that describes our area."

"A person might have other reasons for not wanting to be involved, too, but feels he has to let law enforcement know what he saw."

Pete thought about it some more. "You're right. And one reason the caller might not want to be involved, as you say, is that he's trying to set Ramczyk up."

"Oh, for crissakes, Pete, there you go again. Everything in this case points to that guy. Do I have to go through it all again?"

Pete didn't say anything.

"I have to go, Mr. Thorsen, but is there anything you'd like to share with me? Maybe something you just happened to stumble over in your driveway while trying, ahem, to clear your name?"

"It sounds like you have Ramczyk convicted already, so I don't think I should take up any more of your time."

"I still have five minutes."

"Okay, I'll be brief. I sent the copy of the legal opinion that Frank hit me with to an expert in Chicago for analysis of the signature. I'm waiting to hear back from him. Then I talked to a couple of the investors in the investment pools Bud Stephanopoulis was hawking. Just to try to formulate my defense in case the investors come after me, understand. You'd already talked to both of them."

"The civil side of cases sometimes overlaps with the criminal. Who did you talk to?"

"Tomas Esteban and Kelene Brill."

"Umm," Tessler murmured. "Kelene's quite a babe, isn't she?"

Pete smiled at Tessler's comment. "Quite a babe," he said.

"What did she tell you?"

"Boiling it down, she hates Bud's guts because she thinks he took advantage of her. She wants her money back."

"Any detail? I still have time."

"I don't know whether you got into this with her, but she and Bud were ... seeing ... each other. Bud apparently knew that she had some money from one of her divorces that was sitting in a bank earning next to nothing. From what she tells me, he was pretty clever about the way he drew her in."

"Umm," Tessler murmured again. "But you don't think she's a killer, though, right?"

"I don't think she's a killer. I have a feeling she's capable of doing some nasty things if you get on the wrong side of her, but lying in wait with a rifle and shooting someone ... I'd say probably not. Going forward, I'm not as sure. I found out she took a self-defense course that included firearms training."

There was a pause at Tessler's end before he said, "She didn't tell me about that."

"She'd just completed the course when I talked to her."

"How about Esteban?"

"He wouldn't talk to me."

"Not at all?"

"He wouldn't even give me his name, rank or serial number. He's a strange duck. I'm not sure about him."

"It's that funny voice, right?"

"Partly, I don't know. If I were you, I'd look at him some more. He lost a bundle of money on his investments with Stephanopoulis. He didn't strike me as a pacifist, either."

"I might have talked to him again before we found the murder weapon. Now I don't know. Unless we find some glitch in our case against Ramczyk ..."

"There's no reason you can't go down parallel tracks. At least until you're certain your case against Ramczyk is a lock."

"You're still fixated on the financial scams as a motive for the shooting, aren't you?"

"It was your boss who first raised that possibility, if you'll recall."

"That was then. This is now."

"What was Ramczyk's motive?"

"Oh, God Pete, we've been through this. His mental disorder controlled his actions. He didn't have a motive in the classic sense."

"Maybe."

Tessler's sigh was audible. "I've got to get going," he said, "but when all of this is over, I've been thinking of giving Kelene a call. You know, on a personal basis. I kind of liked her."

TWENTY-FOUR

When Pete got off the phone with Tessler, he saw that Lila McKenzie had called again and he returned the call.

"Ms. McKenzie, this—"

"Lila, please."

"Sorry, Lila. As I started to say, this is Pete Thorsen, returning your call."

"Pete, I'm in Frankfort and wonder if you'd have an hour to talk to me? I could come to your office."

"Talk about what?"

"Gaz Ramczyk."

"I have to warn you, I've already—"

"I know, you declined to represent him when the family came to see you. I'd still like to talk to you."

"Okay, I'm in my office. Do you need directions?"

She laughed. "In Frankfort? I think I can find it."

Pete was down to two client chairs after Ramczyk had made kindling out of the third one. He cleared off one chair and straightened the files on the other to leave space for a guest to put things, then tidied up the rest of his office. He made a fresh pot of coffee and settled in behind his desk again and waited for Lila McKenzie to arrive and try to get him to change his mind.

Ten minutes later, his door opened and a woman in loose-fitting beige pants and a black blouse and a bold necklace with chunky stones burst in. Her dark hair was pulled back and she wore black-rimmed designer glasses. She strolled purposely across his outer office and tossed her briefcase on the half-empty chair.

"Lila McKenzie, Pete. Thanks for making time for me."

Pete shook her hand. By the way she gave a quick squeeze and immediately drew her hand back, he got the impression she was used to bumping fists instead of shaking the old-fashioned way. She sat down in the open chair without being asked and crossed her legs and dug around in her purse. She slid a card across his desk with "PTSD Rehabilitation Institute" on it in bold red letters.

"I'm the head of our legal staff," she said, getting right to the point.

Pete nodded. "Can I get you some coffee or water?"

"Do you have green tea?" she asked.

Pete shook his head. "Sorry."

The look on her face suggested disappointment. "Water's fine then."

He got a bottle of spring water from his small refrigerator and set it on the desk in front of her. She unscrewed the cap and took a swallow and said, "I met with your fellow lawyer earlier this afternoon. Matthew Stroud, if I have the name right. He just about wet his pants when I said I might want to hire him as co-counsel to pave the way with the sheriff so I could get in to see my client."

Pete knew Stroud and could imagine his reaction when faced with the prospect of conflict with the sheriff.

"Mr. Stroud said that you're the tough guy in town and might be better suited for, as he put it, a matter of that sort."

Pete let her talk, feeling amused.

"He proposed that the three of us act as counsel for Mr. Ramczyk and divide the duties among us according to who's best suited to do what."

Pete's smile broadened. "I take it you didn't agree."

Lila rolled her eyes. "I said I wanted to talk to the tough guy first and would get back to him."

"Did the Ramczyks tell you why I wouldn't represent Gaz?"

"They said something about you not being a criminal lawyer."

"That's part of it. I also told them that Bud Stephanopoulis, the guy Gaz Ramczyk is suspected of killing, was a friend of mine. In fact, the day Bud was shot, my eighteen-year-old stepdaughter was jet skiing with him. She could have been killed as well."

Lila McKenzie seemed to consider that. "She *wasn't* killed, though, right? So what you're raising is only a hypothetical justification for your refusal to help someone who needs help."

Pete felt his lips tighten. He stared at her for a long moment and said, "As a lawyer, I thought I was free to represent someone or not represent him. It's my decision. And for you to be so cavalier about my daughter's safety . . ."

McKenzie shrugged. "I was just stating a fact."

"For me, it's more than a fact. I saw blood pouring out of Stephanopoulis when he was floating in the water and all I could think of is that I could have been looking at Julie. I don't know whether Gaz Ramczyk shot Stephanopoulis or not, but I do know I'm not going to represent him."

McKenzie backed off a little and said, "Maybe I was a little clumsy in the way I made my point. I didn't mean to suggest that I was taking your daughter's life cavalierly. But the mission of the PTSD Rehabilitation Institute is to help veterans who come back from wars in places like Afghanistan and Iraq with terrible mental problems because of what they saw or went through. A lot of us think we never should have been over there in the first place, but be that as it may, our returning warriors deserve our help. Our care list totals nearly seven hundred veterans in a six-state area. I and two others on our staff handle legal problems for them when they arise. That's why I'm here."

"That's commendable," Pete said. "You're going to have your work cut out for you in this case. From what I hear, the sheriff's department has a lot of evidence against Gaz, including the murder weapon they found buried in his back yard."

"It's more than his backyard," she said with ice in her voice. "It's a memorial he'd constructed as his way of dealing with the horrors he'd witnessed in Afghanistan."

Now it was Pete's turn to throttle back. "Maybe the sheriff's people could have handled the situation better, but that's still no excuse for Gaz doing what he did. He could have killed one or both of those deputies."

The fire in Lila's eyes signaled she wasn't going to give an inch. "You don't know a thing about PTSD, do you?"

"Not a lot," he admitted.

"That's the problem with our society. We send our young men and women to fight for us, and when they come back, we treat them like a bunch of pariahs and try to lock them up for every bad thing that happens just because they seem to be a little off."

"I'm not saying that we couldn't treat our veterans better."

She looked out the window at the bay for a few moments, then turned to Pete again. "I didn't mean to climb on my soapbox, but the whole thing burns me. Getting back to the issue, though, I can see you're pretty dug in on your position. I can't say I see it the way you do, but that's your prerogative. In the short term, my problem is getting in to see my client. I thought maybe you could help with that."

Pete laughed. "I'm afraid you came to the wrong guy. Not being from the community, I can't expect you to know this, but Sheriff Richter and I don't exactly have a warm and cozy relationship. I've already locked horns with him over one aspect of this case."

"Oh?"

He told her he'd gone to the sheriff's office twice to provide information about Bud Stephanopoulis. The second time, he said, Richter hit him with the bogus legal opinions and suggested that he might have been complicit with Stephanopoulis in his shady securities promotions.

"That's the first I've heard about this."

"It's not common knowledge as far as I know."

"Investment fraud is nothing compared to a murder charge."

"Nothing to you, maybe, but I take my reputation seriously."

Pete could almost see the wheels turning in her mind. She said, "Do you think the financial scams and the murder might be connected?"

"The thought occurred to me, but I really don't know."

McKenzie stared out the window again. Then she said, "Have you seen the memorial at Gaz Ramczyk's house?"

He shook his head.

"I drove out there before I called you the second time. It's a complete mess. After they found the rifle, they made no effort to restore the memorial to the way it was. Not to get off on this again, and I'm not a psychologist or a psychiatrist, but I know enough about PTSD to know that when a vet creates a memorial like Gaz did, he's been deeply scarred by his experiences in the war and is grieving for his fallen fellow warriors. The deputy I talked to in the sheriff's office seemed to be completely unaware of any of this. Or of the trauma Gaz likely experienced when he saw his memorial being desecrated."

"I'm not surprised. Most younger people in law enforcement probably don't even know what PTSD is, much less have an appreciation for its nuances."

"Just so you know, I feel really bad for those two deputies Gaz attacked."

"I understand that one of them has a concussion in addition to his exterior wounds. Gaz is going to have legal problems arising out of that incident even if he isn't the guy who killed Bud Stephanopoulis."

"I know."

"Getting back to your immediate problem, has Sheriff Richter refused to let you see Gaz at all?"

"Not exactly, but it's clear he's stonewalling me. The word I got back through a deputy is that I can make an appointment to see Gaz the day after tomorrow. My problem is I have to be in court in Detroit that day. I want to see him tomorrow before I leave."

"My advice is that you push a little. Stomp your feet. Threaten. That's what I've done sometimes in the past. Most of the time it's worked."

"I thought that if you'd go with me, we'd be making a show of force. Also, having someone local often helps."

"I told you why I don't think it will in this case."

"Will you at least think about it overnight?"

"I will, but I suspect my answer is going to be the same."

"You will think about it, though."

He sighed. "I'll think about it."

She stood and began to gather up her stuff. "What are you doing for dinner tonight?" she asked.

Pete shrugged. "My daughter has been gone for three days. I thought maybe I'd grill a couple of steaks and get reacquainted with her."

"How about this as an alternative. You and your daughter can join me for dinner at Fusion."

He considered it. "Julie loves Fusion. She'll probably prefer that to my cooking. What time?"

She looked at her watch and said, "Seven o'clock?"

"Fine. I assume you won't be embarrassed to be seen dining with a man who has ten yards of bandages on his face."

"You do look like someone who's just gotten back from the front lines. What happened?"

He told her about Gaz Ramczyk's eruption in his office, and she rolled her eyes.

When Pete got home, Julie was sitting cross-legged on a chair on the porch reading a magazine. "How was your lunch?" he asked.

"Wonderful. Susan is really nice. We talked a lot about Cornell and I think I have a better feel for the place now. Of course, I know a lot has changed since she was there. Still, she's on some kind of advisory board at the university and is in touch with the place on a regular basis. It's not like she left campus on graduation day and never looked back or something like that."

"Umm."

"She was kind of sneaky, though, the way she maneuvered the conversation around to Bud's shooting. I mean, she wasn't overbearing or anything, but it was clear to me what she was doing."

"Maybe it was concern. She's a compassionate woman."

"Or maybe it was something she cooked up with my Dad."

"Julie, trust me, Susan and I have spoken exactly once in the past year and you heard every word of our conversation. We didn't cook anything up."

"Whatever. So, what's been happening with the investigation while I've been hiking and lunching?"

"Quite a lot, actually." He told her about the second search at Gaz Ramczyk's place and what ensued when he came home in the middle of the search and put two deputies in the hospital and was now in jail for assault. He also told her about his meetings with Kelene Brill and Tomas Esteban, two investors in Bud's scam investment products. He didn't tell her what he'd learned about Bud's acrimonious departure from Harrison Stryker because he feared it would be awkward if she asked him how he found out. He'd boxed himself in on the Ramczyk office visit so he avoided that as well.

"My God, I go away for a couple of days, and the world goes crazy. Why didn't you call and tell me these things?"

"I didn't want to spoil your outing."

"Spoil my outing! It's not like I'm not involved in all of this. I was ten feet away when Bud was shot, remember?"

"I know you were."

"Geez!"

"Sorry."

"Does Gaz have a lawyer?"

"As a matter of fact, he does. She's in town and I agreed we would meet her at seven for dinner."

Julie wrinkled her nose. "Maybe I'll just find something in the refrigerator."

"We're going to Fusion."

Her interest picked up. "Do I have to dress up?"

"You've been there many times. It's casual."

"I think I'll take a shower and change clothes."

While he was changing himself, Simon Lipscombe, the handwriting expert Angie DeMarco had engaged, called.

"Pete," he said, "I've looked at the letter you sent via Angie. Without an original copy, I can't give you a definitive answer whether it's a forgery or not. Just matching it against samples of your signature, though, I'd say it's probably authentic. I think what might have happened is that whoever produced those letters got ahold of your signature and then used an autopen or a signature machine to apply the signature to the letters."

"That's forgery, isn't it?"

"Yes and no. It's certainly unauthorized use of your signature."

"I don't see the distinction."

"Autopens have been around for a long time. The early ones used a plastic matrix of the original signature. The modern types use a signature smart card or a USB flashdrive to store the signature. They're commonly used in the corporate world and even by some of our presidents. The way we determine whether a signature has been made by autopen or by hand is by analyzing the pressure on the paper. In the simplest terms, with an autopen, the pressure, or the indentation on the paper, is even whereas with original handwriting the pressure tends to vary. The copy you sent me is a photocopy and it's hard to tell, but using some other tests, my opinion is that the signature was applied by autopen."

"And you could testify to that if necessary?"

"Basically. With the various qualifications I just stated."

"Could you put this in a letter to me?"

"I can. I'll send you a draft first to make sure you're happy with it. Then we'll get rid of the drafts."

"It sounds like you've been through this a few times."

"Just a few."

They talked for a while longer, then Pete thanked him and told him where to send his invoice.

TWENTY-FIVE

The man who'd killed Bud Stephanopoulis turned on his television set in time to catch the "Breaking News" segment of the 6:00 p.m. local news. The anchor immediately launched into his lead story about a raid by county sheriff's office personnel early that morning at the home of a suspect in the shooting death of Philippe Stephanopoulis, a Frankfort resident. After some introductory remarks, the screen-shot changed to a reporter standing among piles of earth and a partially-uprooted low white picket fence and a half-dozen white crosses, most of which were lying on the ground or tilted haphazardly.

"It was here," the reporter intoned, "buried in the earth under these crosses representing a memorial of some kind that the sheriff's team found the rifle they believe was used to shoot and kill Mr. Stephanopoulis while he was jet skiing on Crystal Lake."

The man leaned forward on the couch, his eyes intense, hanging on the reporter's every word. After a few more comments, the reporter walked to the driveway that ran along the side of a one-story ramshackle house and pointed to a dark pickup truck and continued. "And while the sheriff's team was excavating the site, the suspect, a long-time area man and Afghanistan war veteran, returned home in this vehicle. After initially appearing confused about what was happening, the suspect suddenly grabbed a shovel from one of the deputies and began to scream and swing wildly."

Then the screen-shot changed again, this time to a sign at the entrance to the local hospital. The camera followed the reporter as he entered the main hospital building and made his way down an interior hallway. He turned, microphone in hand, and said, "This hospital is where the two deputies who were injured by the suspect's sudden and vicious attack were taken. The sheriff's department won't let us near their rooms and hospital personnel declined comment, so we don't know the full extent of their injuries or whether they're life-threatening. Len, back to you."

The news anchor picked up the story and said that the raid on the suspect's home had occurred as a result of a tip the sheriff's department had received the previous night. He gave a few other details about the incident, and then switched to a story about whether swimmer's itch was expected to be a major problem in northern Michigan lakes that summer.

The man who'd been watching the program leaned back and closed his eyes for a long time. *The thug deserves it.* Then he felt a need to see the story again and began to work his remote, switching from channel to channel. He couldn't find another local news broadcast. Maybe all of the stations had gone with the story as their lead at the same time. He closed his eyes again and tried to focus his thoughts. *Now he had to get rid of the other things. Just in case . . .*

He turned off the television and went outside and walked casually to the shed. Seeing no one, he unlocked the padlock and slipped through the door and closed it behind him. The sun was still high enough in the sky to provide light through the flimsy curtails that covered the small windows, and he moved things around to get at the hidden compartment. His priority had to be the duffel bag with the do-rag and ponytail wig and spent cartridges. The kayak and paddle, those he could explain, but not the other things.

He'd previously abandoned the idea of burning everything because he feared someone might notice and become suspicious. As bad, he'd seen a show on television where the police had been able to analyze ashes and scraps of unburned material and piece it all together. And brass wouldn't burn. His new plan was better. He stuffed the do-rag and wig and Ziploc bag with the spent brass under his shirt and began to restore the shed to the way it had been.

The man locked up and walked to his SUV with unhurried steps. After glancing around, he transferred the items from his shirt to a compartment at the rear of the vehicle. He closed the hatchback and hit the lock feature on his key. When it was dark, he'd take a drive. On the way, he'd drop off one of the plastic bags at Goodwill.

Pete walked into Fusion with Julie and saw Lila McKenzie at a window table. Her hair was still pulled back, but her dark-rimmed glasses were gone and her blouse was now forest green with a subtle print. Pete made the introductions.

McKenzie shook Julie's hand and smiled. Her manner seemed warmer than it had in his office a few hours earlier. "Your father tells me you're off to college in a couple of months," she said.

"Yes, Cornell. I'll really excited."

They spent fifteen minutes discussing the college experience. Then the teenager in Julie emerged and she asked McKenzie, "Do you think Gaz is guilty?"

Pete put his hand on Julie's arm, intending to shush her, but McKenzie noticed and said to her, "I really don't know if he's guilty or not. Your sheriff won't even let me in to talk to him. But guilty or innocent, under our system of justice, he's entitled to the best defense I can give him. There's another issue here, too. Gaz has PTSD. That's why I'm involved. The organization I work for provides assistance to veterans with that disorder."

"Why won't the sheriff let you talk to Gaz?"

"Like I told your dad this afternoon, he seems to be jerking me around for some reason. I don't know what his problem is."

"Dad, can you help Lila? You know the sheriff."

"Lila and I already talked about that, Sweetie. I told her I'd think about it."

Julie frowned. "What's there to think about? Gaz obviously needs our help. You told me you had the same kind of problem with Sheriff Richter when your army friend was in jail and you wanted to see him. He didn't want to let you that time, either, but you managed to get in. Why can't you do the same thing now?"

Pete felt two pairs of eyes on him. He loved Julie dearly, but sometimes she could butt into things at the most awkward moment. McKenzie obviously sensed she had an unexpected ally, and kept quiet and waited to see how things would play out.

Trying not to be defensive, Pete said, "From what Lila tells me, Sheriff Richter is willing to let her see Gaz the day after tomorrow, so it isn't like he's taking the position that she can't see him at all. The problem is, Lila has to be in court in Detroit that day. I don't know what the sheriff's reason is for not letting her see Gaz tomorrow. Maybe it's valid, maybe it isn't. I told Lila I'd think about it and see if there's something I can do to help her."

Julie continued to bore in. "It's not fair that a man with PTSD is in jail and can't even see his lawyer."

"I agree," Pete said.

"What did you do in that other case involving your army friend?"

Pete was about to cut the conversation short and tell Julie that he'd talk to McKenzie about it in the morning, but he sensed that would be a mistake given how righteously she seemed to have taken up Gaz's cause. He said, "I know the county prosecuting attorney. I talked to her and got her to intervene with the sheriff."

"Can't you do the same thing again?"

Pete saw it was time to run up the white flag. He turned to McKenzie and said, "Do you want me to try that?"

"How well do you know her?"

"Reasonably well. She knows I don't come to her unless I really feel aggrieved over something."

After shooting Julie a look, she said, "I think you should get your indignation cranked up. What time does the prosecuting attorney get in the office?"

"She's an early bird. She's usually in by seven or seven-thirty. I don't know what her schedule is for tomorrow."

"Let's give her until eight and then call. I'll come to your office about fifteen minutes before that."

Julie glowed. She looked at her Dad and then at McKenzie and said, "I feel like we're really making progress in this case. I remember one of my teachers saying that justice delayed is justice denied. Our job is to make sure justice isn't delayed."

Pete was glad to get off the subject without causing another blow-up with his daughter. He was thinking of suggesting to McKenzie that they call Connie Chapman anyway, but chafed at being pushed into it. When they were alone, however, he intended to emphasize to McKenzie again that he wasn't going to have any other involvement in the case, and he damn sure wasn't going to represent Gaz Ramczyk as co-counsel or otherwise.

"How did you become an expert on PTSD?" Julie asked McKenzie.

"I'm not an expert, I'm a lawyer. But you can't do what I do without learning something about it."

"It's a mental disease, isn't it?"

"I wouldn't call it a disease, exactly. It's a disorder that grows out of a traumatic event or events. Like seeing a comrade get killed in a war, or seeing someone get dismembered by an IED."

"That's like a bomb, right?"

"In a fashion. IED stands for improvised explosive device. They're commonly used by ISIS and the Taliban and other terrorist groups in the Middle East. They cobble together IEDs and plant them where they know military vehicles will be passing, or maybe where soldiers will be out on patrol. A high percentage of the casualties our troops suffer are caused by IEDs."

"What's the connection between IEDs and PTSD?"

"As I said, PTSD is caused by a traumatic event or events. There's nothing more traumatic than seeing a comrade killed or badly injured in combat. Or for that matter seeing young children injured or killed. The critical thing is the trauma a soldier experiences as a result of seeing or experiencing one or more of these violent acts. Some are able to handle it, but others aren't. In many cases, the symptoms of one of these traumatic events don't manifest themselves until months or even years after the event."

"That sounds terrible."

"It is. Someone suffering from PTSD might have recurring upsetting dreams about the traumatic event or suffer emotional distress or physical reactions to something that reminds him of the event. In other cases, the person avoids places, activities or people that conjure up those memories. Still others become irritable or have angry outbursts or exhibit other kinds of destructive behavior. There are many different symptoms."

"What kind of symptoms does Gaz have?" Julie asked.

"I've never met him, but our staff is aware of his case because his parents called the Institute about him over a year ago. From what I'm told, he exhibits aggressive and belligerent tendencies among other symptoms."

When there was a lull in the conversation between Julie and McKenzie, Pete asked, "Is there some significance to the memorial beyond a tribute to his fallen comrades?"

"Hard to say. Maybe he's feeling guilty that they're dead and he's still alive. Or maybe the memorial helps relieve some of the trauma he experienced. Maybe there's some other reason. Whatever, it's clear that the memorial has deep-seated importance because of the way he reacted when he saw the sheriff's people digging it up."

They talked some more about Gaz and then the conversation drifted off to other subjects. When things began to wind down, they called it a night. Pete said he'd be at his office by seven-thirty the next morning and told McKenzie to come over any time after that.

On the way home, Julie was unusually quiet after the way she'd monopolized the conversation at dinner. Pete glanced over at her.

"This is a sad case, isn't it Dad?"

"Very."

"Why didn't you want to help Lila?"

"I *am* going to try to help her."

"Sure, after we ganged up on you. But why don't you want to help her beyond seeing if the prosecuting attorney can get her in to see Gaz in the morning?"

"I explained all of that, Sweetie."

Julie was quiet for a couple of minutes, then said, "I bet Gaz is innocent. I bet the sheriff just thinks he did it because of his PTSD."

"You may be right. But Lila McKenzie strikes me as a competent lawyer who understands these types of cases and will provide him a good defense if he's ever charged."

Julie was quiet again for a few moments. "I had the same impression of her. I mean that she's a good lawyer." Then she added, "I know you aren't going to like this, but women are more compassionate in these types of situations than men are. Gaz is lucky to have Lila in his corner." Then she added as if she were concerned she might have hurt his feelings, "Except for you, of course. You're compassionate."

Pete didn't say anything.

A little later, Julie said, "Could I go with you and Lila in the morning? I wouldn't say anything, I'd just be there to provide moral support."

They were just pulling into his driveway, and he looked her way and said, "I'd love to take you along, but I don't think it would be a good idea. I might have to lean on Connie a bit. I don't want her to feel defensive because three of us march into her office and demand to see Gaz."

"I thought that would be your answer," she said, sounding let down.

They went inside and he followed Julie when she went to the porch and stood looking out.

"When you're finished with Connie," she said, "Can I use your car so I can drive out to Gaz's place and see what they did to his memorial?"

"If you don't mind having company, I'll go with you. I'm curious about it, too."

"What time do you think we'll be able to go?"

"As soon as I see what I can do with Connie."

TWENTY-SIX

When McKenzie arrived at Pete's office the next morning, they made small talk for a few minutes and then he dialed Connie Chapman's direct number.

"Chapman," a woman answered in a snappish voice that suggested the call had interrupted something she'd been doing.

"Connie, this is Pete Thorsen. I have you on the speaker and a lawyer named Lila McKenzie is with me. Lila's from Detroit. She's here on the Gaz Ramczyk case."

"Welcome to our fair community, Lila," Chapman said in a softer tone. "What I can I do for you, Pete? I'm on a tight schedule this morning."

"Lila is with an organization called the PTSD Rehabilitation Institute. The Institute—"

"I know. It helps veterans with PTSD."

"Right. Mr. Ramczyk is in our county jail on assault charges as you undoubtedly know. Lila has to go back to Detroit tonight and needs to see her client before she leaves, but she's run into the same problem with Sheriff Richter I had to call you about last year in another case. He seems to be stonewalling her. Could we stop by your office and see if we can work something out?"

Pete heard an audible sigh come from the speaker. "I have someone coming in in a half-hour and then have to be in court later this morning and I have a meeting after that, so I can't meet with you. But I know you well enough to know that you'll be driving around my building with a bullhorn announcing to the world that we have a failed justice system in our county if I don't get you the relief you think you deserve. Let me call the sheriff to find out what the problem is and I'll call you back."

Pete tapped the off button on his telephone and looked at McKenzie who was smiling at him. "I think I came to the right guy," she said. "You *do* have a reputation up here."

Pete shrugged self-consciously. "Just caught her on the right day. Let's see what she says when she calls back."

While they were waiting for Chapman to get back to them, they rehashed their conversation at dinner the previous night and sundry other things. Thinking back, Pete was grateful that his meeting with the Ramczyk family and the chair-throwing incident never came up. He knew he had to find the right time to say something to Julie, though, hopefully without incurring her wrath again for not saying something earlier.

Chapman called back and said, "I've arranged for Lila to have an hour with her client beginning at ten-thirty. Then the sheriff and key members of his team are going to be tied up for several hours. I know he's not blowing smoke because I'm going over to join them as soon as I'm out of court."

"Is this about the Ramczyk case?"

"As a matter of fact it is."

"Do you want Lila and me to sit in to make sure you have our point of view?"

"This isn't a game, Pete. One of our deputies with two young children at home is in the hospital with a serious concussion because of your client. And we haven't even gotten to what might be the main charges against him."

"Sorry, I didn't mean to make light of it." He thanked Chapman and ended the call.

McKenzie looked at him with a straight face. "You didn't even correct her when she referred to Gaz as your client."

Pete stared back at her. "I didn't think the time was right. But let's get something straight between us. This is it as far as my involvement on behalf of Gaz Ramczyk goes. Don't even try to talk me into anything else."

"I understand. And I also appreciate your help."

Pete nodded, but didn't say anything.

McKenzie looked at the clock on his office wall and said, "Do you have a half hour more to fill me in on what you know about the case?"

"Sure." Pete told her everything he knew, beginning with the day Bud was shot and killed while jet skiing on Crystal Lake with Julie, his conversations with Lydia Vreeland and her arch-foe, Harriet Marlowe, and subsequent events including his two sessions with Sheriff Richter and Detective Tessler. "I think you know about the searches at Gaz's place and the rest of it."

McKenzie appeared to think for a few moments, then, "Do you think the Ponzi schemes Stephanopoulis was involved with have anything to do with his murder? Maybe provided a motive?"

"Possible, I don't know."

"In contrast," McKenzie continued, "I can't think of any motive for Gaz to kill him."

"From what I've been told, Sheriff Richter believes the shooting was a random act of violence by an angry, troubled man so it isn't a question of motive in the sense we usually think of it."

"I think Gaz is being railroaded because of his PTSD."

Pete shrugged. "Good luck proving your case."

Julie was watching from the porch when Pete pulled into his drive-way and she bounded down the steps to meet him. He lowered the passenger-side window and she stuck her head in and asked, "Are you ready to go to the memorial? I thought I'd catch you before you got involved in something else."

Pete smiled. "Get in."

She slid into the passenger seat and buckled up. As he was backing out the driveway, she asked, "Did you meet with the prosecuting attorney?"

"She was busy. We did talk to her on the phone, though."

"And?" she asked, cranking her hand in a circle to coax information out of him as they started back toward town.

He looked at his dashboard clock and said, "Lila should be meeting with her client in about ten minutes."

"Yes!" Julie said, raising both of her arms in triumph.

Pete smiled at her again.

Pete wound through Frankfort and turned on River Road. "Don't you feel good about what you just did?" she asked. "I mean how you helped Lila get in to see Gaz?"

"I'm glad we could work something out."

Julie was quiet for a few moments, then asked, "What do you suppose Lila and Gaz will talk about at the jail?"

"No idea. I'm not a criminal lawyer, as I've told you many times. I expect a lawyer has to just play those things by ear."

"What did you talk about with your army friend when you got in to see him in jail?"

"Jimmy Ray did all of the talking. From the moment I walked in, he rattled on about how he was innocent and was being framed by the North Carolina sheriff and begged me to get him out of there."

"That was true, too, wasn't it? He *was* being framed."

"Yes."

"Maybe it's the same with Gaz. Maybe he's being framed, too."

"Possible. Say, would you help me watch for Ramczyk's place? It's supposed to be right along here."

A half-mile later, they spotted his house, and as they bumped along the rough unpaved driveway and got close, Julie stared and wrinkled her nose and said, "Eeek, this place is a dump."

Pete smiled again, thinking it was the norm for the area he'd grown up in. He parked near the house, and as they got out of his Range Rover, he said, "I see the memorial."

They walked over and stared at the mess that had been created by Sheriff Richter's men. There was no crime tape, but piles of earth dotted the site where the deputies had dug around in the soft soil and everything was in disarray. Crosses had been pulled out of the ground and were scattered around, parts of the low white picket fence cordoning off the memorial had been knocked down.

"This is really disgusting, Dad. You can't blame Gaz for getting upset."

Pete found it hard to disagree. He knew that law enforcement search teams didn't view it as part of their mission to restore premises to the way they had been, particularly where the search uncovered incriminating evidence, but he wished they'd shown some sensitivity in this case.

Julie picked up one of the wooden crosses and read the inscription. "Look at this, Dad." She held up the cross so Pete could see it. It had the name, "Cpl. Rafael Ramirez," and below that the date of his death and words commemorating his service to his country. Pete walked through the mounds of dirt and looked at the other crosses. They all had names and similar inscriptions.

"I can't believe this," Julie said, picking up another cross.

"Do you have your cell phone with you?" Pete asked.

"Are you going to call the sheriff and ask him to send some people out to fix this up?"

"I want to photograph it."

"I don't understand."

"Whatever eventually happens to Gaz on the murder charges, he's going to face assault charges for attacking the two deputies. I want Lila or whoever represents him to be able to show the judge what set him off."

Julie thought for a moment, then said, "That's a great idea. Can I take the pictures?"

"Sure. Just be sure to get photos of each of the crosses and close-up shots as well as shots that show the entire scene. Then we need to document when the photographs were taken and by whom and on what date."

Julie spent a half-hour photographing the memorial and must have taken forty or fifty shots when she turned to Pete and said, "Do you think that's enough?"

Pete had been watching her work and nodded.

They stood together and looked at the decimated memorial. Julie put an arm around her father's waist and said, "It's even sadder when you see this in person."

"It is."

After more silence, Julie said, "I don't have any plans for today. I'm thinking about staying and fixing the memorial so when Gaz comes home, it'll be the way it used to be. Maybe not as good, but a lot better than it is now."

"Are you sure?"

She nodded. "I know none of this is my fault, but I still feel awful that it happened. Maybe if I fix things up, I'll feel better."

Pete thought about that. There wasn't any police tape warning people to stay away so that shouldn't be a problem. Still, he thought about calling Joe Tessler and telling him what they proposed to do. Ultimately he decided against it, though. Involving him would probably wind up elevating something that wasn't a problem into a problem.

"You'll need tools," he said.

"I'll bet there are shovels and stuff in that shed. Buzz must have had tools when he built the memorial."

Pete tried the shed door and found it unlocked. He stepped in and in the gloomy light, he saw a garden rake and shovel leaning against the wall. As his eyes became accustomed to the dim light, he also saw a work bench with small tools. He grabbed the rake and shovel and backed out again, brushing the cobwebs from his face.

"Your choice," he said. "Shovel or rake?"

She looked at him for a few moments. "Does that mean you're going to stay and help me?"

"If you'll let me. A little father-daughter bonding can be a good thing."

"Wow! I'll take the shovel. If you have to shovel dirt, you'll be complaining about your back for the next week." She poked him playfully in the ribs.

He gathered up the crosses and leaned them against the tree and did the same with sections of the low picket fence. Julie busied herself moving the earth back in position to recreate six mock grave sites with carefully shaped rectangular mounds on top of each. Pete followed with his rake, smoothing the mounds and raking the earth between them. When they were finished, Pete went into the shed again and found a sledge hammer that he used to drive the crosses into the earth at the head of each of the mounds. As the final step, they reconstructed as much of the picket fence as was salvageable, leaving the damaged sections leaning against the tree.

They stepped back and admired their work. Julie grabbed the rake and tidied up the mounds some more. When she finished, she gazed at the memorial again.

"I don't know what it looked like before, but I think we did a really good job."

"You did a wonderful job."

Julie beamed appreciatively. "I bet Gaz will be really happy when he comes home."

TWENTY-SEVEN

Julie commandeered the driver's seat, and on the way to town to get something to eat, she said, "Doing good deeds can also be good for your weight. I'll bet we both lost at least two pounds today."

"At least. Before we go to the restaurant, do you mind stopping at the drugstore so I can get some Australian Dream back pain cream? My lower back's killing me."

Julie looked his way and realized he was kidding. "Your back," she said, feigning disgust. "I did the really heavy work. *I'm* the one who should be complaining about *my* back."

Pete laughed.

When they got out in front of Rona's Bay Grille, Julie dangled the car keys in front of him for a second, then dropped them in her purse. "I think I'll hold onto these just in case you lose control and become overserved."

Pete gave her a look feigning hurt feelings.

The restaurant had just opened for the evening, but Harry was already there at his usual table. Jeffrey Talbot was with him. Pete went over to them with Julie following behind.

"Is this a high-level conference to plan the next issue of *The Northern Sentinel*?"

Harry ignored his comment and lumbered to his feet when he saw Julie and rushed to envelop her in a hug. "How's my favorite girl?" he asked. His broad face beamed.

"Hungry. Dad and I missed lunch today."

"It wasn't because he didn't want to spend the money, was it?" Harry asked, smirking as he shot a look at Pete.

Julie shook her head. "We were at Gaz Ramczyk's house fixing up his memorial that the police made such a mess of."

"Have you changed your stripes or something?" Harry asked Pete with the same smirk. "Usually it's other people cleaning up after you."

Pete shrugged. "You know what they say about consistency being the hobgoblin of small minds and all that."

Talbot looked uncomfortable, like he was caught in the middle of family banter that whizzed past him like bats in a deserted church.

"Jeffrey, have you met Pete's daughter, Julie?"

Talbot shook his head and stood. "Nice to meet you, Julie. I teach English at the high school."

"Jeffrey's a heck of a writer, too," Harry said. "He does the poetry column for my newspaper. Have you ever read it? Or is your dad too cheap to get you a subscription at school so you can keep up with news from the north country?"

Julie smiled awkwardly and didn't say anything. Pete rolled his eyes.

Talbot sorted through his leather portfolio and extracted a sheet of paper. "Here's one of my better columns," he said to Julie in a modest tone. "Some people think Charles Lamb, the poet featured in the column, wasn't actually one of the Lake Poets, but he certainly was associated with them. This piece is about his formative years."

Julie scanned the column. "I know the Lake Poets," she said. "William Wordsworth and that bunch."

Talbot's face lit up. "Right, William Wordsworth and Samuel Taylor Coleridge and Robert Southey and some others."

Julie's face grew solemn and she began to quote:

> I wandered lonely as a cloud
> That floats on high o'er vales and hills,
> When all at once I saw a crowd,

Talbot's eyes widened and he picked up where Julie left off:

> A host of golden daffodils;
> Beside the lake, beneath the trees,
> Fluttering and dancing in the breeze.

"That's it," Julie said. "I should have remembered the rest of it. That's from Wordsworth's daffodils poem, right?"

"Right!" Talbot said, rubbing his hands together. "Do you know *A Night Thought*?"

Julie frowned as she seemed to think. "I can't quite place that one."

"Lo! Where the Moon along the sky . . ."

"Right, right! The moon and everything."

Pete's cell phone burred. He saw that it was Joe Tessler and got up and walked away from the table to take the call.

"Pete, I thought you'd want to know this. The ballistics tests came back. They confirm that the rifle we found in Ramczyk's memorial is the weapon that was used to kill Stephanopoulis."

"Umm."

"Frank's holding a press conference tomorrow morning at ten to announce this latest development."

"Thanks for giving me a heads-up."

"I thought you might want to caucus with your co-counsel, that McKenzie woman, and—"

"I'm not her co-counsel, Joe. All I did was help her get in to see her client."

Tessler didn't say anything for a while, then, "That's not the way it came off when we talked to her after she was done with Ramczyk. She implied that the two of you were teaming up and started to rant and rave about how she's going to mount this giant PR campaign about veterans with PTSD, how they aren't getting the treatment they deserve, how we're railroading Ramczyk just because of his condition, and blah, blah, blah."

Pete rolled his eyes. "Once more, I'm not representing Ramczyk in any capacity. I'm not his lead counsel, I'm not his co-counsel, I'm not his anything counsel. If Lila McKenzie puts on a show of some kind, she'll be doing it on her own."

"You better straighten her out then."

"Getting back to the press conference, is Connie going to be there?"

"She has a conflict. I guess she had a meeting already scheduled that she can't get out of."

"I'm surprised that Frank didn't set his press conference for a time when she's able to be there. She's the one who's going to have to prosecute Ramczyk if charges are brought against him."

"Just between you and me and the tooth fairy, and strictly off the record, I think Frank and Connie got their signals crossed on this one. Frank had already announced the press conference before he found out about Connie's conflict. He felt committed and doesn't want to change it."

"There's not something else going on here, is there? Like a disagreement between Connie and Frank on whether you have a strong enough case to proceed?"

"What gave you that idea? There's no disagreement."

"I don't know. Just my nose. How about fingerprints? Did they find Ramczyk's prints on the rifle?"

Tessler hesitated for a moment, then said, "No, the piece has been wiped clean, just like the brass we found at the murder scene. That's why we believe we're dealing with a clever killer here who knows what he's doing. Ramczyk was in special ops in the military and probably knows all the tricks. It's one more thing that points to him."

"But you didn't find his fingerprints on the rifle."

"I just said we didn't and explained why we think that is."

"Mmm. It seems to me you guys have more than a few holes in your case—no motive, no fingerprints, no eyewitnesses to the murder."

"We have eyewitnesses," Tessler said defensively.

"You've got two elderly women who *claim* they saw a guy who resembles Gaz Ramczyk in the vicinity of where the shots came from. They didn't say they actually *saw* him fire the rifle. Even their accounts are inconsistent. I know because I talked to them."

"You talked to them? Why may I ask?"

"They're my neighbors. Neighbors talk to each other once in a while."

"They live over a mile away from you. This was Pete Thorsen at it again, sticking his nose into a law enforcement matter and conducting an investigation on the side, wasn't it?"

"I haven't made a secret of the fact I've been poking around, but it's because of the bogus legal opinions. I have a right to clear my name."

"I don't think the two old ladies had anything to do with those legal opinions," Tessler said dryly.

Pete smiled, sensing that the detective was ready to throw in the towel, and said, "They're my neighbors, as I said."

Pete heard a sigh, then, "Getting back to the McKenzie woman, if you talk to her—and I'll accept at face value what you said about not being her co-counsel—you might want to suggest that we'd be open to plea negotiations in view of the PTSD issue. Frank and I are convinced that Ramczyk is guilty as sin, but as long as he's off the streets, a plea might be the way to go."

"If I see her and the subject comes up, I'll mention it."

Pete returned to the table and sat down. Three pairs of eyes stared at him.

"Something happen in the Ramczyk case?" Harry asked.

Pete saw no reason to be evasive since Richter was holding a press conference the following morning anyway, and said, "The ballistics tests on the rifle they found buried in Ramczyk's memorial came back. It's the weapon that was used to kill Bud Stephanopoulis."

Julie's eyes widened, then tears began to roll down her cheeks. She got up from the table and hurried in the direction of the ladies' room.

Talbot seemed concerned and asked, "Will she be alright?"

"She's been emotional about all of this and needs time to adjust," Pete said. "I don't know if you're aware of it, but she was jet skiing with Stephanopoulis the day he was shot. The fact that Ramczyk is suffering from PTSD bothers her, too. Like many people her age, she's full of empathy. She'll be okay after she works through everything."

Talbot stared out the window.

"As we've talked about before," Harry said, "Sheriff Richter doesn't believe Gaz really has PTSD. He remembers him from his high school days. He thinks he's using PTSD as a smoke screen."

"It's more than a smoke screen, Harry," Pete said.

"Hey, I'm just telling you what Richter thinks. We need to cut him some slack on things like this. He's lived in this community all of his life. Long-time residents know people from the time they were born and have insights that those of us who've moved here more recently lack."

Pete didn't say anything.

Harry shifted his gaze to Talbot. "How long have you lived here, Jeffrey?"

"Since college. When I graduated, I accepted a teaching position at the high school. I liked the community and stayed."

"Do you remember Gaz from his high school days?"

Talbot's brow furled for a few moments. "Vaguely. I believe he was on the football team or something."

"You never had him in class?" Harry asked.

"Not that I recall. If I did, he wasn't a memorable student. It's a fault of mine. I tend to remember only the exceptional students." He looked at Pete. "Like I suspect your daughter is."

"Did Detective Tessler say where they were on the case?" Harry asked Pete. "Murder charges and everything?"

Pete shook his head. "He said there's a press conference tomorrow morning to announce the results of the ballistics tests."

Harry picked up his cell phone and scrolled through his messages. "Here it is," he said. "Ten o'clock at the County Government Center."

Julie came back from the ladies' room and joined them again. She appeared more composed.

"Well, I'm going to be on my way," Talbot said. "Julie, it's been delightful meeting you. I hope you'll take a poetry class in your first year of college. You obviously have a sensitivity for words and the emotions a poem seeks to convey."

He patted her shoulder and left.

"Nice guy," Pete said.

Harry nodded. "He is. What I don't understand is why he's still teaching English here. You'd think that with his intellectual bent, he'd be at a college somewhere."

They got their dinner orders in and the conversation switched to other topics, including the upcoming race for president and the two likely candidates and their respective platforms. Pete and Harry both held moderate political views, but liked to get after each other whenever the conversation turned to these things. Julie was mostly quiet as the barbs flew back and forth across the table.

Rona joined them and looked disapprovingly at the ribeye steak and double-baked potato that Harry was attacking with gusto. Harry made a show of leaving a sliver of the steak on his plate when he pushed it away with a satisfied expression. The potato was completely gone, though.

TWENTY-EIGHT

The next morning, Pete went for a run along the lake, and when he got back, Julie was still sleeping. He shaved and showered and grabbed something to eat. Then he settled into his favorite chair on the porch and flipped through the latest issue of *Golf Digest*. As he studied an article on bunker shots, his bugaboo as a golfer, his mind drifted off to his telephone conversation with Joe Tessler the previous evening. Finding the rifle in Gaz Ramczyk's backyard certainly wasn't a plus for him, but the anonymous telephone call that led to the discovery bothered him. Maybe Julie had it right. Maybe Gaz was being set up just like Jimmy Ray Evans had been.

Bud's financial entanglements nagged at him, too. Since he'd first seen the bogus legal opinion and then started to poke around, he'd become increasingly struck by the difference between Bud's public posture and the apparent reality of his life. No matter how you sliced it, it appeared that Bud had made a lot of enemies, from the partners at Harrison Stryker who'd taken it on the chin on account of his shady client, to investors who'd lost money in his more recent Ponzi schemes.

Pete leaned back and thought about calling Harrison Stryker to see if he could find someone who would be willing to talk to him about Bud. He knew that was a longshot, though. When he was managing partner of Sears & Whitney, if someone he didn't know had called looking for information about a former partner, he knew what his response would have been. Name, rank and serial number and nothing else.

Still, it might be worth a try. He pulled up Harrison Stryker's website on his laptop and scrolled through the list of the firm's bankers, but didn't recognize any of the names. He flipped through the documents he'd taken from Bud's house again. The name Marvin Kratz popped up repeatedly, either as the addressee on correspondence and memoranda or as one of the persons copied. He found Kratz's name listed on the website; he was the firm's managing director, which made sense in view of the other documents.

He heard water running upstairs, which meant that Julie was finally up. He stared at the telephone, debating whether a call was worth it, and heard the water stop. Finally he picked up the phone and dialed Kratz's direct number given on the website. After a couple of rings, a woman came on the line and said, "Mr. Kratz's office, Rose Cummings speaking."

"Ms. Cummings, my name is Pete Thorsen. Is Mr. Kratz in?"

"May I tell Mr. Kratz who you're with?" she asked in a businesslike voice that didn't invite casual chit-chat.

"I'm a lawyer in Michigan. I'd like to speak to Mr. Kratz about Bud Stephanopoulis. Mr. Stephanopoulis used to be with your firm."

"I'll see if he's available."

She put him on hold for a couple of minutes, then came back on the line and said, "I'm sorry, Mr. Kratz is in a meeting. Would you like to leave a message?"

"Do you expect him to be in his meeting long?"

"I really can't say, sir. He's with a client. I'll give him a message you called if I can have your telephone number."

He gave it to her, and after he hung up, he gazed out at the lake thinking that was about the response he'd expected. Julie came to the porch with her wet hair wrapped in a towel. "I heard your telephone conversation, Dad. Who were you calling about Bud?"

"Good morning," he said. "I called the managing director of Harrison Stryker, Bud's former investment banking firm, but I couldn't get past his secretary."

"Why did you call him?"

"Curiosity. With everything that's happened recently, I've been wondering about Bud's relationship with the firm."

"I don't understand."

"I was going to go fishing."

She looked at him blankly. "You're not talking about actual fishing, are you?"

Pete laughed. "No, it's a term we use when we're probing for information and aren't sure what to ask."

"You still must have *some* idea of what you're going to ask."

"In my telephone conversation with Joe Tessler last night," he lied, "I got the impression that Bud might have had a financial dispute with his investment banking firm at the time he left." He hated to mislead her again, but couldn't very well confess that he'd broken into Bud's house.

"What kind of dispute?"

"I don't know the details. I gather there were lawsuits against the firm, and Bud and the other partners had to contribute money to settle them."

Julie went to the kitchen and got a cup of coffee and returned. She cradled the mug in her hands and sipped coffee and looked out at the lake. After a while, she said, "I don't think Gaz did it."

"You may be right."

She took another sip of her coffee. "I bet if we teamed up, we could prove Gaz is innocent."

"Back to teaming up, huh? You forget, Gaz already has a lawyer."

"Yeah, but Lila's a lawyer, not an investigator."

"I'm not an investigator, either."

Julie looked at him sharply. "Dad, this is your daughter you're speaking to, and I'm trying to have a serious conversation. I *know* you've done a lot of investigating in the past. And I *know* you've been doing *some* investigating in this case already."

"Only to the extent it involves the phony legal opinions. That's one of the reasons I called the managing director of Harrison Stryker. I'm trying to get additional information about Bud to find out what was going on."

Julie looked out at the lake. She said without looking at him, "Well, I think Gaz is innocent."

She went to dry her hair, and when she came back, she asked, "So, what are we going to do today?"

"I hadn't thought about it. Any ideas?"

"I thought I'd hang out with you. Maybe pick up a pointer or two about being a crime-fighting investigator." She smiled impishly.

"The first thing is, you need to start wearing a trench coat with the collar turned up even when the weather's hot."

They both laughed.

"We could always have a dad-daughter lunch in a couple of hours," he said.

"Let's do that. Then, unless you need to get back because of your *very* busy schedule, we can do some shopping. You know, to recharge our batteries after hours and hours of doing battle with bad guys. I need to stop at The Bookstore to say hello to Dwight and Barbara Reed and stock up on reading material for the rest of the summer. Then we can go to Crystal Crate & Cargo so I can check out the earrings. I have about nine pairs that aren't pairs anymore because half of them are missing."

"Sounds like a plan. First, though, I'm going to stop at Sheriff Richter's press conference and hear what he has to say about the rifle they found. Want to come?"

When they pulled into the County Government Center parking lot, Pete saw two television crews in front of the building and maybe fifty other people milling around waiting. Harry was in front, close to the microphones. A few minutes after 10:00 a.m., Sheriff Richter came out of the building, followed by Joe Tessler and a deputy Pete didn't know. The television cameras began to grind. Julie seemed mesmerized by it all.

"Thank you for coming," Richter in a voice that sounded a bit pompous. "I'd like to update you on the Bud Stephanopoulis murder investigation. We just had an important breakthrough in the case. Two days ago, we discovered what we now know is the murder weapon." He held a rifle encased in a plastic sheath over his head, turning slightly to his right so people standing there could get a good view of it, then turning to his left for the same reason.

"We found the weapon buried in the backyard of a suspect in the case, a Mr. Alfred Ramczyk who lives a couple of miles outside of Frankfort. Around here, Mr. Ramczyk is commonly called Gaz. He's well-known to the sheriff's department, having been arrested on a number of occasions for a variety of offenses."

Richter went on to say that they'd had ballistics tests performed on the rifle and had established conclusively that it was the weapon used to shoot Mr. Stephanopoulis, one of the community's leading citizens. Richter provided some more detail and then opened the session to questions. Harry and several other reporters clamored for attention at the same time, and the sheriff patiently began to answer their questions as he called on them. Pete could tell that Richter reveled in the attention.

Pete checked his watch. He'd already heard all of this from Tessler, only in more detail, and suggested to Julie that they leave. She insisted on staying longer, but Pete was finally successful in coaxing her away. He'd deliberately parked on the edge of the lot to facilitate an early getaway.

They went to The Mayfair Tavern for lunch, and Julie kept up a running soliloquy about the press conference, gushing about how interesting it had been and saying she'd learned things she could never get from a book. Then she was back to Gaz Ramczyk, restating her conviction that he was innocent. She kept emphasizing that she could tell from Sheriff Richter's eyes that he didn't really think Gaz was guilty either.

On their way out of the restaurant, they almost bumped into three men who were just coming in. One of them was Tomas Esteban. Pete had never seen the other two before. Esteban was talking to one of his companions in his strange voice and started to step to the side to let them out. Then he saw Pete and his lips tightened and his eyes darted around until finally he looked away.

"Tomas, good to see you again. This is my daughter, Julie."

Esteban didn't say anything. His eyes flicked toward Pete again for a brief moment before he took another step to the side.

"I think we're clogging up the door," Pete said to Julie as he guided her through the opening between the three men.

When they got into Pete's Range Rover, Julie said, "Did you know those men, Dad?"

"One of them."

"The one in the middle, the shorter one?"

"That's Tomas Esteban. He lost money in one of Bud's investment scams. I tried to talk to him the other day, but he wouldn't have anything to do with me. I don't know what his problem is."

Julie looked at him and said, "He didn't seem very happy to see you."

Pete shrugged. "Like I said, I don't know what his problem is."

On the way to downtown Frankfort, Julie said, "Is that man a suspect in Bud's case?"

"I believe he's on the sheriff's list. And he's kind of a strange character. Beyond that, I don't know anything."

"He looks mean."

"Second lesson of detecting. Just because a person looks mean doesn't mean he's guilty of something."

When they got to The Bookstore, Julie's attention shifted to socializing and shopping. The Reeds were happy to see her and Julie found five books she wanted. Then it was on to Crystal Crate & Cargo where she chatted with Sally Berlin and her sales ladies and replenished her supply of earrings. Leaving the store, Pete said to Julie, "Why don't you drive home so I can call Marvin Kratz at Harrison Stryker again."

She snatched the keys from his hand and settled in behind the wheel with a satisfied expression and eased out of their parking spot. Pete suppressed a smile as he punched in Kratz's number.

"Mr. Kratz's office, Rose Cummings speaking."

"Ms. Cummings, this is Pete Thorsen again. We spoke this morning. Is Mr. Kratz out of his meeting yet?"

"Yes sir, but he had to leave to meet another client."

"Will he be back today?"

"I'm afraid not. He's having dinner with the client after their meeting. Can I have him call you in the morning?"

"Please. Do you have my number?"

She read off his cell phone number. He confirmed that was it and ended the call.

"No luck?" Julie asked.

"He's in another meeting and then has a business dinner. Let's see if he calls back in the morning."

"What if he doesn't?"

"I'll decide then."

"If he doesn't call back, we could go to Philadelphia and demand to talk to him."

"We?"

"Sure. As part of the team, I could support you. Two people look more formidable than one. Besides, I've never been to Philadelphia. The trip could do double-duty as a father-daughter pre-college trip."

He smiled at her. "Let's see what happens in the morning."

"It wouldn't even cost you anything, if that's what you're worried about. I have more than enough money in my bank account for a ticket because I've been so frugal."

"That's good to know. The frugal part, I mean."

"Do you think I spend a lot of money?"

He tried to look thoughtful. "No, I really don't," he said after a while.

"You're not saying that just to be nice, are you?"

"Of course not."

Julie was quiet for a while. Then she said, "When we get home, I'm going to check Philadelphia's website and make a list of places I think we should see."

Pete hoped that Kratz would call him in the morning. He hadn't decided to go to Philadelphia if Kratz didn't call, and if he did go, he wondered how he'd talk Julie out of joining him without causing another rupture in their relationship.

TWENTY-NINE

Julie's face was plastered to the window, searching for landmarks, as the Boeing 737 circled over the city and went into its glide path toward one of the runways at Philadelphia International Airport. Kratz hadn't called him back that morning, and when he put in another call to Rose Cummings, it confirmed his impression that he was being given the run-around. Julie pressed her case for a trip east, and Pete eventually relented. With reservations he left unsaid.

"I think I saw Independence Hall back there," Julie announced, her voice brimming with excitement.

Pete, who had the aisle seat, couldn't see anything but rooftops as they approached the runway.

When they were at the gate, they retrieved their carry-on luggage from the overhead compartment and stood in line to get off the plane. They took a taxi to their hotel, which was a couple of blocks from Harrison Stryker's offices, and checked in. It was still light and would be for several hours. They decided to walk around and see some of the sights before finding a place to have dinner.

The steps in front of the Philadelphia Museum of Art, immortalized in the *Rocky* movies, was one of the stops on Julie's list. She stared up at them for a few moments, then began to jog in place. She looked at Pete and said, "It's hard to believe I'm standing at the bottom of the steps where Rocky did his training. Should we run up like he did?"

Playing Rocky wasn't on Pete's personal bucket list, but he tried to be a good sport and said, "Why not?"

Julie started up with a bounce in her step and Pete followed. Halfway up, he felt the strain in his thighs and began to suck air. He took his time and didn't try to keep up with Julie. When he reached the top, she was waiting for him, continuing to jog in place and feinting with her hands as if warming up for a championship fight.

"Going down is easier," she said and was off.

She was right, Pete grudgingly admitted, it was easier. She was waiting for him again when he got to the bottom. He tried not to show his exertion.

"Do you think Sylvester Stallone actually ran the steps in those movies? Or was it a stand-in?"

"No idea," Pete said, resisting the temptation to put his hands on his knees.

"Want to go again?" Julie said, jogging in place some more and feinting with her hands again.

"No, this Rocky is done." He watched Julie race up the steps and then back down.

She continued her jogging in place routine, directing several left jabs his way. Brushing a wisp of hair away from her face, she said, "I feel like I could take on that—what was that boxer's name?"

"Apollo Creed?"

"Yeah, that's right, the mean guy."

"All boxers are mean."

Julie acted like she hadn't heard him and said, "Have you rested enough so we can go again?" She resumed jogging in place and looked up at the steps.

"Nope, I'm done. I'm going to conserve my strength in case I need to protect you from some goons tomorrow."

Julie started up again, and when she reached the top, she jogged in place as she gazed out over the cityscape for a while before starting back down. Pete smiled when she pulled up beside him, laboring just a little. "Ready for some dinner?" he asked.

After a stop at their hotel, they found a seafood restaurant that was only half-full and got a table and settled in. They immediately began to peruse their menus and got their orders in without dallying. When their appetizers came, Julie said between bites of her stuffed shrimp, "What's the game plan for tomorrow?"

"No real game plan. We're going to show up at Harrison Stryker's offices about 9:00 a.m. and ask to see Marvin Kratz. We'll play it by ear from there."

They walked into the Harrison Stryker reception room at the time they'd planned. Pete introduced himself to the receptionist and said Julie was his assistant. He asked to see Marvin Kratz.

"Do you have an appointment?"

"We've been trading telephone calls. I spoke to his secretary, Rose Cummings, several times. Mr. Kratz knows we're coming," he said confidently.

The receptionist looked at him skeptically, but reached for the phone on her desk and dialed a number. She spoke in a low voice, then hung up and said, "Ms. Cummings will be out in a minute."

They moved to the seating area and waited for Cummings to appear. Finally, a dour woman in a nondescript gray suit with a hemline below her knees and sensible shoes appeared and came over to them. "Mr. Kratz has a very busy schedule today, Mr. Thorsen. I'm afraid he can't see you without an appointment."

"Look, Ms. Cummings. I've been calling for two days, trying to talk to him. I appreciate that he's busy, but all I need is a half-hour of his time. It's about Bud Stephanopoulis who used to be with this firm." He deliberately raised his voice when he said Stephanopoulis's name.

"I'm sorry," Ms. Cummings said, shaking her head. "If you want to make an appointment, I'll see if I can fit you in. It won't be this month, though. Maybe July . . . or possibly August. I'll have to see what's available."

"I need to see Mr. Kratz now," Pete said in the same loud voice. "Bud Stephanopoulis was murdered a few days ago. I represent some of the investors in financial products he was promoting. I have reason to believe they were put together when Mr. Stephanopoulis was still with Harrison Stryker. If we have to, we'll sue this firm along with other defendants we've already identified. I'd prefer not to do that, but we will if we have to."

"Mr. Thorsen—"

"Is Mr. Kratz in his office?" he asked, starting in the direction Cummings had come from.

"Please Mr. Thorsen, I told you, Mr. Kratz is busy."

Pete saw two men approaching, both in black suits that looked like they'd been bought off the rack at some discount store. *Crap, security people.*

"Mr. Thorsen," the lead man said when he reached them, elbowing Rose Cummings out of the way, "I'm going to have to ask you and your assistant to leave." He grasped Pete's arm and steered him toward the elevator. His assistant did the same with Julie. When the elevator door opened, the security men nudged them in and the lead pushed one of the buttons. They all stood in silence as the elevator started down. The elevator door opened at the lobby level and the lead man pointed, indicating they should get out.

When they'd been herded away from the elevator bank, the lead guy moved close to Pete with their chests nearly touching and said in a low voice, "Don't come back. If you do, I'm going to call the police and press charges. Or maybe I'll have one of our people who specializes in matters like this deal with you." He bumped Pete with his chest and turned and headed toward the elevators with his assistant hurrying to keep up.

Pete watched them disappear and shook his head. He hadn't expected *that*.

"That was really rude," Julie whispered. "Why won't Mr. Kratz talk to us?"

"I don't know. We must have struck a sensitive chord when I asked about Bud."

As they stood in the building lobby deciding what to do, a man came up to them and slipped a note into Pete's hand, then continued toward the drug store in the corner.

Pete unfolded the slip of paper and glanced at it. It said, "Meet me in the bar at Luigi's at 5 p.m." It gave the address. He showed it to Julie.

"This is like one of those spy movies," she said with wide eyes. "Who was that man?"

"No idea."

"Do you think we should meet him?"

Pete thought about it for a few moments. "I do. He obviously didn't want to be seen talking to us. I suspect he wants to tell us something about Bud."

He checked his watch; it was 9:30 a.m. They went to a corner of the lobby with seats and he spent fifteen minutes on the phone with the airline changing their return tickets to the 8:00 p.m. flight.

They spent the day at Independence National Historical Park, much of the time browsing around Independence Hall and the Liberty Bell Center. Julie seemed mesmerized by the bell. "It really does have a crack in it," she whispered to her father. The guard standing nearby smiled.

They took a side trip to the Reading Terminal Market, which supposedly was America's oldest farmer's market. Pete had been checking his watch periodically the entire afternoon, and when 4:00 p.m. came, they caught a taxi to the restaurant where they were supposed to meet the nameless man.

Luigi's looked like a family-run Italian restaurant. The bar was small and separated from the eating area by a divider made of wooden dowels that extended from a fabric-covered base to the ceiling. A half-dozen stools lined the bar and three postage-stamp tables covered with red-and-white checked tablecloths hugged the opposite wall.

"This looks like a Mafia place," Julie whispered as they walked in.

Pete smiled. "I don't see Tony Soprano. Maybe he eats later."

They took one of the tables, and a bartender appeared from nowhere and took their orders. After bringing their Diet Cokes, he disappeared again. Pete and Julie made small talk, speaking in hushed voices. They were grateful when a couple came in and took one of the tables in the dining area. The couple's voices made their conversation a little less conspicuous.

Promptly at 5:00 p.m., the man who'd slipped the note into Pete's hand walked in, and after chatting briefly with the waiter who was hovering over the couple in the dining area, crossed to the bar. He extended a hand and said, "Hunter Pusateri."

Pete introduced himself and Julie.

The bartender appeared again and brought a glass of something that looked like Campari and soda and set it in front of Pusateri. After exchanging a few words with him in what Pete thought was Italian, the bartender disappeared again.

"If you like Italian food, this is the place," Pusateri said, taking a sip of his drink. "And I say that not just because my uncle owns the place."

"I love Italian food," Julie gushed.

"Maybe you should stay for dinner after we finish talking." He turned to Pete and said, "Sorry for the cloak and dagger stuff in the lobby, but I didn't want anyone to see me talking to you."

"I understand."

"I couldn't help but hear the ruckus you caused in our reception area, asking to see our managing director about Bud Stephanopoulis. That's a sensitive subject around the firm."

"I gathered as much. In case you're not aware of it, Bud was shot and killed while he was jet skiing on a lake in Michigan."

"I heard that. And you're the attorney for a bunch of investors in financial products Bud was peddling."

"Not yet," Pete said, skirting the issue, "but I am involved in the mess. I found out Stephanopoulis was dummying up legal opinions under my name and including them in the packages he gave investors. I'm trying to unravel what's been going on."

Pusateri smiled and shook his head. He said, "Sounds like Bud. I'll tell you what I know, but first we need to have an understanding. None of what I tell you came from me, okay?"

"Agreed." Julie nodded, signifying that she agreed as well.

Pusateri played with his swizzle stick. "Where to start," he mused. "Bud and I both came to Harrison Stryker about eighteen years ago, give or take. He came from a small firm where he'd been for a few years. I joined right out of college. Harrison Stryker was never one of the really top-tier firms like, to give you one example, Goldman Sachs. But it was still a pretty darn good shop. Once you get past the seven or ten year-mark at Harrison, there's a lot of pressure on you to produce business. M&A work, securities offerings, that sort of thing. The stuff that generates big bucks for the firm."

"Sounds a lot like law firms," Pete said.

"Were you in a corporate firm?"

Pete nodded.

"You know what I mean, then. Big firms always say they don't have an eat-what-you-kill culture, but most of them do. With some, you can probably hang on if you're not a big producer, but you're going to be on a diet, you know?"

He twisted his swizzle stick into various shapes while Pete waited for him to continue. "Bud was a business producer from the time he walked in the door. Some of the stuff he brought with him from the small firm we picked up in the merger. A lot of our top people thought it was garbage business, but it produced revenue so they held their noses and listened to the cash register chime. About eight or ten years ago, Bud brought in this high-flying firm that was putting together deals and Harrison started to underwrite them. Then one went sour and a bunch of the investors sued and the crap hit the fan. After that, another deal sprung leaks.

"The Securities and Exchange Commission began to investigate and civil lawsuits were filed all over the place. When the dust settled, a number of our younger bankers who'd worked on the deals were barred by the SEC from being involved in the securities industry for five years. Bud, while he was investigated, managed to walk even though many of us thought that he had to know about his client's fraud.

"When the smoke cleared, Harrison Stryker had seven investor class-action suits against it. Our lawyers managed to get the lawsuits consolidated and eventually settled them. Harrison Stryker got nicked for ninety-two million dollars as a result. The firm's capital wasn't sufficient to cover the settlement amount so a capital call went out. That resulted in a lot of angst and recriminations among the partners, and during the process, Bud was ousted from the firm."

"That's when Bud had to kick in about seven million dollars, right?"

"That was part of it. A group of our partners sued Bud personally, and I heard he settled that lawsuit for close to ten million."

"So you're saying the whole thing cost him seventeen million, more or less."

"More or less."

"Were the deals his client was pushing Ponzi schemes?"

"That's what a lot of us concluded."

"From what I can tell, Bud was running the same kind of scams in Michigan before he was shot."

Pusateri shook his head. "Old dogs don't learn new tricks."

"Who were the people sanctioned by the SEC?"

"There were five. In no particular order, their names were Larry Albright, Effie Zepp, Wayne Jessup, Leslie Wallace, and Aaron Isaacs."

"Are any of them still with Harrison Stryker?"

Pusateri laughed derisively. "No, they're long gone. The firm was afraid that cutting them loose right away would be an admission of guilt, but as soon as everything was settled, they were history. Scapegoats, fall guys, whatever you want to call it."

"Do you know how I can get in touch with these people?"

"Larry Albright, you'll have to wait until you get to the pearly gates to talk to him. He committed suicide a year after the firm gave him the boot. Last I heard, Effie Zepp and Aaron Isaacs were still in the area. Leslie Wallace and Wayne Jessup have fallen off the face of the earth as far as I know."

Pete knew that his next question would sound a little bit like asking a man accused of murder whether he really did it, but decided to ask anyway. "A lot of people at Harrison Stryker obviously were hurt by what Bud Stephanopoulis did. Does anyone come to mind who might have felt aggrieved enough to kill him?"

Pusateri laughed, derisively again. "How about a hundred people? The five I just mentioned who had their careers and reputations ruined, plus, obviously, the partners who had to pony up to pay the settlements. In my case, I lost my house and capital in Harrison Stryker and what savings I had apart from what was in my 401(k), which they couldn't touch. Oh, and my wife divorced me and got custody of our two kids."

"Umm."

"But before you add any of the Harrison Stryker partners to your list of suspects, I should tell you that I checked on when our friend Bud was shot. That whole week, all of the partners, including me, were at a retreat at some crap-hole in the Poconos discussing the latest plan management had developed to resuscitate the firm. Kratz knew that a lot of us thought the plan was a joke so he required everybody to sign in in the mornings and again before the afternoon sessions."

"That sounds like a pretty good alibi."

"I'm happy to hear you say that."

Pete shook his head. "Are you going to stay with the firm as it rebuilds?"

"No. I've decided to move on with my life. Kratz doesn't know it yet, but I just concluded arrangements to move to a startup shop that's going to specialize in middle market companies looking to sell out to lock in the owners' gains or to go public to raise capital. That's why I decided to talk to you. To do my part to wipe the slate clean."

THIRTY

Pete and Julie delayed their flight again until the following day to see if they could locate Effie Zepp and Aaron Isaacs. Both were listed in the Philadelphia telephone directory. He tried Zepp first.

"Hello," a woman said in a weary-sounding voice.

"Ms. Zepp, my name is Pete Thorsen. I'm a lawyer and I'm calling at the suggestion of Hunter Pusateri. I'm not far from your house. Would you have time to talk to me if I come by? It's about Bud Stephanopoulis."

The phone was quiet for a few moments, then, "Someone told me he was dead."

"Who told you that?"

"A person I used to work with at my former employer."

"Harrison Stryker?"

"Yes."

"You're right, Mr. Stephanopoulis is dead."

"Why do you want to talk to me?"

"A man I know is accused of killing him. I think he's innocent. I have reason to believe Stephanopoulis's death had something to do with investments scams he was running in Michigan. They sound similar to what got Harrison Stryker and a lot of its people in trouble. You worked for Bud. I'd like to confirm some things with you."

After a pause, she said, "I'm trying to put that nightmare behind me. I don't think I can help you."

Pete heard an infant crying in the background. "Please, Ms. Zepp," he said, "it's important. It won't take long."

"I have to go." The connection went dead.

Pete looked at Julie and said, "She hung up."

"I couldn't hear her end of the conversation. Was she defensive? Belligerent?"

"Neither. She just sounded weary. I heard a baby crying in the background."

"Why don't you try her again in a few minutes? Turn on the charm."

Pete smiled at her and waited fifteen minutes, then dialed again. The same tired voice answered.

"Ms. Zepp, I really do hate to pester you, but I have some questions that only you can answer. If now isn't a convenient time for you to talk, name some other time and I'll be there."

"You again."

"Yes, and I'm not going to go away. It's important."

After a moment, she asked, "Will this take long?"

"An hour at most. Maybe less."

"Could you come at eight? I'll have my baby fed and bathed by then."

"I'll see you at eight."

Pete ended the call and looked at Julie and grinned. "Was that charming enough?"

She rolled her eyes. "That sounded more like a threat than charm."

"But I made the threat in a charming way, right?"

She rolled her eyes a second time.

They grabbed something to eat at the hotel coffee shop and then took a taxi to Effie Zepp's apartment building. It was a boxy four-story faded yellow brick structure that looked forty or fifty years old. Pete found Zepp's name on the board in the lobby, pushed the button, and waited for her to buzz them in. Her apartment was on the fourth floor so they took the elevator up and Pete knocked on her door.

After a minute, the door opened and baby smells greeted them. A woman who was maybe in her mid-thirties with short ash-blonde hair stood with her hand on the knob and said, "Mr. Thorsen?"

"Yes. This is my daughter, Julie. I hope you don't mind me bringing her along."

She let them in, and as they were talking, a man with dark horned-rim glasses and jeans who looked about Zepp's age came out of another room with an infant in his arms. She was wrapped in a pink blanket and he bounced her gently as he walked. "Hi," he said, "I'm Aaron Isaacs. This is Tina. I'd shake your hand, but . . ."

Pete hadn't expected to see Isaacs there. He glanced at Effie Zepp's left hand and didn't see a ring and wondered what their relationship was. Regardless, having him there eliminated the need to track him down.

Julie peeked at the baby wrapped in the blanket and extended her forefinger. A little hand reached out and grabbed it. Julie looked at Effie with a big smile and said, "Cute!"

Effie smiled awkwardly, obviously pleased with her comment. She cleared some Pampers and rattles and other items from one of the couches, and said, "Please, sit." Effie, Aaron and the baby took the couch opposite them.

"We thought all of this was behind us," Aaron said.

"It might be out here," Pete said, "but in Michigan it's just getting started. We're trying to unravel the threads and figure out what's going on. We know the gist of what happened at Harrison Stryker and that you're aware Bud is dead. Just to explain why we're here, I'm a victim of Bud Stephanopoulis like the two of you and a lot of other people." He told them that he'd discovered Bud had been forging his signature on fake legal opinions and then using the opinions in connection with his scam investment products.

Aaron looked him up and down. "Are you being investigated by the SEC?"

"Not yet."

"Why don't you just tell the investors you didn't write the opinions?"

"When people lose a lot of money, they're usually not satisfied with casual answers. They either want their money back or iron-clad proof that you weren't complicit in the scam."

Effie Zepp seemed sympathetic, but Isaacs looked like he thought Pete was making a big deal out of nothing.

Pete added, "My reputation is something I take seriously, and when someone drags it through the muck . . ."

"Aaron didn't mean anything," Effie said, apparently sensing that he'd been put off by Isaacs' comment. "It's just that we've been through so much. We didn't have any idea what was going on with Bud's client. What one of us did was always kept separate from what everyone else did. We had no way of knowing. That's what we told our lawyers and the SEC when it investigated. Obviously, they didn't believe us. We all went to good schools and worked so hard and now this . . ."

"Have you thought about some way you can clear your names?"

"We tried, believe me. Bud, who was our big friend before all of this hit, suddenly wouldn't have anything to do with us. When I found out I was pregnant, I tried to call him, like, ten times to ask for some help, but he wouldn't even return my calls."

"The guy's an asshole," Aaron said. "He was an asshole when we worked there, then he became a bigger asshole. Now he's a dead asshole. I say good riddance."

"Aaron . . ."

The baby started to cry and Isaacs picked her up and walked to the kitchen, probably to get her a bottle.

Pete chose his words carefully, and said, "Of the five of you who were debarred by the SEC, I know that Larry Albright is dead. How about the other two?" He looked at his notes and added, "Leslie Wallace and Wayne Jessup."

"I heard that Wayne is on the West Coast. I'm not worried about him, he'll be okay. He's the kind of guy who'll give someone he doesn't like the middle finger salute and walk away and never look back. Leslie is the one I worry about. She came from such a poor background and worked so hard and overcame so much. She was such a star in everything she did in life, too, including at Harrison Stryker. Everyone thought she'd eventually be the firm's first female managing director. Then all of this happened . . . It's so unfair."

"Where is Leslie from? Does she still have family?"

"I don't know. She was so depressed the last time I talked to her. I just wish she'd call. Aaron and I have each other, but Leslie . . ."

"Have you tried to call her?"

"Only about twenty times. Her landline has been disconnected and her cell rings and rings, but there's never any answer."

"Could you give me her cell phone number?"

Effie went to another room and came back with a slip of paper and handed it to him.

"I have to ask you a question," Pete said, "and please don't take this the wrong way. Is Leslie capable of violence?"

Effie Zepp looked at him as if she were stunned by his question. "Leslie? I don't think she could shoot a gun or use a knife if her life depended on it." She thought about it again for a while. "I know what you're asking, but no, not Leslie. Never. She's competitive in the way she approached work, but underneath, she's a gentle, sensitive soul."

Pete thought about that and finally turned to Julie and asked, "Do you have any more questions for Effie?"

Julie shook her head sadly and said to Effie, "You'll get through this. You're a strong woman. And you have a beautiful baby. And Aaron, too. You'll be okay."

Effie wiped her eyes.

"Have you and Aaron found other jobs?" Pete asked.

"Oh sure," Effie said, sarcasm dripping from her words. "After the baby is asleep, I crunch numbers part-time for a small accounting firm for the princely sum of fifteen dollars an hour. That's gross. Aaron is the assistant manager for a mom-and-pop shoe store. We're living the American Dream."

Going down the elevator, Julie brushed a tear from her cheek and said, "The more I hear about this, the sadder I become. Bud is dead and all of the lives he's ruined . . ."

Pete pulled her close and kissed the top of her head.

Pete called a taxi on his cell phone, and while they were waiting for it to come, he punched in Leslie Wallace's cell phone number. No answer.

THIRTY-ONE

The next morning, Pete went to his office to check on his mail and telephone messages. Harry had called — four times — and Joe Tessler had called once, but aside from that, there was nothing other than telemarketing calls. It wasn't like the old days when he was king of the roost at Sears & Whitney and came back from a business trip to a stack of telephone messages and copious notes from his secretary reminding him of a dozen commitments he had that day. He thought about how times had changed and sighed.

After staring out the window at the bay for a while, he picked up the telephone and dialed Tessler's number. His call went to voicemail. He gazed out the window some more, then got up and walked down to *The Northern Sentinel*'s offices. He half expected to see Harry huddled again with Jeffrey Talbot, but he was alone.

"Well," Harry said, dropping his pen on the top of his desk, "the wanderer is back. It must be nice to have nothing to do so you can extend your visit to Philly from one day to three."

Pete forced a grin. "You know what I always say about flexibility."

"You're not going to give me that hobgoblin nonsense again, are you?" Harry asked with a disgusted look on his face.

"You know who said that? Ralph Waldo Emerson."

"You expect me to believe that? You made that up."

Pete shrugged. "Check it out."

Harry shot him a look.

"So, what's been happening around here?"

"Well, for one thing, you missed out on a fishing outing with your best friend. It was a perfect day, too. I was even going to drive. But it's too late, now. I'm back to running an important newspaper. You missed the window of opportunity, as they say."

"Sorry."

"The other thing is, I was surprised not to see you at Sheriff Richter's press conference."

Pete waved a hand at him. "I knew what he was going to say. I didn't want to waste my time," he lied, not acknowledging that he and Julie had watched most of it from the fringes of the crowd.

"But the biggie is that Gaz Ramczyk is out of jail."

"*Really*," Pete said. "Did they drop the charges against him?"

Harry shook his head. "Yesterday morning, your friend from Detroit—what's her name, Nina McKenzie—went before—"

"Lila McKenzie."

"Lila, whatever. She went to the judge and argued that Gaz shouldn't be held because he's a decorated vet, that he's not a flight risk, and blah, blah, blah. The judge released him on his own recognizance pending trial on the assault charges. He has to wear a leg bracelet so they can trace him if he tries to flee. But that's it, he's out."

"Didn't Connie argue that he should be held because he's also under suspicion for murder?"

"I guess she did, but the judge said they can't hold him on just the assault charges. If they weren't ready to bring murder charges, they had to release him."

"Umm."

"Did you learn anything useful in Philadelphia?" Harry asked.

Pete told him about the trip, including his meetings with Hunter Pusateri, Effie Zepp and Aaron Isaacs.

"Incredible. And the inside guy you talked to said Bud had to cough up seventeen mill to get out of the mess?"

"That's what he said."

Harry whistled. "That's a lot of bread."

"For anybody."

"Much as I hate to admit it, I guess you were right when you said that maybe Bud wasn't as rich as we thought he was."

"Thanks for the compliment. Knowing the story of what really happened at Harrison Stryker explains a lot of things, including why he was running his scams up here. He must have been broke or close to it because of what he had to fork over in the settlements. But here's the important thing—we now know that a whole lot of people had a motive to kill him."

"Do you think it could have been someone from Harrison Stryker?"

"Possible, but there's a complicating factor. According to Pusateri, the firm had a retreat in the Poconos the week that includes the day Bud was shot. He claims they had mandatory sign-ins twice a day. That would seem to give all of the bankers pretty good alibis."

"If it's true."

Pete nodded. "If it's true."

"Are you going to check it out?"

"I wouldn't know where to start. The managing director of Harrison Stryker, a guy named Marvin Kratz, won't talk to me and there are or were almost a hundred bankers at his firm. Besides, trying to check them out would involve me in the murder investigation and we both know I'm not doing that. I'm just trying to clear my good name."

"Uh huh," Harry said dryly, shooting him a look. "How about those five younger people?"

"I talked to two of them — Zepp and Isaacs — and I seriously doubt it was either of them. Larry Albright is dead. That leaves Leslie Wallace and Wayne Jessup. Nobody has any idea where they are."

Pete could see Harry's mind working. Finally, Harry said, "Are you going to tell Joe Tessler what you uncovered?"

"He called while I was in Philadelphia, probably to tell me about Ramczyk. I called him back, but he didn't pick up. When I do talk to him, I intend to pass on what I just told you."

Harry seemed to think some more. "Have you run the scandal through the computer databases? Something that big, there should have been quite a lot of coverage in the financial press at least. Maybe you'll see something that's inconsistent with what people have been telling you."

"You know, every now and then you manage to come up with something that borders on a good idea."

"No need to be a wise guy. Do you want me to run the search? You've distracted me from what I was doing anyway."

"Can't hurt." He grabbed a piece of paper and wrote the name Harrison Stryker on it to be sure he had the right spelling, followed by Marvin Kratz, Hunter Pusateri and the names of the five younger employees.

Harry scanned the list and said, "There was a girl from Frankfort named Leslie who was quite a star a while back. A great soccer and volleyball player, valedictorian of her class, that kind of thing. She was in the *Sentinel* a lot during her high school days. She went to college some place out east and I kind of lost track of her. It'd be too much of a coincidence for her to be the same person."

"Was her last name Wallace?"

"No, I don't think so. Just a minute." He started poking the keys of his computer and few minutes later looked up and said, "Lehr, Leslie Lehr. I should have remembered that. We wrote about her a lot. As I said, she was a star."

Pete's interested picked up. "What did her family do?"

"What do you mean?"

"Was she from one of the town families—the daughter of a store owner, for example—or was she from the farm?" He remembered how it was when he was growing up. The "townies," as they were called, ran everything and the farm kids were at the bottom of the heap. As Effie Zepp described Leslie Wallace, it seemed unlikely that she was a daughter of the merchant class.

"You know, I don't remember exactly. Hold on." He thumbed through the local telephone directory and said, "There's a Lehr family that lives south of Benzonia. If that's Leslie's parents, she probably wasn't a town resident. That's just a guess, though."

"Okay."

"If you want, I can probably find her picture in our archives."

"Can't hurt."

Pete waited while Harry poked at his keyboard again and kept looking between his monitor and keyboard. Finally his printer started to grind and several sheets of paper shot out. He went over to the machine, and after looking at them, handed them to Pete.

"The top one is probably best. Of course, that was taken at least a dozen years ago. I'm sure she's changed a lot."

"Understood," Pete said as he studied the photographs.

Harry plugged the other names into his search engine and soon zeroed in on the scandal that had enveloped Harrison Stryker. Several of the stories gave essentially the same narrative that Pete had been able to piece together. Most of them quoted the former managing director of Harrison Stryker or its public relations person. Two of the stories referred to the SEC's settlement with the firm and said five employees had been debarred by the SEC, but didn't give their names. Bud Stephanopoulis and another senior banker at the firm were both mentioned in several of the stories, but were said to have declined comment.

After thanking Harry, Pete took everything he'd printed out and walked back to his office. He settled in behind his desk and read the stories more carefully. He saw no inconsistencies between the press accounts and what Hunter Pusateri and Effie Zepp had told him, although some of what they'd said hadn't made it into print.

Pete tried Joe Tessler again, but his call went to voicemail for the second time. He drummed his pen on his desktop as he gazed out at the bay, then tried Leslie Wallace's cell phone number again. No answer and no voicemail greeting. He spread the three photographs of Leslie Lehr in front of him. The best one, the headshot, looked like a photo from a school yearbook. The girl who looked back at him had curly dark hair framing her face, and even though the photograph was grainy, her sparkling eyes danced on the paper.

He knew he was talking himself into something, but wondered whether Leslie Lehr and Leslie Wallace were the same person. And wondered how he could find out. He remembered Kelene Brill telling him that she'd attended several gatherings at Bud's house when he'd given presentations to prospective investors. Maybe Bud had an assistant at the presentations. After trying Tessler again without success, he dialed Brill's number.

"This is Kelene," a woman's voice purred.

"Pete Thorsen, Kelene. Do you remember me?"

Her voice changed a little. "Of course I remember you. You're going to get my money back for me."

"As far as I know, the probate estate hasn't even been opened yet. Claims can only be filed after the probate estate is open. Besides, I'm still assessing whether I want to represent the investors."

"I really need that money."

"I understand. Are you going to be home a while? I'd like to come by and ask you a few more questions."

A pause, then, "We could talk over lunch. I don't know about you, but I'm hungry."

He hadn't been expecting that, but recovered and said casually, "Sure, we could have lunch. Do you want to meet somewhere? Or should I pick you up?"

"I think it would be nice if you picked me up. I'm old-fashioned. I think a man should always pick up the girl."

Pete blanched at the inference.

Pete picked up Kelene Brill at her house shortly before noon. Her perfume filled the car and he cracked his window slightly to let some of the aroma out. She seemed pleased with his choice of the Coho Café as a lunch venue.

When they were seated on the screened porch overlooking the marina, she scanned the drink card, and apparently seeing nothing that struck her fancy, asked the waitress if the bartender could make her a Pink Silk Panties. Pete frowned, wondering what the hell that was, and ordered an iced tea with extra lemon. Her expression was the same as it was at her house that day when he'd declined her offer of a drink.

"You told me when we talked that you attended some of the get-togethers Bud held for people who were interested in his investment products. Did—"

"Boy, you don't even let a girl get settled before you start talking business, do you?"

"Sorry, we can eat first and then discuss my questions if you like."

She took a sip of her pink-colored martini and folded her arms under her breasts and leaned forward. "No," she said, "let's get the boring stuff out of the way. Then we can eat and get to know each other."

"As I was saying—"

"I went back and checked. I did go to *three* of slimeball's presentations."

"All at his house?"

"Yes, at the log mansion."

"Did Bud give the presentations alone or did he have someone helping him?"

She frowned. "You mean like Vanna White changing the letters?"

"Yeah, kind of like that. Did he have anyone with him handing out papers or helping with PowerPoint presentations, that sort of thing?"

Kelene looked thoughtful. "It was just slimeball, I think." She thought some more. "Maybe he had someone help him, I just don't remember."

Pete pulled the head shot of Leslie Lehr from the manila envelope he had with him and showed it to her. "Do you remember if this woman was at any of the presentations?"

Kelene squinted at the photograph for a few moments, then dug around in her purse and pulled out a pair of rhinestone reading glasses and put them on and examined the photograph again. She looked up at Pete and said, "This looks like a high school girl."

"It is, but it's the only picture I have of her. Look at the photograph again, then visualize what she might look like ten or fifteen years later. Did you see a woman who resembled her at any of the presentations?"

She studied the photograph again, then shook her head. "No, I'm sure I didn't. I kept an eye on the women at the presentations in case any of them got too friendly with slimeball, you know? I don't remember seeing anyone who looked like this bimbo. Bud was a jerk, but he wasn't a pedophile. At least I don't think he was."

"How many potential investors were at the presentations? Approximately."

Kelene finished the last of her martini and seemed to think. "I don't know, maybe fifteen. Or it could have been twenty."

"All from around here?"

"No, the only people from around here were me and the Mexican. Or the dog killer or whatever I'm supposed to call him. The others were from Grand Rapids, Detroit, places like that. And some of the Mexican's friends were there, but they weren't from around here. At least I don't think they were."

They got their orders in and the conversation shifted to other things and Kelene had a second Pink Silk Panties. Pete was itching to get on his way, but waited patiently for her to finish the martini. When they got back to her house, she invited him in, but he politely declined, pleading that he had to get back for an afternoon meeting.

THIRTY-TWO

When Pete checked his messages, he saw that Joe Tessler had returned his call while he was at lunch with Kelene Brill. He called him back. This time he was successful.

"You're a hard guy to get ahold of," the detective said.

"I could say the same about you. I understand you guys released Gaz Ramczyk."

"More properly, the judge released him. Gave us a big lecture about due process and all that bull."

"Due process is more than bull."

"I know, I know, a figure of speech, okay?"

"Why haven't you brought murder charges against Ramczyk? You said it was a slam dunk case after you found the rifle. With murder charges, you could have continued to hold him, right?"

"Unless that senile judge granted him bail. Connie's still evaluating our evidence against Ramczyk. I guess she's been busy."

"Umm," Pete murmured. "Are you in your office or out and about somewhere? I have something I'd like to talk to you about when you have a minute."

"What is it?"

"In the process of digging around for background on the bogus legal opinions, I discovered some things I think you should know."

"Like what?"

"It's complicated and there are documents and everything. The best thing would be for us to get together so I can lay it out for you."

"Does this impact the murder case?"

"It might, you'll have to decide for yourself. But it's something I believe you should at least know."

After a pause, Teller asked, "Are you in your office?"

"Yes."

"Let me stop by in a half-hour or so."

When Tessler walked in, he looked like he hadn't had a good night's sleep in a week. He glanced at Pete's coffee pot and walked over and helped himself to a cup.

He sat down and took a gulp of coffee and shook his head. "Tired," he said.

"Frank been working you hard?"

"That, and woman issues. I'll tell you, the personal stuff takes more out of you than chasing down ten serial killers." He shook his head again.

Pete looked at him sympathetically. "I'll get right to it, then, before you fall asleep on me."

He handed Tessler a stack of paper held together by a large black clip. "You can read these news stories later, but the gist is that Bud Stephanopoulis was at the center of a scandal at his Philadelphia investment banking firm some years ago. It involved a client of his who was promoting what can be best described as Ponzi-scheme investments. A lot of people were ruined as a result. Bud himself skated, but he was pushed out of the firm. Later he got his comeuppance when he was forced to kick in about $17 million to settle investors' lawsuits and suits brought against him by his fellow partners. I think that's why he was running his scams in our neck of the woods. He was broke as a result of the settlements and was trying to recoup."

Tessler chewed on this for a while, then said, "This is part of your Ramczyk didn't do it, someone with a financial motive did theory, right?"

"Basically."

"But you have no names, right? Or have you come up with somebody?"

"Nothing specific from the Philadelphia scandal, at least not yet. I think a starting point has to be Esteban and Brill. There must be other disgruntled investors, too."

"We talked about this before. I'm sure Kelene didn't do it."

"Okay, but that still leaves Esteban and a flock of others. Kelene told me that at the three investor presentations she attended, most of the people there were from Grand Rapids and Detroit, with some from Panama."

A grin spread across Tessler's face. "Can you imagine Frank's reaction if I told him I wanted to go to Panama to interview unhappy investors?"

"I'm not suggesting you go to Panama. Take a harder look at Esteban. Then get a list of investors in Bud's deals and do what you always do, start digging. Grand Rapids and Detroit aren't that far away."

"I don't know," Tessler said, shaking his head.

"I'm not suggesting that you drop your case against Ramczyk. I'm suggesting you go down parallel tracks while you see if you can patch up the holes in that case."

Tessler looked thoughtful again. "Frank is still convinced Ramczyk's the one."

Pete shrugged. "Maybe he is. But I keeping thinking of the philosophy of my old mentor in the CID, cast a wide net and then narrow things down."

"You say that a lot, but there are different ways to work a case."

Pete shrugged again. "Just a suggestion."

Tessler stood to leave and said, "I'll read this stuff over tonight and see whether there's anything that changes my mind."

Pete nodded.

Tessler looked at him and said, "You do agree that Kelene Brill had nothing to do with this, right?"

"I have no way of knowing."

"She seems like too nice a lady."

Pete puttered around his office for an hour, brooding about the way Bud Stephanopoulis had covered up his past as well as what he was doing locally. His thoughts shifted to Leslie Lehr and he studied her photograph again. Then he picked up the telephone and called Effie Zepp. When she answered, he heard baby Tina crying in the background.

"Sorry to bother you again, Effie, but do you have a photograph of Leslie Wallace?"

For a few moments, all he heard was crying. Then she said, "I don't believe so. Why?"

"I have this feeling Leslie might be from the small town in Michigan where I live."

"Is it a poor community?"

"It's mixed. The county as a whole is one of the poorer areas of Michigan. But it's also a lake community where a lot of people with money have seasonal homes."

More silence, then, "That could be where she's from, I just don't know. I know she's from the Midwest, that's all. Sorry I can't be more specific."

He thanked her and hung up. He needed some air and walked down to the marina and sat on a bench and looked out. After a while, he punched in the number of the landline at his house. After four rings, it cut over to voicemail and he left a message for Julie that he'd be home in an hour. She was tubing with her friend Sarah and apparently hadn't gotten back yet.

He went back to his office and called Effie Zepp's number again. This time Aaron Isaacs answered.

"Aaron, Pete Thorsen. Is Effie there?"

"You again. What are you calling about now?"

"I'm trying to determine whether Leslie Wallace is a girl who was born and raised in the area where I live."

"Oh, God!" The line went dead.

Pete shook his head and dialed Effie's number again.

Isaacs answered, and when he realized who was calling, he said in a snarly voice, "We're getting tired of this, Thorsen. We're trying to put all the crap about Bud Stephanopoulis behind us and get on with our lives. I don't know what your racket is, but I'm getting sick of you calling every two minutes and dredging up the past."

In the background, he heard Aaron and Effie carrying on a heated conversation. After a minute, Effie came on the line and said, "Do you have another question?"

"Yes, I'm sorry to disturb you again, but if I email you a photograph, would you look at it and tell me whether the person is Leslie Wallace?"

"Of course." He got her email address and warned her that the photograph he was sending was ten or twelve years old. He scanned Leslie Lehr's photograph into his all-purpose printer and emailed it to Zepp.

Ten minutes later, she called back. "It's definitely her. Her hair has changed and things like that, but that's definitely Leslie."

THIRTY-THREE

Pete called Harry McTigue, and when he answered, said, "Well, we did it."

"Did what?"

"Confirmed that Leslie Wallace, the woman at Bud's former investment banking firm, Harrison Stryker, is Leslie Lehr."

A pause. "No kidding."

"Nope. You know that headshot of the girl you pulled off the computer for me? I just emailed it to a woman in Philadelphia who used to work with Leslie Wallace when they were both at Harrison Stryker. She knows her well and just told me there isn't any question that Leslie Wallace and Leslie Lehr are one and the same."

"Just with different names."

"Right. Maybe she got married. Or she might have changed her name for some other reason. Either way, it's the Leslie from right here in our little town."

"Does this mean you're going to buy me dinner?"

"I'm not only going to buy you dinner, but you can order the dessert of your choice. On one condition. That you tell me when Bud bought his house on Shorewood."

Harry was quiet for a few moments, then said, "It was before you bought yours, I know that. Maybe twelve or thirteen years ago? Something like that. In that range anyway."

"Do you know if Leslie Lehr was still in high school at the time?"

More silence. "Maybe. At least she probably was in college. Why is that important?"

"One more question first. Can you think of any way Bud would have known Leslie?"

"I don't know, she got tons of publicity. If he didn't know her personally, he almost certainly knew who she was. She was a star, like I said, and she was in the newspapers all the time. In a small community like this . . . But I don't understand what you're getting at."

"What would you say the chances were of Leslie Lehr ending up at Bud's investment banking firm if she didn't know Bud?"

"I don't know. She probably had her pick of a lot of job opportunities, being a star and all. Maybe she interviewed there and got hired."

"Just serendipity, huh? I don't think so. Too much of a coincidence. Either Bud recruited her or she went to him for a job. Either way, I think they knew each other before she went to work there."

"Okay, let's say you're right. What difference does it make?"

"I don't know if it makes *any* difference. But think about it for a minute. A young woman who was a star knew a man at Harrison Stryker who was one of the biggies at the firm. The man gets the firm entangled in what became a major scandal involving a client who was running Ponzi schemes. The young woman and four others at the firm become fall guys in the scandal and have their lives and careers ruined. The young woman disappears. Bud turns up dead."

"Are you suggesting that Leslie might have killed him?"

"I'm not sure what I'm saying. All I know is that, the more I think about it, the more I'm inclined to believe Gaz Ramczyk isn't the killer.

I think Bud's murder had something to do with the shady investment deals he was involved with."

"Intuition, huh?"

"Intuition backed by logic and facts."

"So what time are we going to meet for that dinner you owe me?"

"I need to check with my daughter first and I'll call you. Do you mind if she comes along?"

"Of course I don't mind. Then I'll have somebody interesting to talk to while I enjoy my delicious meal."

The man who'd killed Bud Stephanopoulis picked at his food and thought about his conversation with the clerk in the hardware store. *That thug is out of jail. How could they let him out with all the evidence they have against him?*

He used the remote to change channels, searching for the local news. He found a station with the anchor in the middle of yet another follow-on story about the zoning dispute. Then he moved on to a story about a dispute between Native Americans and sportsmen over fishing rights in an Upper Peninsula river, then the weather report, then the sports. Nothing about that thug being released from jail.

The man clicked off his television and sulked about the injustice. *He deserves to be locked up, for crissakes. Look at what he did to those deputies.* As he sat there, his anger shifted to Pete Thorsen. *He's the guy who's screwing things up. Always nosing around, looking for things, poking here, poking there. He was scumbag's friend, too. And he's tight with that idiot detective. If they happened to stumble on to something . . .*

When he went outside, the sliver of salmon on the western horizon was dissolving into gray. He stood and listened to the crickets for a few minutes, then walked to the shed and unlocked the padlock. He fumbled around for the flashlight on a shelf and worked the slide and cast the dim beam on the boxes of junk cluttering one corner. There was one more item he had to get rid of.

He moved the boxes aside with his foot and dropped to his knees and pulled up the loose board. He felt around in the opening until his fingers touched the canvas bag, then took it out and replaced the board and shoved the junk back to where it had been. He put the flashlight on the shelf again and slipped outside, making sure the padlock was secure.

After closing the kitchen blinds, he loosened the bag's drawstring and removed the partial box of .223 cartridges and placed it on the small table. He found a pair of latex gloves under the sink, and after putting them on, emptied the cartridges from the box, taking care that none rolled off the table. Then he began to carefully wipe each cartridge with a cloth before he returned it to the box. When he was finished, he wet the cloth and scrubbed the outside of the box before putting it back in the bag.

He looked at the cloth. The detective shows on television were full of cases where DNA had been used to solve crimes. He wondered if his DNA could be detected from the cloth. Or if they could tell that the cloth had been in contact with live ammunition. He didn't know, but he wasn't going to take any chances. He stuffed the cloth into the bag and would bury that as well.

Driving north on M-22, he thought about Thorsen some more and his anger began to rise again. *Meddling sonofabitch!* He passed The Manitou with the cars of patrons lining both sides of the road and continued on a couple of miles until he came to a dirt road. He turned in and parked safely away from the highway. He opened the hatchback, pulled on his latex gloves, and took the bag and his shovel and trudged into the woods.

Harry perused the dessert menu and settled on a chocolate brownie concoction with a generous scoop of vanilla ice cream. Pete and Julie agreed to split a piece of key lime pie.

Harry eyed Pete with a smirk on his face, like he'd already decided his friend wasn't going to be candid with him, and asked, "So what's your plan now that you know Leslie Wallace is the same person as Leslie Lehr and that Bud knew her before she went to work for Harrison Stryker?"

"I don't have a plan."

Harry rolled his eyes. "I *knew* that's what you were going to say."

Pete flashed his innocent look. "I'm just being honest."

"Maybe you should talk to Leslie's father," Harry suggested. "You said he lives south of Benzonia, right?"

"Right. At least he used to."

Julie jumped in and said, "I think Uncle Harry has a good idea, Dad. We should talk to Mr. Lehr. He might know about Leslie and Bud. He might even know where Leslie is."

Harry said, "Lehr's first name is Art. He's listed in the telephone book. I can get the address for you if you don't have a directory."

"I have one."

"Are you going to talk to him?" Harry asked, pushing for an answer.

"Let me think about it."

Harry and Julie looked at each other.

The conversation shifted to other things, and after a while, they called it an evening.

On their way home, Julie said, "I don't understand why you're so hesitant to talk to Mr. Lehr, Dad. How else are we going to find out what we want to know?"

"Right."

"Let's do it in the morning, then. It would be better to see him in person instead of just calling him on the phone. You can tell a lot by the way someone acts. You can't see those things when you just talk to someone on the telephone."

"I agree."

She was quiet for a few moments, then asked, "Can I go with you if you decide to go? I wouldn't be any trouble. Things worked out pretty well when I went with you to Philadelphia, didn't they? We're a team, right?"

"They worked out very well. And yes, we're a team."

"I can go then?"

"Let's decide in the morning. If I go, you go, how's that?"

Her face brightened.

THIRTY-FOUR

After Pete checked on the address and oriented himself on the county map, they headed for the Lehr farm. Julie kept up a drumbeat of conversation about everything from the new puppy her friend Sarah's family had just gotten to the number of days she had until she had to leave for college to the text message she'd just gotten from Susan Ettleman asking whether she'd made any progress on the two books she'd recommended.

She cracked the window and inhaled deeply. "It smells so much different out here."

"Farm country."

"Is this what it smelled like where you grew up, Dad?"

"It's been a while, but it's similar as I recall."

"This is like being in real America," Julie said, breathing in deeply again.

Real America, Pete thought, reflecting on his youth and how he'd wanted to get out of northern Wisconsin. It was a lot easier to romanticize farm life if you'd never had to live it.

"We must be getting close, Dad. That mailbox we just passed had 1144 on it."

They continued on down the two-lane asphalt road that was in need of pothole patching. Several mailboxes later, they came to the Lehr farm driveway. Pete turned in the gravel road and headed for the farm buildings at the top of the gentle rise. The house, a clapboard structure with a rooftop dish that seemed to be a fixture in farm country, needed a paint job and the barn's spine sagged like a broken-down plow horse. A dome-capped silo nestled close to the barn and a utility shed stood between the house and barn.

They got out and looked around. Pete pointed to a silver SUV that looked like the newest thing there and said, "Someone must be home."

They walked around the barn and saw a man in bib overalls and a railroad-style striped cap pitching manure onto a pile with a broad-tined fork. "Hello," Pete called.

The man glanced up, and from the look on his weathered ruddy face, seemed to be trying to place them. Finally he said, "If you're selling something, I'm not buyin' so you're just wasting your time."

"We're not selling anything, Mr. Lehr. We'd just like to talk to you for a few minutes."

The man stuck the tines of his fork into the ground and leaned on the handle with folded hands and stared at them. "What about?"

"Your daughter and a couple of other people."

"My daughter doesn't live here anymore," he said curtly.

"We know she doesn't live here. That's not what we want to talk to you about."

He took one hand off the fork's handle and said, "I've got work to do. I don't have time to talk to strangers who barge in asking a bunch of personal questions."

"We know you're busy, but this shouldn't take more than fifteen or twenty minutes. Can we sit at that picnic table and talk?" He waved a hand toward the table with built-in benches under a shade tree, thinking it would be a more relaxed setting than standing around in a sloppy barnyard.

Lehr didn't move. "Who are you?" he asked, scowling.

"I'm Pete Thorsen, a lawyer in Frankfort. This is my daughter, Julie. I represent a group of investors who might have claims against a person you know."

"Who?"

"Philippe Stephanopoulis. He goes by Bud."

At the mention of Bud's name, Pete thought he saw a change in Art Lehr's body language. "Don't know the man," he muttered.

"Your daughter did. Can we sit down and talk?"

"I ain't sitting down," Lehr said. "Anything else you got to say, you can say it right here. You got two minutes."

Pete abandoned the idea of getting Lehr in a more relaxed setting, but at least he would have preferred to get closer so he could better read his reaction to his questions. He looked at the slop Lehr was standing in and forgot about that as well. He said, "Stephanopoulis was the man who was shot while he was jet skiing on Crystal Lake. It's been all over the news. Does that joggle your memory?"

Lehr didn't say anything right away, then, "I didn't recognize the name."

"Okay, fine. When did your daughter Leslie first meet Mr. Stephanopoulis?"

"How do you know she knew him?"

"She worked for him in Philadelphia for at least five years."

"I don't know anything about it."

"I find that hard to believe. How about a man named Gaz Ramczyk? Do you know him?"

Lehr scoffed and spit into the slop. "That delinquent? Everyone around here knows him. Or knows *about* him."

"Did Leslie know him?"

"How would I know?"

"This is a small community. I thought you might know."

"Leslie's a good girl. I don't think she'd give a bum like Ramczyk the time of day."

Pete considered that for a moment, then said, "Gaz is one of the suspects in the Stephanopoulis murder case. He also was in jail until a day or two ago when a judge let him out."

"It's probably that damn fool, Frank Richter. That never would have happened if Bill Haskins was still sheriff."

"I gather that you think Gaz killed Bud Stephanopoulis, then."

"How the hell would I know? He probably did, though. Goddamned leach, sucking disability benefits off the government while he hangs out in the bars with every whore in the county and spends his days shooting all of those guns."

"Some people believe Gaz is being set up. That he's innocent."

Lehr spit into the slop again. "Innocent? He's nothing but a goddamned criminal."

"Mmm," Pete murmured. "At least some people think there might be a connection between the shooting and the Ponzi-scheme investments Stephanopoulis was peddling. The things your daughter Leslie worked on with him."

Lehr stared at them. "Are you accusing my daughter of something?"

"I'm not accusing her, but—"

"This conversation is over." Lehr started to pitch manure again.

"Have you talked to Leslie recently, Mr. Lehr?"

Lehr ignored them.

"Leslie left her job in Philadelphia and moved out of where she used to live," Pete said. "Can you give us her new address?"

Lehr pitched more manure and didn't respond.

"Has she moved in with you again?"

Lehr looked up and pointed the times of his fork at them and said, "That's really why you're here, isn't it? You're fishing around for personal information about my daughter. I told you, this conversation is over. You need to move on." He started working again.

"How long has it been since you've been in contact with Leslie, Mr. Lehr?"

Lehr turned around again, and even from fifty feet away, Pete could see his face turning a deeper shade of red. "Didn't I just tell you to leave?"

"Mr. Lehr —"

Lehr pointed the tines of his pitchfork at them and said, "Get off my land and do it now. You're trespassing on private property."

Pete wedged one of his business cards into a crack in a nearby fence-post. "I'm leaving my business card with my telephone numbers. Call me if you recover your memory." He walked back to his Range Rover with Julie hurrying to keep up.

On their way out the driveway, Julie said, "I'm glad you're not like that. He's terrible."

"He's a farmer. A lot of them aren't comfortable around strangers." He thought about his father.

"Did you see that target on the dead tree?" Julie asked. "He must practice shooting every day. The target has more holes than paper."

Pete had noticed that, too. He looked at Julie and said, "Don't read too much into the target. People in this area tend to be hunters. Maybe he likes to hone his marksmanship skills in preparation for deer season."

"I wasn't so much thinking about hunting as I was about Bud getting shot." She folded her arms and shuddered even though it was a warm day.

"Understand," he said, not wanting the conversation to go in that direction.

"I thought it was scary."

Pete kept quiet.

Just before they came to the county road, he noticed a new fence at the northern edge of Lehr's property and wondered about it. Everything else on the farm looked so run-down, but the fence was pristine.

Julie had been looking out the window on her side and seemed to be thinking. She turned back to him and said, "Do you think it was useful to have me along?"

"I do. You're a terrific observer of people. Plus, it's wonderful to take a drive in the country with my daughter."

"Thanks."

"Besides not being friendly, did anything else strike you about Art Lehr?"

After appearing to think for a while, she said, "I think he misses not having his daughter around."

"I agree. Anything else? Like, what was your impression when I asked him about Bud and Gaz Ramczyk?"

More thinking, then, "He hates Gaz, that's the easy one. Bud, I don't know. Maybe he *didn't* know him."

"Leslie knew him, we know that. Do you think he was being evasive when I asked about Bud?"

Julie thought some more and said, "He *did* act kind of funny."

"That's what I thought, too."

She was quiet for a few minutes. "I keep thinking about that target with all of the bullet holes." She shuddered again.

A mile later, she said, "How do you think Rae handles the situation when she runs into someone as unfriendly as Mr. Lehr?"

"She probably breaks his arm and then forces him to apologize."

Julie laughed. "Or maybe she takes out her piece and shoots off one of his toes."

THIRTY-FIVE

"**D**o you know where I can find copies of old high school yearbooks?" Pete asked when Harry answered his telephone.

"You mean yearbooks from our high school?"

"No, I mean from the high school in Saddlestring, Wyoming."

"Geez, you don't have to be so touchy. I don't have copies of the yearbooks. The public library might. If they don't have them, I'm sure the high school does. That's probably your best bet."

"The school year's over. Is there likely to be anyone around who could let me in?"

"I don't know. You can always call Jeffrey. I bet he has a key to the building."

"I'd just as soon not bother him. He'd probably give me a pop quiz on *The Sagas of the Icelanders*. I'll try the school and see if anyone is around."

"What are you looking for?"

"I went to see Art Lehr. He was evasive when I asked him about Leslie and Gaz Ramczyk and Bud Stephanopoulis. I thought I'd try the yearbooks and see if they have any useful information."

"Pete Thorsen the sleuth, on the hunt again."

"Just trying to clear my name because of the bogus legal opinions."

"Un huh. I'll be interested if you find anything. Dinner tonight?"

"Lovely idea. Julie is having another sleepover at her friend Sarah's house."

"You buying to make up for your rude behavior when you called?"

Pete sighed. "Again? Okay, I'll buy, but no dessert. I wasn't *that* rude."

The high school's front door was unlocked and Pete went in. When he didn't see anyone, he called, "Anyone here?" No one answered, so he followed the corridor signs to the administrative offices. The lights were on and he entered and called again. A neatly dressed woman with shoulder-length gray hair appeared from one of the offices in back.

"Can I help you?"

"My name is Pete Thorsen. I do freelance work for Harry McTigue at *The Northern Sentinel*. I'm thinking about writing some color pieces on people in the community. Do you have copies of the school yearbooks going back fifteen or twenty years I could look at as part of my research?"

She sized him up for a moment, then said, "What specifically are you looking for? Maybe I can help. I'm the school principal."

"That's kind of you, but at this stage, I'm just trying to generate ideas. I thought the school yearbooks might be a good place to start."

"Our library has copies going back almost fifty years. You're free to look at them as long as it won't take you more than an hour. I have to leave and lock up when I go."

He said an hour would be fine and she led him to the library, pointed to the shelves with the yearbooks, then disappeared again. He'd already figured out when he thought Leslie Lehr would have been in high school, and took the volumes for those years to one of the tables and started to look through the indices at the end of each book. He was off on his calculation by a year, so he replaced that volume and took the right one. He started with the latest yearbook and made notes of the pages where Leslie's name appeared. She was mentioned seventeen times.

He was flipping through the yearbooks when he heard footsteps. He looked up and saw Jeffrey Talbot coming around the corner.

"Marian told me you were here. You're looking for people to do profile pieces on for the *Sentinel*?"

"Right. I haven't produced anything for Harry recently, and he was on my back about it last night when we were having dinner. I thought I'd better get busy."

"You can only do so many Norwegian pieces, huh?" he said, glancing at the yearbooks spread out on the table.

Pete laughed. "That's what the boss thinks."

Talbot eyed the yearbooks again. "I talk to Harry regularly and he never mentioned anything about human interest pieces."

"It's something we came up with last night. People like to read profiles of people they know."

"I see."

"What are you doing here? It's summer vacation. I thought teachers coveted their time off and liked to stay away during vacations."

"Good teachers, the really committed ones, never *really* take vacations. We're always trying to add to our base of knowledge, to improve for the benefit of our students."

"I'm impressed. That's what all teachers should do."

"Anything I can help you with? This coming year will be my twentieth year at the school. I know this community and its people pretty well."

"I just might take you up on that after I come up with some ideas. Maybe we can have lunch someday when you're free."

"I'm usually available. We can talk about *The Sagas of the Icelanders* at the same time. It would be wonderful if we can find a way to collaborate."

When Talbot was gone, Pete resumed looking through the yearbook for Leslie's senior year. In the class picture section, he found the same photograph of Leslie that Harry had pulled up from his archives. Moving on, he found photos of her playing basketball and softball; playing the lead in the school play; riding down Main Street perched on the back seat of a convertible in a strapless dress, surrounded by her homecoming court; giving a speech in her capacity as student body president; and finally addressing her classmates as valedictorian on graduation day. In each case, there was a write-up ranging in length from a sentence to a paragraph or more.

Toward the end of the book, he saw an entire page devoted to Leslie's selection as the winner of the Aegean Merit Scholarship, which the blurb said was awarded to the outstanding student in the graduating class. He stared at the scholarship reference and remembered the name of the company Bud had been using as the sponsor of his local investment products. The similarity between the scholarship's name and Bud's investment company might be a coincidence, but he doubted it. It seemed to corroborate his hunch that Leslie's relationship with Bud predated the time she joined Harrison Stryker.

Pete went to the index again and looked for the name Ramczyk. It wasn't there. He opened the volume for what would have been Leslie's junior year and checked that index. Leslie was listed on numerous pages again. He continued down the alphabet and this time found Ramczyk's name. There were nearly as many entries for him as there were for Leslie. Captain of the football team and second-team all-state; scoring champ of the basketball team; all-conference baseball player; homecoming king. No academic honors though.

He continued to flip through the pages, and in the school life section, his eyes immediately locked on a photograph of a couple sitting together on a swing under a gnarled tree, holding hands. It was Leslie Lehr and Gaz Ramczyk. Over the photograph was a caption, "Dream Couple," and it was surrounded by a random collection of kitschy hearts. In smaller letters below the photograph, there was a quote from each of them, telling of their aspirations and plans for a life together. Staring at the photograph, Pete suspected that their relationship was hardly a secret around town. How could Art Lehr not have known about it?

He turned to the scholarship section of the yearbook, but the Aegean Merit Scholarship wasn't mentioned. He checked the earlier editions of the yearbook as well, but found no reference to it there, either. He opened the volume from Leslie's senior year and read the write-up again. It didn't disclose the scholarship's sponsor.

Out of curiosity, he checked the earlier editions of the yearbook to see what they had to say about Gaz Ramczyk. Beginning with his freshman year, he'd been the starting running back for the football team and in his sophomore year, he'd made first-team all-conference. Granted, the small high school wasn't exactly a national football powerhouse, but it was still clear that he'd been a pretty darn good high school player. His other athletic accomplishments were covered in detail as well.

Pete went to the copying machine against the wall, but not surprisingly, found he needed either coins or a password to use it. He had neither. He checked his watch and saw that his hour was almost up. He walked back to the principal's office and knocked on her doorjamb.

"Excuse me, I'd like to make copies of a few pages from the yearbooks. Fifteen at most. I don't have any quarters, but I'll be happy to pay you."

The principal gave him the password and reminded him that she had to leave in a few minutes. He went back to the library and got the machine working and copied the pages that were of most interest to him and reshelved the yearbooks. He shut off the lights and went back to the principal's office and dropped a five-dollar bill on her desk. She protested that that was unnecessary, but he insisted, thanked her, and left the building.

He got in his car and headed home to pick up Julie and take her to her friend Sarah's house. On the way, he considered telling her what he'd discovered about Leslie, but decided to wait. He might learn more that night.

When Pete got back from dinner with Harry, darkness had settled over the lake. He changed into the same clothes he'd worn the first time and got his tools out again and assembled the rest of his equipment. Then he got on his bike and headed for Shorewood Drive. The moon was just rising over the lake, and as he pedaled along, the sky seemed brighter than the night of his first visit. He would have preferred pitch-black, but it was what it was and he pedaled on.

He grinned when he thought about the story Harry had told him at dinner. After running into Pete at the high school, Jeffrey Talbot had gone directly to the *Sentinel's* offices and confronted Harry about the project Pete said he was working on for him. Harry spent five minutes boasting about how quick on his feet he was in situations like that, then said he told Talbot a story that more or less jibed with Pete's. Neither Pete nor Talbot received a dime for any of the work they did for Harry, but apparently professional rivalry wasn't limited by financial reward.

Pete got on Shorewood, and after laboring on the uphill stretch again, he reached Bud's driveway. He thought there were a few more houses with lights on before, but like the first time, he didn't see anyone outside. He put his bicycle in the brush where he'd hidden it the first time and walked down the driveway to the house, keeping an eye out for anyone he hadn't noticed before.

When he got to the side door, he glanced around to make sure everything was still clear, then dropped to his knees and began working with his tools. He felt the same anxiety he'd felt before and was relieved when he heard the tumblers move. He quickly took the flashlight from his teeth and switched it off and opened the door. As soon as he was inside, he disarmed the alarm system again.

He took a deep breath and made his way through the dark house to Bud's study. After making sure the blinds were still fully closed, he clicked on his flashlight and adjusted it so the beam was wider. He checked his watch and gave himself ten minutes. No way he was going to stay a half-hour like last time.

Then he began to quickly go through the file drawers, scanning the handwritten labels on each of the folders. The bottom drawer was filled with a potpourri of personal files. He saw a thin folder captioned "Scholarship." *Ah*, he thought. He laid the folder on his nylon carry bag and continued to search, looking for anything with Leslie's name on it. He found nothing. Then he went back to where he remembered seeing a "Miscellaneous" folder. It was stuffed with papers and he didn't want to take the time to look through it so he took the entire file.

He checked his watch again; his time was up. He scanned the room to make sure everything was the same as when he entered it, then left and hurried toward the mudroom. He armed the security system again and slipped out the door. Everything was still quiet, and importantly, there was no dog.

Back in his lake house, he got a bottle of water, put a Billy Joel CD in his player, and settled down on his porch to look through the files he'd taken. The scholarship file contained correspondence between Bud and members of the high school administration over a six-month period. The essence of it was that Bud had agreed to fund a scholarship for the "most outstanding" member of the graduating class. The scholarship was worth $100,000 over a four-year period. Bud retained final say regarding the student to whom the scholarship was awarded. Leslie Lehr had been chosen as the first scholarship recipient.

Billy Joel was just beginning "Piano Man" when Pete finished looking through the file. He was right, the relationship between Bud Stephanopoulis and Leslie Lehr *did* pre-date the time she joined Harrison Stryker. How it had started wasn't as important as the fact it existed. He took a swallow of his water and began sorting through the "Miscellaneous" file. It included many letters and emails relating to Leslie, including several that offered her summer jobs with Harrison Stryker LLC after her sophomore and junior years in college.

THIRTY-SIX

Pete left a note for Julie saying that he'd be back later that morning, then headed for Art Lehr's farm again. He'd been awake much of the night trying to figure out why Lehr had been so evasive when he'd asked about Bud Stephanopoulis and Gaz Ramczyk. It was clear both of them had a special connection to his daughter that he had to know about unless he never ventured out of his barnyard.

He parked next to Lehr's silver SUV, and when he got out of his Range Rover, he saw him across the field on his older-model John Deere tractor. He walked that way, and when he got closer, he saw that Lehr had wrapped a heavy chain around a large tree stump and was trying to remove it. He called, "Mr. Lehr, I need to talk to you for a minute."

Lehr looked up, like he'd noticed Pete for the first time. He moved the tractor's shift to neutral and stared at him for a few moments, then said in an irascible voice loud enough for Pete to hear over the idling tractor's engine, "What are you doing here? I told you before I had nothing more to say to you."

"I know what you said. I want to know why you lied to me."

"You sonofabitch! Coming on my property and calling me a liar! Get out of here or you're going to get hurt." He worked the tractor's gear shift and the machine started forward and the chain around the stump tightened.

Pete stepped in front of the tractor. "Shut off your engine and let's talk."

The stump's roots broke free from the ground with an explosive crack and the tractor surged forward. The sound startled Pete, but after taking a step or two back, he remained in the tractor's path. It continued to come at him with the stump thumping along behind. When Pete saw that Lehr wasn't going to stop, he jumped to one side to get out of the way, but tripped and sprawled backward. He got up just as Lehr steered the tractor toward him again. He stepped to his left again and grabbed at Lehr's leg as the tractor passed. Lehr kicked free and Pete backed away further. He noticed the lever-action rifle in the scabbard alongside the seat. Like the .30-30 his father used to have.

"Okay, Mr. Lehr," he said, brushing himself off, "your next visitor is going to be from the sheriff's office."

Lehr finally stopped and glared at him from his perch atop the John Deere. "You're trespassing on my property! Now get out of here!"

Pete backed away a few more paces. "What are you hiding?" he asked.

Lehr started toward him with the tractor again. "Get!" he screamed.

Pete retreated further. "Okay, okay, I'm leaving. But you're in big trouble, Mr. Lehr."

He walked toward where his Range Rover was parked and periodically glanced over his shoulder to see what Lehr was doing, hoping he didn't have his rifle out. When he got to his vehicle, he saw that Lehr was off his tractor and adjusting the chain around the tree stump. *Crazy bastard,* he thought.

Back on the county highway leading to Benzonia, the new fence caught his eye again. On a whim, he turned in the neighboring farm's driveway. In contrast to the Lehr place, it looked relatively prosperous and a whole lot larger. The buildings had been freshly painted and the equipment looked almost new. He parked near the house, and seeing no one outside, went to the front door and knocked. A minute later, a woman with silver hair and a white patterned blouse hanging loose over grey slacks opened the door.

"Hi," she said in a friendly voice, "can I help you?"

Pete was grateful that not everyone in northern Michigan farm country was as surly as Art Lehr and handed her one of his business cards. "I'm Pete Thorsen," he said. "I'm a lawyer in Frankfort. I have a client who is interested in acquiring farm properties," he lied. "Do you own this place?"

"Half owner. My husband and I own it jointly. My name is Evelyn Stojak."

"Nice to meet you," he said, looking around. "Good looking place. It must be a lot of work to keep it up the way you do."

She rolled her eyes. "You wouldn't believe the work. We're fortunate to have a great hired hand. Who's your client?"

"I can't disclose that right now. He wants to remain anonymous at this stage. We've just started to look around."

"Most people want to sell their farms these days, not buy one."

"I know. Tough times for farmers, huh?"

"Real tough. We're in a trough where prices are low and costs for fertilizer and other necessities are high."

"The farm to the south seems to be one that's fallen on hard times."

"Art Lehr's farm?"

"Yes. I just talked to him. He wasn't very friendly."

Mrs. Stojak lowered her voice, like she was concerned he might hear her, and said, "I don't know how much longer he's going to be able to hang on, frankly. He's down to forty acres now."

"When you say he's down to forty acres, what do you mean?"

She said in the same low voice, "When his daughter got in trouble and had to hire a lawyer, we bought his other forty from him. He came to Martin—that's my husband—and said he wanted us to have first crack at it because he knew us and our two farms adjoin. We jumped at the chance. We've got two hundred acres now. We figure only the larger farms are going to survive."

"I saw a new fence between your farm and the Lehr farm. Was that put in after you bought forty acres from him?"

"Yes. The old fence was falling down and we needed a new one anyway. The purchase gave us an excuse."

"When did you buy the property from Mr. Lehr?"

Evelyn Stojak's brow furrowed and she said, "About two years ago, I think."

"What did you pay if I may ask?"

She smiled and shook her head and rubbed one forefinger against the other several times. "Shame, shame, Mr. Thorsen. Marvin and I both graduated from the Michigan State College of Agriculture. You don't think I'm going to tell you the price so you'd know what to offer as an opener, do you?"

Pete laughed. "You can't blame a man for trying. You said the Lehr girl got into trouble. What was that about?"

"Leslie's a sweet girl, but like a lot of young people these days, she's ambitious and didn't want to be a farmer. She had a good job with some company out east, but then the company got into trouble with the government. That's about all I know."

Pete talked to her for a while about other things, thanked her and left, emphasizing that he was just in the exploratory stage of his work for his client and might be back to them if there was any interest.

When he was a couple of miles down the road, he pulled to the side and called Joe Tessler. For once, Tessler answered right away.

"I was just going to call you," Tessler said, "and find out if you have any plans for lunch. I can bring you up to date on the Ramczyk case. I also have a few personal things I'd like to get your thoughts on."

"I can't imagine what the personal things involve."

"Don't be a wise guy. Are you free?"

"What time do you want to meet at the bakery?"

"How about eleven-thirty. That'll give me time to wrap up a couple of things here."

Pete checked in with Julie, who'd gotten back while he was at the Lehr farm. She said her plans for the day were to spend time at the beach and read. After chatting with her for a few minutes, he left to meet Joe Tessler at Ebba's Bakery. They got their sandwiches and drove to the Elberta overlook. It was one of those rare days when there were no other vehicles around to get Tessler's dander up. He seemed to be in a good mood and ate his lunch as he gazed out at Lake Michigan.

"So, what's happening with the case?" Pete asked casually.

Tessler took a bite of his pickle and crunched on it for a few moments. "Connie is still dragging her feet, saying she'd be more comfortable if we had additional evidence against Ramczyk."

"Sounds like me, huh?"

He stuffed the rest of the pickle in his mouth, and while he was chewing, mumbled, "I guess. No prints on the weapon, conflicts in the description of the suspect."

"So what's next?"

"I don't think I've ever seen Frank so on edge as he has been this past week. He spends half his time bad-mouthing lawyers and the other half ticking off reasons he's convinced Ramczyk is guilty." He took the last bite of his sandwich, and with his mouth full, added, "I finally got him to let me widen the investigation."

"Does that mean you're going to look into the disgruntled investor angle further?"

Tessler nodded while he continued to chew. He swallowed and said, "That's my plan. I talked to Tomas Esteban again. And that woman, Kelene Brill. That's one of the things—"

Pete sensed where he was going and interrupted, saying, "I think what you're doing is wise. As I said before, besides Esteban and Brill, I'd get a list of investors in Stephanopoulis's deals and see who else you might want to look at."

"I have no idea where to get a list."

Pete realized he had to be careful not to stick his foot into something and said, "Promise you won't say anything about this to Kelene?"

Tessler looked at him suspiciously. "I guess."

"That day I stopped to see her? When she was in the kitchen, I saw a copy of an investor's list on her bookcase." Pete grinned. "I sort of borrowed it, shall we say."

Tessler rolled his eyes. "And you're going to let me be the second borrower, is that what you're saying?"

Pete nodded. "I'll get it for you when you drop me off."

Tessler swiped his napkin across his lips and looked at Pete again. "I don't want you to think that broadening our investigation means we're not going to continue to go after Ramczyk. I'm still going to be looking at him pretty damn hard to see if we can patch up any holes in our case."

"Understand. Staying on Gaz Ramczyk for a minute, I understand he was quite a high school jock. Second-team all-state in football, good basketball and baseball player, big man around high school."

"Yeah, that's the good side. I wasn't around here in those days, but according to Frank, he was also dealing dope, getting into fights all the time, was a suspect in a couple of burglary cases. Stuff that goes beyond the things you normally see in a delinquent his age."

"He used to date a girl named Leslie Lehr who was quite a star in her own right."

"That doesn't surprise me. A lot of girls are attracted to the jock bad boys."

"I looked at the high school yearbooks from those days. Gaz and Leslie were a hot number. I forget how one of the yearbooks described them—the ideal couple or something like that. I got the impression he was more the choir boy than a delinquent."

Tessler's eyebrows rose. "You looked at the yearbooks? Maybe when we have a couple of days, you can explain what that has to do with clearing your name on account of the bogus legal opinions."

"Just being thorough," Pete said innocently. "When I was in the army—"

Tessler rolled his eyes. "Okay, okay, I heard that story before."

"Old habits die hard," Pete said, grinning.

"Is there a point you're going to get to?"

"There is. Bud Stephanopoulis was also close to Leslie Lehr before she became employed by Harrison Stryker. I don't think it was a pedophile thing, more that he was her benefactor. Funded a scholarship for her, got her summer internships at his investment banking firm, got her hired by the firm after she graduated from college. Remember that stuff I gave you about the financial debacle in Philadelphia? That might play into this, too."

Tessler furled his brows. "I still don't see where you're going with this."

"Leslie was from this area and her father still has a farm south of Benzonia. I went to see him twice. He lied to me the first time and tried to run me over with his tractor the second time. Something is going on."

"Run you over with his tractor?"

"He was working in his field, trying to get an old stump out of the ground. Some of the things he said the first time didn't square with what I learned later, so I asked him about it. The next thing I knew, his big John Deere tractor was coming at me. He keeps a rifle on the tractor, too."

Tessler's eyes widened. "Did he threaten you with the rifle?"

"No, but I was getting nervous."

"Did he say anything, or did he just start at you with his tractor?"

"He accused me of trespassing on his property."

Tessler nodded a couple of times. "That'll probably be his defense. You were on his property uninvited and didn't leave when he asked you to."

"Joe, I'm not interested in pressing charges against him. I'm interested in getting to the bottom of all of this. He must have some reason for lying to me about Gaz Ramczyk and Stephanopoulis."

"If I'm following you, I think you're suggesting that this Leslie girl, Lehr's daughter, might have had something to do with the murder."

"Or maybe Lehr himself. The final thing you should know is that Lehr had to sell off half his farm to help his daughter pay her legal bills incurred in the scandal I told you about. Maybe Lehr blamed Stephanopoulis for ruining his daughter's life. He's angry as hell. You might want go out and question him."

"So this is your latest theory."

Pete nodded.

Tessler looked at him and said, "You know how you're always accusing Frank of flailing around? Think about what you've told me the past few days. First, Stephanopoulis's shooting wasn't a random act of violence, but instead had a financial motive behind it. Now you're saying that maybe the motive wasn't financial, but some other kind of grudge was involved, like Stephanopoulis ruined a young woman's life and her father took revenge. Do you see my point? About flailing around, I mean?"

"The path of true investigations doesn't always run smooth."

Tessler rolled his eyes again.

"I think you should look at Lehr, Joe, but it's up to you."

"Let me think about it," Tessler said. "Getting back to Esteban, I got some more information about him. I checked him out with the police in Panama. He's got a bad reputation down there. Got into an argument with some guy, and a few days later, they found the guy in a ditch. They suspect him of being involved in the drug trade, too. Might have some connection to one of the cartels, they're not quite sure. It's pretty clear he hated Stephanopoulis because of the money he lost in the Ponzi scheme. Kelene thinks he's a really bad actor, too."

"How did you happen to talk to her?"

Tessler looked like he was considering how to answer Pete's question. "That's the thing I wanted to talk to you about."

Pete sensed what was coming. "You didn't."

"No, no," Tessler said hastily, "nothing like that. You don't really think I do something like that with a person of interest in a murder case, do you? Do you think I'm an idiot?"

"What happened then?"

"Kelene called and suggested we meet for a drink. I didn't see anything wrong with it as long as we were, you know, just talking."

"You didn't go to her place, did you?"

Tessler's face showed his indignation. "No, Sherlock. We went to the hotel bar where you seem to like to take your women. Quiet, a nice place for conversation."

"Kelene got you smoking again, didn't she?"

"Why do you say that?"

"I smell fresh cigarette smoke in your car."

"Hey, I only had one or two, just to be social, you know? Then I had one when I took a drive around the lake to think about things. I hardly think that's *back* to smoking."

"You want my advice, Joe? Friend to friend? Stay away from Kelene until this is over. That was your first instinct, remember? I still think it's the thing to do."

"The different circumstances don't change your perspective?"

"Nothing has changed. You still have an unsolved murder on your hands and she's at least a person of interest."

Tessler glanced at his dashboard clock and said, "I've got to get going. I have a meeting with Frank in a half hour to assess where we're at. I'm going to wear my flak jacket to ward off his shots against lawyers."

On the way back to drop Pete off, Tessler said, "If I decide to pay Art Lehr a visit, with or without Frank's approval, are you interested in going with me?"

The question surprised Pete. "Sure," he said. "Should I bring my Viking bow to protect myself in case a range war breaks out?"

Tessler chuckled. "No weapons necessary. I'll have mine, which is all we should need." He was quiet for a few moments, then added, "A nice trip to the countryside will also give us an opportunity to continue our discussion about the other stuff."

Pete resisted the impulse to roll his eyes again. "I'll get the investor list for you."

THIRTY-SEVEN

essler called in mid-afternoon, after his meeting with Sheriff
Richter was over, and said he was going to see Art Lehr and asked
Pete whether he still wanted to go along. Pete said he did, and told
Julie where he was going. She didn't say anything, but seemed disap-
pointed not to be invited.

On the way to the Lehr farm, Tessler confessed that he'd decided it
wasn't necessary to clear the visit with the sheriff since they'd already
decided to expand the investigation into Stephanopoulis's murder. Tessler also admitted that his decision had been influenced by his reluc-
tance to tell the sheriff that he'd gotten the tip about Lehr from one Pete
Thorsen. In the circumstances, he thought that might push him right
over the edge.

Tessler used the remainder of the driving time to rehash their earlier
conversation about whether it was really necessary for him to stay away
from Kelene Brill until the investigation was over. Pete kept repeating
the advice he'd given him during their lunch a few hours earlier.

When they got to Lehr's farm, his SUV wasn't parked in its usual spot in front of the house. They decided to give it an hour to see whether he came home. While they waited, they sparred over what kind of music to listen to and finally compromised on a classic country station. Tessler lowered the volume so Pete could refresh his memory about his prior visits to the farm and his conversation with Evelyn Stojak. Following that, Tessler segued back to personal issues and his relationships with his estranged wife Taty in Chicago and Sheree Starr and Kelene Brill locally. Pete was about to go into overload when he saw Lehr's SUV coming up the driveway.

They got out and waited for him. Lehr pulled up alongside Tessler's Acura and stared through his open driver's-side window. Even with his cap brim shading his eyes, it was evident he wasn't pleased to see them. When Lehr didn't exit his vehicle, Tessler flipped open the leather case in his hand to display his sheriff's department shield and stepped closer to the SUV to show it to him. "I'm Detective Tessler from the sheriff's department," he said. "I think you've met Mr. Thorsen. We'd like to talk to you for a few minutes."

Lehr took his time getting out of his SUV and said, "About what?"

"Bud Stephanopoulis. He's the man who was shot and killed while he was jet skiing on Crystal Lake."

Lehr looked at Tessler for a moment, then shifted his gaze to Pete and glared. "I already told this yahoo with you that I didn't know the man."

"We have reason to believe you did."

Lehr's gaze didn't waver from Pete. He jabbed his forefinger in his direction and said, "Is he with your department?"

"No, Mr. Thorsen is a private citizen, but he does work for us from time-to-time. I asked him to come along because of the earlier conversations the two of you had. Mr. Thorsen said you tried to run him over with your tractor. That's a serious matter."

"I didn't try to run him over."

"Mr. Thorsen claims you did."

"He was trespassing on my property and I asked him to leave. He refused. I was working to get a stump out. It broke free and the tractor started forward. He was standing in the way. That's it."

Pete said, "Bull. You tried to run me over."

Tessler stepped between them. "Okay, okay, that's enough. I'll interview the two of you separately on that issue. My main reason for being here, Mr. Lehr, is to talk about the murder of Mr. Stephanopoulis. This will probably take a while. Is there some place we can sit down and talk?"

Lehr was still glaring at Pete. "I don't want this yahoo on my property."

"He stays," Tessler said.

"Okay, then I'm not going to talk," Lehr said. He started toward his house.

Tessler called after him, "Mr. Lehr, you've got a choice. You can talk to us here, or I'll put these handcuffs on you and take you to the jail where you'll stay until you *do* talk." As Tessler spoke, he unhooked a set of plastic restraints from his belt and dangled them in the air.

Lehr looked back at him. "You got no cause to take me to the jail."

"I disagree. What's it going to be?" Tessler dangled the restraints again.

Lehr put his hands up and backed away. "How long will this take?" he asked. "It's milking time. I got to get to my cows."

"Probably an hour. Maybe less if you cut the crap."

"That's too long."

Tessler sighed and shook his head. "You're wasting time, Mr. Lehr. It's either talk here or talk at the jail. You decide."

Lehr seemed to consider his options. "Over there," he mumbled in a resigned voice, pointing to the picnic table.

When they were settled, Tessler asked him, "Now I understand you claim you didn't know Mr. Stephanopoulis, is that right?"

"How many times do I have to say it, I didn't know him."

Tessler made some notes in his spiral notebook, then looked up and said, "Are you aware that Mr. Stephanopoulis endowed a college scholarship for you daughter?"

"I don't know anything about any scholarship."

"If you don't know anything about the scholarship, how did your daughter Leslie pay her college expenses? Did you pay them?"

Lehr waved a hand and said, "Look at this place? Does it look like I could afford to send her to college? I told her that lots of folks have done just fine without one of those college degrees, but she wouldn't listen."

"That's not what I asked. I asked how your daughter paid her expenses if she didn't have a scholarship?"

"And I told you I don't know anything about it."

"I don't believe you, Mr. Lehr," Tessler said, "but let's move on. Next question: Are you aware that Mr. Stephanopoulis arranged to get your daughter summer jobs with his investment banking firm in Philadelphia so she could earn extra money to pay expenses that her scholarship didn't cover? The firm is called Harrison Stryker."

"I just knew she never came home. I could have used her help on the farm, too, I know that."

"You don't seem to know much about your daughter, do you Mr. Lehr? Maybe you know something about this, then. Mr. Stephanopoulis was instrumental in getting your daughter hired permanently at Harrison Stryker, a job that would have been highly coveted by most college graduates, wasn't he?"

"I don't know who was responsible for that. Leslie was a good student. Everyone probably wanted to hire her."

Tessler made some notes in his spiral notebook, then looked up and asked, "Are you aware that when a big scandal hit Mr. Stephanopoulis's investment banking firm and they needed scapegoats to get out of it because of the regulatory people in Washington, D.C., your daughter and four other younger employees were fired and had their careers ruined? All five, by the way, worked for Mr. Stephanopoulis, who just skated in the whole thing."

"What's that mean, he skated?"

"It's an expression. It means he got off free and clear, without any consequences."

Lehr shrugged. "I don't know anything about it."

Tessler shook his head and said, "Mr. Lehr, I don't know why you keep lying. I happen to know for a fact that you sold off half your farm to pay your daughter's legal bills. If the bills weren't for the matter I just described, what were they for?"

"That's private."

"Private. In a murder case, nothing is private. I know you're lying."

Lehr sat sullenly and didn't say anything.

Tessler looked at him disgustedly, and said, "Do you know Alfred Ramczyk? People around here call him Gaz."

"I told this yahoo," Lehr said, jabbing a finger at Pete, "that he's a delinquent who's been around this area for years."

"My question was, do you know him?"

"No, I don't know him. I only know *of* him."

"Mr. Lehr," Tessler said, shaking his head disgustedly, "how can you sit there and say these things? We know that Gaz Ramczyk was your daughter's steady boyfriend during their high school days. How could you not know that?"

"Why are you asking me all of these things?"

"I'm asking, Mr. Lehr, because we know a lot about you and I wanted to see if your answers coincide with what we know. They don't. You're lying, plain and simple. The fact is you had a powerful motive to kill Bud Stephanopoulis. He lured your daughter away to college out east and got her hired by a firm where he was a big shot. Then he walked away from her and four other talented young people when the crap hit the fan. All of their lives were ruined as a result. You had to sell off half your farm to help your daughter pay her legal bills." Tessler stared at him for a long moment to let his words sink in, then added, "You know what I'm thinking, Mr. Lehr? I'm thinking maybe you killed Stephanopoulis to get revenge for what he did to your daughter."

"That's crazy!"

Pete watched Tessler and was impressed with the way he bored in. He'd obviously soaked up everything he'd told him even though at the time he'd seemed to treat the information casually.

Tessler didn't let up. "And here's something else I'm thinking, Mr. Lehr. After you shot Stephanopoulis, you've been trying to set up Gaz Ramczyk for the crime. You hate him for personal reasons and he's an easy target. He comes back from the war, having seen all of those horrible things . . . People who haven't experienced that themselves might think he's crazy and will do anything to anybody. You know what, Mr. Lehr? I'm thinking that you might be behind everything."

"I'm not going to listen to this crap anymore!" Lehr screamed as he scrambled to his feet. "I know my rights! Get off my property and don't come back without one of them warrants." He gave the picnic table a shove and Pete and Tessler put up their hands to keep it from tipping over on them.

They watched as Lehr stalked towards his barn and went inside.

Pete nudged Tessler in the ribs as they got up from the table and said, "God, Joe, that was brutal. You can be a tough S.O.B. when you want to."

Tessler grinned. "Years of practice. You can't be a weenie if you work homicide for the Chicago PD."

Driving out Lehr's unpaved driveway, Pete asked, "What do you think?"

"I don't know if he did it or not, but I think you're right, the guy's flat out lying. That is, of course, if all of the information you fed me is true."

"It's true, trust me."

"It'll stand up in court if that's where all of this takes us?"

"It'll stand up. I pieced the whole picture together."

"It's amazing what turns up when you investigate some bogus legal opinions, huh?"

"Hey, I've just been casting a wide net, like I was taught."

"Oh," Tessler said, looking away toward a field of young corn, "not that line again."

When Tessler didn't say anything else, Pete asked, "So, has Art Lehr moved up to number one on your suspect list?"

Tessler thought for a while. "I'd say I have three number one suspects: Lehr, Tomas Esteban and Gaz Ramczyk, and not necessarily in that order."

"You won't give up on Gaz, will you?"

"Not unless the facts establish that someone else did it. That lawyer of his, your friend Lilly McKenzie—"

"Lila," Pete corrected him. "And she's hardly my friend. I only met her a few times."

"Whatever. She's pretty slick, I'll give her credit for that. She's been playing the PTSD card for all it's worth, trying to milk sympathy for her client. But I haven't forgotten about the possibility that old Gaz went out for target practice one day and Stephanopoulis just happened to be in the wrong place at the wrong time."

"I said before and I'll say it again, he's almost too easy a target."

Tessler was quiet for a while, then said, "Well, if he didn't do it, there sure as hell were a lot of people lined up who wanted a crack at Stephanopoulis. The more I see of this case, the more I think that you were the only friend the guy had."

Pete grunted. "Friend or patsy?"

THIRTY-EIGHT

When Pete got home, Julie was sitting in a chair on the beach reading one of the books Susan Ettleman had recommended. She pumped him about the meeting with Art Lehr, and he gave her a top-line summary, basically saying that Lehr had been hostile and evasive, but that Joe Tessler had been ruthless with his questioning. She wanted to know what he'd asked, and he gave her another top-line summary. He had to do a soft-shoe around how he got some of the information he'd fed to Tessler, but his answers seemed to satisfy her.

After they finished talking, Pete said he was going to town to do a few things at his office. Driving along Main Street, he decided to stop at *The Northern Sentinel*'s offices first to check in with Harry who'd called a couple of times. Knowing him, he probably was looking for a dinner companion that evening. He parked right in front, and as soon as he opened the door, he saw Jeffrey Talbot huddled with Harry again. It was too late for him to back out gracefully, so he strolled in and said casually, "It looks like the top level staff is hard at work again."

Harry looked at him over his half-glasses and said, "Did your daughter tell you I called to invite you to an important editorial meeting?"

Pete shook his head. "She must have forgotten."

Harry had that look in his eyes that always telegraphed his sense that there was some news he should ferret out. He said, "She told me you and Detective Tessler had gone out to Art Lehr's farm to talk to him some more about the murder case. How did that go?"

If Harry had been alone, Pete would have laid everything out for him. He didn't feel comfortable doing that with Talbot there, particularly since his interest seemed to pick up at the mention of the murder investigation. He had the impression that Talbot fed on gossip nearly as much as he did on poetry.

Pete chose his words carefully and said, "With investigations, most of what law enforcement does is go around and talk to people. This was one of those occasions. All pretty routine."

"As a neophyte in these matters," Talbot said, "why were you with the detective? Do you have a part-time arrangement with the sheriff's department like you do with the *Sentinel?*"

Pete laughed. "No, I don't think Sheriff Richter would be interested in having me part-time even if I were available. I've just become personal friends with Joe Tessler and he likes to bounce things off me now and then, particularly about his love life. I wasn't doing anything so I agreed to ride along with him."

"Not doing anything," Harry interjected dryly, "except ignore my calls about the editorial meeting."

"Sorry, what did I miss?"

Talbot shifted in his chair and fussed with some papers, like he was pretending not to be there. Harry glanced at him and said, "Jeffrey has an idea for a color piece and I thought you should be here because of the project you're working on."

"I'm not trying to steal your thunder, Pete," Talbot hastily interjected, "so don't get the wrong impression. But I've had this idea about doing a piece on a family from the Arcadia area for some time. They came here by covered wagon in the mid-nineteenth century, before the Civil War, and were genuine pioneers. Wonderful story. I was just presenting it to Harry to see if he'd be interested. Then I was going to check with you to make sure it wasn't something that might infringe on your community profiles idea."

"Sounds interesting," Pete said. "What's the family's name."

"That's what makes this so exciting," Talbot said, his emotions visibly rising. "It's Coleridge, like the poet, Samuel Taylor Coleridge. I haven't run a genealogy check yet to see if the families are related, but you can just imagine what we could do with the story if it turned out that they are."

"That would be something," Pete said.

Talbot babbled on for a while, then said to Pete, "I know you love to write. Have you ever tried fiction?"

"I've played around with a couple of things. Nothing I've ever tried to get published."

"If you ever go to a fiction writer's conference, I'll bet you hear the phrase 'suspension of disbelief' at least ten times. That's what good fiction writers try to do, draw their readers so into the story that they feel they're actually a part of it. In other words, they get their readers to suspend their disbelief and live the story. Those words were first coined by Samuel Taylor Coleridge."

"Interesting."

Talbot's expression changed from excitement to concern. "Is the story about the Arcadia family something you're already working on?" he asked.

Pete shook his head. "It sounds like it's a great idea, though."

Talbot exhaled in relief and turned to Harry with the excited look back, obviously looking for a sign that he should proceed.

Pete had witnessed Harry's stoic demeanor when he wanted to put off a decision on some matter before, and watched as he made a show of giving the idea serious consideration. He drummed his pencil on his desktop a few times and made some squiggles on his legal pad. "It strikes me as a wonderful idea, Jeffrey. Give me a week to think about it. I want to review the personal interest pieces I've already got queued up. How do you think you'd spin the story if I'm able to give you the go ahead?"

It was like a dam giving way under the pressure of floodwaters. Talbot poured out his ideas, many of them woven together with the lives and times of the famous Lake Poets in early nineteenth century England. Fifteen minutes later, after the reservoir was dry, Pete took advantage of the lull and asked, "Jeffrey, you've taught at the high school for a long time. I was—"

"Going on twenty years," Talbot said proudly.

"Right, twenty years. Do you remember having a student in any of your classes named Leslie Lehr?"

Talbot looked at him with blank eyes. "Golly," he said, "I've had so many students over the years. What did she look like?"

"Back in those days, at least, she had short dark hair and a face right out of a teen glamour magazine. Average height, maybe a little taller. Very bright."

Talbot frowned as he appeared to think. "That description could fit a lot of my students over the years. At that age, most of the girls are dolls, if you'll pardon my use of a sexist term."

"I was just wondering. Leslie Lehr was a real star, I'm told. If you had her in a class, I'm sure you'd remember her."

Talbot looked thoughtful. "I've kept records of most of my classes going way back. If it's important, I can look through them and see what I find."

"When you have time," Pete said. "Here's my phone number." He handed him one of his business cards.

They talked about other things for a while. Then Talbot said to Pete, "When does your daughter leave for college?"

"Mid-August, six or seven weeks from now. She's been invited to walk-on for the women's soccer team at Cornell and has to be there early for that. Walk-ons, as you might know, have the potential to become regular team members and maybe even earn an athletic scholarship, but aren't quite there yet."

"College athletics are a big commitment," Harry said. "Does Julie know what she's getting into?"

"She says she does. She feels that she can handle both the academics and one sport. I know her, she has her head screwed on right. If it turns out to be too much, she'll drop soccer. Assuming they'll want her on the team, that is. There's no guarantee they will."

"Is she planning to take a poetry class?" Talbot asked. "I was so impressed with her at dinner that night. Not many entering college freshmen are able to quote Wordsworth like she did."

"I don't know what her current course lineup is. It changes every now and then. She doesn't have to make her final choices until registration."

"I really hope she takes poetry classes. I don't want to sound corny, but poetry feeds a person's soul. It nourishes the inner person, if you know what I mean."

Harry nodded sagely. "What's Julie doing to get ready for soccer?"

"She just started running again because endurance is a big factor."

"The two of you can run together," Harry said with a faint needling tone in his voice. "A father-daughter team."

"Oh sure, she only runs about three times as far as I do. Besides, I like to run in the mornings and she prefers nights."

Harry frowned and appeared to think. "Maybe I'll add running to my workout routine. You know, for balance."

Pete had been waiting for a chance to get back at Harry for the barbs he'd been directing his way and said, "Maybe if I learn to drive an ambulance, I can be a volunteer paramedic and follow behind you. You know, just in case you need resuscitation."

"Very funny," Harry said, shooting him a look.

Their banter bounced back and forth for a while and Talbot listened to them, seeming a little bewildered again by how two friends could go at each other like Pete and Harry did. Finally he gathered his papers, said goodbye and left.

Harry looked at Pete and said, "Anything else you want to tell me about the interview with Art Lehr? I got the impression you didn't want to say too much with Jeffrey here."

"I think Tessler is going to look at him some more. I can't figure out why Lehr's lying the way he is unless he's hiding something."

They talked a little longer and then Harry asked, "You available for dinner tonight? You can bring that daughter of yours along if she's not doing anything."

"I'll see what her plans are."

Harry got that faraway look in his eyes and he tapped his pen on his desktop a few times. "I should have asked Jeffrey if he wanted to join us. He and Julie got along so well last time." He checked the clock and said, "Maybe I'll give him another fifteen minutes and then call him at home. He doesn't carry a cell phone."

Pete rolled his eyes. "Whatever."

"What?" Harry said. "I thought you liked Jeffrey. He's one of the smartest guys in town."

"And also one of the most pedantic."

Harry glared at him and shook his head. "You Norwegians are always so judgmental. That's one of the reasons you're not revered around the world the way we Scots are."

Pete threw up his hands in surrender.

"Let's let Julie decide," Harry said. He put his desk phone on the speaker and dialed a number. When a female voice answered, he said, "Julie, this is Uncle Harry. I'm here with your father. We were talking about having dinner tonight. Are you interested in joining us?"

"That sounds wonderful! I've been sitting around the cottage all day going stir crazy."

"Your dad and I were just trying to decide whether we should invite Jeffrey Talbot. He's the local high school teacher you met that night a week or so ago."

"I remember him. He's a nice man. We can have a little party. That's what I liked about school. There were always people to get together with and talk and everything. Up here at the lake, everyone is so standoffish."

"Wonderful."

THIRTY-NINE

The next morning, Pete was getting some roadwork in after all of the talk the previous day about running and exercise. As he loped east on South Shore, he thought about dinner the night before. Jeffrey Talbot had eagerly accepted Harry's invitation to join them, and must have immediately turned to researching the names of Cornell professors who specialized in poetry of one stripe or another. As soon as he arrived at the restaurant, he'd begun pressing notes into Julie's hands and chattering animatedly about professors whose courses she should take. Pete suffered patiently through the dinner, but Julie seemed to enjoy it.

When he returned to his cottage after his run, he went through his morning routine and then had a bowl of plain shredded wheat for breakfast since he had no berries or bananas in the house. After eating, he called Joe Tessler who answered right away.

"Have you thought about getting a warrant to search Art Lehr's place?"

"For once, I'm way ahead of you. I laid everything out for Frank this morning before he left for the health club and I'm sitting here working on an affidavit we can take to the judge to get a warrant. I think we should be able to make a pretty good case for probable cause."

"Good. Anything else?"

"Yeah. You know why Frank didn't grill me that hard about getting a warrant to search Lehr's place?"

"No idea."

"Your friend Lilly is raising all sorts of hell about our treatment of Gaz Ramczyk. She's made half the press people in the country aware of his case and we've got reporters calling our office every five minutes demanding to know why we're hounding a veteran who's suffering from PTSD even though — her words now — we've got absolutely no case. I tell you, that woman's on a friggin' vendetta against us and we haven't even brought charges against her client except for the assault stuff and he even got out of jail after that. She's turning the guy into some goddamned war hero who's deserving of sainthood. To cap it off, I understand she's convinced a TV station from Detroit to send their top investigative reporting team up here later today with a camera crew. Lilly herself plans to come."

Pete gave up reminding Tessler of McKenzie's correct first name and said, "And Frank's not happy about it, right?"

"Batshit would be a better way of putting it. He's ranting about lawyers again. Strategy-wise, we figure the best thing to do is to let McKenzie play her game for a while, then upstage her by showing that Ramczyk is only one of *several* suspects we're investigating. That's why I need to get back to this affidavit."

"Anything I can do to help?"

"I've been trying to keep you out of it so I don't do something else to make Frank's mood worse."

"Use your own judgment. Personally, I don't care whether he knows I'm involved or not. He's the one that got me into this mess in the first place by laying that bogus legal opinion on me like it was a confession to a string of axe murders."

"That seems like small potatoes the way this thing is going."

"People keep saying that, but to me it isn't small potatoes. Anyway, my offer stands. I'll be happy to help with the affidavit if you want. I assume Connie is involved. I have a pretty good relationship with her."

A pause, then, "I'm about to go over to her office. You can join us if you want."

When Pete walked in, Tessler was already going over a draft of the affidavit with Connie Chapman. She handed Pete a copy of the draft.

After reading it, he said, "I'm not an expert, but this strikes me as kind of thin."

Both Chapman and Tessler looked at him.

"I think we can beef it up," he explained.

"If you have some suggestions," Chapman said, "feel free to add them. Just remember this is an affidavit. What we say has to be grounded in fact."

Pete began to flesh out the draft by incorporating a lot of what he'd learned while poking around on his own. He reconsidered a couple of his inserts and crossed them out and rewrote them. He also revised the part of the draft affidavit pertaining to his second visit to the Lehr farm when Art Lehr tried to ram him with his tractor.

Chapman read his revisions and said, "I agree this is stronger. The question is whether all of it is true."

"It's true."

"I understand the stuff you uncovered in Philadelphia; your daughter can corroborate that if necessary," she said. "It's some of the other things that concern me."

"Take my word for it, Connie, it's all true. The part about the scholarship Leslie Lehr got should be easy to support if we have to. The rest is true, too."

Chapman continued to look skeptical. "It's not the scholarship that bothers me. It's some of the other things . . ."

"Again, I stand behind everything I've added." He hoped his word would satisfy her since he obviously couldn't come clean about how he'd obtained some of the information.

Tessler kept looking at his watch, conscious of the time passing and the dog-and-pony show Lila McKenzie had orchestrated for that afternoon. In the end, Chapman signed off on the affidavit, but asked Pete to give them a backup affidavit without specifically addressing the source of some of his information. With that, Pete left them to finalize the affidavit and take it to the judge and try to get a warrant to search Art Lehr's farm.

Julie was interested in going to the press conference and Pete thought it would be a good educational experience. They arrived at County Government Center parking lot just before the announced time. The parking lot was already half-filled and crews from three television stations were setting up their operations. Their cameras were trained on the bank of microphones in front of a panel truck that was decorated with red, white and blue swirls and had prominent lettering identifying it as a PTSD Rehabilitation Institute vehicle. Lila McKenzie stood talking to another woman. She saw him and came over.

"Nice of you to come, co-counsel."

"Ha ha. I just thought I'd stop by and learn some lessons from the professionals about how to try a case in the court of popular opinion."

McKenzie didn't smile. "Or more accurately, how to shine the spotlight on an insular community that's all for war, but when the brave men and women who've fought for them return home scarred from the horrors they've endured, how they come under suspicion for every crime, large or small, that happens in the area."

"We've been over this before, Lila. I think you're overstating things."

"Am I? We both know that's what's happening to Gaz Ramczyk."

Pete shrugged. "That's why we have a criminal justice system, to determine guilt or innocence."

"Oh really? You call it justice when a redneck local sheriff tries to rail-road a veteran with PTSD and slaps him in jail even though he hasn't filed murder charges against him?"

"C'mon now, Lila, you know Gaz's arrest had nothing to do with the murder investigation. It was because he assaulted two law enforcement officers. He could have killed them. One suffered a serious concussion he's going to be dealing with for a long time."

"And why did Gaz assault them, as you say? Was it because he found them digging up a memorial he'd created to his fallen war comrades? A memorial that's sacred to him and is his way of dealing with the trauma he experienced? To jail him in those circumstances . . ."

"He's not in jail. He's free pending what happens on the assault charges."

McKenzie scoffed. "Free? He's got a monitoring device shackled to his leg like he's a convict in a prison chain gang. He can't even use the toilet without someone knowing about it."

"Lila!" a man standing by the microphones called. She looked that way and then walked over. She huddled with her team for a few moments, then stepped to the bank of microphones.

Julie whispered in Pete's ear, "She seems a lot tougher than she did that night at dinner."

"Gearing up for battle."

The cameras started to grind as McKenzie gazed around the crowd for a few moments. "Ladies and gentlemen," she finally said, "thank you for coming. This is a sad day for the Frankfort community and, indeed, for the entire country. A war hero who spent six long years in our armed forces, much of that time deployed in the hell-holes of Afghanistan and Iraq, returned home to repair his life only to find himself the victim of local law enforcement. A convenient target because of his condition."

She beckoned behind her and Gaz Ramczyk shuffled forward with his head down. Pete thought he looked a lot crisper than the last time he'd seen him. His camo pants and khaki T-shirt looked freshly laundered and pressed and his star-spangled do-rag looked new. McKenzie placed her hand on his shoulder and said, "This is Gaz Ramczyk, a young man who was born in this area, grew up here, went to school here, and regaled all of you with his exploits on the football field and basketball court and baseball diamond. After years of service to our country, Gaz returned home to try to put his life together again. You see, Gaz has been diagnosed as suffering from Post-Traumatic Stress Disorder, or PTSD for short, because of the horrors he experienced in Afghanistan and Iraq. For those of you who aren't familiar with PTSD, I'd like to have Dr. Naomi Turner, the head of our Institute, give you a brief overview."

Dr. Turner took the mic, and after summarizing her professional credentials, said she'd been head of the PTSD Rehabilitation Institute in Detroit for over twelve years. During that period, she said, she'd seen countless veterans returning from the wars in the Middle East who were suffering from PTSD. She went into a ten-minute discourse on the causes and symptoms of the disorder. She concluded by saying that she'd seen Gaz Ramczyk on two occasions and was certain he was suffering from PTSD and had referred him to other mental health professionals who concurred with her diagnosis. She said that the Institute had been funding medications to treat his disorder for the past year.

McKenzie took the mic again and proceeded to lay out a scathing indictment of the local sheriff's department and its "uncaring" and "harsh" and "knee-jerk" focus on Gaz Ramczyk for the murder of Bud Stephanopoulis. She stressed that he'd been provoked into his actions when he came home and found a horde of sheriff's deputies desecrating the memorial he'd constructed on his own property as his way of coping with the loss of his comrades in arms. By the time she finished, more than a few people in the crowd were dabbing at their eyes.

After McKenzie and Turner answered a stream of questions for twenty minutes, the cameras shifted to Sheriff Franklin Richter who'd been standing off to the side with Joe Tessler and two deputies. Richter tried to give a dispassionate summary of where they were in the case, stressing that Gaz Ramczyk was only one of several suspects they were investigating for the murder. He denied that they'd been harsh or unfair in their treatment of Ramczyk, and emphasized that Gaz was free in the community while the investigation proceeded. After McKenzie's spellbinding performance, Richter's presentation came off as flat and dull and pedantic.

McKenzie flashed a triumphant grin Pete's way as she helped her fellow members of the Institute load their props into their panel truck and prepare for the drive back to Detroit. Sheriff Richter was standing with Joe Tessler, watching them, and for a moment, Pete thought the sheriff was going to flip them the bird. Richter said a few words to Tessler, then spun on his heel and stomped toward the County Government Center's door.

Pete caught Tessler's attention and walked over to him. "Did you ever hear a bigger pile of crap?" Tessler asked. "Listening to her, you'd think we'd put Ramczyk in a set of stocks on Main Street where everybody could see him and then encouraged people to poke him with sticks and brand him with hot irons."

"I agree it was over the top."

"Over the top! There wasn't a speck of truth in anything she said. And not a word of sympathy for those two deputies he put in the hospital. Not one friggin' word!"

Pete let him vent some more, then asked, "Did you get the warrant?"

"I just got a text message from Connie saying the judge finally signed it. Do you know what the guy was doing for most of the day? Fishing. We pay those judges a lot of money, and the goddamn guy was out fishing instead of tending to his job."

"So when do you plan to go out to the Lehr place?"

Tessler glanced at his watch and thought for a few moments. "Maybe in the morning. I have to round up a team and do our prep work. Lehr seems like a bit of a nut case. I don't want to go out there alone."

"Do you want me to go?" Pete asked.

Tessler looked at him and decided he was kidding. "No, I think you'd better stay away this time." He appeared to think again. "Of course, if I'm ever going to be able to get Frank to go along with adding you to the team, it's probably now. He's desperate for a breakthrough in this case."

FORTY

When the late evening news came on, the man who'd killed Bud Stephanopoulis slumped on his couch and watched as the anchor made his talking-head introduction. The image on the screen changed to the County Government Center parking lot and the patriotically-painted panel truck with "PTSD Rehabilitation Institute" on the side and that woman standing in front of the microphones. Her words barely registered. He knew what she was saying, though. It was all a bunch of lies.

He'd seen Thorsen, too, when the television cameras panned the crowd before the press conference began. Then he'd seen him again later, bending the ear of that detective, probably trying to talk him into doing God knows what. He's probably the one who got that woman from the PTSD Rehabilitation Institute involved. The guy's dangerous, and he wished he would just go away. He dropped the remote on the couch and rubbed his temples for a while, trying to clear his mind.

Then he clicked off the television and went outside and looked up at the sky. The blanket of stars didn't comfort him like it usually did.

Instead, anxiety flooded his body. *Had he done something that might put that idiot sheriff onto him? How about the stuff in his shed? Was everything gone?*

Feeling tense, he unlocked the padlock and slipped inside the small building. He cast his flashlight's beam around the clutter for a few seconds before he moved the Sunfish to one side and pushed the workbench out of the way. He squeezed into the gap and removed the pegboard and piece of insulation. The compartment was empty. He flashed the beam across the floor and looked, but didn't see anything. He put everything back the way it had been, then checked under the loose floorboard to confirm that he hadn't missed anything there, either.

He left the shed and locked up. As he stood looking up at the sky again, he felt some of the tension drain from his body. The half-moon had cleared the horizon while he'd been double-checking the shed and it gave the night a peaceful feeling. He admired it for a while, then went into his house again and got the box out of his closet and began to look through it. Normally that comforted him, even exhilarated him, but tonight it didn't. He had too much on his mind.

After returning the box to the closet, he clicked off the lamp next to the couch and sat in the darkness for a while, feeling cold in spite of the June weather. He went to his bedroom and got a blanket and wrapped it around his shoulders and went back to the couch. He stared into the darkness some more and watched as the moonlight filtering through the windows created exotic shapes on the wall and moved slowly across the room.

Restless, he went outside again and got in his SUV and began to drive. When he came to the north shore of Crystal Lake, he drove west, meeting other vehicles only occasionally. He turned left on M-22 and proceeded along the west end of the lake. The moon was higher in the sky now and gave the water a soft sheen. A deer jumped out of the bushes and crossed right in front of him, prompting him to jam on the brakes. He breathed in deeply and tried to settle his nerves.

He knew where Thorsen lived, and when he came to his driveway, he stopped on the opposite side of the highway and looked in. Lights were on in his house, but the surrounding area was mostly dark. In the distance, he saw a vehicle approaching and he pulled onto the highway again and proceeded south, going slowly. The vehicle dimmed its lights out of courtesy, and when it was past him, he watched in his rearview mirror until it was out of sight.

South Shore Drive was just ahead and he considered making a U-turn to go past Thorsen's house again. Instead, he turned left and followed the road east along the lake. A half-mile along, he thought he saw something flash in the moonlight. When he got closer, he saw that it was a woman with neon strips on her shoes and top, out for a run. He watched intently as he got closer to her, hugging the opposite side of the road and maintaining his slow speed. *That's Thorsen's daughter.* She gave a little wave as he passed, but paid no other attention to him. He watched in his rearview mirror to make sure she didn't turn to look back.

Pete kept checking his watch the next morning, anxious to hear from Joe Tessler about his search of Art Lehr's place. Tessler finally called about noon.

"Are you home?"

"I am."

"I'm on my way back from the Lehr farm. Let me stop by and fill you in before I go to the office and brief Frank."

Tessler arrived a half-hour later. Julie was at the beach, reading, and when Tessler drove in, Pete saw her look up from her book. She waited until the detective was on the screened porch with Pete, then got up from her chair and wandered casually towards the house, beach towel slung over one shoulder and book in hand. She came up the steps with her flip-flops slapping the wood, and when she was inside, she poked her head through the French doors and said, "Hi, Joe."

Pete, not wanting to appear to be excluding her, said, "Joe and some of his people just searched Art Lehr's place. He's about to tell me about it. Want to join us?"

"Sure," she said. She disappeared and was back in about thirty seconds in a cover-up with a bottle of water in her hand.

"I'm glad I had three of our deputies with me," Tessler began, "because for a while, I thought things might get dicey. I presented the warrant and Lehr spent about ten minutes staring at it. I finally started to paraphrase the language of the warrant and tell him what it authorized us to do, when all of a sudden he threw the thing back at me and said he had nothing to say to us and walked away. I followed him because I was afraid he might be going to get one of his guns."

Julie listened with widened eyes.

"Lehr went out by his barn and started to work like we weren't even there. I had one of the deputies watch him and the rest of us began our search. Talk about firearms. Between his house and the one he keeps on his tractor, we found five long guns and two pistols."

"Were any of them .223 caliber?"

"None of the ones we found."

"There are lots of places to hide weapons on a farm," Pete said. "How thorough of a search did you make?"

"Pretty thorough. We searched all of the buildings, the hay loft, the silo, looked for places that were dug up where he might have buried something, checked the machinery, things like that. I'm not saying we couldn't have missed something, but we did a pretty thorough job."

"Anything else?"

"We found a lot of memorabilia relating to his daughter, Leslie. Pictures, copies of newspaper articles, awards going back to the time she was in 4-H Club, everything you can imagine. All in a cardboard box he keeps in a closet."

"Did you take the stuff with you?"

"We didn't because I wasn't sure our warrant covered it. Plus, when we were looking through the box, Lehr came into the house and went crazy. That's the only time he said anything after he told us he wasn't going to talk."

"I can understand that, Dad," Julie said. "Think of how you'd react if someone said he was going to take the things you've been saving in that file cabinet since I was three years old?"

Pete knew she was right.

"One more thing," Tessler said. "I don't know if you noticed it when you were there, but the guy obviously target practices a lot. A paper target we found pinned to a dead tree was peppered with bullet holes. We found eighteen spare targets in that shed of his, too. Even by this area's standards, the guy burns through a lot of rounds."

"Dad and I noticed the target when we were out there," Julie said.

Tessler nodded. "Do you know what one of our junior deputies said? He's only two years out of the police academy, and he said one of their guest lecturers told the cadets that things like that can be a sign of deep-seated anger. He takes a gun out and starts blasting away to relieve tension. That's consistent with the way the guy acts in general."

"Getting back to the memorabilia, how carefully did you look through it?"

"Reasonably carefully. Besides the items I mentioned, there was a ton of stuff from her high school days. Things parents like to keep. Old tests, things she wrote, essays and the like. But we didn't make an inventory if that's what you're getting at. There were probably two hundred items in that box."

Pete didn't say anything for a while, then, "So, where does that leave us?"

Tessler looked at him, then at Julie, and said, "I came out here to talk to you personally, because when we were about to leave, Lehr said something like, 'Thorsen is behind this, isn't he?' It was clear that you aren't exactly his favorite person. I tell you this because I know you, the way you like to keep digging and everything. You need to stay away from Lehr. I don't know if he killed Stephanopoulis, but I have the feeling the guy's on the edge and could be dangerous."

"You took all of his guns."

"We *think* we took them all, but we can't be sure. I'm not kidding, Pete. My advice is to stay clear of this guy."

"Before you go, is there any way I can get a look at the things Lehr has from Leslie's high school days?"

Tessler frowned. "What exactly would you be looking for?"

"I don't know. But the more I think about it, the more convinced I am that Leslie is involved in this somehow. Something in the memorabilia might shed light on her relationship with Bud. You can never know too much."

Tessler stared at him for a long time, then a grin spread across his face. "You've finally dropped the pretense that your poking around doesn't involve the murder, haven't you?"

"I think you should talk to Connie about getting an expanded search warrant," Pete said. "I'll join you if you want."

FORTY-ONE

"Pete, Connie Chapman. Have you talked to Joe since his people searched the Lehr farm?"

"A couple of hours ago."

"Then he probably told you that things got ugly."

"That's what he said."

"I went through seven kinds of hell getting our search warrant approved. When Judge Trimble finally got back from his fishing outing, I caught him at his house. You're not a litigator so you probably don't know the judge, but the closer he gets to retirement, the crankier he gets when it comes to the Fourth Amendment."

"You obviously satisfied him because he signed the search warrant."

"He signed it, but I'm still worried. According to Joe, Lehr was ranting about you harassing him and that the sheriff's department is now doing the same. If Lehr gets lawyered up, I'm concerned that something might come back to bite us. And it's not just that evidence found in the search might be barred. I'm worried about a civil lawsuit, too."

"I told you, we can support everything in that affidavit."

"That's the reason for my call. I think it'll look better if we already have a file with supporting evidence rather than if we scramble around if and when the doo-doo hits the fan. It'll make it look more like we had probable cause for the search from the get-go."

"Makes sense."

"You said you have documents to support the affidavit. Can you drop off copies so I can start to build a file?"

"Sure, give me a day or so to collect them. Did Joe mention my suggestion that you get an amended warrant so we can take a closer look at the memorabilia relating to his daughter? Assuming you feel an amended warrant is necessary, that is."

Chapman paused for a long time. "Do you really think we need to look at that stuff again? Joe looked through it and said he didn't see anything."

"There may not be anything, but I think we should be sure. Do you think the warrant is broad enough to cover the memorabilia?"

"Geez, I'd hate to go back to Judge Trimble."

"You might not have to if you think the warrant is broad enough."

She was quiet for a minute and he assumed she was reading the warrant. "Looking at this," she said, "I think you could interpret it as extending to the documents. I'm not sure Judge Trimble would see it the same way."

"Do you want to tell Joe he can go ahead without an amended warrant then?"

"Pete, you can be a real pain in the rear. If I say yes, you better tell me that we're going to find something."

"I can't give you any assurances. But given that the investigation hasn't turned up a solid case against anyone yet, I think we need to have a look."

Chapman sighed. "I'll tell Joe. And ask him to coordinate with his new boss."

As Pete started to gather documents for the prosecuting attorney, he realized that he should have copied more pages from the yearbooks. He checked the time and wondered if the principal was at the school again. The telephone directory listed only the general number and a hotline number for parental use. He called those numbers and got recorded messages that the school was closed for the summer. The school building was only a dozen blocks away; he decided to drive over and see if he'd get lucky and catch Marian there a second time.

When he arrived, he saw two cars parked in front and hoped that one of them belonged to the principal. The front door was unlocked again and he wound his way through the corridors to the administrative offices. When he got close, he heard voices. He walked in and saw Jeffrey Talbot talking to the principal. He said, "Am I interrupting a high-level school conference?"

They both looked mildly surprised to see him. Talbot said, "More yearbook research?"

Pete tried to maintain a sober expression and said, "Actually, I wanted to see what the school library has in the way of works on the Lake Poets. I'm thinking of doing a piece on the Coleridge family in Arcadia."

After initially blanching, Talbot saw he was kidding and said with a touch of pride, "We do have quite a nice little library here. Very competitive with the libraries of other high schools of similar size around the state. There aren't many public high schools that have eleven scholarly works on the Lake Poets."

"Very impressive," Pete said. "Marian, I need to copy a few more pages from the yearbooks that I should have copied the first time. Can I use your copying machine again?"

"Feel free. You still have a credit from the last time you were here."

"Thanks, but I'll keep track of the number of pages I copy and pay on my way out. Do my part to support the school."

"Do you remember how to find the library?" she asked.

"I do."

"Anything I can do to help?" Talbot asked.

"Thanks, but I'm one of those creatures who thinks better when he's alone."

"It wouldn't be a problem. Marian and I were just kibitzing about the new school year. Nothing we can't do later."

"Let's stick with the game plan we discussed and have lunch when I get some ideas we can kick around."

He started to walk out again when Talbot interrupted a second time. "Remember that day in Harry's office when you asked me about a girl named Leslie Lehr? I must have had a brain fart or something at the time, if you'll both pardon my barnyard language. Maybe too many thoughts about Samuel Taylor Coleridge rumbling around in my head. Of course I remember Leslie. Great student, fabulous person. If I remember correctly, she's the first member of her family ever to go to college."

"Umm," Pete murmured.

"I've lost track of her, though. I believe she went to college somewhere out east. Are you considering her for one of your profiles?"

"You're way ahead of me Jeffery."

Pete found the library and carried the four yearbooks from Leslie's years in high school to a nearby table and put Post-it notes on the pages he wanted to copy. Then he reacquainted himself with the mechanics of the dated machine, plugged in the access code, and began the copying process. When he was finished, he put the yearbooks back on the shelf, turned off the lights, and walked back to the administrative offices.

Talbot was still there, talking to Marian. Pete gave her another five-dollar bill to pay for the copies. He brushed aside her protests over the amount again, and asked, "One question before I go. What's the story behind the Aegean Merit Scholarship? It was awarded once, and from what I can tell, never again."

Marian frowned. "When was it awarded?"

Pete looked at his sheaf of papers and gave her the year.

"That was before I came."

"Do you know, Jeffery?" Pete asked.

Talbot appeared to think. "Boy, that was a long time ago. I vaguely remember it. As I recall—and don't hold me to this—the sponsor decided not to continue the scholarship."

"That's kind of what I thought might have happened. Another question. Bud Stephanopoulis, the guy who was shot, had a company called Aegean Capital Partners LLC. The scholarship also had Aegean in the name, which seems a bit of a coincidence. Was Stephanopoulis or his company the scholarship donor?"

Talbot thought again. "I'm really not sure about that, either. I can't say if there was a connection or not."

"No problem, just curious." Pete said his goodbyes and left.

Back in his office, Pete went through the pages he'd copied from the yearbooks to see what he could use to support the affidavit. For a parent, that was like going through the life of a model high school student created for others to emulate. He particularly enjoyed some of the testaments to Leslie's athletic career because of the success Julie had enjoyed at her prep school. He looked at the "Favorites" page from Leslie's senior year, which listed her favorite pig-out food, her favorite historical character, her favorite rock band, her favorite movie actor, her favorite color, and . . . Near the bottom of the list, she'd named Jeffrey Talbot as her favorite teacher. He smiled. If Leslie hadn't left a lasting impression on him, he certainly had left one on her.

FORTY-TWO

The man who'd killed Bud Stephanopoulis slowed to a near stop again when he came to Thorsen's driveway. Like last time, it was one of the few houses in the area with lights on. The man increased his speed a bit when he saw a vehicle's headlights round the bend in the road behind him. The vehicle caught up to him at the junction of M-22 and South Shore Drive and he let it pass. He proceeded on until he came to a narrow side road that ran along the south end of a field that was used for youth recreational activities. He turned in and parked near some tennis courts, enjoying the quiet.

Ten minutes later, he pulled out and turned left on the highway, then right again on South Shore. As he drove along the lake, the moonlight shimmered on the water, turning it into a blanket of dark molten silver. His headlights picked up a couple walking their dog, a large animal, like a Russian wolfhound. He veered left as he passed them and the woman waved her hand in appreciation. He continued on, and while he met a couple of vehicles, he didn't see any other dog walkers or runners.

When he came to the end of South Shore, he reversed directions and headed west again. He turned right on M-22, and when he came to Thorsen's driveway, he slowed like he had before. He passed at a crawl, and when he came to a place where the road widened at bit on the opposite side, he made a U-turn and pulled over and parked snug against the embankment.

He sat there for a half-hour, watching the road. When he saw a flash near Thorsen's driveway, his pulse beat faster. *Maybe she was running tonight after all.* He saw the flash again farther south on M-22, and turned off his headlights so he could see better, but didn't see additional flashes. He started his engine and pulled onto the highway, using only his daytime running lights. In the distance, he saw an oncoming vehicle and switched his headlights back on.

He turned left at the junction, continuing to look for flashes, but didn't see any. He didn't want her to see him drive past so he turned into a horseshoe drive that served a half-dozen houses along the lake and parked near some lilac bushes where summer residents often parked during the height of the season. He shut down his engine and turned off the lights. Then he leaned back and waited. Ten minutes passed, then twenty, then a half-hour. Nothing. What if someone saw him sitting there in his car? He tilted his seat back more so he'd be less noticeable, but could still see the road.

After nearly an hour, he saw flashes again. They bobbed up and down, like the rhythm of a person running. He moved his seat more upright so he could see better. She came into view, running smoothly, passing right in front of him, a hundred feet away. He watched until she faded into the semi-darkness and all he could see was an occasional flash. Then the flashes stopped. She probably turned on M-22, he thought. He twisted his wrist so he could see the face of his watch in the moonlight. He'd give her ten minutes.

When the allotted time was up, he started his engine and turned on his running lights again. He eased out of the horseshoe drive onto South Shore, then turned his headlights on as he turned right on

M-22. The road ahead was clear as he drove along at little more than idle speed. He slowed further to a near stop when he approached the Thorsen driveway and looked in again.

"How was the run?" Pete asked.

"Wonderful. You know that old fairy tale about the porridge not being too hot and not too cold? That's the way it is tonight. Perfect for running."

"You should sleep well."

"You know, I'm not even tired. I realize it's past bedtime for you older men, but if you can keep your eyes open for a while, it'd be a great night to sit on the porch and look at the moon and talk."

"Sounds like a plan. Just promise you'll nudge me if I doze off."

"How about if I kick your shin?"

"That'll get my attention."

"I'll be back in five after I take a quick shower."

When Julie came back, she was wrapped in a robe and licking an orange Dreamsicle. "Is there any news about the investigation I don't know?" she asked.

Pete filled her in on the search of the Lehr farm. He didn't remember whether he'd mentioned it, so he also told her about his visit with Evelyn Stojak and how she'd told him that Art Lehr had been forced to sell them part of his farm to raise money to pay his daughter's legal bills.

"That's terrible," she said, shaking her head. After thinking for a few moments, she added, "Remember that day when we were at Mr. Lehr's farm and I said I thought that he misses his daughter?"

Pete nodded. "I think you were right on the money."

"Wow, a compliment. Does that mean you're going to keep me on your investigating team?"

"I don't see why not."

Julie looked pensive and said, "The story is gradually coming out, isn't it Dad?"

"Gradually, but things are still murky."

"Meaning?"

"There seems to be a lot of people who had a motive to kill Bud, but that's where it seems to stop. You can't charge a person with murder just because he — or she — had a motive."

"There's only one she, right?"

"That we know of. That woman Kelene Brill I told you about."

"Women don't kill as many people as men."

"Have you heard about Bonnie and Clyde? She was as bloodthirsty as he was. More, even."

"Yeah, but that was a movie."

"A movie based on real characters. Bonnie and Clyde were real-life gangsters during the Great Depression."

She looked at him coyly and said, "That was eons ago. The female species has evolved a lot since then."

"Right."

"Seriously, Dad, who do you think killed Bud?"

"I'd only be guessing."

"Go ahead and guess. I'm not asking you to forfeit something if you're wrong."

"It would be tragic, but it's looking more and more like Leslie's father had something to do with it."

FORTY-THREE

"You're convinced it's worth the flack to take another look at Lehr's memory lane stuff, huh?" Tessler asked.

"I do."

"Connie told me you convinced her we should take a more expansive reading of the existing warrant."

"Are you comfortable with that?"

"I'd like to have more specificity, but given how everything we try to grab onto in this case seems to go nowhere, I figure we have to take a chance."

"So, what's the plan?"

"I don't have one," Tessler said. "I understand you're my new boss. I thought you'd give me orders."

"I suppose the next time you see me, you'll salute, right?"

"Yeah, maybe using my middle finger. Seriously, though, any ideas?"

"I think you should press your search team into action again and go out and commandeer the box. When you bring it back, I'll go through it with you. Hopefully, we'll find something that steers you in the right direction."

"Like I told you, the last time we touched that box, Lehr went bananas. A better plan might be for you to come with us. If we can't take the box without starting World War III, you can go through it right on the spot."

Pete sat in the front seat of Tessler's Acura and two cruisers with a pair of deputies in each followed behind. Pete thought that was overkill, but Tessler argued that a show of force was usually the best approach. Tessler used the driving time to rehash the increasing complexities of his love life. When they reached Lehr's driveway, they saw his SUV parked near the house. The law enforcement caravan pulled in and parked behind the SUV and everyone got out. Of the six of them, only Pete was unarmed even though he was the one most likely to be the target of Lehr's ire.

Lehr must have heard them arrive because he came out of his barn. When he saw the six men, four in uniforms, arrayed in front of him, he stopped, clearly taken aback.

"Mr. Lehr," Tessler called, "we're here to complete our search." He waived the warrant in the air. "Are all of your buildings unlocked?"

Given the distance, Pete couldn't tell if Lehr was staring at him, but it was a fair assumption he was. He kept back and let Tessler handle things. Lehr didn't move. He also didn't say anything.

"Did you hear me?" Tessler called.

Lehr continued to just stare at them.

Tessler and two deputies started toward him. "As you know, Mr. Lehr, our warrant entitles us to enter any of the buildings on your premises with or without your permission. We'd prefer to do it with your consent, though, just like last time we were here. Do you consent?"

Lehr finally spoke, and the tone of his voice was more temperate than Pete expected. "You already searched every damn place on this farm."

"We didn't complete our search. That's why we're here now."

Pete watched the scene play out, and with Tessler's continued pressure, Lehr's will to resist seemed to wither. He waved his hand and turned and shuffled back into the barn. The two deputies with Tessler hurried after him.

Tessler came back to where Pete was standing and said, "That was easier than I expected. Let's get you in the house before the old coot sticks his head out of that barn again." He told one of the remaining deputies to go through the pretense of searching outside and motioned for the other to follow him. As soon as they entered the house, Pete smelled stale food in the stuffy space and saw what a mess the house was. Dishes littered the sink, the kitchen garbage can overflowed with refuse, old magazines were scattered around. Tessler fanned the air in front of his face and said, "Jesus, I forgot how much this place needs a good airing out."

Tessler hurried down the hall and came back with a large corrugated box and plopped it on the kitchen table. He fanned the air again. "It's all yours, Sherlock. Don't tarry. Vince is going to watch the door in case Mr. Lehr decides to pay you a visit. I'm going to do my searching out in the fresh air."

Pete wanted to join him, but opened the box and began looking through it. Like everything else in the house, it was disorganized and items had been tossed in willy-nilly. Either that or Tessler's people had made a mess of it the first time they searched. In either case, it was the opposite of his file on Julie which was organized according to year and activity.

On top of the clutter was a rumpled watercolor of a farm scene with a child's depiction of animals, all Holstein cattle except for one chicken. It had been signed by Leslie with a prominent scrawl, and seeing it brought back memories of Julie's childhood. He laid the watercolor on the table and reached in for a handful of other documents—the ubiquitous 4-H Club certificates and awards, school grade reports, yellowed clippings from *The Northern Sentinel* chronicling the exploits of sports teams Leslie had been on. He was tempted to read some of them, but reminded himself of his charge to go through the box quickly and then leave, hopefully without a confrontation with Art Lehr.

He took another batch of documents from the box and saw copies of applications to various colleges and universities—the University of Virginia, Hamilton College, the University of Michigan, Princeton. He scanned them and put the Michigan application on top of his leather portfolio. There were more grade reports and copies of tests and the results of standardized examinations. He found a copy of a poem Leslie had written. The grade, an A+, was in the left-hand corner, followed by the word "Fabulous!" in red ink. It was from an English class taught by Jeffrey Talbot. He put the poem with the University of Michigan application.

There were more press clippings, including an article from the *Traverse City Record-Eagle* listing the all-state women's soccer team on which Leslie had been named to the third team. He saw more poems authored by Leslie in Talbot's English class, always with an A+ and always with an additional superlative in the margins. He added the poems to his pile. He found a letter from Talbot to Lehigh University, urging her admission and extolling her capabilities and virtues. He added the letter to the pile as well.

There was more artwork by Leslie and still more grade reports and copies of tests and newspaper clippings. Then he found a letter from the high school scholarship committee advising Leslie that she'd been awarded the Aegean Merit Scholarship. The letter was signed by Jeffrey Talbot, the committee chair. He read the Post-it note attached to the letter and shook his head and added the letter to his separate pile. He found a copy of Leslie's speech as valedictorian of her graduating class. It was too long to read, so he added it to the pile.

Pete continued to methodically sort through the memorabilia, adding some of the items to his take-along pile, included a yellowing newspaper photograph of Leslie dancing cheek-to-cheek with a boy at the homecoming dance. Finally, he reached the bottom. He put the mass of items he wasn't going to take with him back in the box and returned the box to the closet. Then he unzipped his portfolio and slipped the papers he'd put aside in and zipped it again.

When he stepped outside, he saw Tessler standing next to Art Lehr. Lehr was talking with his hands, and even a couple of hundred feet away, he could hear Lehr complaining about the search. Then Lehr's eyes fixed on Pete.

"What's that yahoo been doing in my house?" he screamed. He started toward him, but Tessler blocked his path.

"I know he's not a police officer," Lehr continued. "If something's missing, I'm going to file a complaint!"

Tessler tried to calm him down, and Pete could hear him remind Lehr of the first time they were there when he'd told him that Pete occasionally did work for the sheriff's department. Lehr kept trying to get around Tessler, and Joe kept blocking him. Two deputies hurried over and assumed the restraining duties.

Tessler came to where Pete was standing by the house and asked in a low voice, "You done?"

Pete nodded.

"Let's get out of here, then, before the loon finds a shotgun and starts blasting away."

Tessler pulled a U-turn on Lehr's patchy grass and headed out the driveway. Pete glanced around and saw that the deputies were getting into their cruisers, as well. When they were on the highway back to Benzonia, Tessler said, "Well, did you find anything?"

"Maybe. I need to study it."

"What's that supposed to mean?"

"Just what I said."

"Pete, I'll try to put this in a nice way, you know? Connie and I put our butts on the line and I told my boss a half-truth, all because we trusted you when you said there might be something in that box that's useful to our investigation. Now you go coy on me again."

"Sorry, I don't mean to be coy. The things I took wouldn't mean anything to you, but they might to me after I've studied them. I want to talk to someone first before I tell you what I'm thinking."

"Who's the someone?"

"I'll tell you after I talk to him."

Tessler raised both hands and slammed them down on the steering wheel again. "Oh, for crissakes . . ."

When Pete got back to town, he stopped to see Harry and asked him to suggest the names of three or four area people who'd be candidates for human interest profile pieces. Harry seemed to sense there was something Pete wasn't telling him and peppered him with questions. Pete deflected the questions and Harry eventually gave up and put on his thinking cap and came up with the names of four people he thought would be interesting or colorful candidates. Pete thanked him and went back to his office.

He set up a lunch date for noon the next day, then settled in with the documents he'd taken from Art Lehr's house and the other documents he'd accumulated and began to study them. And to figure out a game plan.

Darkness was settling over the area, and the man who'd killed Bud Stephanopoulis was edgy. To ease his anxiety, he got in his SUV and drove around. Aimlessly, on side roads and through villages.

As always, he was drawn to the lake and pretty soon he found himself headed west on Crystal Drive. He turned south when he came to M-22 and continued to follow the lake. He knew he shouldn't do it, but when he came to the access road, he turned in and bumped along the rutted path until he reached the water. He got out of his vehicle and went to the beach and sat on the soft sand and gazed out. After a while, his eyes shifted to where he knew the rotten stump was and he stared in that direction for a long time. Then he thought about the invisible woman, and his anxiety began to rise again. He got up and dusted off his seat and climbed into his SUV. He turned around, and just with his running lights on, started back to the highway.

When he came to Thorsen's driveway, he slowed as he always did, looking in. He came to South Shore and followed the road along the lake to the horseshoe driveway where he turned in and parked where he'd parked before. He shut off his engine and lights and tilted his seat back. He wondered if she was running tonight.

As he sat there, he tried to identify the constellations he could see from the front seat of his vehicle. Then he saw a flash and his attention picked up. *That's her.* She emerged from the shadows, loping along the road, looking graceful. She disappeared from view, and he waited anxiously for her to reverse directions and come back. Each minute seemed like an eternity. Finally, he saw flashes again, and then her graceful stride. He followed with his eyes until she was gone. He leaned back in his seat, looking at the sky again.

FORTY-FOUR

When Pete walked into the restaurant, Jeffrey Talbot was already there. A yellow legal pad and three Bic pens, one with red ink, were on the table next to his right hand. Talbot got to his feet and shook Pete's hand and said a few words in greeting. They both ordered iced tea and Pete told the waitress they needed a half-hour to talk before they placed their lunch orders.

"You moved fast," Talbot said. "I'm anxious to see who you've identified for your first profile." He sounded uneasy, like he feared Pete might have come up with a name that would relegate his piece about the Coleridge family to second place.

Pete shoved his pad across the table so Talbot could read the names. "Here's what I've come up with so far. Do you know any of these people?"

Talbot studied the list and put check marks by two names. "I know these two. I know *of* the others, but don't know them personally. Millie Keiler, I think she'd be an excellent choice. She has two college degrees, hand-washes her clothes because she's an outstanding steward of our environment, runs a private shelter for animals in the area. Of the four, she's the one I'd focus on if I were you."

"Mmm."

"I'd be happy to interview Millie if you like. I've met her several times."

"I'll keep that in mind. How about the others on my list? Any comments on them?"

Talbot went through them one by one and told Pete what he knew. Then he found a reason to switch the conversation to the Coleridge family and his voice recovered some of its usual breathlessness. He said his research indicated that they very well *might* be related to Samuel Taylor Coleridge. After monopolizing the conversation for twenty minutes, he asked, somewhat hesitatingly, whether Pete would be put off if he suggested to Harry that they lead off with a profile of the Coleridges. Pete said that it wouldn't bother him personally, but they'd have to leave the decision to Harry.

They got their lunch orders in, and Pete used the break to switch the conversation to other matters. "Teaching high school students must be a real challenge. How large are your classes?"

Talbot frowned and appeared to think about Pete's question. "On average, my English classes run about twenty-five students, I'd say. I teach two sections, so you'd need to double that to come up with my English teaching load. Plus, I have other teaching responsibilities, of course."

Pete nodded. "If you take fifty students a year over twenty years, that comes to a thousand. That's a lot of students. I can understand why you wouldn't remember Leslie Lehr right away."

Talbot appeared not to know what to say at first, then recovered and said. "And you have to double those numbers again when you take into account the other courses I teach. With that many students, all of them start to blend together after a while."

Pete nodded again. "But when you did remember Leslie, you seemed to think highly of her."

"Very solid student," he said solemnly, nodding. "Motivated, too. She wanted to get away from the farm as I recall. Why are you asking about her? She isn't a candidate for a profile, is she?"

"I don't know, she might be. Everyone I've spoken to seems so high on her. That's my approach to these things, assemble a lot of possibilities and then cull the list."

"There's a problem with Leslie, though. She hasn't lived in the community for years, so she doesn't really fit your concept."

"Good point. Maybe she'd be a good candidate for some other piece, but not for the profiles we're considering."

While they were eating, Pete asked some more questions about Millie Keiler, and Talbot took advantage of every opportunity to redirect the conversation to the Coleridge family. When there was another lull in the conversation, Pete asked, "How does your high school handle scholarship awards? Is there a committee?"

"Yes, why do you ask?"

"I keep thinking about the Aegean Merit Scholarship that was awarded to Leslie Lehr. If that scholarship was a one-shot thing, do you think it would have gone through the committee? Or is it more likely that it was handled informally?"

Talbot seemed guarded again. "I don't know offhand, but my guess is that it probably was handled informally. If it became a recurring award, then it's something the committee would have handled."

"Mmm. Have you ever served on the scholarship committee?"

"Only as an alternate for a couple of years. With so many other responsibilities . . ."

"A person can only do so much, right? The reason I asked about the Aegean Merit Scholarship is I continue to believe Bud Stephanopoulis — the man who was shot — might have been the sponsor. The name of his company and the scholarship name, they're so similar. That day at the high school, you and Marian didn't seem to know anything about it. Any thoughts since then?"

Talbot shook his head. "Not really."

"Okay. If you don't know anything about the scholarship, you probably don't know whether the donor ever came through with the money, either."

Talbot shook his head again. "Sorry."

"Just wondering. I heard that Art Lehr, Leslie's father, had to sell off half his farm to help his daughter out financially. I thought it might have had something to do with the scholarship sponsor not coming through."

"Gosh, Pete, I wish I could help you . . ."

"No, no, I understand. I thought I knew Stephanopoulis pretty well, but the more I find out about the guy now that he's dead, the more I think he might have been a bad apple. Making a show of granting a poor high school girl a scholarship, then not coming through with the money, sounds like something he might do. He's gotten me in trouble, too. Keep this under your hat, but I found out the guy was peddling scam investment products and forging my signature on phony legal opinions to help draw in investors."

Talbot's eyes widened. "That sounds serious."

"It is. And I'll tell you something else, off the record again. You know that the sheriff has been focusing on Gaz Ramczyk, that veteran with PTSD? I've gotten to be friends with Joe Tessler, the detective, and he tells me that they're now looking at people who might have had a grudge against Stephanopoulis. Financial, personal, whatever."

Talbot's voice dropped and he said, "Does that mean Gaz Ramczyk isn't a suspect anymore?"

"They haven't announced it, but that's what I'm reading into some of the things they've said."

"Gaz is a bad actor, too, you know."

"I know that's the scuttlebutt, but the sheriff and his people are beginning to think Gaz's lawyer might be right, that his PTSD has been giving people the wrong impression."

"Some of us remember Mr. Ramczyk from his high school days, before he was in the army. He was always involved in bad things in those days."

"So you *do* remember him, huh?"

"It takes a while for some of these things to come back, but I guess your questions about him tickled something in my memory bank."

Pete nodded sagely. "I understand. I'm a relative newcomer to the community, but after hearing what everyone says about Leslie Lehr and what many are saying about Gaz Ramczyk, I was really surprised to see this in one of the yearbooks." He handed him the photograph of Gaz and Leslie sitting on a swing together he'd copied from one of the yearbooks.

Talbot looked at the photograph. "I don't remember them being this close," he said after a few moments hesitation.

Pete nodded. "I suppose it could be an example of the yearbook editors trying to conjure up a teen romance. Believe me, having a daughter that age of my own, I've seen some of the things they come up with."

"That could be it," Talbot said, looking at his watch. "Pete, I'm really sorry, I'd love to stay and talk some more, but I have to meet someone else in a half-hour. Think some more about Millie Keiler and whether there's anything I can do to help you."

"I will. And remember, please don't mention any of the things we talked about to anyone else."

"Don't worry about me, Pete. I'm good at keeping my mouth shut."

When Pete got back to his office, he clicked on his miniature recording device and listened to his conversation with Jeffrey Talbot. He played the recording again and jotted down everything Talbot had lied about. Pete gazed out at the bay for a long time, then called Joe Tessler. Predictably, he didn't answer. He left a message for him to call back as soon as possible.

FORTY-FIVE

The man who'd killed Bud Stephanopoulis stood at the counter and shifted from one foot to the other as he waited for the bank manager to approve the withdrawal of his entire account balance in cash. *What's taking so long? Incompetent idiots!* Finally the manager appeared and whispered in the cashier's ear and she began to carefully count out almost five thousand dollars in cash. The man tried to act businesslike as he verified her count before stuffing the bundles of currency into his briefcase and leaving the bank.

As he drove on to the other two stops he had to make, he considered again whether he should rent a small U-Haul so he could take more of his possessions. He decided to stick with his previous decision and take only what would fit in his SUV. A trailer was too easily spotted in case they started to look for him, which he feared they would.

When he got home, he began to lay out the things he'd take with him, making sure he didn't overlook any of his favorite shirts and sweaters. He finished sorting through his possessions, and then got the box out of his closet and set it next to the pile. Just being close to it aroused deep emotions in him. He knew he shouldn't take the time, but he couldn't resist opening the box and looking through it. As he flipped through the pages, powerful memories came back and the fear that clutched his insides since he left the restaurant receded a little. He slid the picture of her, the best one he had, from its plastic sheath and raised it to his face and inhaled. He could almost smell her scent.

He shook off his reverie and closed the box again. Then he looked out his bedroom window at the shed. Was there anything in there he needed to take? He ticked off in his mind the items he'd disposed of, cataloging where he'd buried each of them. He wondered if he should look through the shed one last time just to be sure, but resisted the temptation. He had to leave.

No one was around when he opened his front door, and he began to carry things to his SUV. When he finished, he went inside again and used the bathroom for the final time. He strolled through the modest house, looking at the furniture and the bookcase he'd built and the kitchen he'd remodeled himself. This was the last time he'd be there. He wasn't going to miss it, though; Dove Cottage is what he was going to miss.

He closed the door behind him and locked it. No use making things easy for the people who'd come looking for him. He took a final look around, then got in his SUV and drove out the driveway. As he passed the houses of people he knew, he felt sad that he couldn't say goodbye. They didn't mean anything to him, but they were good people.

As he passed the Shell station, he glanced at his gas gauge. It showed full. He'd stopped to fill his tank on the way back from the bank, just as he'd periodically filled the tanks of various vehicles he'd owned over the years. On his way out of town, he was careful not to exceed the speed limit. He couldn't afford to be pulled over by the police. He continued to observe the higher limit when he got on the highway.

He turned on Dead Stream Road and proceeded on until he came to a secluded driveway that was all but obscured by foliage. The bushes on the sides and the overhanging tree branches brushed his SUV as he drove through the leafy tunnel. Then the drive opened up and his heart jumped as it always did when he saw the small structure in front of him. Its pristine white exterior and gray slate roof gleamed in the sunlight and the red roses added dabs of color.

The man parked, and after admiring the structure a few moments more, went over and ran his hand over the rough exterior, feeling the texture, letting it excite him. In previous incarnations, it had been a boathouse, but some sensitive soul had converted it into a cottage. He'd added the stucco to the exterior himself to give it a more authentic look. In a burst of extravagance, he'd hired a contractor to replace the shingle roof with one made of slate, and had also replaced the door with one that looked like it had been hewed from planks. The black iron fixtures he'd added made it look rustic.

He walked around the perimeter of Dove Cottage, losing himself in the ambiance. On the front side, he dropped to his knees and began to pluck some weeds that had sprouted in the rose bed. Finally satisfied, he got up again and brushed himself off and unlocked the door and went inside. He looked around, the familiarity of everything calming him, like an old friend, and he made a mental checklist of things he'd take when he left.

Then the exhilaration faded and depression set in. The thought of never being able to return to Dove Cottage overwhelmed him. It was all that scumbag's fault. Until he messed up her life, everything was so perfect. Even long distance, it had been wonderful. He craved one more perfect night.

He took a worn leather-bound volume from the shelf and walked to the water's edge where he adjusted the beach umbrella and sat down and opened the book. He knew each of the poems by heart, but there was something comforting about holding the book and savoring the words with the lake country all around him. Platte Lake in front, and behind him, Little Platte Lake, and not far away, Loon Lake.

After losing himself in the splendor for two hours, he looked at his watch and saw that it was almost 7:00 p.m. One part of him wanted to leave, to get as far away as possible, but another part wanted to stay just a while longer.

He parked in the circle driveway of a cottage that must have been splendid at one time, but now was in disrepair and overgrown with unruly hedges and other foliage. It could be depressing in the daylight, but at night, his favorite time, it was perfect. He hid in a break in the hedge along the road which gave him a clear view and waited and hoped this wasn't the night she took off from running.

Finally, far down the road, near the highway, he saw a flash and his heart beat faster. He peered into the semi-darkness, straining to see. *There it was again.* Another flash, closer this time. He clutched his flashlight tighter and worked his thumb back and forth over the slide. He could see her now, loping toward him in the moonlight. Then headlights appeared as a vehicle turned onto South Shore and headed his way. He stepped back in the hedge to avoid the lights, and the vehicle passed with a soft *whoosh.*

He breathed out and moved closer to the road again. When he regained his night vision, he saw her a hundred feet past him and the taillights of the vehicle that had messed up his plan were fading into the night. Frustrated, he was tempted to throw his flashlight into the lake, but regained control of his emotions and realized she had to pass him again on her way back. He knew she always ran on the other side of the road on her return leg so he crossed over and positioned himself in some brush on that side. He breathed deeply and worked the slide on his flashlight some more, hearing the soft buzzing sound, as he waited.

In the distance, a dog barked and then another joined in. All around him, the quiet was disturbed by the gentle sounds of the night as he waited and continued to clutch his flashlight. He knew that it worked because he'd tested it on his leg. He watched for flashes from the east. Then he saw one. A minute later, he saw another. He watched intently until she came into view, running smoothly, her reflective tape occasionally flashing in the moonlight.

He gripped the flashlight tighter as she came closer. She was a hundred feet away now. He edged a little closer to the road, readying himself. She was even with him when he leaped out and pressed the flashlight to the back of her thigh and held it there.

FORTY-SIX

Pete checked the time. It was past 10:00 p.m. and Joe Tessler still hadn't returned his calls. He tried his cell phone again, but didn't leave another message. He'd already left two.

He changed the CD on his player to a Gordon Lightfoot collection and stewed as he half-listened to "Early Morning Rain." *Where is the guy?* He suspected Sheriff Richter had finally let him take a few hours off and he probably was romancing one of his many quality lady friends somewhere. Out of the rain, most likely. Someplace with a nice comfortable bed. He didn't begrudge him a little relaxation now and then, but he needed to talk to him.

Lightfoot had moved on and was warning Sundown not to go creeping 'round his backstairs when Pete got up and looked at the scattered lights around the lake and thought some more about his lunch with Jeffrey Talbot. Then he glanced at his watch again and saw that it was 10:30 p.m. and wondered why Julie wasn't home. Maybe she'd stretched out her nightly run, he thought. He went back to dissecting his conversation with Talbot.

When it got to be 11:00 p.m. and Julie still wasn't home, Pete dialed her cell phone number. He heard the familiar grating tune that was her cell's greeting start to blare from upstairs. *Great, she didn't take her phone with her.* When another fifteen minutes passed and she still hadn't showed, his concern ramped up and he wondered whether something had happened to her. Maybe she'd sprained her ankle and was lying along the road and couldn't continue.

He got in his Range Rover and tracked her normal running route. When he came to where South Shore ended, he zigzagged away from the lake and took Shorewood all the way to M-115, and looped around and then took a road back to the lake. He followed South Shore home, scanning both sides of the road, but saw nothing. When he got back to his house, he confirmed that Julie wasn't there and called the emergency room at the hospital. The person who answered said that no one had been brought in that evening. He called the sheriff's office and was told they hadn't received a call about a young woman, either.

Julie was now his sole focus, and he got into his Range Rover again and drove along the route he'd just taken, only this time instead of taking South Shore, he took a road that intersected with M-22 and went home that way. Nothing.

Back on his screened porch, he stared into the night and the subliminal fears he'd been suppressing broke free from their constraints, and the times he'd gotten Julie into trouble in the past as a result of his incessant poking around in some case came flooding back. He thought about what he'd been doing recently and got the same cold feeling in the pit of his stomach he'd felt before. He grabbed the telephone and dialed the sheriff's office again. When the night deputy answered, Pete identified himself and asked the deputy if he knew where Detective Tessler was. He didn't so Pete told him he was concerned that his daughter might have been kidnapped.

"How long has she been missing?" the deputy asked.

"Since about nine o'clock."

"Morning or evening?"

"Evening," he said, having a feeling he knew what the deputy was going to say.

After a long pause, the deputy said, "Sir, if she's not home in the morning, call back and we'll look into it."

Pete slammed the telephone down and tried to calm himself so he could think logically. He ticked off in his mind the people he might have rubbed the wrong way while looking into Bud Stephanopoulis's murder. There were several, but his brain wasn't functioning the way it normally did and he knew he couldn't sit around analyzing the matter to death. He grabbed his cell phone and jumped in his Range Rover and spun out of the driveway, his wheels squealing as he turned onto M-22. He'd try the closest one first. And the one with whom he'd had the most recent contact.

He screamed down the highway toward town at ninety miles an hour, passing two other vehicles on his way. He slowed a bit when he entered the city limits, but still navigated the streets at a reckless speed. He came to Talbot's street on the edge of town. There were only three houses on the block and he tried to identify the right one. He saw the street number tacked on a tree and turned in the gravel driveway and skidded to a stop.

The house was dark and no vehicles were parked outside. Pete grabbed a flashlight from his glove box and hurried to the detached garage at the end of the drive and directed the beam through a small window. The garage was empty. He went to the front door of the house and tried the knob and found it locked. He worked his way around the perimeter, shining his flashlight in each window. He saw a room that appeared to be a bedroom and put his face close to the glass and looked in. He couldn't see anything, so he took one of the bricks that was holding up the end of a downspout and used it to break two of the windowpanes. He put his hand with the flashlight through one opening and looked through the other. The room was a mess. An open suitcase was on the bed, and the floor was littered with clothes and other items.

It was well after midnight. Talbot didn't strike him as a night owl, and from the mess in his bedroom, it looked like he'd left in a hurry. Pete went to his Range Rover and lifted the hatchback and found a tire tool and old rag in the side compartment. He hurried to the shed, and after wiping the padlock with the rag, inserted the tool in the padlock's hook and pried until the hasp gave way. Then he pried some more and finally was able to open the door. He cast his beam around inside and was relieved to see only clutter.

Tomas Esteban was the next one on his list and he was tempted to descend on his house next even without Joe Tessler. As he stood there, though, he thought about Talbot some more. The guy was always a little high-strung, but he seemed even more so during their lunch. He'd clearly lied to him, too, which is what he wanted to talk to Tessler about. He seemed too mild mannered to be a killer, but he sure as hell had a motive if everything he'd uncovered were true. He also remembered the way Talbot had fawned over Julie at the two dinners. Now Talbot seemed to be gone and Julie was missing, too. *Jesus Christ!*

Pete punched in Harry's number, and after a while, he answered in a voice that suggested he'd been roused from a deep slumber.

"Harry," Pete said, "sorry to wake you, but I've got a problem. Julie's disappeared and I'm trying to track her down. Do you—"

"What do you mean, disappeared?"

"I don't have time to explain. I need the high school principal's name. I know her first name is Marian. I need her last name."

"What do you—"

"Harry, goddamn it, I don't have time! I just need her friggin' name!"

"Okay, okay, give me a minute."

After what seemed like an hour, Harry said, "It's Marian Unger. Couldn't you tell me what—"

"Do you have a phone number for her? Not the school number, her home number."

Harry's end went quiet again, then, "I think this is it. She's the only Unger in town." Harry gave him the telephone number.

"Thanks," Pete said.

"Is there anything—"

"I have to go, Harry."

Pete punched in Marian Unger's telephone number and a few moments later, her familiar voice answered, "Marian Unger speaking."

"Marian, this is Pete Thorsen. You probably remember me. I stopped at the school a couple of times to look at the yearbooks. I'm sorry—"

"Glad to see that I'm not the only one in Frankfort who's still up at this hour, Pete. I'm reading a Dennis Lehane novel and can't put it down."

"Good writer. Say, the reason I'm calling is that I have to reach Jeffrey Talbot about something. He's not at his house and his landline doesn't seem to have a message service. Does he have a cell phone?"

"The reason you don't get his voicemail alert is probably because the machine is filled. Jeffrey is one of those souls who can't be bothered about earthly things. He doesn't have a cell phone, either, because he thinks it might interfere with his ethereal processes."

"How do you reach him then?"

"Usually by email. Or wait for him to drop in."

"Did he say anything to you about leaving town? To take a vacation or something?"

"He didn't mention anything."

"Any suggestions, then?"

"Have you tried Dove Cottage?"

"What's that?"

"A lot of the romantic poets used to live in the English lake district. A couple of them—Wordsworth and somebody—called their place Dove Cottage. Jeffrey has a little cottage on Platte Lake that he's given the same name."

"Do you know if he has a landline there?"

Marian Unger laughed. "Did William Wordsworth and the others have a landline in *their* Dove Cottage?"

"How would I find this place?"

"I've been out there twice, and it's not easy. The first thing is, if you're coming from this direction, don't turn on Platte Road. You'll be on the wrong side of the lake if you do. You have to continue on until you come to

Dead Stream Road, then turn right. Jeffrey doesn't have any signs or house numbers, either. What I do is watch for a sign that says 'The Clouds.' It's a big wooden thing with blue and white clouds on it. Dove Cottage is the first or second driveway beyond that. It's just a tunnel through the brush. I scratched my car when I was there the first time. The second time, I parked on Dead Stream and walked in."

When Pete got off the telephone with Marian Unger, he knew he had to make a decision. He could chase around the area and confront men he knew would be hostile. And lose valuable time while he did it. Or he could continue to try to find Talbot. He went with his gut.

FORTY-SEVEN

J oe Tessler finally called back when Pete was headed north on M-22 toward Platte Lake at close to a hundred miles an hour. He slowed to take the call.

"What's the emergency?" Tessler asked.

"A lot of things. The most important is that my daughter, Julie, is missing. She went on her nightly run and didn't come back."

"Did you call our office and report it?"

"Twice. The deputy I talked to the first time said that they hadn't gotten any reports about a young woman. The second time, another deputy implied I was a paranoid parent and should call back in the morning if she wasn't home. Oh, and I also checked with the hospital. Nothing."

"I know you probably don't want to hear this, but our second guy was probably right. We get calls from parents all the time saying that one of their kids has been kidnapped. The next morning, the kid's back home again. She was out sowing some oats just like our guy said."

"Not Julie, Joe, I know her too well. I'm convinced her disappearance has something to do with my poking around on the Stephanopoulis case."

Tessler didn't say anything for a while, then, "Do you suspect someone like Art Lehr? Or Esteban?"

"Possibly, but there's another guy I've been zeroing in on, too. That's why I've been calling most of the afternoon and evening. He's a local high school teacher."

"A high school teacher," Tessler repeated.

"He has a little place on Platte Lake. I'm on my way there now. I need you to meet me."

"Ah, Christ, Pete, I just got home, and I have to get up again in four or five hours. Can't this wait until the morning?"

"If you're with some goddamned bimbo, just say so. I'll do it by myself." He ended the call and accelerated again. His leg twitched from the tension and he held his thigh to make it stop. He flashed past the turn-off for Platte Road and the remorse he felt began to overwhelm his other emotions. *How many times can I put Julie at risk because I've been stupid enough to get involved in something?*

His cell phone burred and he saw that it was Tessler calling again. *Screw him,* he thought. A couple of minutes later, the phone burred again. This time he slowed and answered.

"I'm on my way," Tessler said. "How do I get there?"

Pete summarized the driving instructions Marian Unger had given him and told Tessler to look for his Range Rover.

He turned on Dead Stream Road and accelerated again. He whizzed past driveways and signs for cottages and periodically caught glimpses of the lake with the moon bathing its calm surface. A couple of miles down, he slowed and kept an eye out for The Clouds sign Marian had described. He saw it and slowed further watched for the tunnel she'd described. He passed it at a crawl and saw a couple of lights, but couldn't tell whether they were coming from Dove Cottage or another place.

Fifty feet past the driveway, he pulled over next to some bushes and parked. He got out and squeezed the car door shut behind him as carefully as he could. In the quiet night, the click still sounded like a rocket exploding over the lake. He winced and started for the driveway, but then stopped. If Talbot had taken Julie, he could be armed. He went back to his Range Rover, and opened the driver's-side door again and grabbed the tire tool he'd used to break into Talbot's shed. He closed the door carefully and winced again when the click disturbed the night.

Pete crept through the leafy tunnel until it opened up after a hundred feet and he saw Dove Cottage gleaming in the moonlight. Talbot's light-colored SUV was parked in front. On the side of the house he could see, two small windows were tucked near the roofline and another was next to the front door. Some sort of elevated structure perched on the roof, like a low bell tower.

He stood quietly for a long time and studied the scene. When he was satisfied that no one was outside, he stepped quickly to the vehicle and saw that it was crammed with clothes and other things. He stayed in the shadows as he moved toward the house and crouched beneath one of the windows. He raised up carefully and peered through one corner and saw Julie sitting in a straight-backed chair with tape over her mouth and her hands and feet tied. Jeffrey Talbot sat across from her with a book in his hands.

FORTY-EIGHT

Pete saw Talbot's mouth moving, but couldn't hear his words. It was obvious he was reading to her, though. He watched for a few minutes, transfixed by the sight. Then he moved to the front of the small house and put his hand on the doorknob and tried to turn it. It was locked.

He crept back to the side and peered in the window again. Talbot was on his feet now and the tape across Julie's mouth had been peeled to one side. He was holding a glass to her lips. As she drank, he ran his free hand through her hair. She jerked her head away. Pete couldn't tell what she'd said, but she must have told him to stop. Talbot continued to stand over her with the glass of water. Pete saw his lips move again and he held the glass close to her lips a second time and she drank some more.

Talbot went to the kitchenette in one corner and began to slice fruit of some kind. An apple, maybe, or a peach. When he was finished, he untied one of Julie's hands so she could use it to eat and placed the plate of fruit on a postage stamp table next to her. Pete saw his mouth move again, but like before, couldn't hear what he was saying.

Pete crouched down and checked his watch. He didn't remember the exact time he'd last talked to Tessler, but he should be here by now. He raised up and peered in the window again. Talbot had retied her right hand, but hadn't put the tape across her mouth. He was back to reading to her.

He sank back down and leaned against the wall, his hand clutching and re-clutching the tire tool. He needed a plan. A big problem was that he didn't know what kinds of weapons Talbot had. Even with Tessler here, that would be an issue. There was no way they could get to him without breaking the door down, and that would give him plenty of time to react.

His cell phone burred. Alarmed at the noise, Pete hastily reached in his pocket to shut off the sound. It was Tessler again.

"Pete, I've got tire problems and I'm putting my spare on. I'll be there as soon as I can."

"Talbot has Julie," Pete whispered. "I'm outside his house watching them through a window. He's reading to her."

"Reading?"

"I can't talk anymore. I'm afraid he'll hear me. Get here as soon as you can." He ended the call and rose up and peered in the window again. Talbot was still reading. He sank down and tried to think. He needed to lure the goddamned pervert outside, but how? He thought about creating some noise, but worried that Talbot either wouldn't fall for it, or if he did come out, he'd bring Julie with him. Either way, he'd be alerted that somebody was around. That might increase the risk to Julie. As long as Talbot was just reading, she didn't seem to be in any immediate danger. He decided it was best to wait for Tessler.

For the next half-hour, Pete periodically peered in the window to make sure nothing had changed. Then he thought he heard something, like a chair leg scraping across a wood floor. He raised up again and saw that both Talbot and Julie were on their feet. Julie was still tied up, but it looked like Talbot had loosened the bounds on her ankles to permit her to walk but not take long strides. Tape covered her mouth again.

Pete watched Julie shuffle toward the door with Talbot holding her arm, guiding her along. He reached for the knob and opened the door and guided her outside. *What's he doing?* Pete crept around to the other side of the cottage where he'd have better cover. Talbot continued to guide Julie toward two beach chairs that rested on the narrow strip of sand along the water. He held her elbow and helped her sit in one of them. Then he took the chair opposite her and opened his book and began to read again. Pete could hear him now, but not well. No question it was poetry, though.

They were probably a hundred feet away from where Pete was crouched in the tall dune grass. His pulse beat faster as he tried to come up with a plan. *He'd never have a better chance.* Rushing Talbot was the first thing that came to mind, and maybe the only thing he could do, but from that distance the guy would have too much time to react. He had to get closer. He studied the trees and bushes around him, plotting a route he could take. His army obstacle course training came back to him and he remembered how he'd been taught to inch along on his belly, using his elbows and knees to propel him. It seemed like a century ago, but he remembered the basic technique. The gentle lapping of the waves against the shore and Talbot's voice would provide a little cover if he should make some noise. He thought again of waiting for Tessler to get there, but decided that would be worse. A vehicle stopping at the end of the driveway would alert Talbot that something was up.

Pete clutched the tire tool and knew he had to go. He began to wriggle through the grass and around bushes, always keeping an eye on Talbot to be sure he hadn't heard him. The mosquitoes were far worse than when he was in the open and it took all of his willpower not to swipe at the back of his neck. Talbot continued to read and occasionally looked up at the night sky before he resumed. Pete had covered less than half the distance to Talbot, maybe only twenty-five or thirty feet.

He rested for a few moments, then began to inch forward again, feeling as he went to be sure there weren't sticks in his path that would snap under his weight and cause Talbot to notice him. The dune grass ended a few feet in front of him, and he knew it was a close as he was going to get on his belly. Talbot was maybe fifty feet away, now, and he could hear his voice clearly. "Oft she is hid from the mortal eye, or dimly seen . . . ," he intoned, periodically gazing skyward.

Julie continued to look straight ahead at Talbot. *Don't look this way Julie.* Pete tucked his knees under him, trying not to move the grass, and tightened his grip on the tire tool. He exploded out of the grass and covered twenty-five feet before Talbot realized what was happening. Talbot lurched to his feet when Pete was ten feet from him and threw his beach chair into his path. Pete tripped over the chair and pitched headlong into the sand. He kicked the chair away and scrambled to his feet again, thinking of nothing except getting his hands around Talbot's neck. Talbot continued to back up and frantically reached into his pocket. He pulled out a flashlight and pointed it just as Pete drove his shoulder into him. Pete heard a buzzing sound and felt his side go numb.

Pete tried to get up, but his body didn't respond. Talbot came at him with the flashlight again and the buzzing sound filled the night air like a bunch of angry wasps. Pete still had a death grip on the tire tool, and even though he felt like he was moving in slow motion, he swung at Talbot and the steel caught his arm. Talbot dropped the flashlight and screamed in pain. He kicked at Pete and tried to recover the flashlight. Pete could barely move, but he threw the tire tool at Talbot just as his hand reached out. The tool hit him somewhere and he screamed again.

Talbot stood ten feet away from Pete and Julie, holding his arm and a crazed look in his eyes. Then he whirled away and ran toward his SUV. Pete was regaining feeling in his body and forced himself to his feet and hobbled after him. He caught Talbot just as he was climbing into his vehicle. He heard fabric tear as he hauled him back by his collar and threw him to the ground. Talbot raised his hands to protect himself, but Pete was all over him and swung wildly and felt some of his punches connect. When Talbot tried to crawl back toward his vehicle, Pete stayed after him. He grabbed his shirt collar again and hauled him back and banged Talbot's head against the SUV. He banged it again. And again.

"Stop, Pete! You're going to kill him!"

Pete's felt someone's arms around him and his chest heaved and rage churned through his body. He kept trying to get at Talbot.

"That's enough, Pete. The guy's out."

Pete let Tessler move him back a few feet, then stared at the figure on the ground in front of him. He tried to get at him again, but Tessler continued to restrain him.

FORTY-NINE

When Pete and Julie walked into the conference room, Connie Chapman was already there along with Sheriff Richter and Joe Tessler. Pete didn't know the other man, but Chapman introduced him as Homer Eaton, one of the assistant U.S. attorneys for their district.

"I thought we should get everyone together," Chapman said, "so we can assess where we're at. Julie, I think all of us pretty much know what happened that night when Talbot jumped you with a stun gun and took you to the place he calls Dove Cottage, but interrupt at any time if you feel there's something we ought to know. Joe, do you want to lead off and tell us about the search?"

"Sure," Tessler said. "After we rescued Julie, we searched both of Mr. Talbot's dwellings as well as his vehicle. We didn't find anything really useful in the dwelling searches, except we inferred from the mess in his Frankfort house that he planned to flee the area. That's corroborated by some other things, too, as I'll explain as we go along.

"The vehicle is where it gets interesting. Besides a ton of books about poets and poetry, many of which seem to have been pilfered from the high school library, and a bunch of clothes, the first thing we found is four humongous scrapbooks." He tapped the foot-high stack in front of him. "They contain all kinds of memorabilia pertaining to a girl named Leslie Lehr who's the daughter of Art Lehr, a farmer who lives south of Benzonia and one of the suspects in the Stephanopoulis murder case. Newspaper clippings, certificates, photographs, school papers, a gazillion poems Leslie had written in Talbot's high school English class, recommendation letters from Talbot to various colleges and universities, information about a college scholarship that was granted to Leslie and, we believe, funded by Mr. Stephanopoulis.

"Next, we found eleven letters Talbot wrote to Leslie over the past two years," he continued, tapping a smaller stack of documents. "Each of the letters is marked, 'Not at this address. Return to sender.' The letters are heavy on poetry and full of language suggesting romantic intentions. We're not sure whether the letters came back because Leslie refused to accept them or because she moved and didn't leave a forwarding address."

Julie chimed in and said, "When Mr. Talbot kidnapped me and took me to Dove Cottage, he called me Leslie several times. It was like he confused me with her."

Tessler nodded several times and made a note in his spiral notebook. "I'm glad you mentioned that, Julie. That's very helpful. The third thing—"

"One minute, Joe," Chapman said. "Julie, do you think what you just said is the reason Mr. Talbot kidnapped you? That in his mind he confused you with Leslie?"

Julie looked at her father.

"We don't know," Pete said. "The kidnapping doesn't seem to be the usual kind. We're not even sure Talbot intended to take Julie with him when he left."

"Strange," Chapman said. "Okay, Joe, continue."

"As I was saying, the next thing we found in Talbot's vehicle was almost five thousand dollars in cash and a withdrawal slip from a local bank indicating Mr. Talbot had closed out his account. This further corroborates our conclusion that Talbot intended to flee the area. And last, we found a set of Vermont license plates." He held up plates encased in a plastic sheath. "We believe Talbot planned to switch plates on his vehicle to the Vermont set to throw off law enforcement, which is also consistent with our conclusion that he intended to flee. That's pretty much it from me. There's a lot more detail in my written report."

Sheriff Richter hadn't said anything, but now he looked at Pete and said, "Mr. Thorsen, I've been sitting here wondering about something. How did you know Talbot had your daughter?"

Pete sensed where he was headed and said, "I didn't. I guessed and happened to be right."

"You know," Richter said, "most people would give a little more complete answer when law enforcement asks them a question."

Pete shrugged. "After you gave me the bogus legal opinion letter in your office that day, I felt I had to start looking around so I could establish that I had nothing to do with Mr. Stephanopoulis's investment scams. In the process, I learned some things about your case. Talbot and I both do freelance work for Harry McTigue's paper, and in a couple of conversations I had with him, including the day of the kidnapping, he said things I knew weren't true and I got suspicious. I'm just guessing, but he must have been concerned I was onto him. When Julie didn't come back that night, he was one of the people I suspected. I tried his house first because he was closest. I got lucky."

"What did Mr. Talbot say that you thought wasn't true?"

"A number of things. He said he didn't remember Leslie Lehr when I was positive he knew her very well. He said he was never on the high school scholarship committee when I had documents that showed he not only was on the committee, but he was the chairman and sent a letter to Leslie informing her that she'd been awarded the Aegean Merit

Scholarship. He said he didn't know Bud Stephanopoulis, but I was sure he at least knew who he was and didn't like him. Things like that."

"It sounds to me, counselor, that you were sticking your nose into law enforcement matters again rather than just looking into legal opinion issues."

Pete shrugged again. "Sometimes things run together. If I discovered something I thought might be relevant to the murder investigation, I passed it on to Detective Tessler. In fact, I had a call in to him about Talbot the night Julie was kidnapped. I think he'll confirm that."

Tessler nodded his agreement.

The sheriff didn't look convinced.

Chapman was aware of the history between the two and stepped in and said, "Pete, you have an interesting theory that we might have a twofer here, that Talbot might be guilty not only of kidnapping, but he might also be the one who shot Bud Stephanopoulis. Do you want to tell the group about our conversation?"

"Yes, but I'd like to make clear it's as much the theory of a psychiatrist I know as it is mine. As we all know, Talbot is obsessed with the so-called Lake Poets. You can't be around the guy for five minutes before he starts to talk about them and quote from their work. He seems to live in a fantasy world and even named the place he owns on Platte Lake Dove Cottage.

"At some point, he became enamored with Leslie Lehr, probably when he first had her in one of his English classes. She was a great student, apparently had a flair for poetry, was pretty. From all appearances, Talbot became extremely covetous of Leslie. I think that explains a lot of the stuff you found in his vehicle."

"Pete," Chapman said, "let me interrupt. Do you think Talbot's relationship with Leslie was sexual? Or was it purely platonic?"

"I have no idea, but it's clear he was jealous of others who became close to her. Two of them were Gaz Ramczyk, Leslie's boyfriend during her high school years, and Bud Stephanopoulis. I don't know how the relationship between Leslie and Stephanopoulis started, but he became her benefactor at some point. He funded a college scholarship for her, got his investment banking firm to give her summer jobs, got her hired on a permanent basis by the firm. The firm is Harrison Stryker LLP in Philadelphia, by the way.

"Fast forward to a couple of years ago. Harrison Stryker got into a lot of trouble due to a client that had been selling Ponzi-scheme investments that Bud had to know about. There were civil lawsuits against the firm and a major investigation by the SEC. In the fall-out, Leslie Lehr—I understand her name is Wallace now—and four other junior people at Harrison Stryker were canned and barred by the SEC from working in the securities business for five years. I—"

"How do you know all of this?" Richter asked.

"From press accounts, largely. I also talked to some people in Philadelphia who corroborated everything."

His answer seemed to catch Richter off guard and he didn't ask a follow-up question.

"Anyway, to conclude, I believe Talbot was convinced that Stephanopoulis had ruined Leslie's life, so he killed him. Then he tried to pin the murder on Gaz Ramczyk, who he hated for other reasons."

When Pete was finished, Richter shook his head and scowled. "I listened to you pretty darn carefully, and I didn't hear you mention one thing that amounts to concrete evidence in support of your theory."

"It was more of a psychological analysis than an evidentiary one."

"Who's the psychiatrist that fed you all of this?"

"Susan Ettleman. She's done work for your department before. Back when Bill Haskins was sheriff. You might want to talk to her directly."

"Frank," Tessler said, "what Mr. Thorsen just told us at least establishes motive. Plus, we know that Talbot was tromping around Ramczyk's place. Tests the lab did on soil residue found on the floor of Talbot's vehicle matches the soil of Ramczyk's memorial."

When Richter didn't say anything right away, Pete said, "If what I just said isn't true, Sheriff, how do you explain why Talbot clearly intended to flee the area?"

"Maybe he planned all along to hit you up for money and knew he couldn't stay around here."

"Possible, but I don't think so. I think he feared that I knew more about him than I actually did and decided he had to scram for that reason."

Richter screwed his face up and after a few moments, said, "Well, maybe we'll get lucky and Talbot will confess. Assuming he recovers his memory, that is. I'm told he has a bad concussion. He's being held in special confinement until he recovers enough for us to question him." He paused before saying to Pete, "That's something else I've been wanting to ask you about. Exactly how did you subdue Talbot?"

"I jumped him while he was reading poetry to my daughter. We were wrestling around on the ground when Detective Tessler arrived and put cuffs on him."

"Do you know how he suffered those head injuries?" Richter persisted.

Pete looked at him and said, "It all happened so fast. We were close to his vehicle. He must have hit his head on something."

Richter scoffed audibly. "You weren't trying to punish him because of what he did to your daughter?"

Chapman stepped in again before he could respond and said, "Well, at least we have Talbot on kidnapping charges, which is a felony. There doesn't seem to be much doubt about that regardless of what we're able to prove in the murder case. Any way you cut it, he's looking at a long prison term."

On their way to lunch, Julie said, "You know, Dad, Leslie is the real victim here. I mean Bud is dead and everything, but he really did a lot of bad things. I'm not saying he deserved it, because no one deserves to be murdered. But he did some bad things and ruined a lot of people's lives. Leslie is the victim, not him."

Pete nodded.

As they were pulling up to Rona's Bay Grille, Julie said, "You know all of those scrapbooks Joe had? I bet Mr. Lehr would like to have them."

"He probably would," Pete said, thinking about the mishmash of memorabilia he'd gone through at his house. "But the scrapbooks are evidence. I don't think we'd be able to take them."

"I don't mean now. I mean after the case is over. I'm going to ask."

FIFTY

Julie slid into the passenger seat and said, "Susan asked me to tell you hello."

"That was nice of her." Julie had been seeing Susan Ettleman once a week since the kidnapping incident, and even though he was dying to know how things were coming, he steeled himself and refrained from prying.

On their way out of Traverse City, she said, "Does Susan have a new boyfriend or something?"

"No idea," Pete said. "Why do you ask?"

"You know how she always wears dark suits? I mean they're nice and everything, but nobody would accuse her of exactly being flamboyant. When I walked into her office this morning, I saw this woman in a shocking pink pantsuit looking for something in a file cabinet. I thought, did I go in the wrong office or something? Then she stood up and I saw it was Susan. Wow!"

"Maybe she's branching out."

"You men don't pick up on these things the way we women do. I bet she has a lunch date with some hot new man."

"Could be."

Julie was quiet for a while, then, "Dad, I made a decision about something. Please don't think this is something Susan and I cooked up. I mean, I've talked to her about it a couple of times, but this has been strictly my decision."

"And what's this weighty decision?"

"I've decided to defer college for a year. It's called taking a gap year."

Pete almost slammed into the car in front of him. After he'd regained his composure, he said, "Are you sure? Everything is all set. You've gotten into a good school, you've been in contact with your roommate, you've decided on your first semester classes, everything."

"I just feel I'm not ready."

Jumbled thoughts banged around in his head. "Have you given any thought to how you're going spend the next year, then?"

"I'm going to try to find Leslie."

ABOUT THE AUTHOR

Robert Wangard is a crime-fiction writer who splits his time between Chicago, where he practiced law for many years, and northern Michigan. *Victim* is the seventh Pete Thorsen novel. The first six, *Target, Malice, Deceit, Payback, Stalked* and *Framed,* have been widely acclaimed by reviewers. *Payback* was also named as a 2014 INDIEFAB Book of the Year Finalist. Besides his novels, Wangard is the author of *Hard Water Blues,* an anthology of crime-fiction short stories. He is a member of Mystery Writers of America, the Short Mystery Fiction Society, and other writers' organizations.

Readers:
• Robert Wangard's books are available in both print and as e-books in independent bookstores and online at amazon.com and bn.com.

• Did you enjoy *Victim* or one of the author's other books?
If so, please post a review on the appropriate book pages
on amazon.com, bn.com and goodreads.com. Thanks.

www.rwangard.com